Gud

BOOK TWO:
THE YELLOW
WHALE

Translation, Layout, and Editing by Mike Kennedy

ISBN: 978-1-942367-88-8

Library of Congress Control Number: 2018962462

10 9 8 7 6 5 4 3 2 1

CHAPTER ONE
SILENCE!

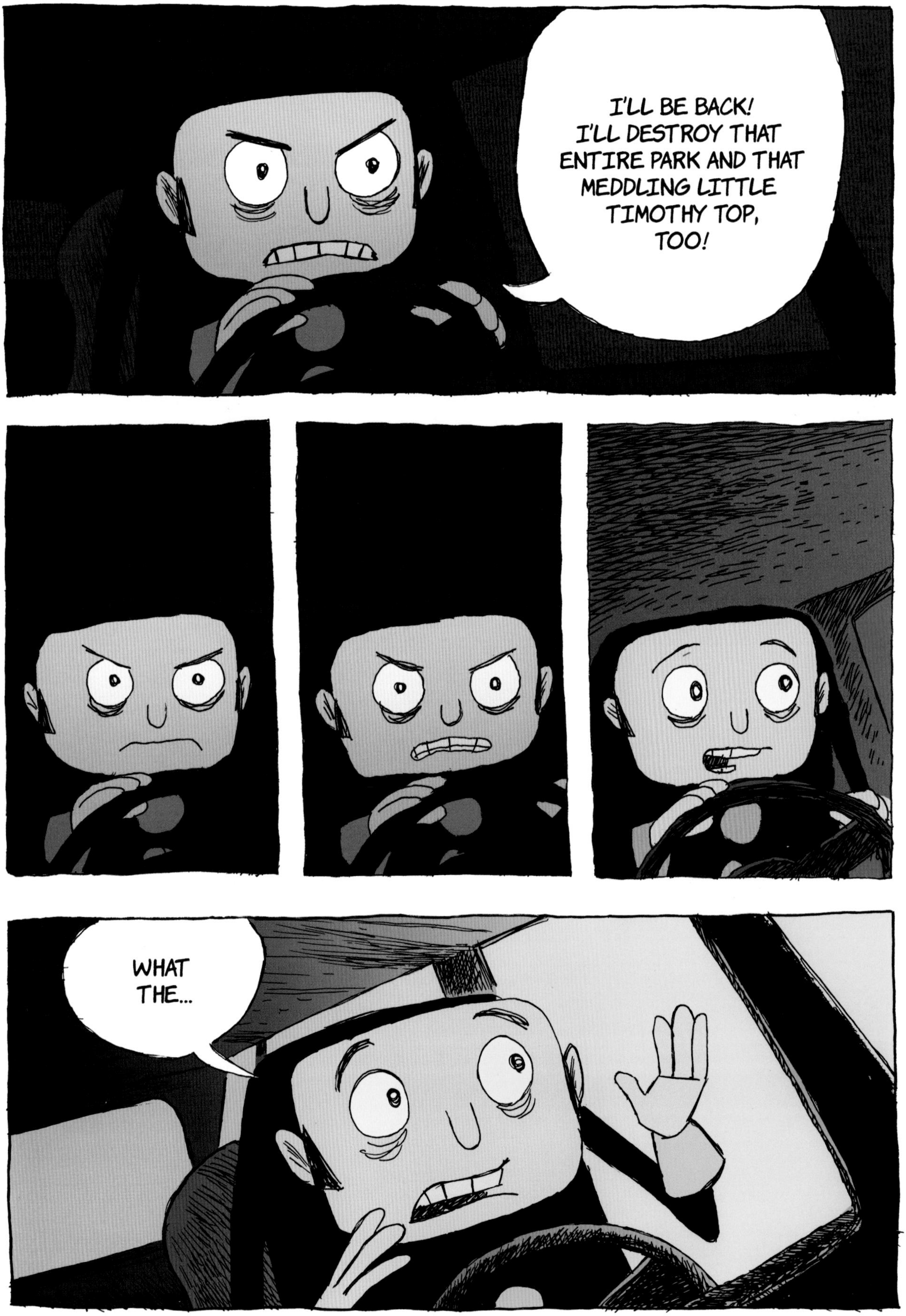
I'LL BE BACK! I'LL DESTROY THAT ENTIRE PARK AND THAT MEDDLING LITTLE TIMOTHY TOP, TOO!
WHAT THE...

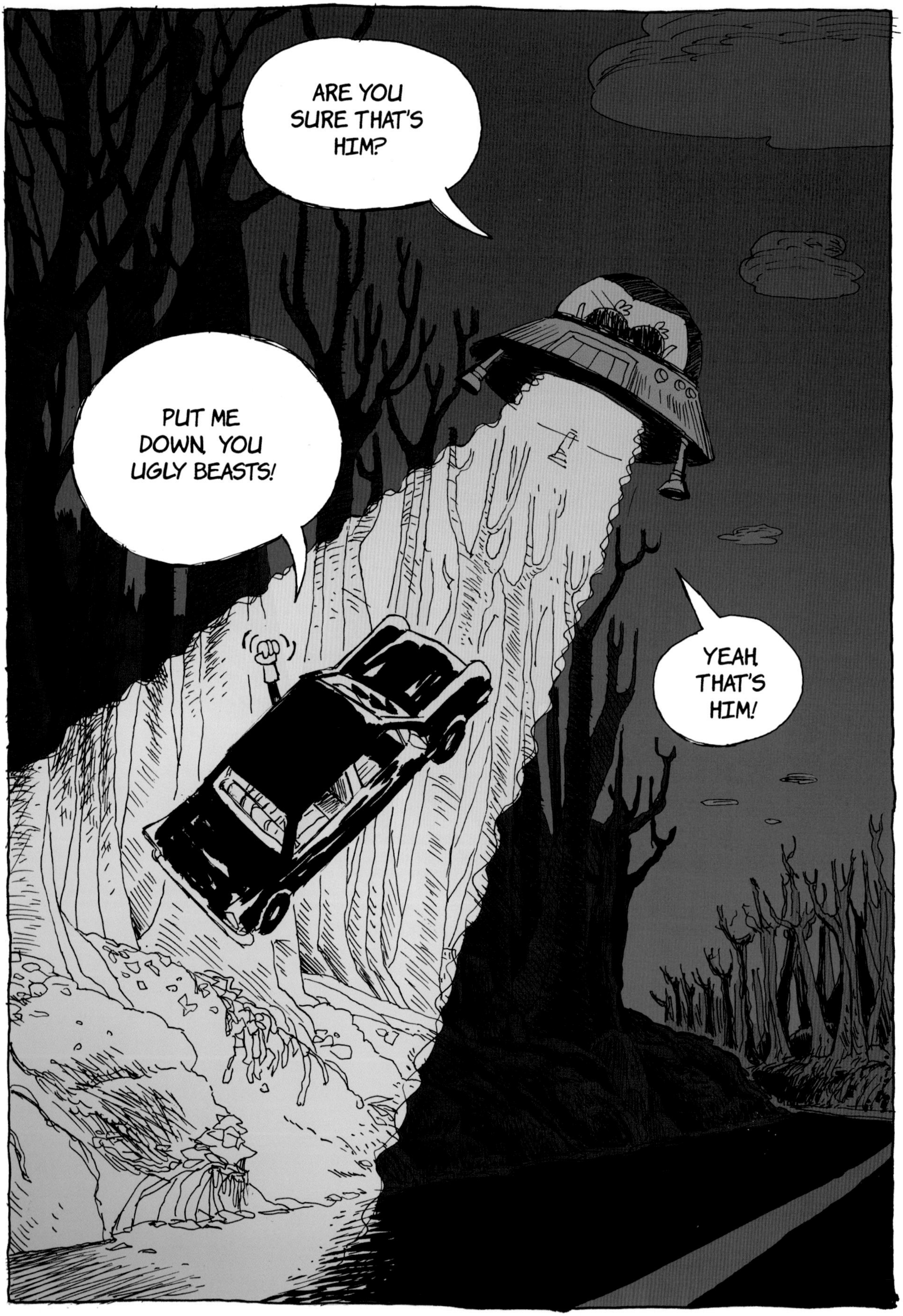
ARE YOU SURE THAT'S HIM?
PUT ME DOWN, YOU UGLY BEASTS!
YEAH, THAT'S HIM!

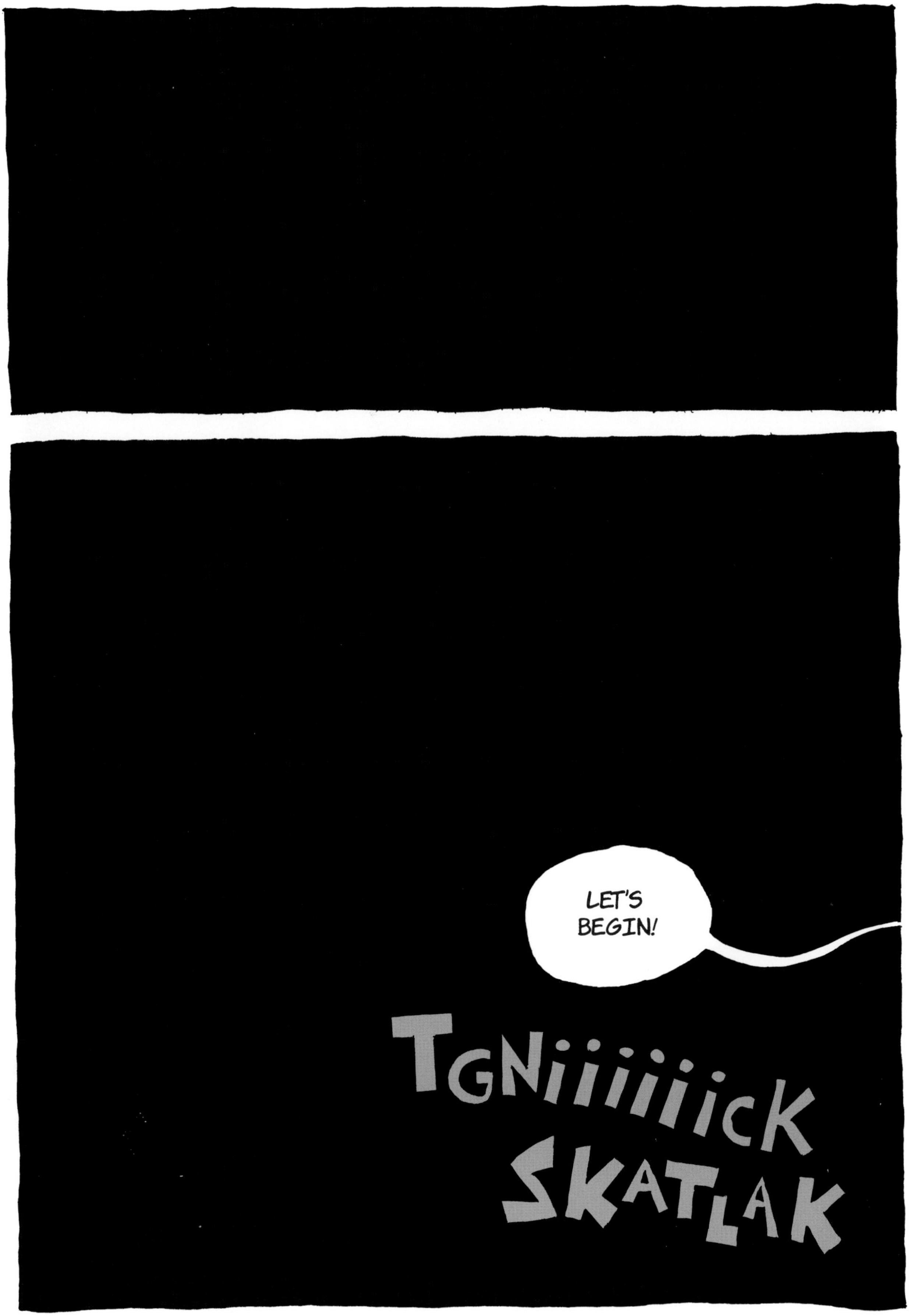
LET'S BEGIN!
TGNiiiiiick
SKATLAK

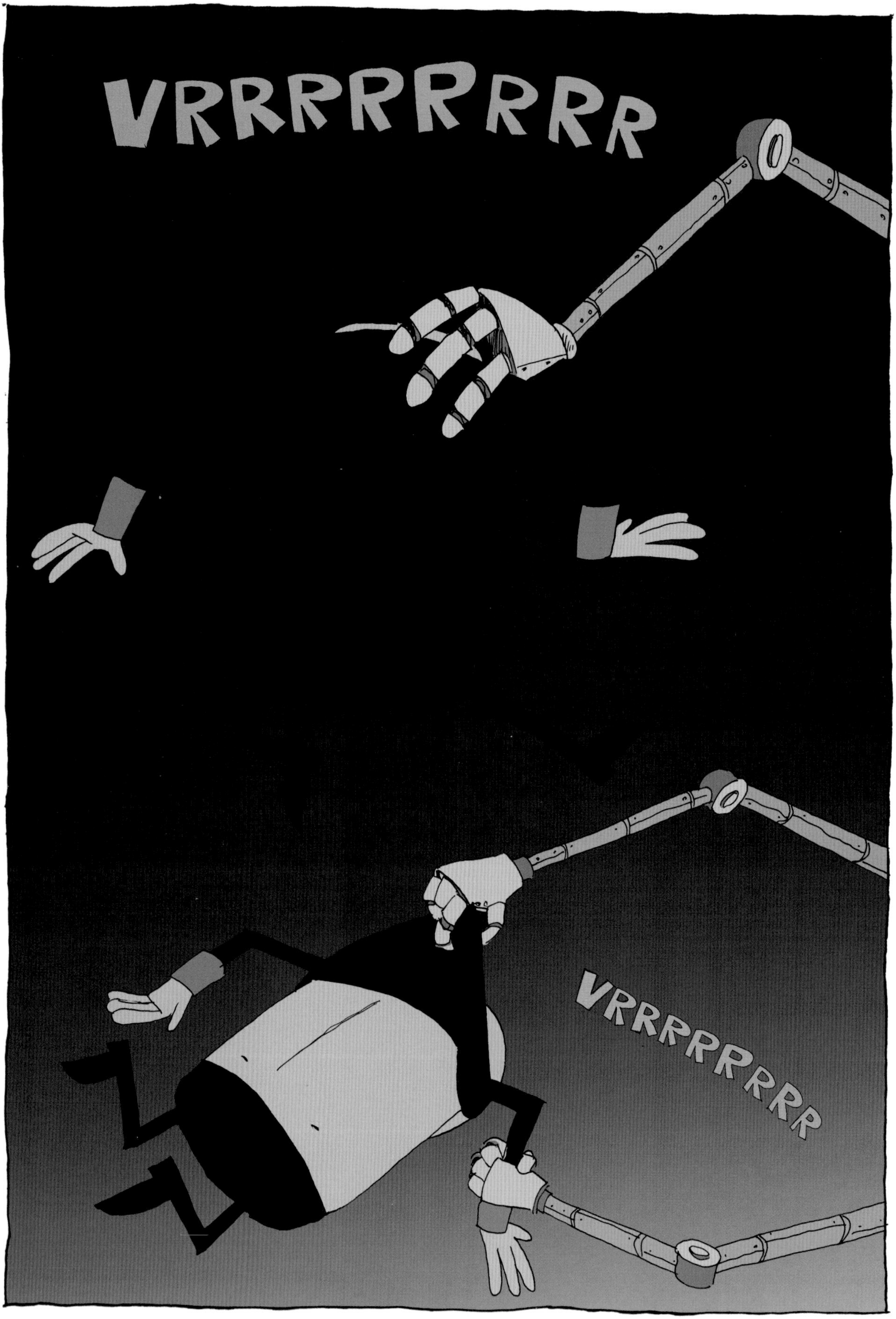
VRRRRRRRRR
VRRRRRRRRR

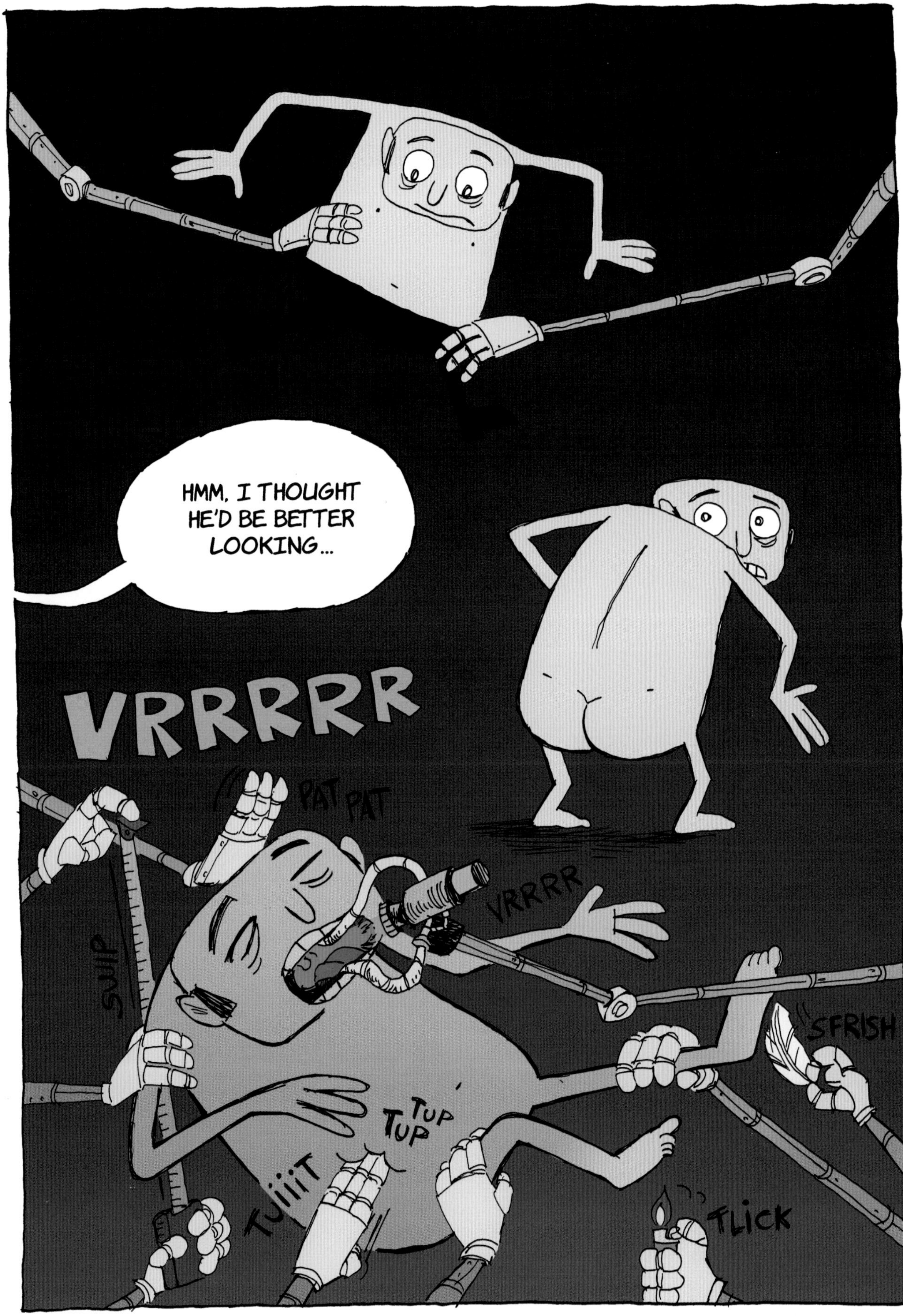
HMM, I THOUGHT HE'D BE BETTER LOOKING...
VRRRRR
PAT PAT
VRRRR
SWIP
SFRISH
TUP TUP
TUiiiT
FLICK

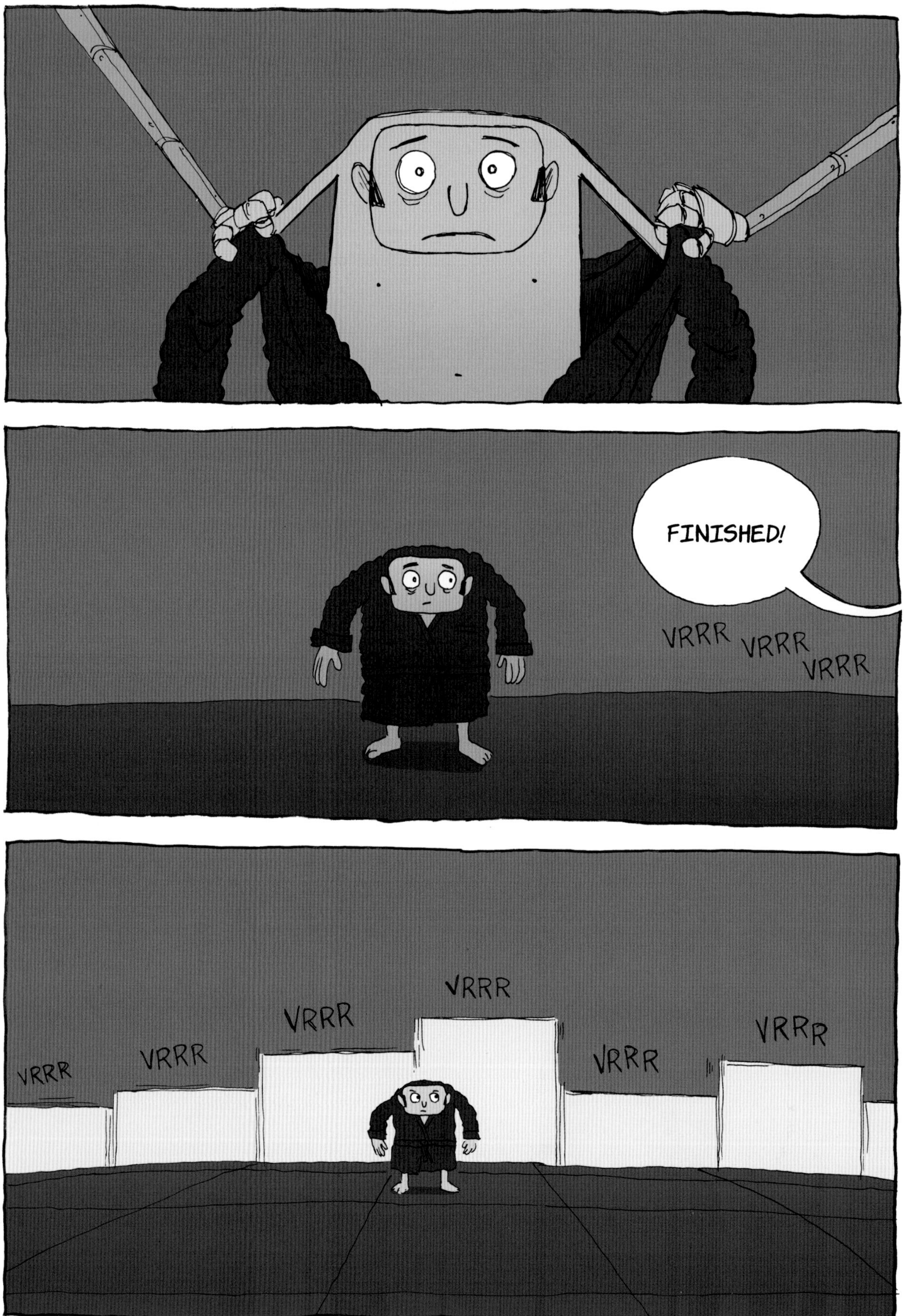
FINISHED!
VRRR VRRR VRRR
VRRR
VRRR
VRRR
VRRR
VRRR
VRRR

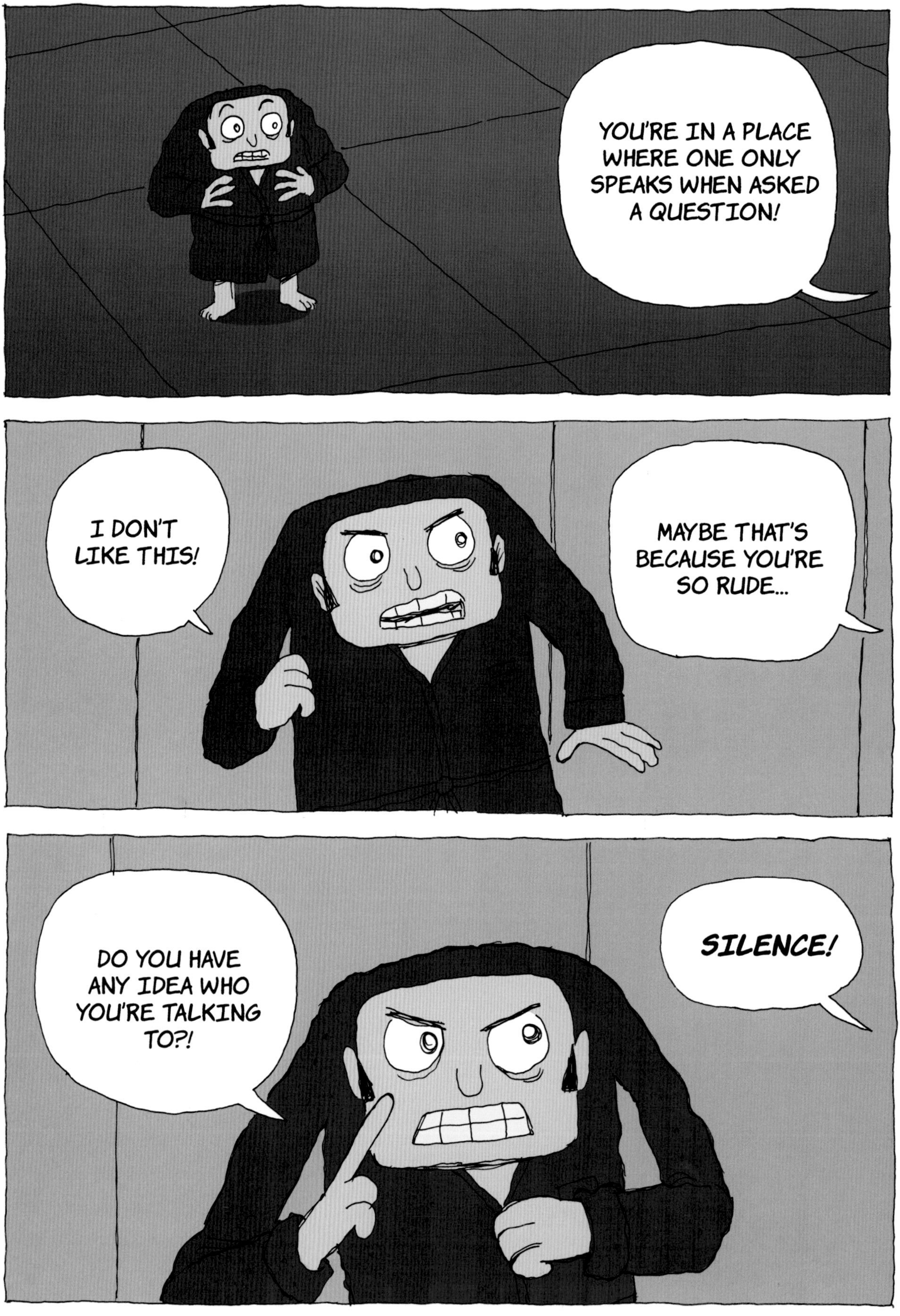
YOU'RE IN A PLACE WHERE ONE ONLY SPEAKS WHEN ASKED A QUESTION!
I DON'T LIKE THIS!
MAYBE THAT'S BECAUSE YOU'RE SO RUDE...
DO YOU HAVE ANY IDEA WHO YOU'RE TALKING TO?!
SILENCE!

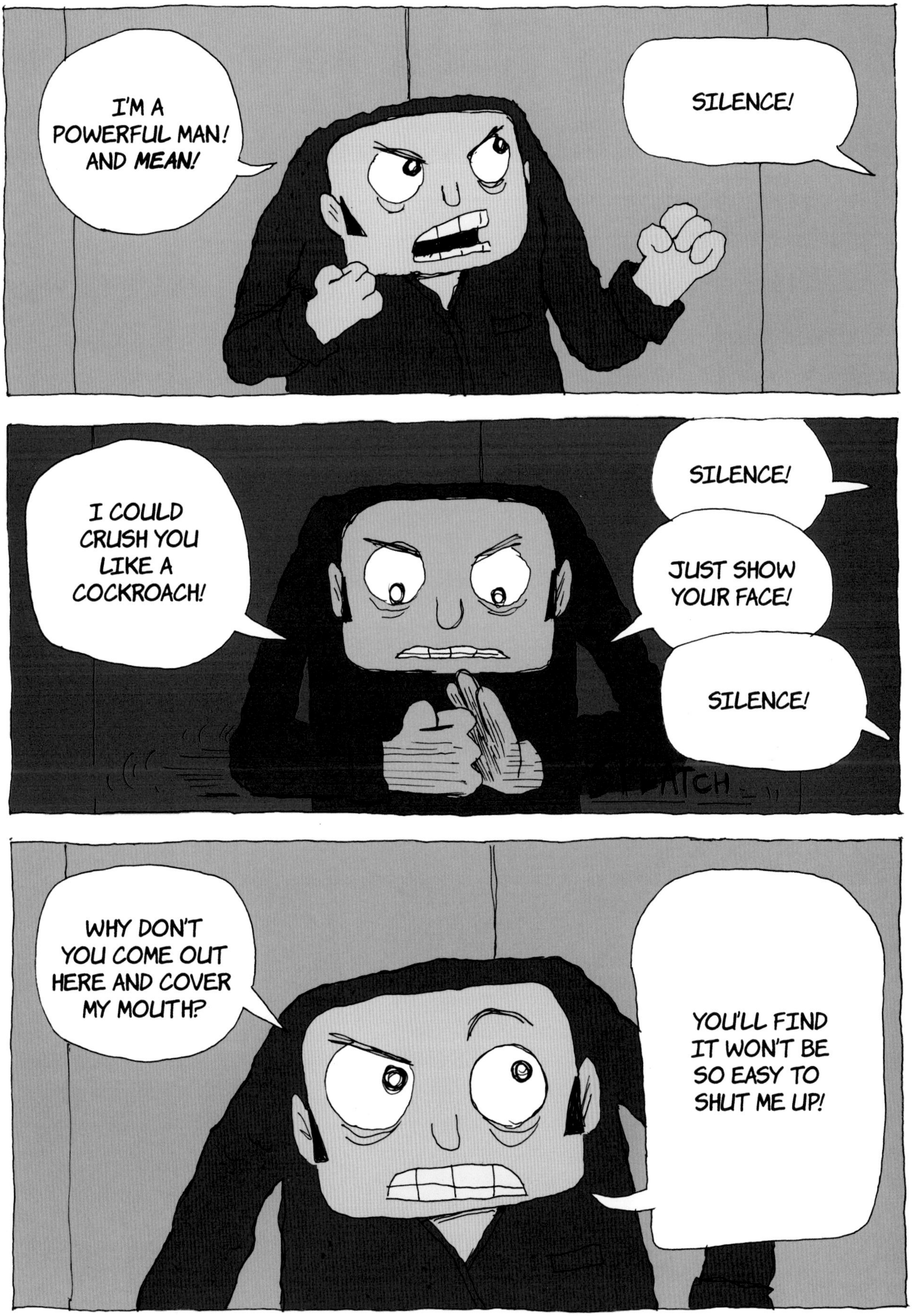
I'M A POWERFUL MAN! AND MEAN!
SILENCE!
I COULD CRUSH YOU LIKE A COCKROACH!
SILENCE!
JUST SHOW YOUR FACE!
SILENCE!
WHY DON'T YOU COME OUT HERE AND COVER MY MOUTH?
YOU'LL FIND IT WON'T BE SO EASY TO SHUT ME UP!

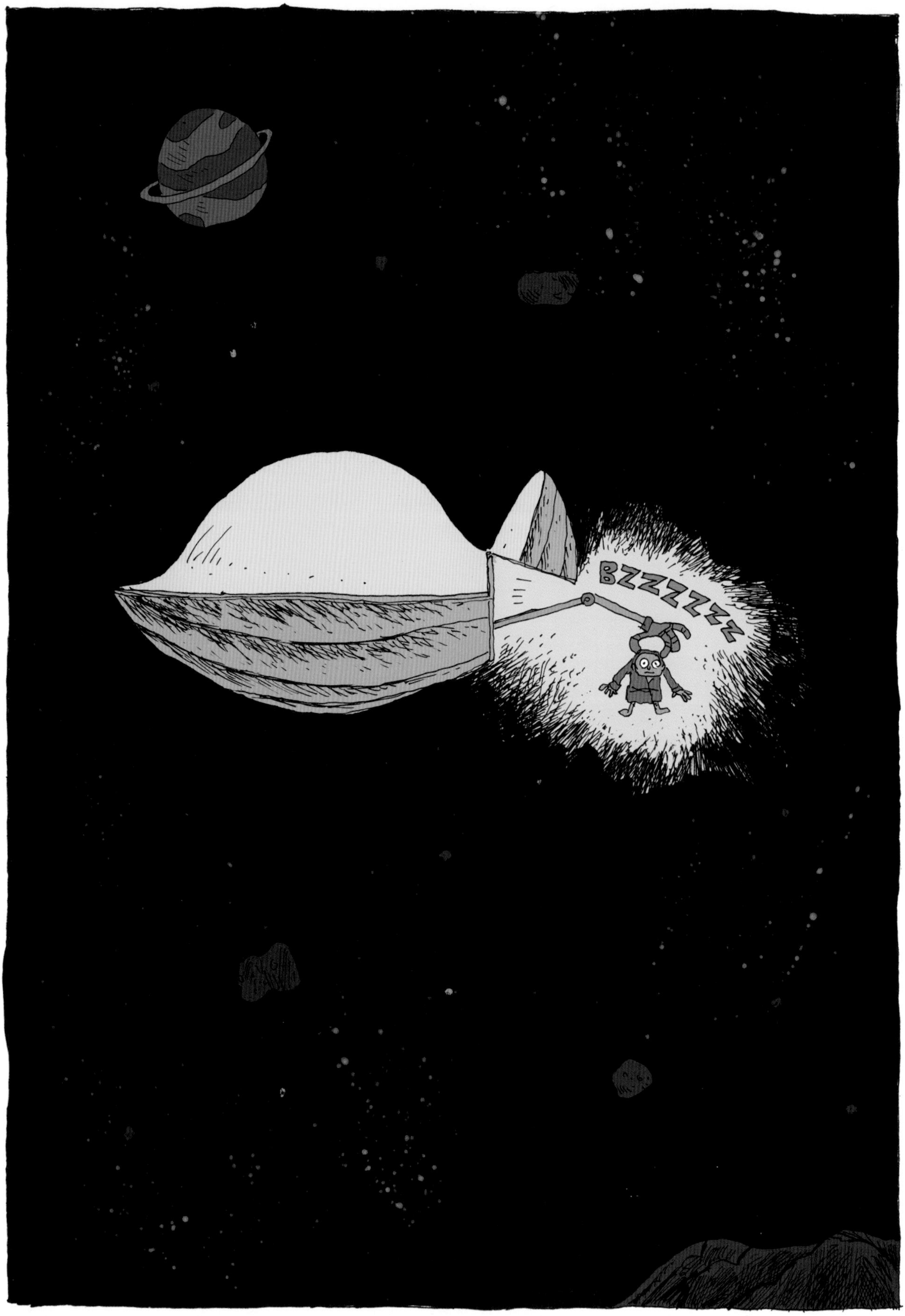
BZZZZZZZ

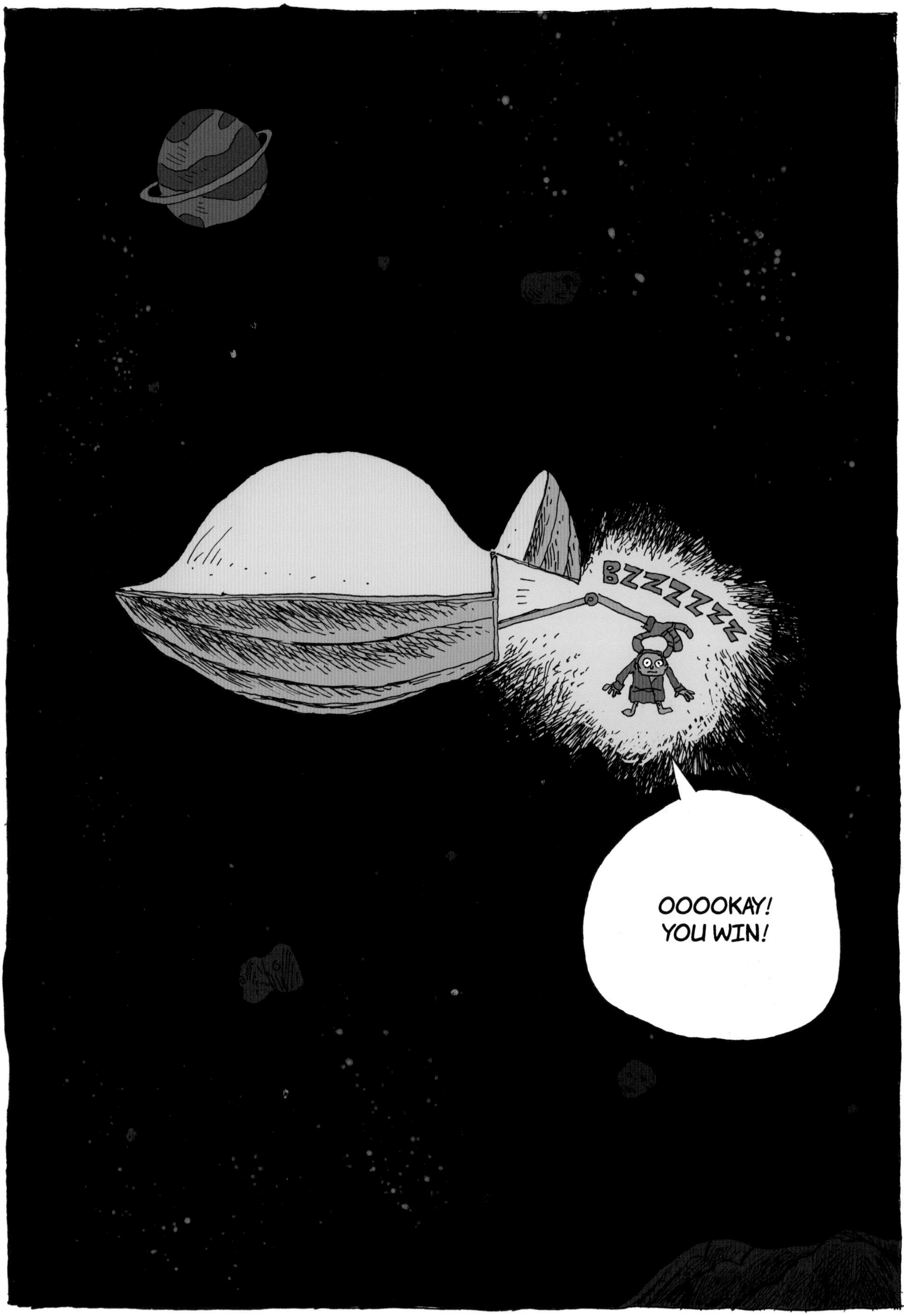
BZZZZZZZ
OOOOKAY! YOU WIN!

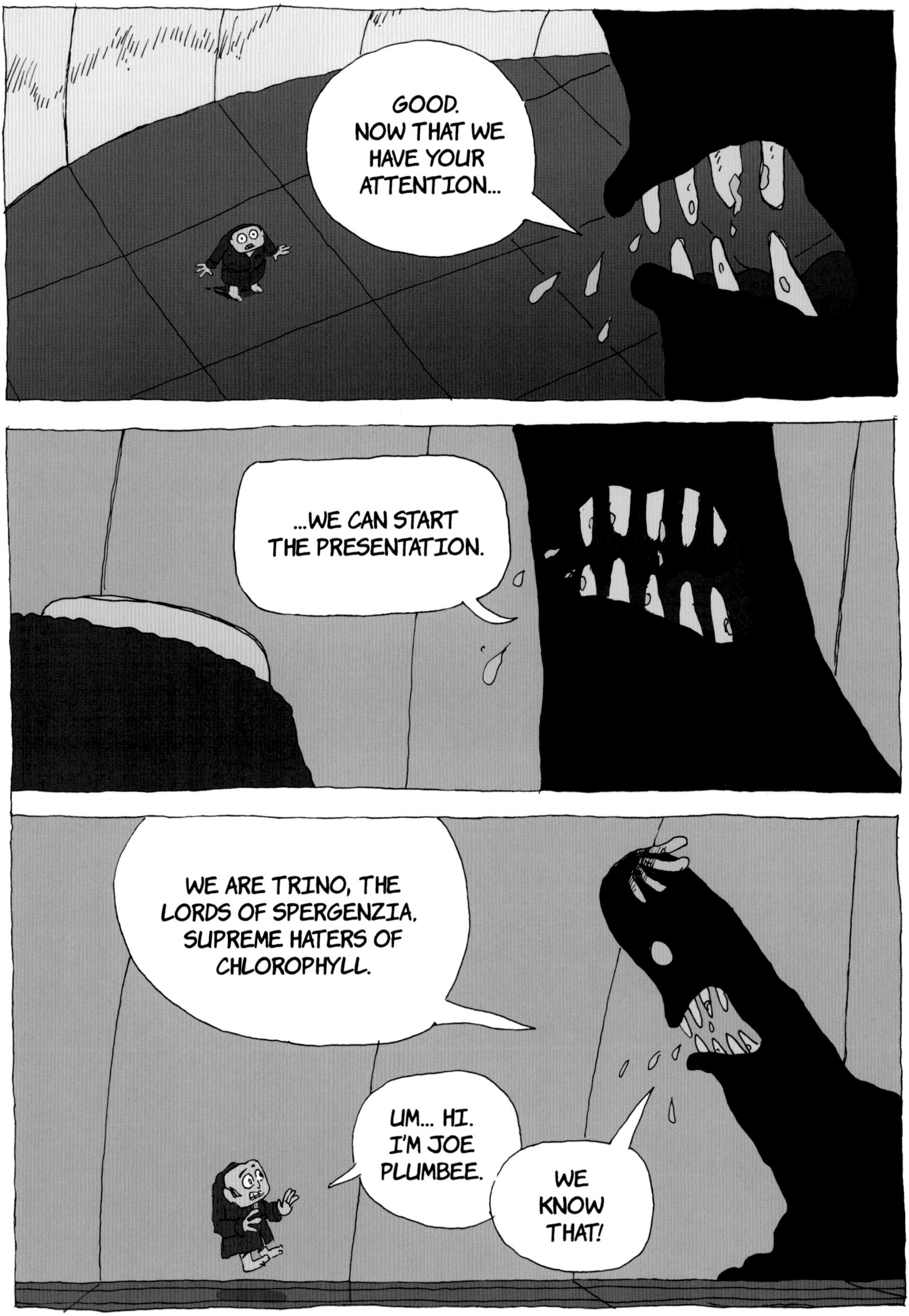
GOOD. NOW THAT WE HAVE YOUR ATTENTION...
...WE CAN START THE PRESENTATION.
WE ARE TRINO, THE LORDS OF SPERGENZIA, SUPREME HATERS OF CHLOROPHYLL.
UM... HI. I'M JOE PLUMBEE.
WE KNOW THAT!

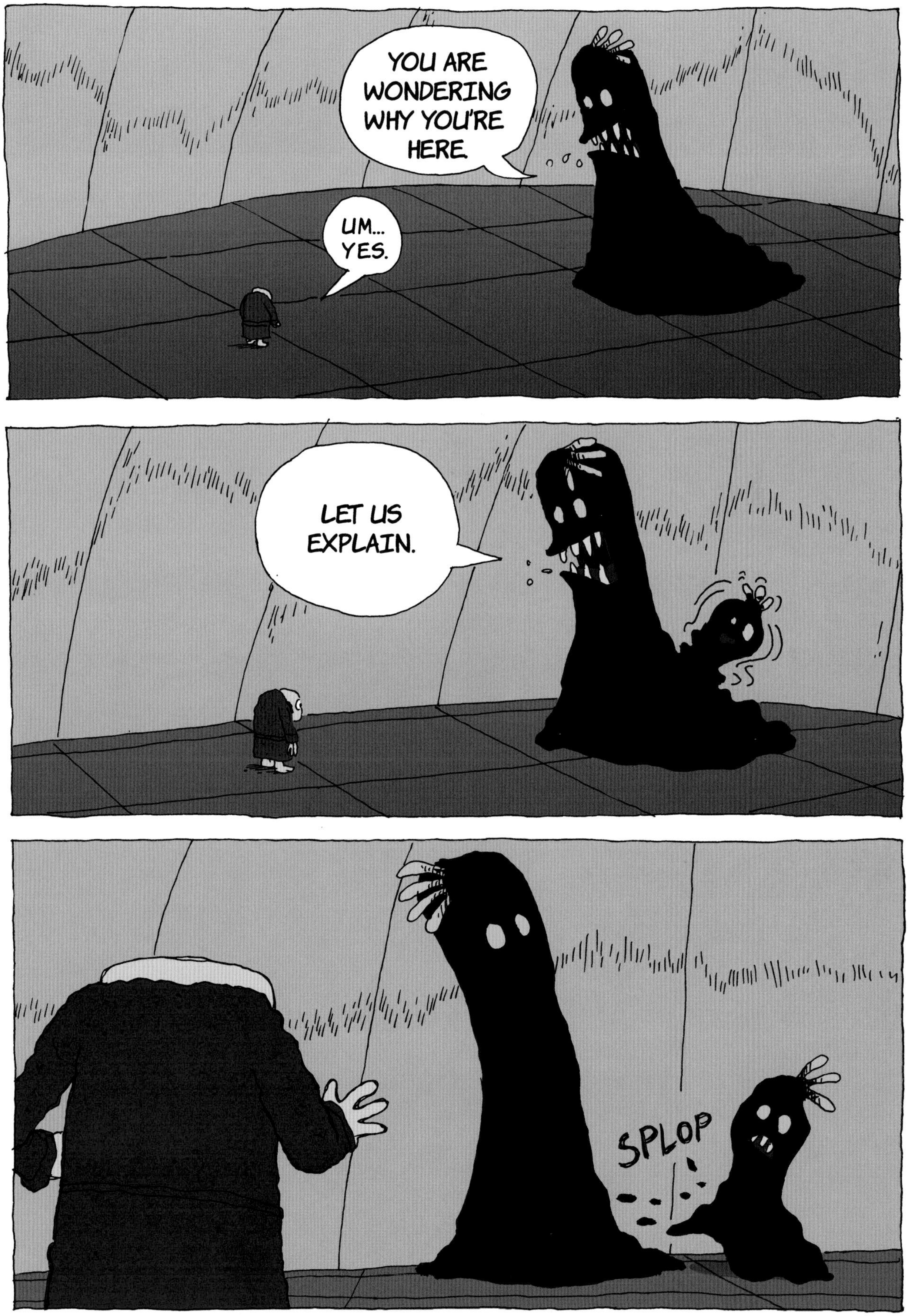
YOU ARE WONDERING WHY YOU'RE HERE.
UM... YES.
LET US EXPLAIN.
SPLOP

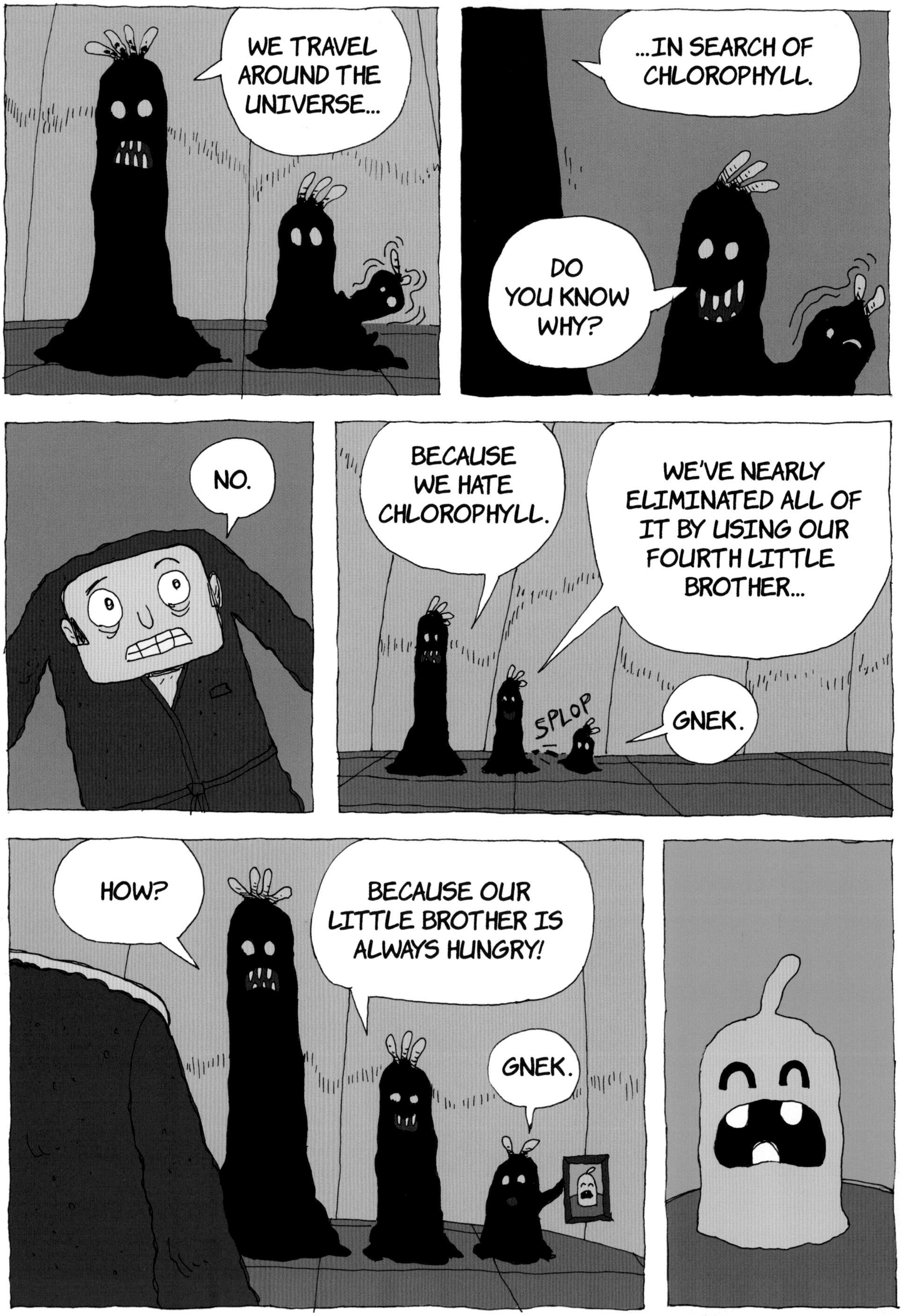
WE TRAVEL AROUND THE UNIVERSE...
...IN SEARCH OF CHLOROPHYLL.
DO YOU KNOW WHY?
NO.
BECAUSE WE HATE CHLOROPHYLL.
WE'VE NEARLY ELIMINATED ALL OF IT BY USING OUR FOURTH LITTLE BROTHER...
SPLOP
GNEK.
HOW?
BECAUSE OUR LITTLE BROTHER IS ALWAYS HUNGRY!
GNEK.

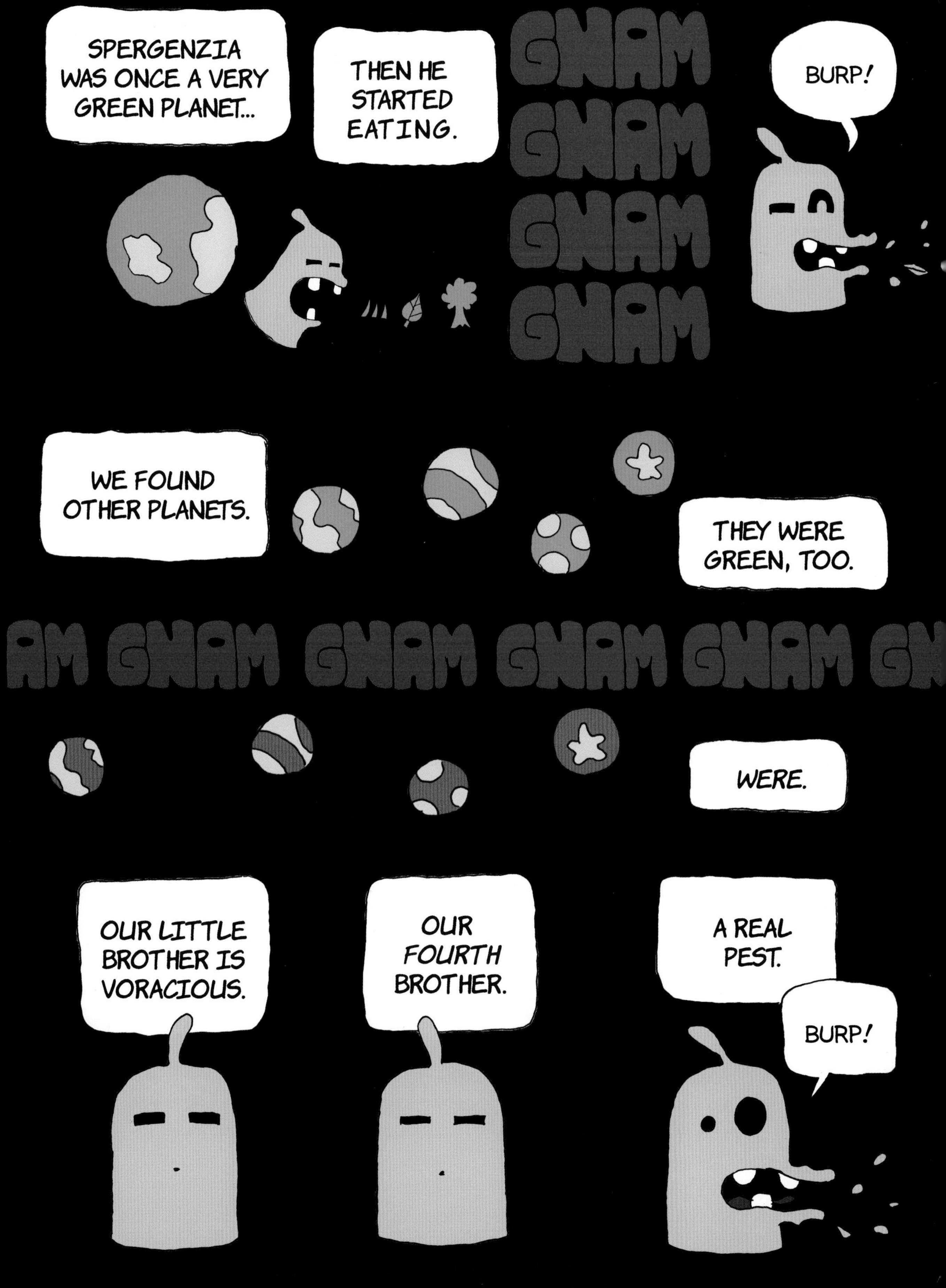
SPERGENZIA WAS ONCE A VERY GREEN PLANET...
THEN HE STARTED EATING.
GNAM GNAM GNAM GNAM
BURP!
WE FOUND OTHER PLANETS.
THEY WERE GREEN, TOO.
AM GNAM GNAM GNAM GNAM GN
WERE.
OUR LITTLE BROTHER IS VORACIOUS.
OUR FOURTH BROTHER.
A REAL PEST.
BURP!

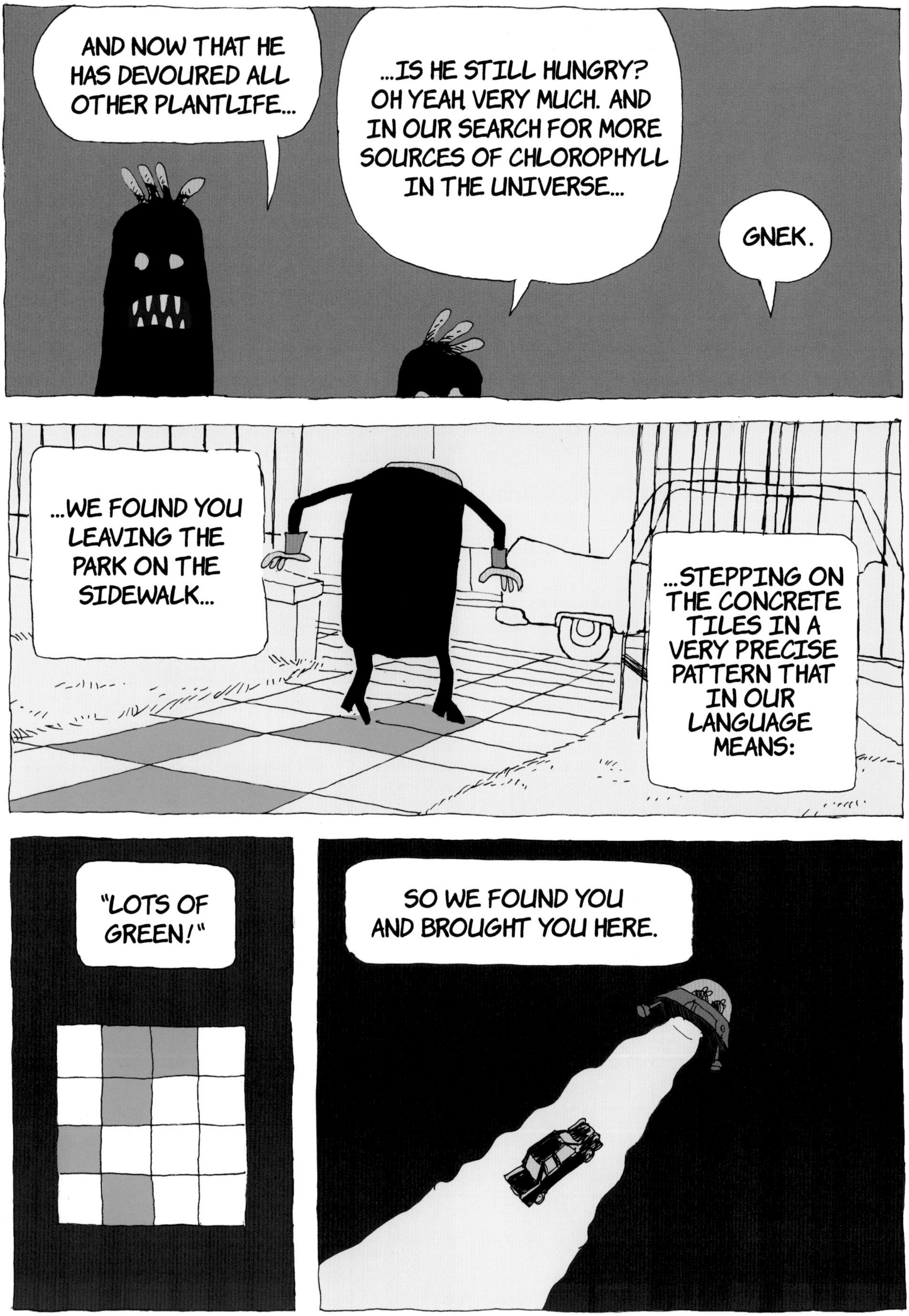
AND NOW THAT HE HAS DEVOURED ALL OTHER PLANTLIFE...
...IS HE STILL HUNGRY? OH YEAH, VERY MUCH. AND IN OUR SEARCH FOR MORE SOURCES OF CHLOROPHYLL IN THE UNIVERSE...
GNEK.
...WE FOUND YOU LEAVING THE PARK ON THE SIDEWALK...
...STEPPING ON THE CONCRETE TILES IN A VERY PRECISE PATTERN THAT IN OUR LANGUAGE MEANS:
"LOTS OF GREEN!"
SO WE FOUND YOU AND BROUGHT YOU HERE.

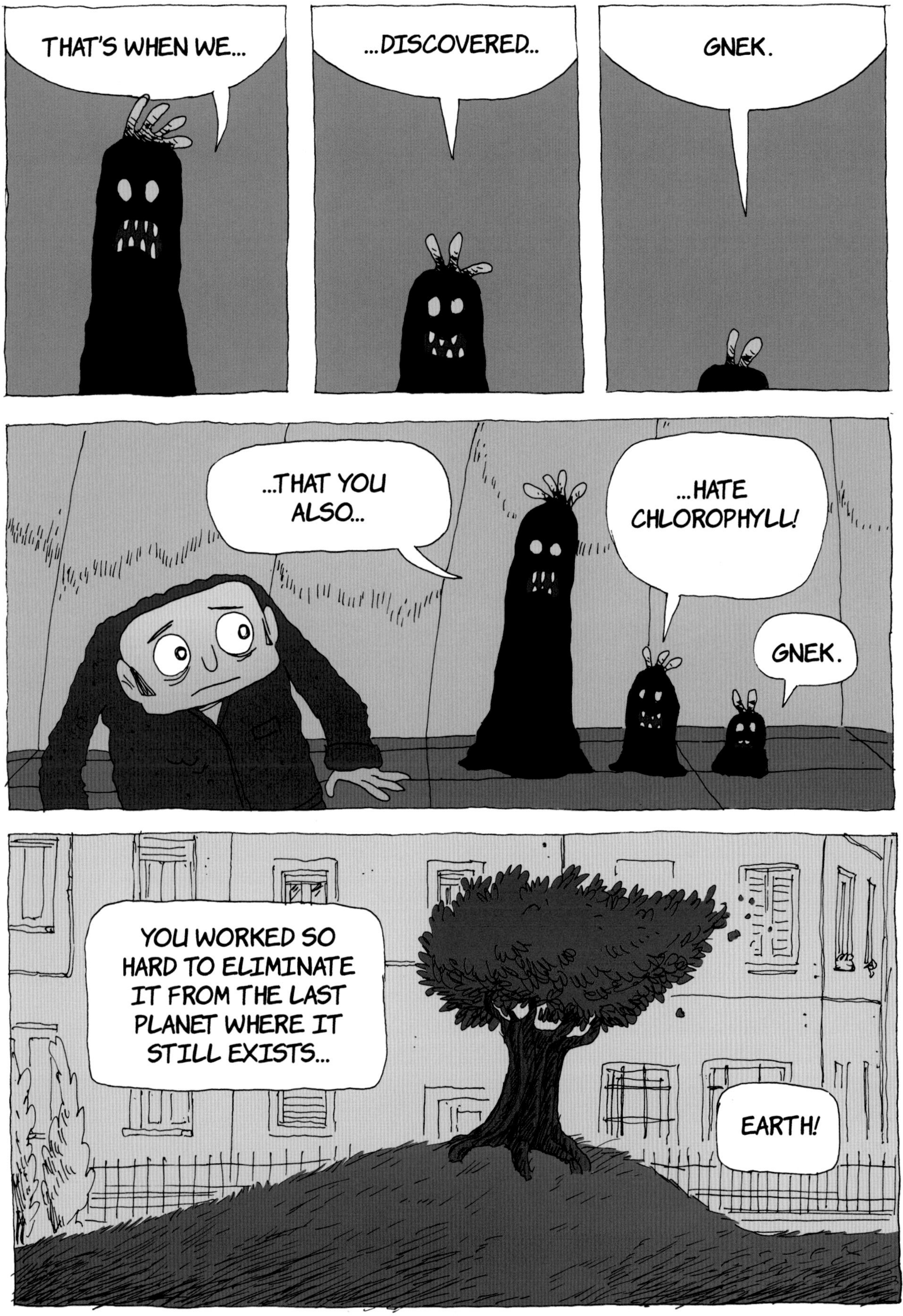
THAT'S WHEN WE...
...DISCOVERED...
GNEK.
...THAT YOU ALSO...
...HATE CHLOROPHYLL!
GNEK.
YOU WORKED SO HARD TO ELIMINATE IT FROM THE LAST PLANET WHERE IT STILL EXISTS...
EARTH!

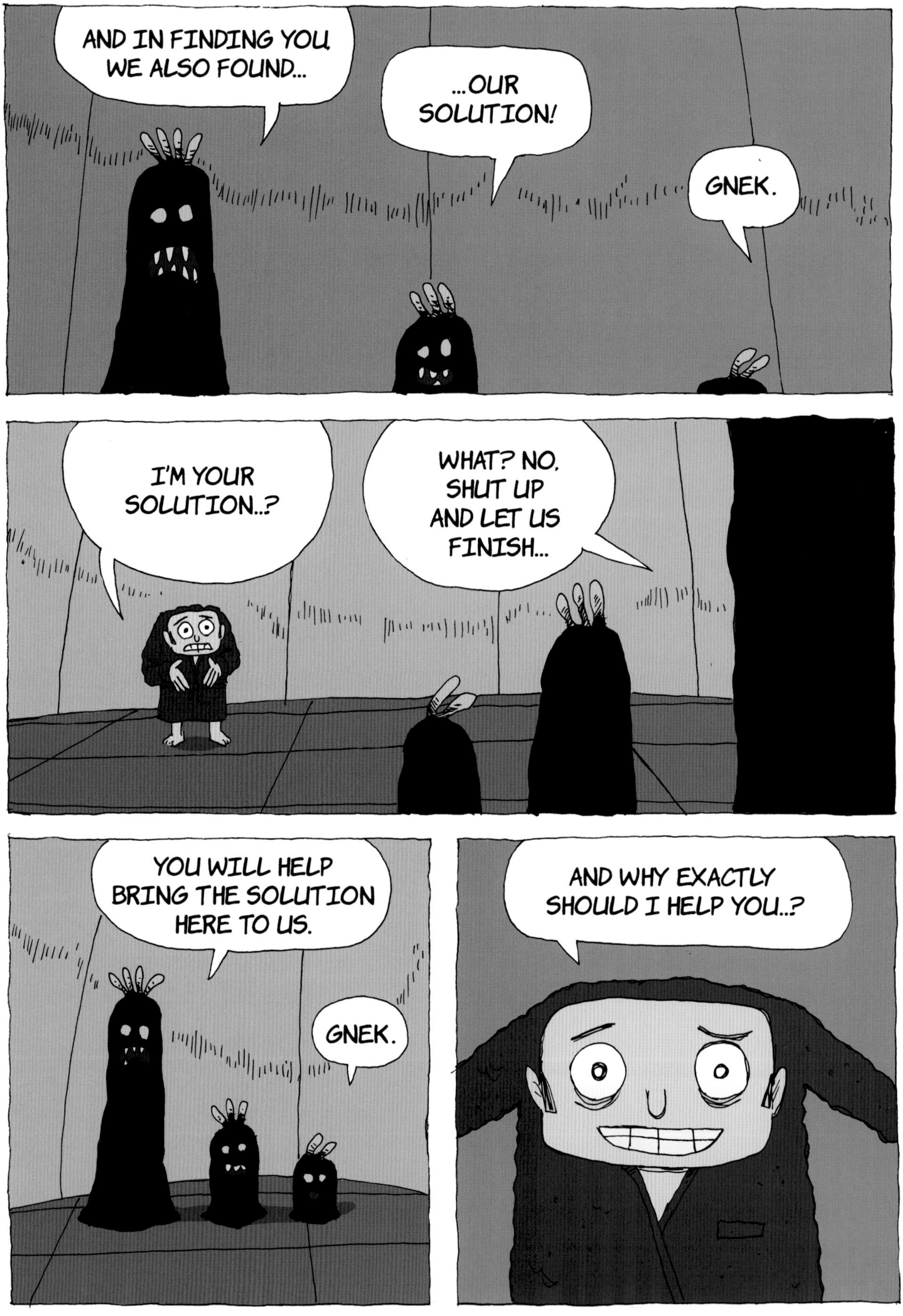
AND IN FINDING YOU, WE ALSO FOUND...
...OUR SOLUTION!
GNEK.
I'M YOUR SOLUTION..?
WHAT? NO. SHUT UP AND LET US FINISH...
YOU WILL HELP BRING THE SOLUTION HERE TO US.
GNEK.
AND WHY EXACTLY SHOULD I HELP YOU..?

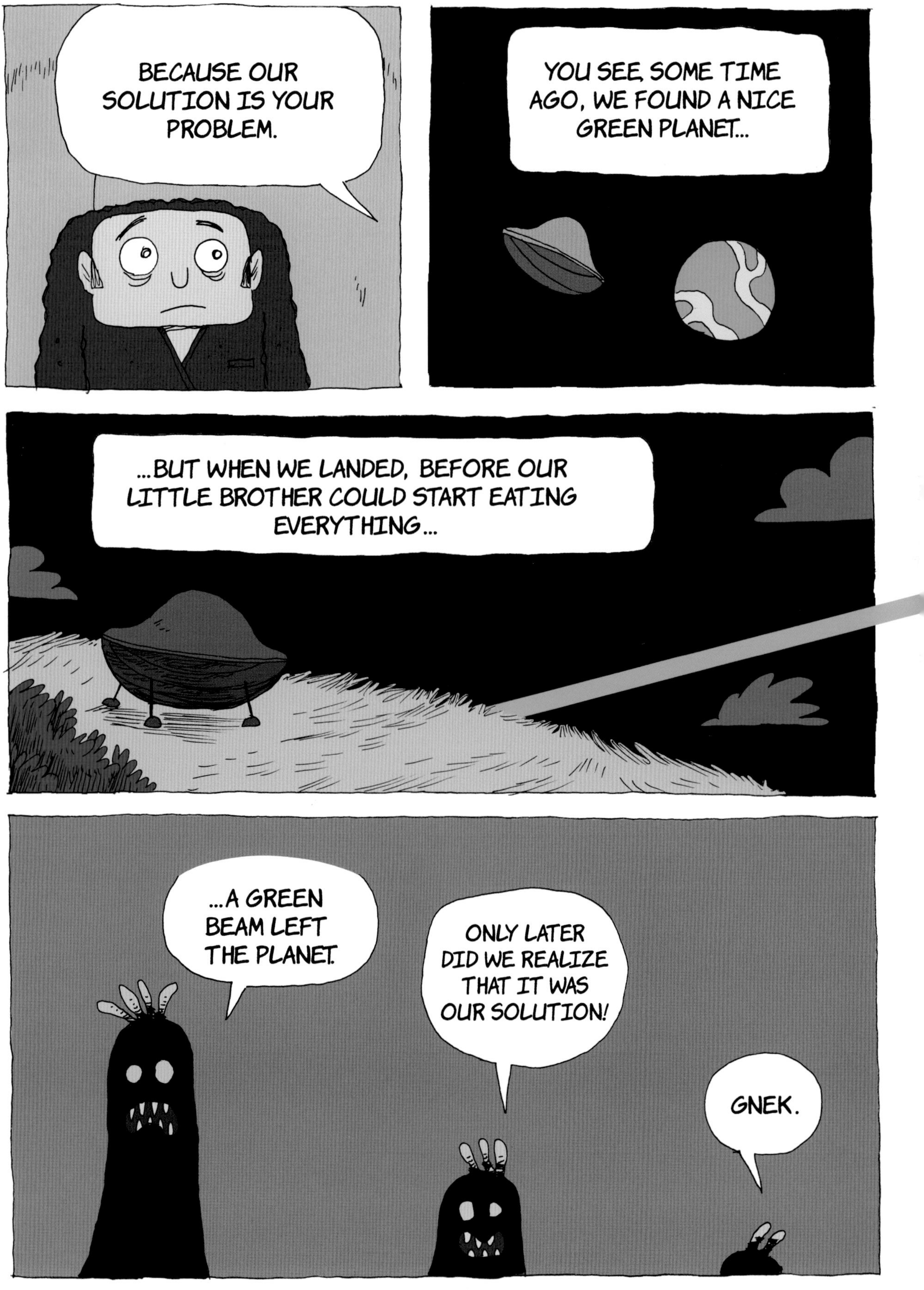

BECAUSE OUR SOLUTION IS YOUR PROBLEM.
YOU SEE, SOME TIME AGO, WE FOUND A NICE GREEN PLANET...
...BUT WHEN WE LANDED, BEFORE OUR LITTLE BROTHER COULD START EATING EVERYTHING...
...A GREEN BEAM LEFT THE PLANET.
ONLY LATER DID WE REALIZE THAT IT WAS OUR SOLUTION!
GNEK.

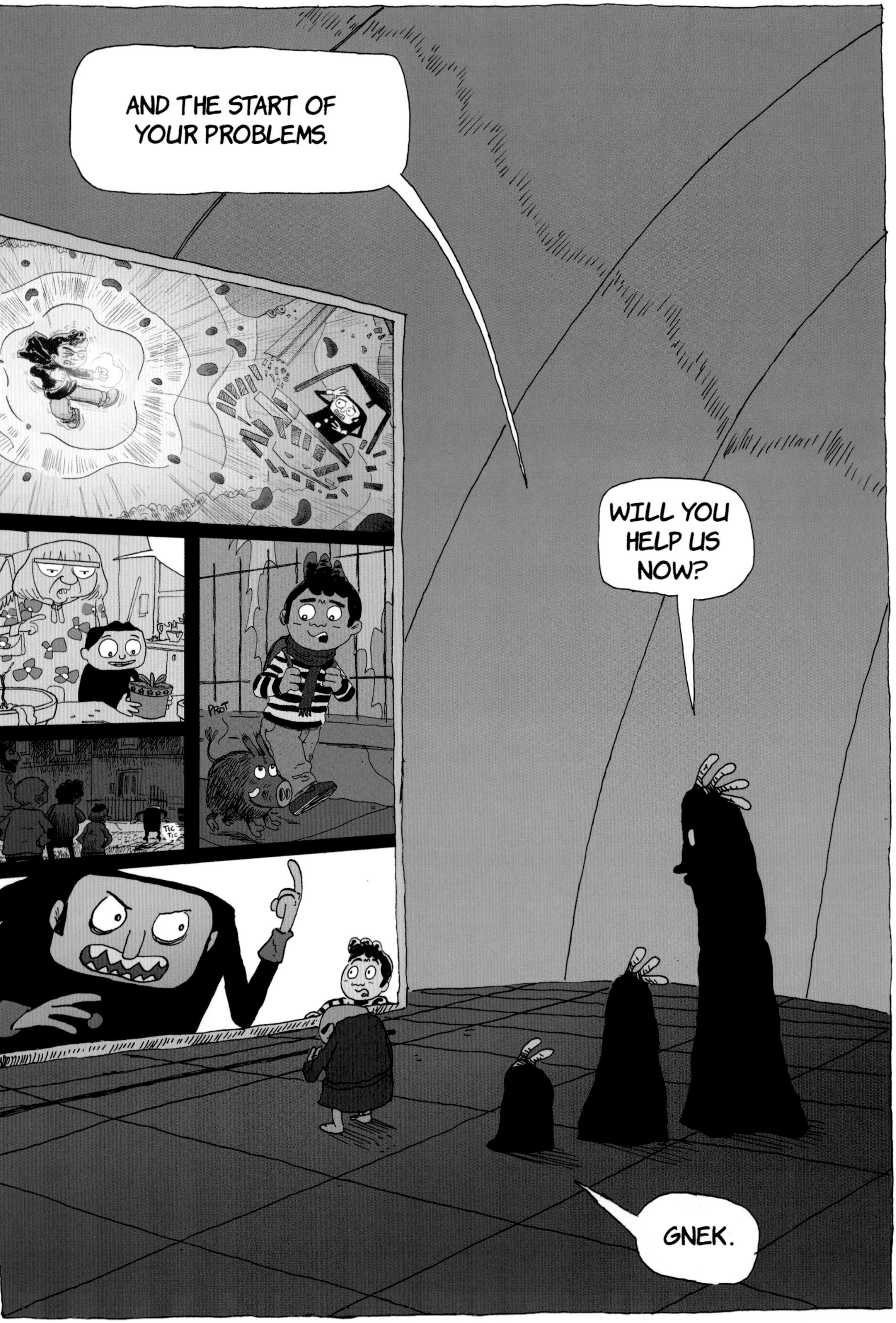
AND THE START OF YOUR PROBLEMS.
PROT
TIC TIC
WILL YOU HELP US NOW?
GNEK.

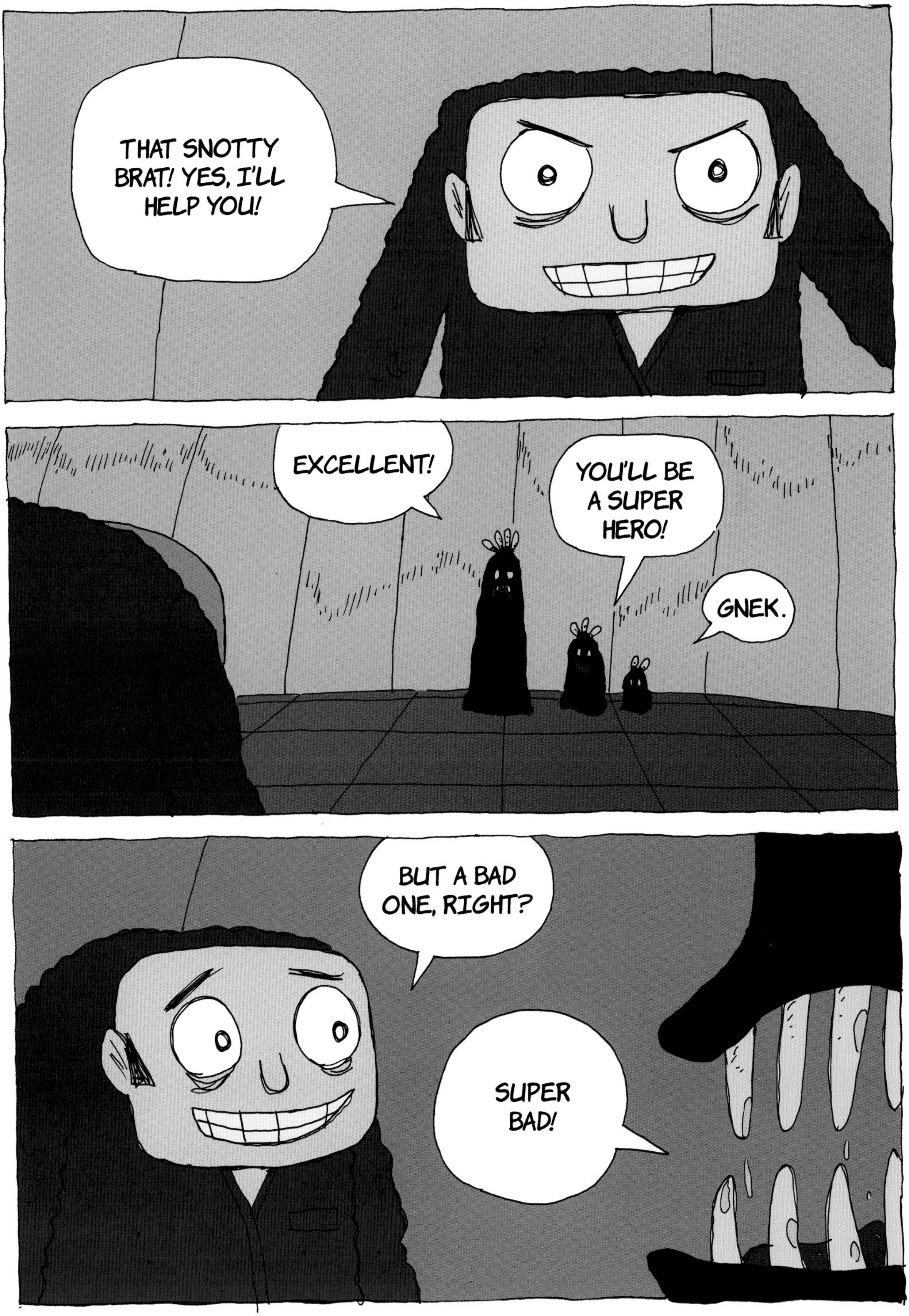
THAT SNOTTY BRAT! YES, I'LL HELP YOU!
EXCELLENT!
YOU'LL BE A SUPER HERO!
GNEK.
BUT A BAD ONE, RIGHT?
SUPER BAD!

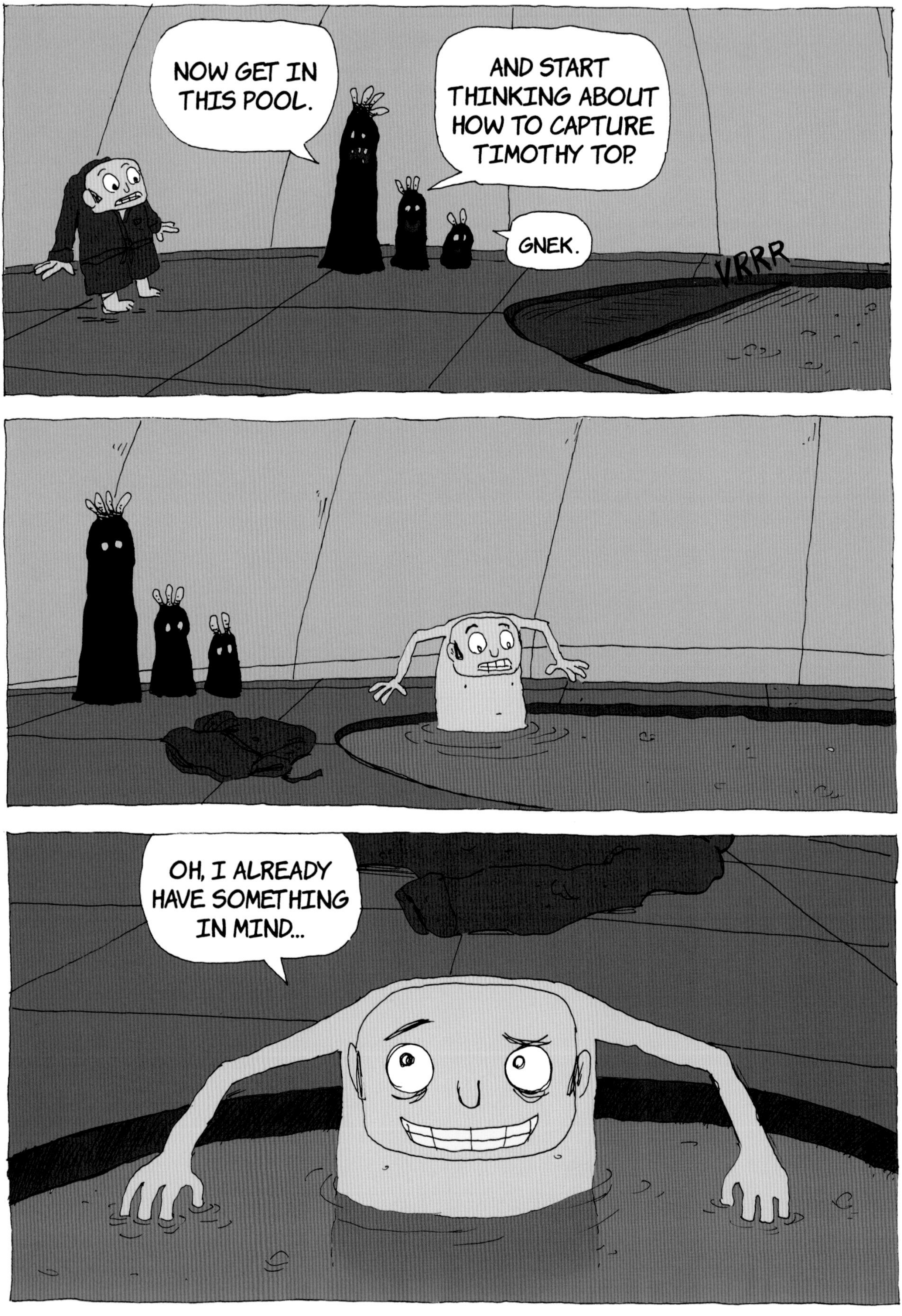
NOW GET IN THIS POOL.
AND START THINKING ABOUT HOW TO CAPTURE TIMOTHY TOP.
GNEK.
VRRR
OH, I ALREADY HAVE SOMETHING IN MIND...

CHAPTER TWO
FOURTH GRADE

SGRUFL
SGRUFL

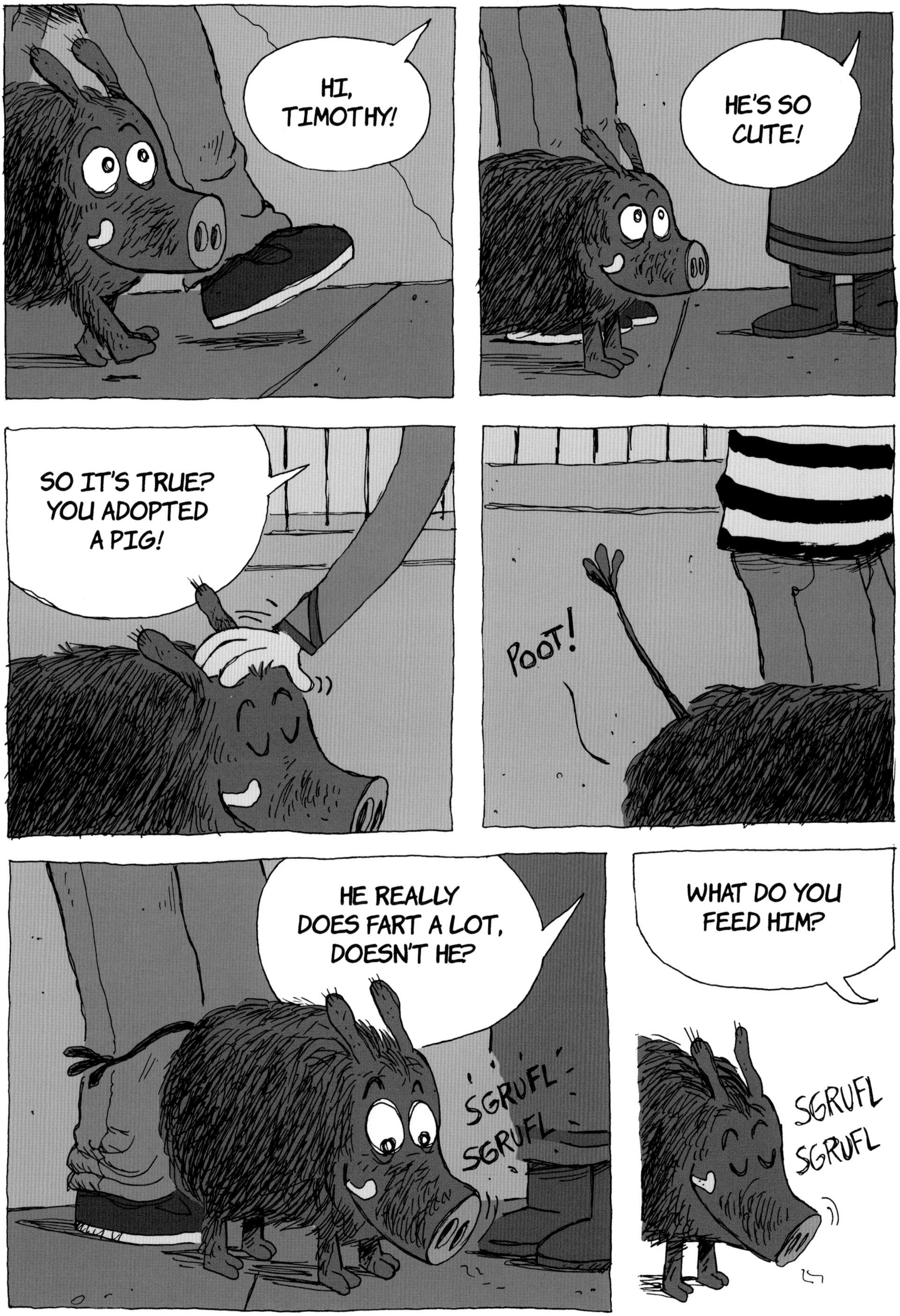
HI, TIMOTHY!
HE'S SO CUTE!
SO IT'S TRUE? YOU ADOPTED A PIG!
POOT!
HE REALLY DOES FART A LOT, DOESN'T HE?
SGRUFL SGRUFL
WHAT DO YOU FEED HIM?
SGRUFL SGRUFL

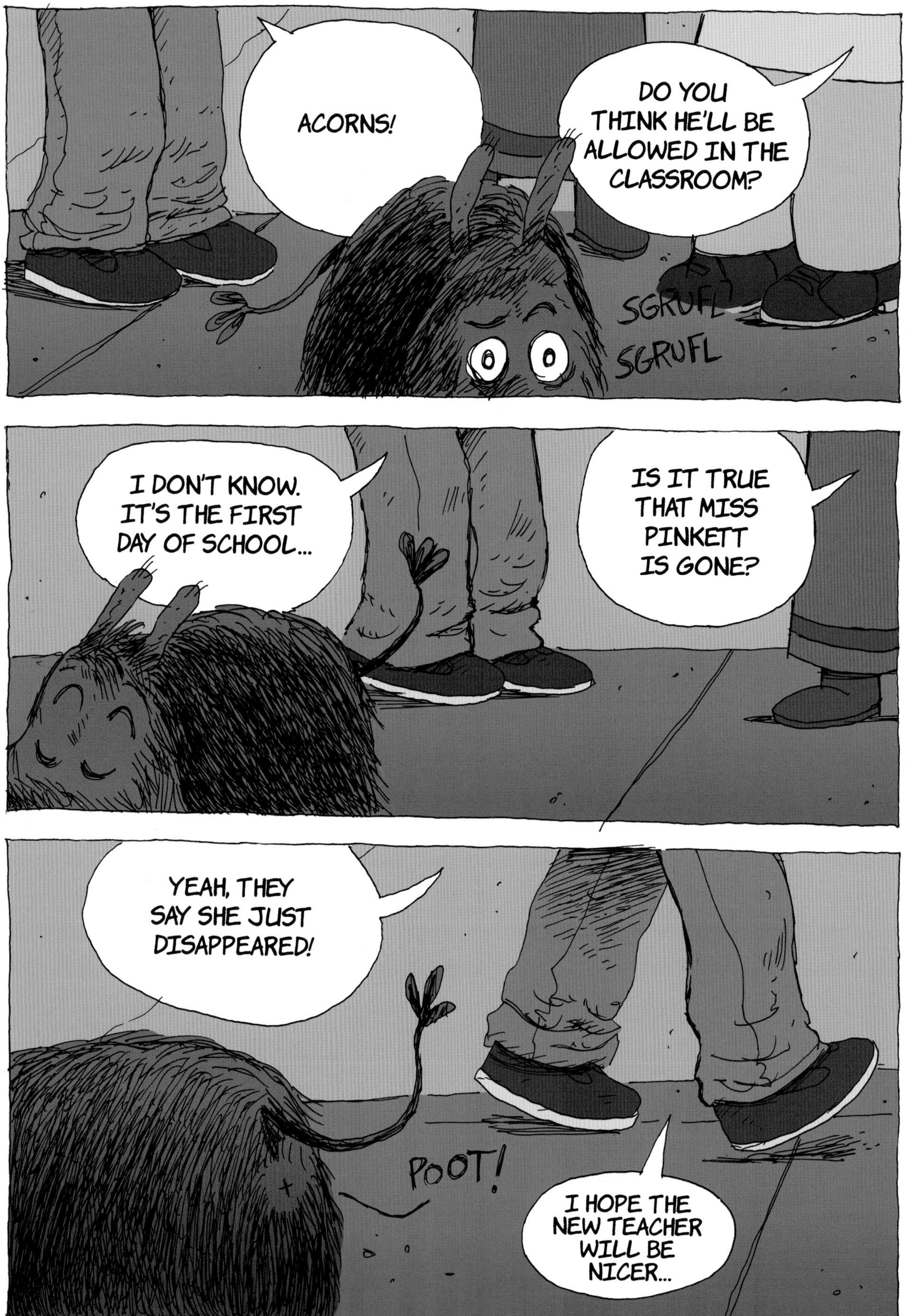

ACORNS!
DO YOU THINK HE'LL BE ALLOWED IN THE CLASSROOM?
SGRUFL
SGRUFL
I DON'T KNOW. IT'S THE FIRST DAY OF SCHOOL...
IS IT TRUE THAT MISS PINKETT IS GONE?
YEAH, THEY SAY SHE JUST DISAPPEARED!
POOT!
I HOPE THE NEW TEACHER WILL BE NICER...

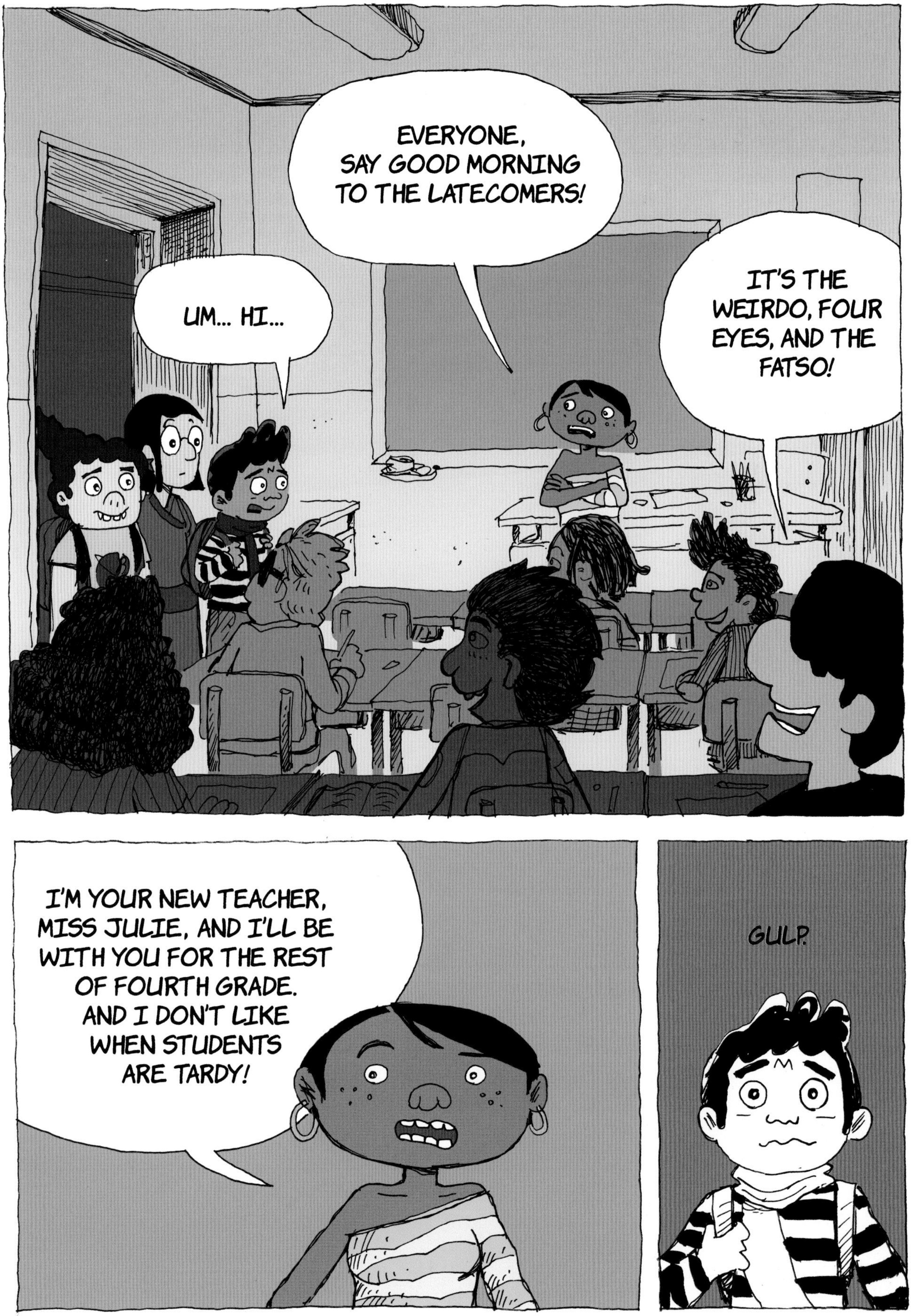
EVERYONE, SAY GOOD MORNING TO THE LATECOMERS!
UM... HI...
IT'S THE WEIRDO, FOUR EYES, AND THE FATSO!
I'M YOUR NEW TEACHER, MISS JULIE, AND I'LL BE WITH YOU FOR THE REST OF FOURTH GRADE. AND I DON'T LIKE WHEN STUDENTS ARE TARDY!
GULP.

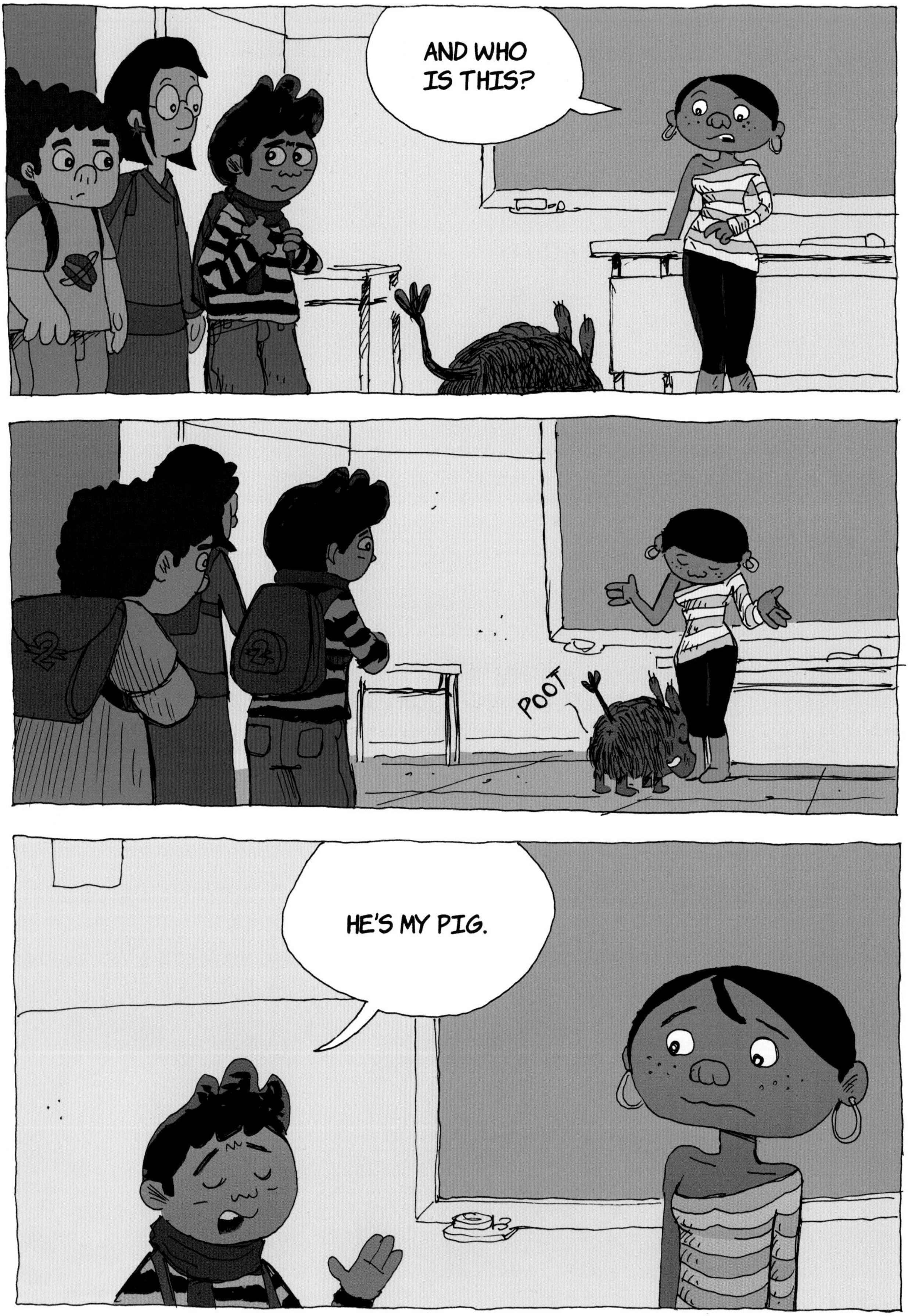
AND WHO IS THIS?
POOT
HE'S MY PIG.

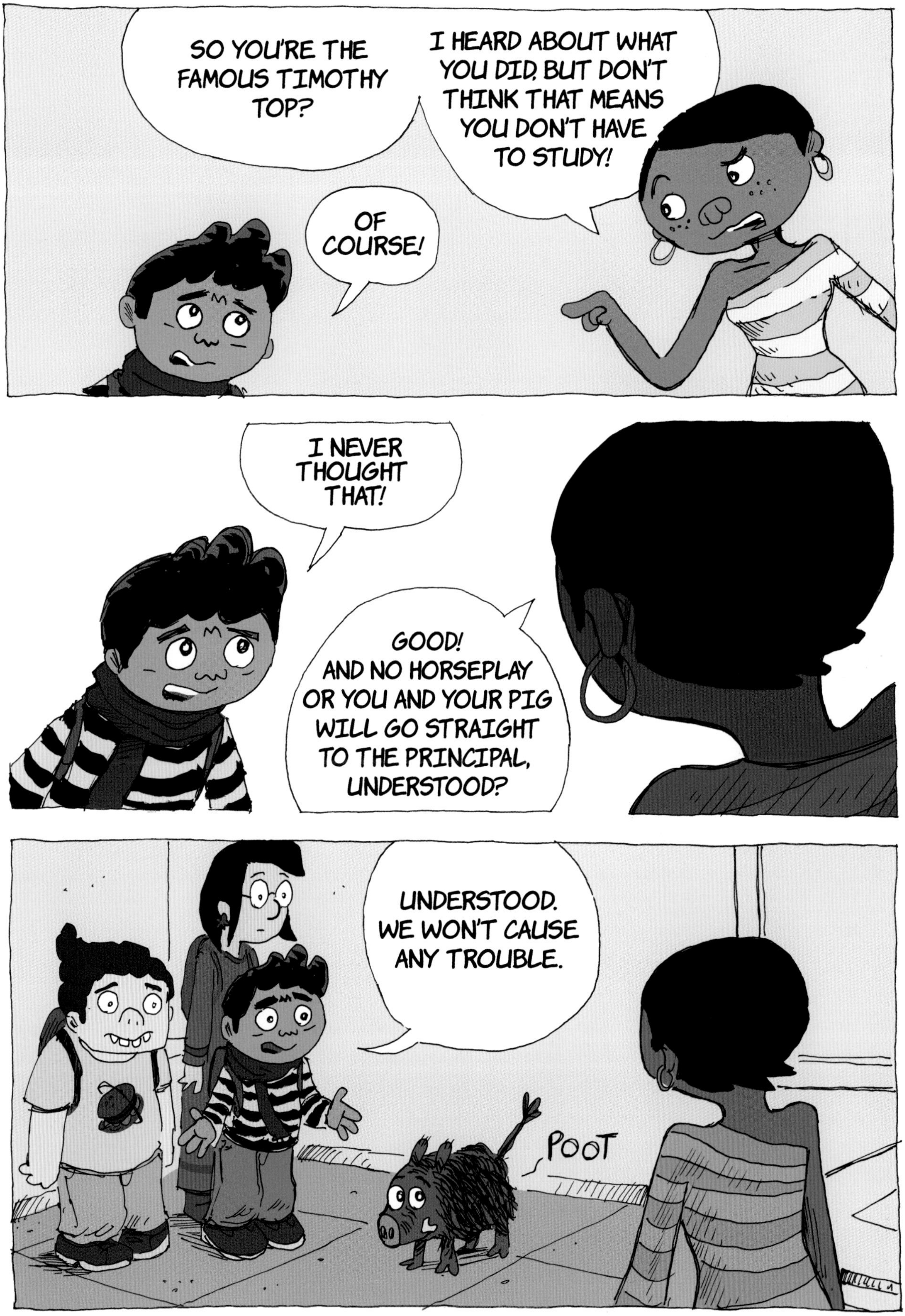
SO YOU'RE THE FAMOUS TIMOTHY TOP?
I HEARD ABOUT WHAT YOU DID, BUT DON'T THINK THAT MEANS YOU DON'T HAVE TO STUDY!
OF COURSE!
I NEVER THOUGHT THAT!
GOOD! AND NO HORSEPLAY OR YOU AND YOUR PIG WILL GO STRAIGHT TO THE PRINCIPAL, UNDERSTOOD?
UNDERSTOOD. WE WON'T CAUSE ANY TROUBLE.
POOT

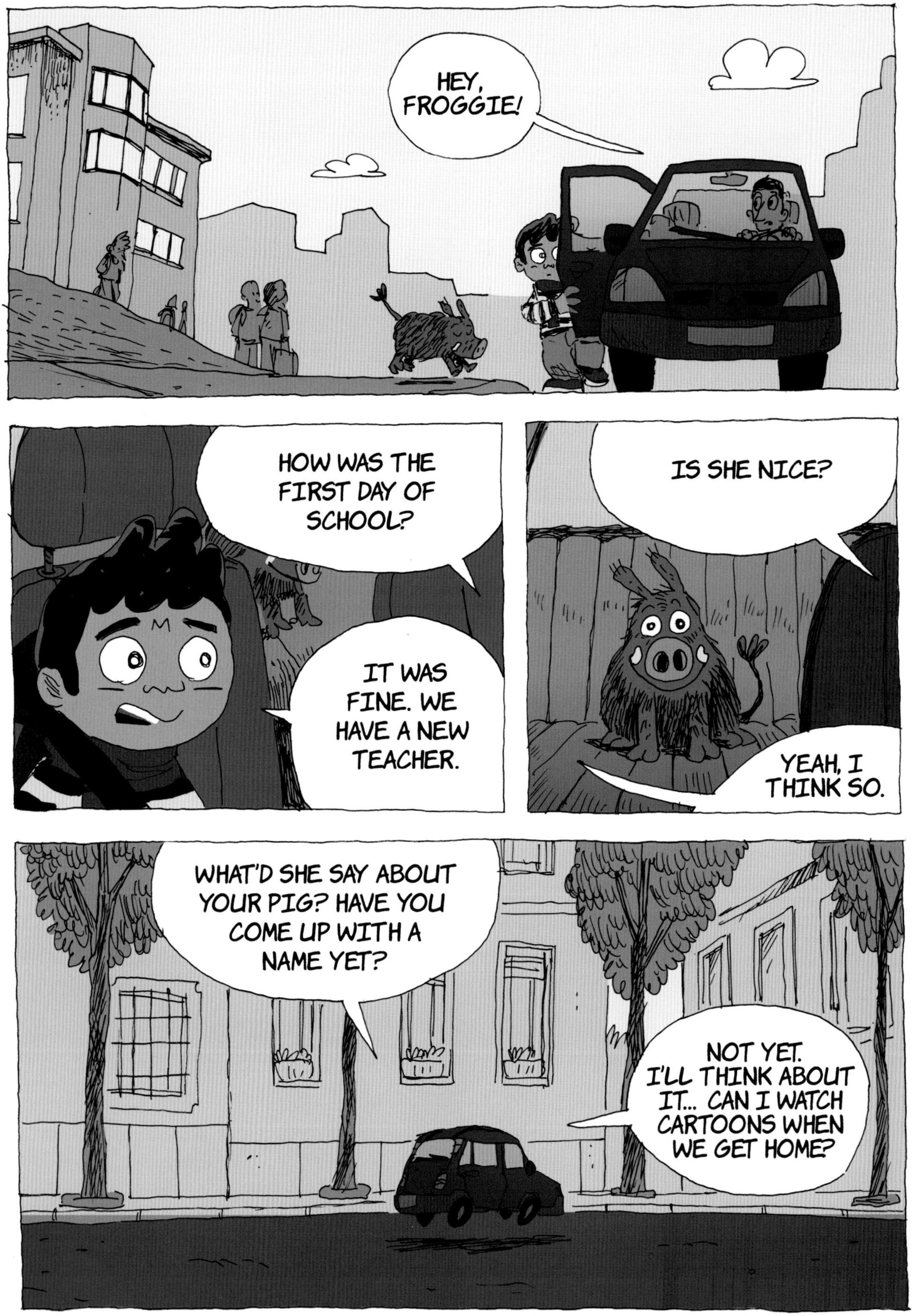
HEY, FROGGIE!
HOW WAS THE FIRST DAY OF SCHOOL?
IT WAS FINE. WE HAVE A NEW TEACHER.
IS SHE NICE?
YEAH, I THINK SO.
WHAT'D SHE SAY ABOUT YOUR PIG? HAVE YOU COME UP WITH A NAME YET?
NOT YET. I'LL THINK ABOUT IT... CAN I WATCH CARTOONS WHEN WE GET HOME?

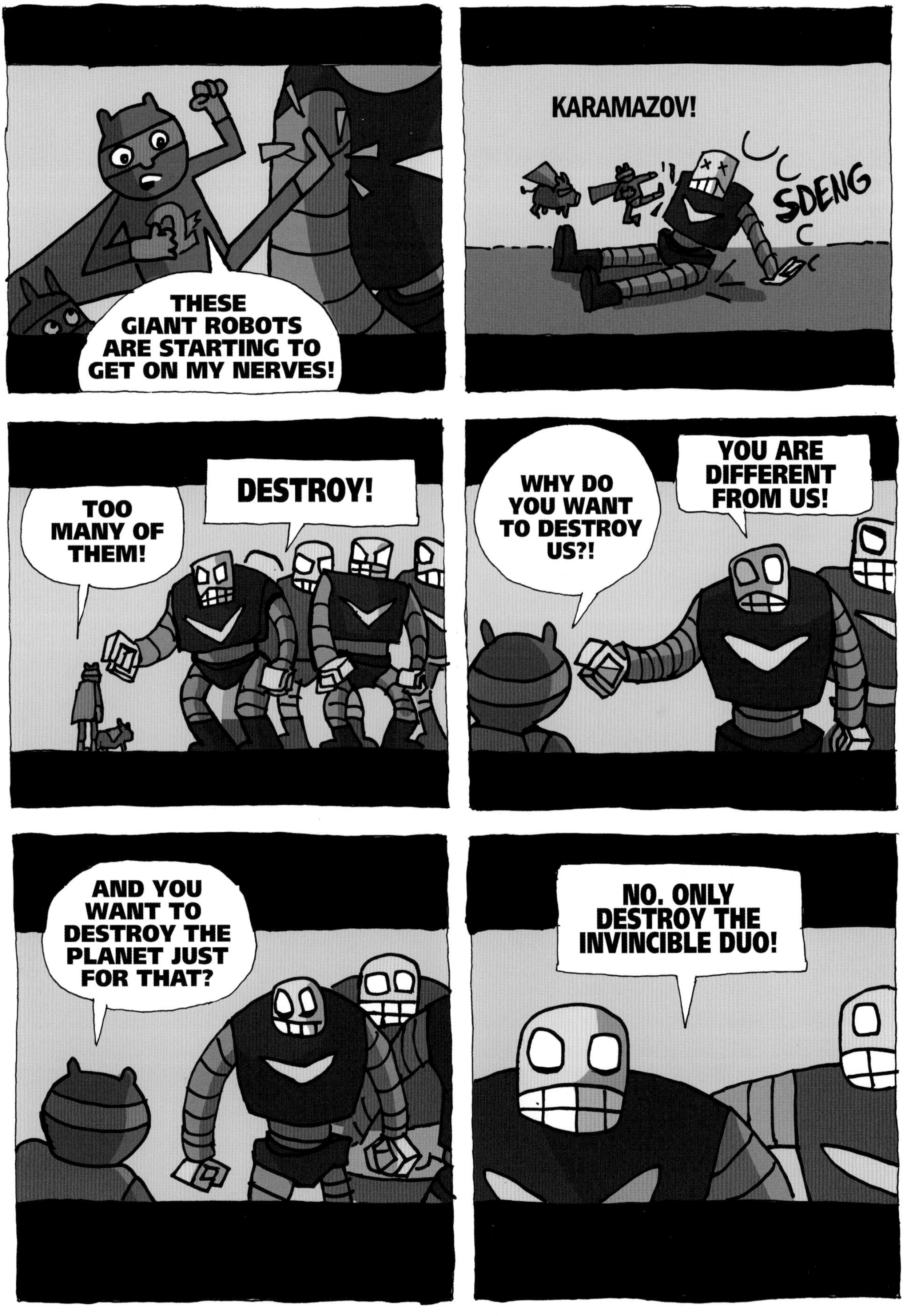
THESE GIANT ROBOTS ARE STARTING TO GET ON MY NERVES!
KARAMAZOV!
SDENG
TOO MANY OF THEM!
DESTROY!
WHY DO YOU WANT TO DESTROY US?!
YOU ARE DIFFERENT FROM US!
AND YOU WANT TO DESTROY THE PLANET JUST FOR THAT?
NO. ONLY DESTROY THE INVINCIBLE DUO!

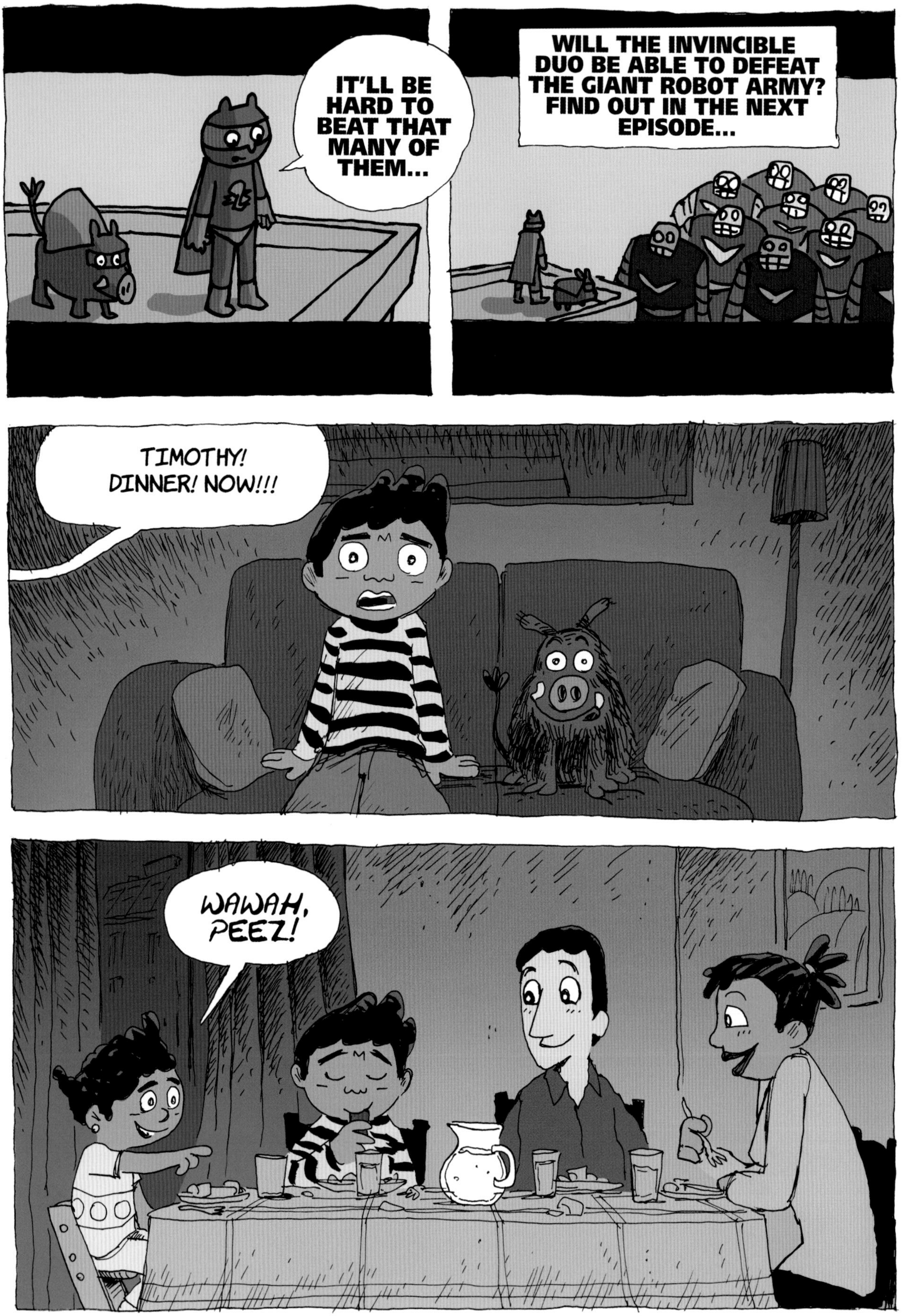
IT'LL BE HARD TO BEAT THAT MANY OF THEM...
WILL THE INVINCIBLE DUO BE ABLE TO DEFEAT THE GIANT ROBOT ARMY? FIND OUT IN THE NEXT EPISODE...
TIMOTHY! DINNER! NOW!!!
WAWAH, PEEZ!

CHAPTER THREE
ELECTRA ALLEN

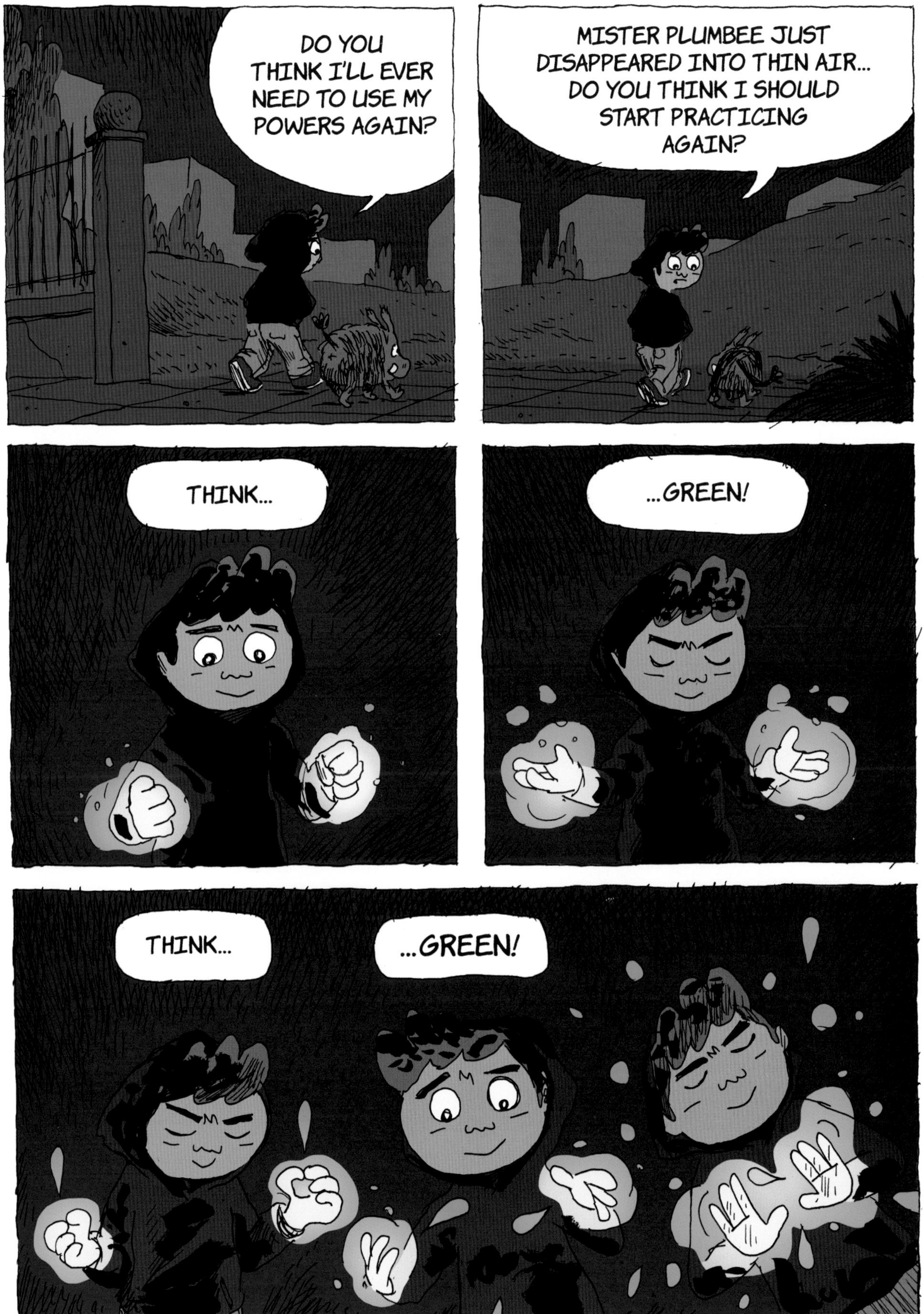
DO YOU THINK I'LL EVER NEED TO USE MY POWERS AGAIN?
MISTER PLUMBEE JUST DISAPPEARED INTO THIN AIR... DO YOU THINK I SHOULD START PRACTICING AGAIN?
THINK...
...GREEN!
THINK...
...GREEN!

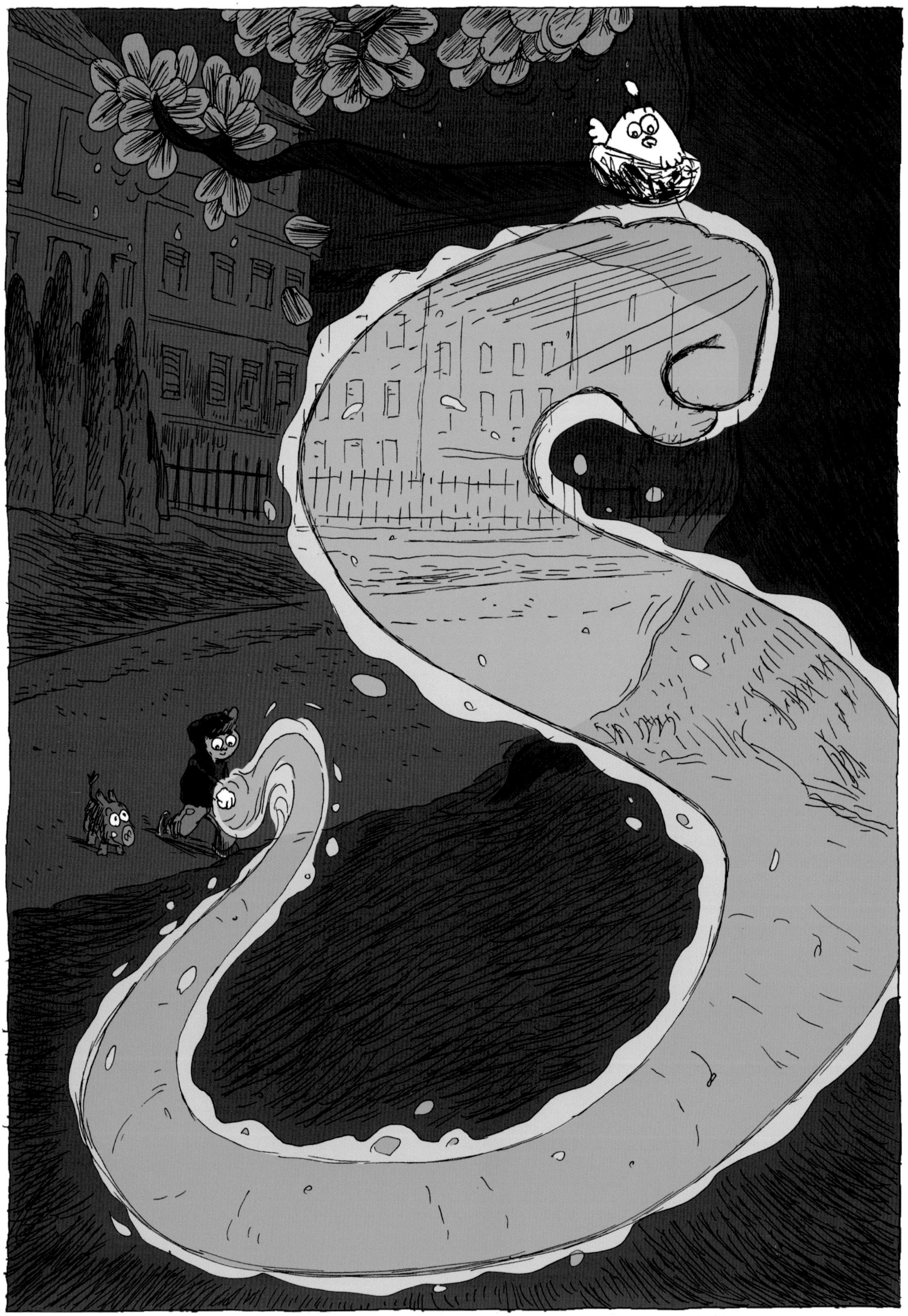

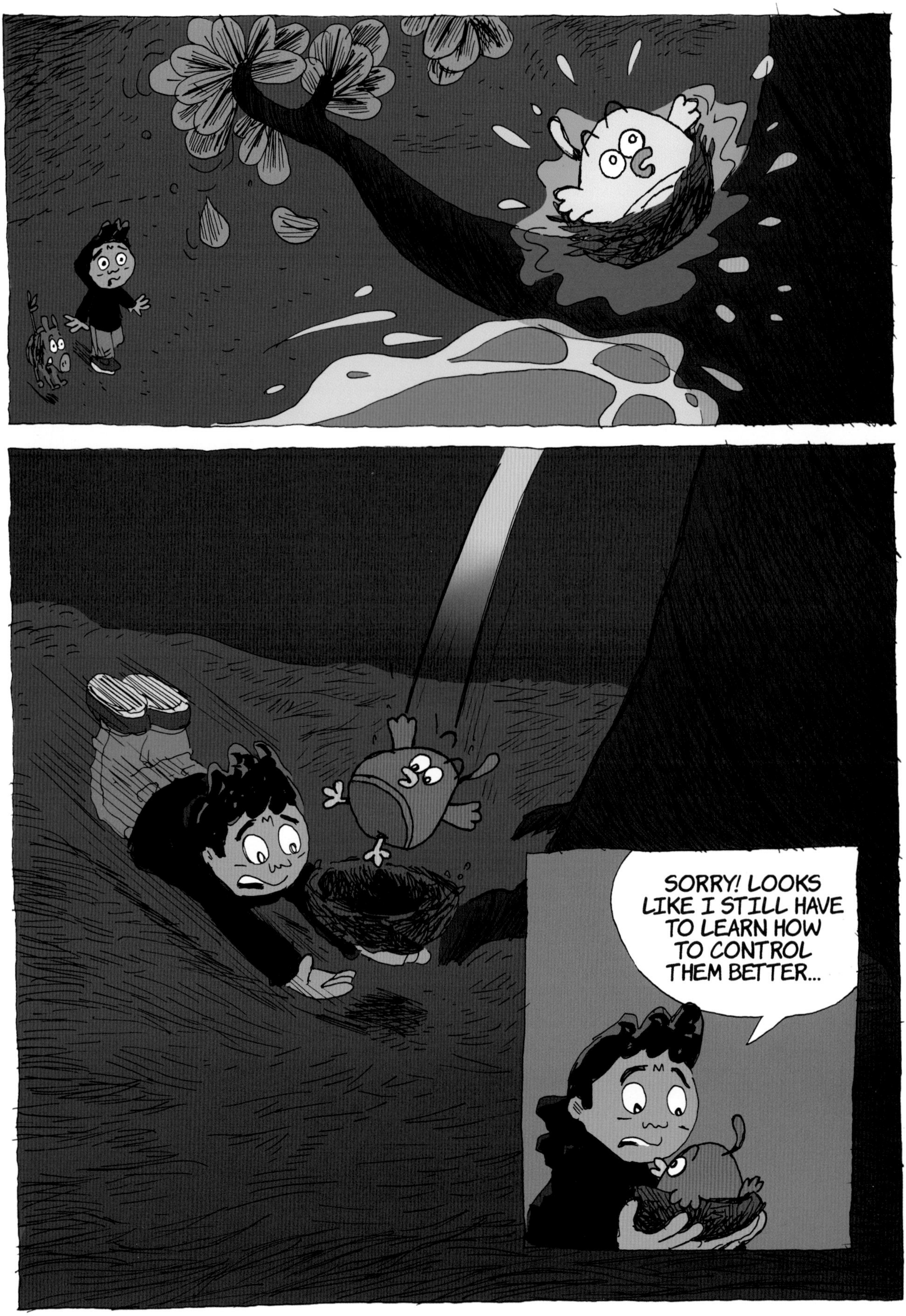
SORRY! LOOKS LIKE I STILL HAVE TO LEARN HOW TO CONTROL THEM BETTER...

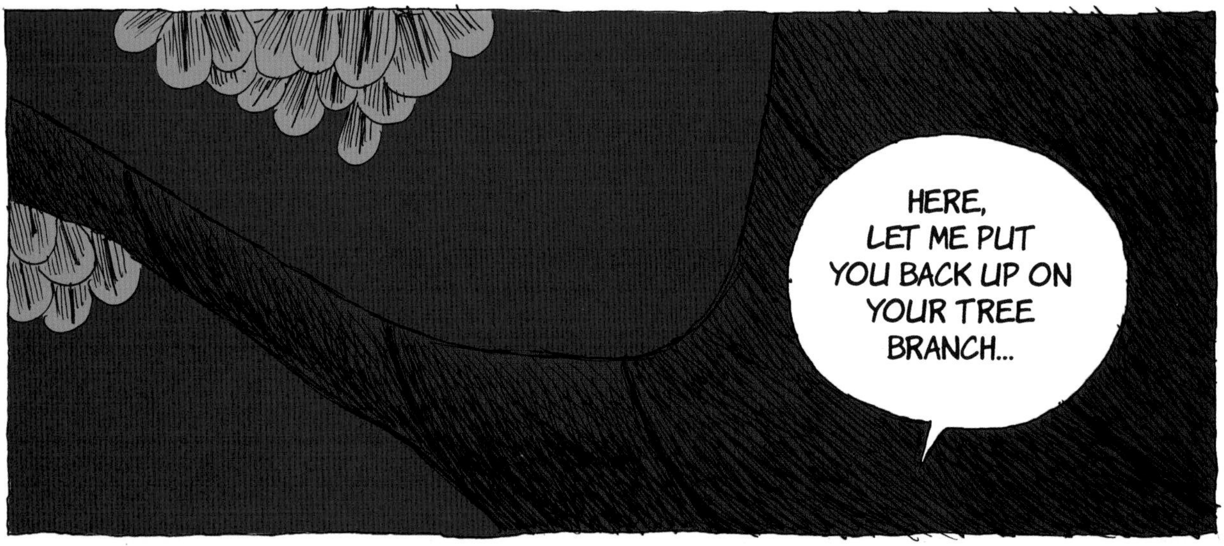
HERE, LET ME PUT YOU BACK UP ON YOUR TREE BRANCH...

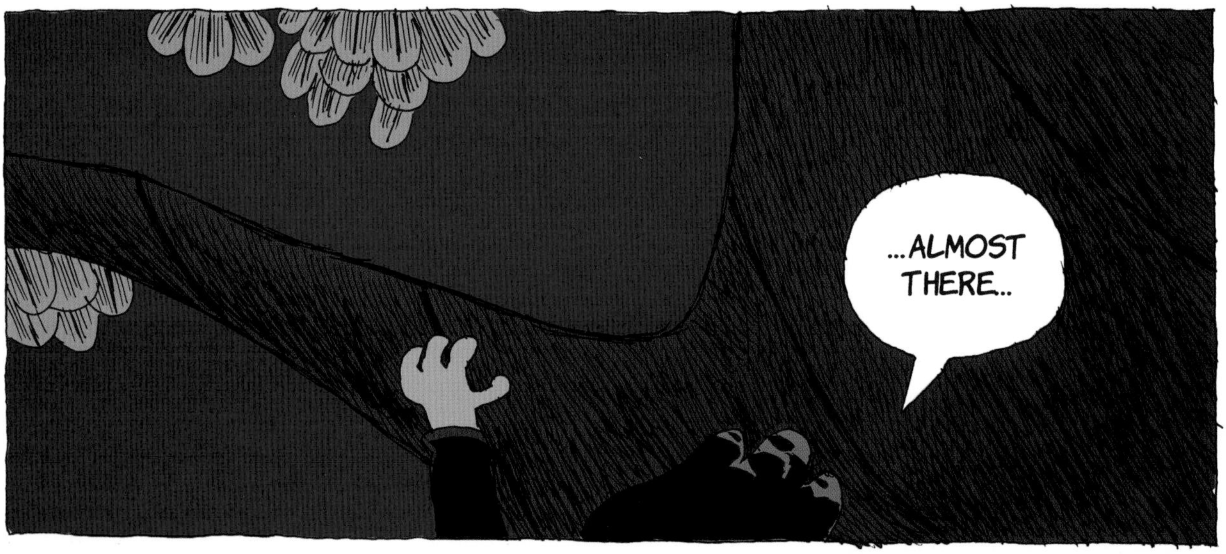
...ALMOST THERE..

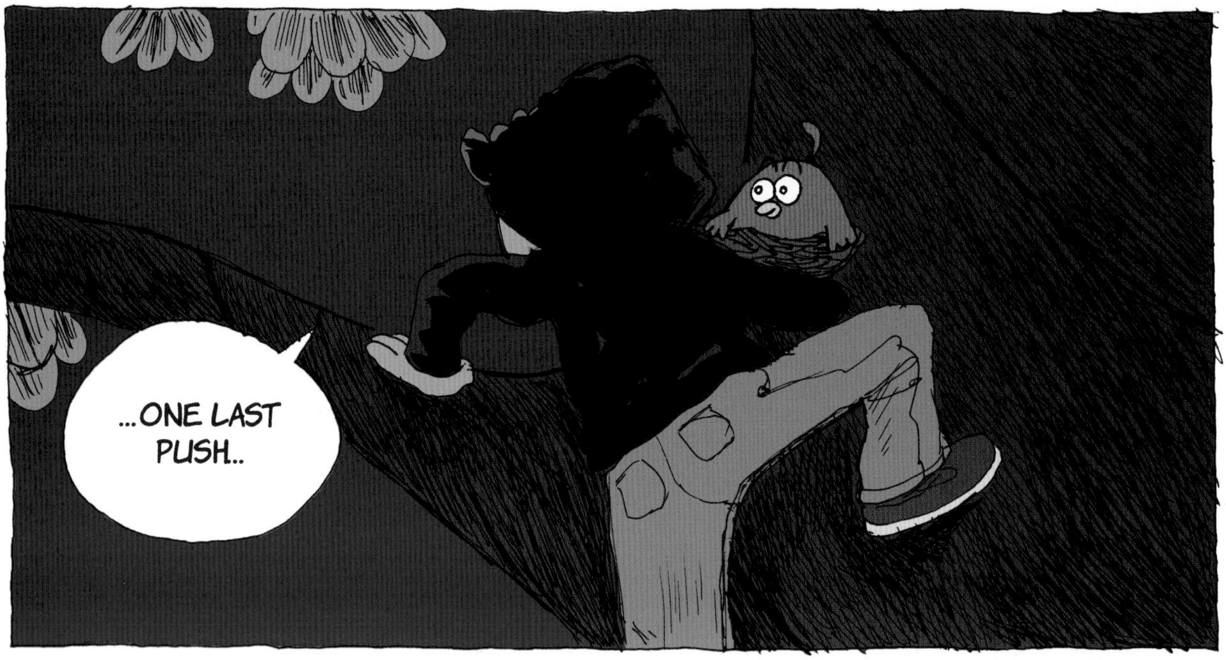
...ONE LAST PUSH..

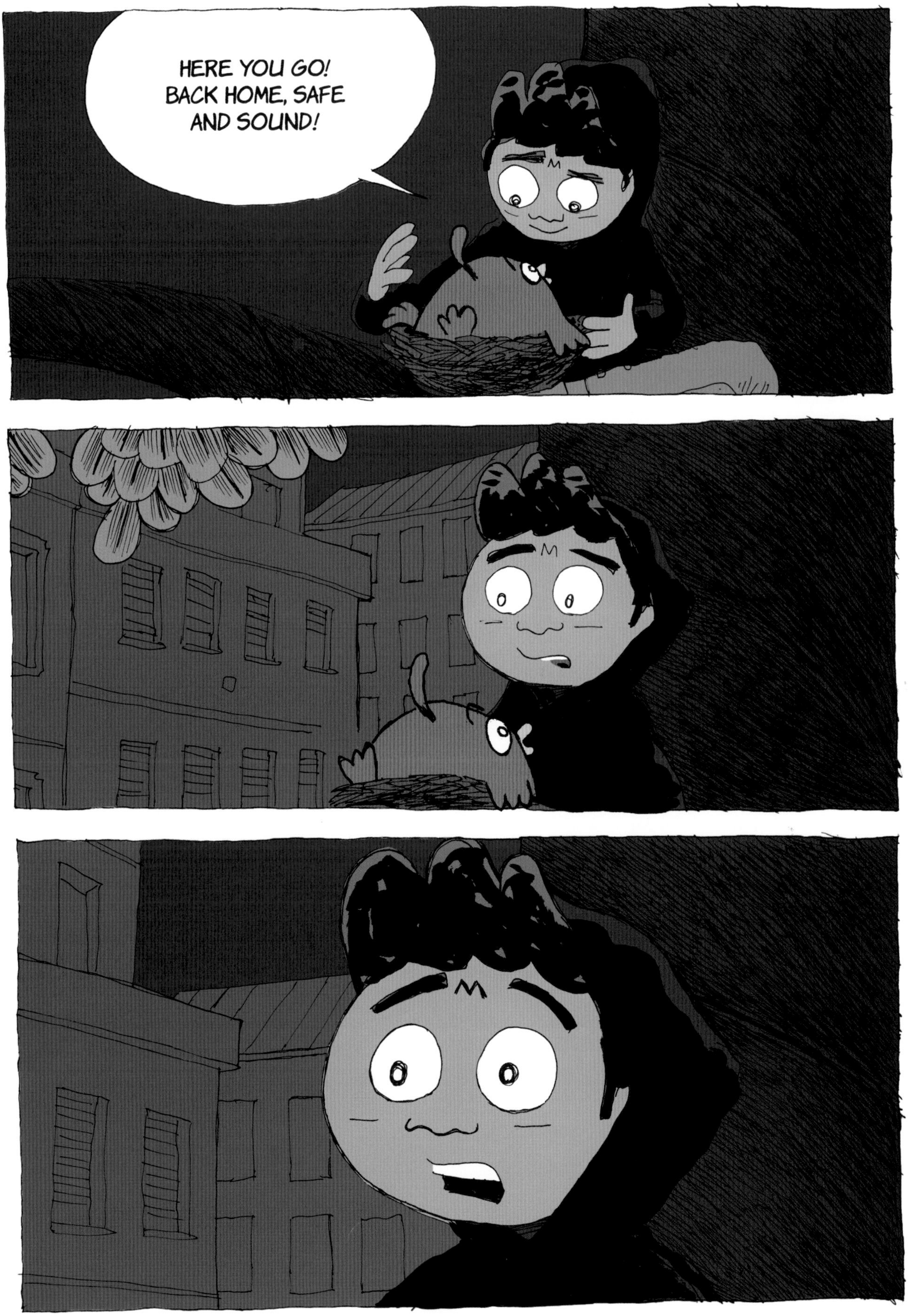
HERE YOU GO! BACK HOME, SAFE AND SOUND!

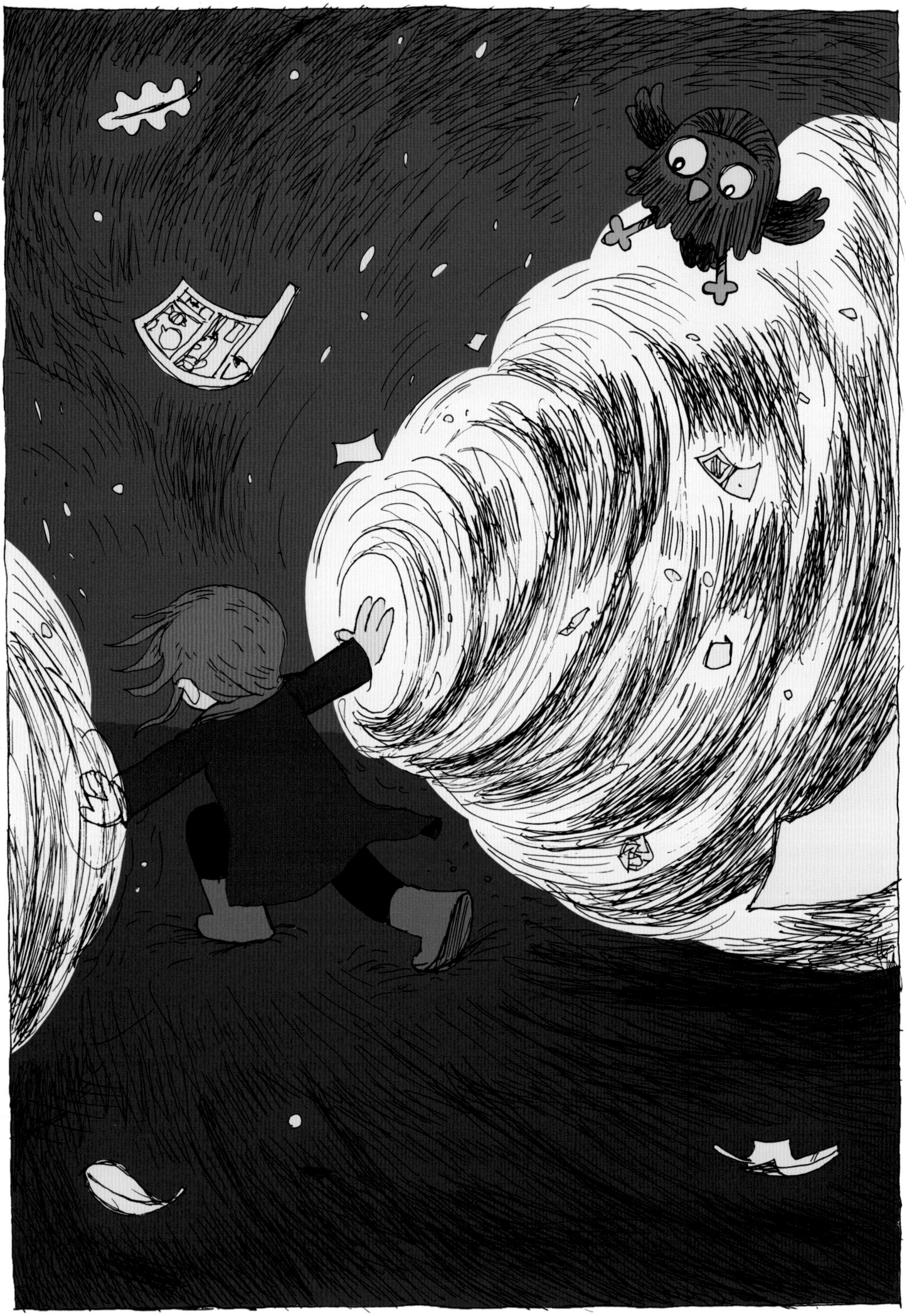

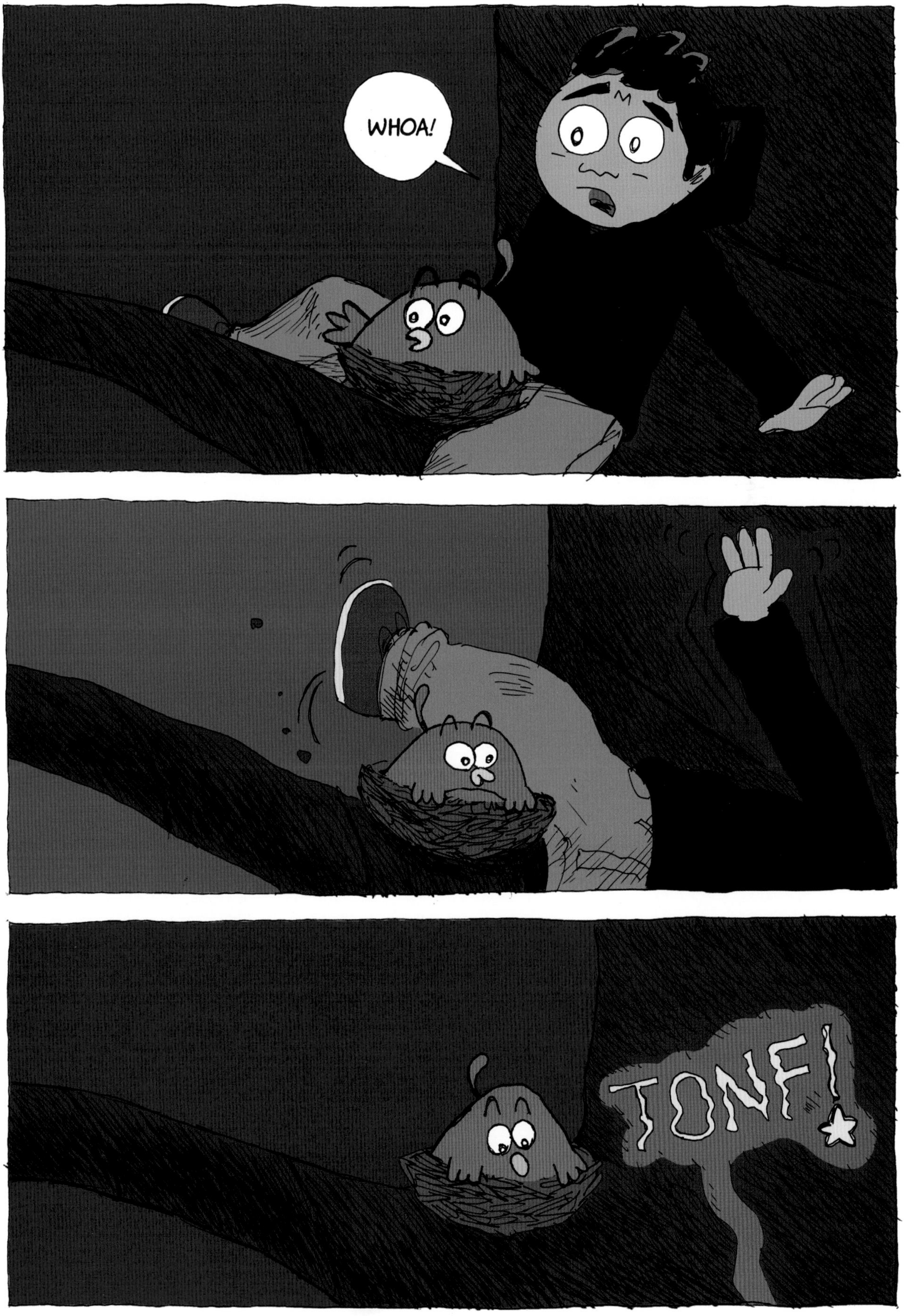
WHOA!
TONF!

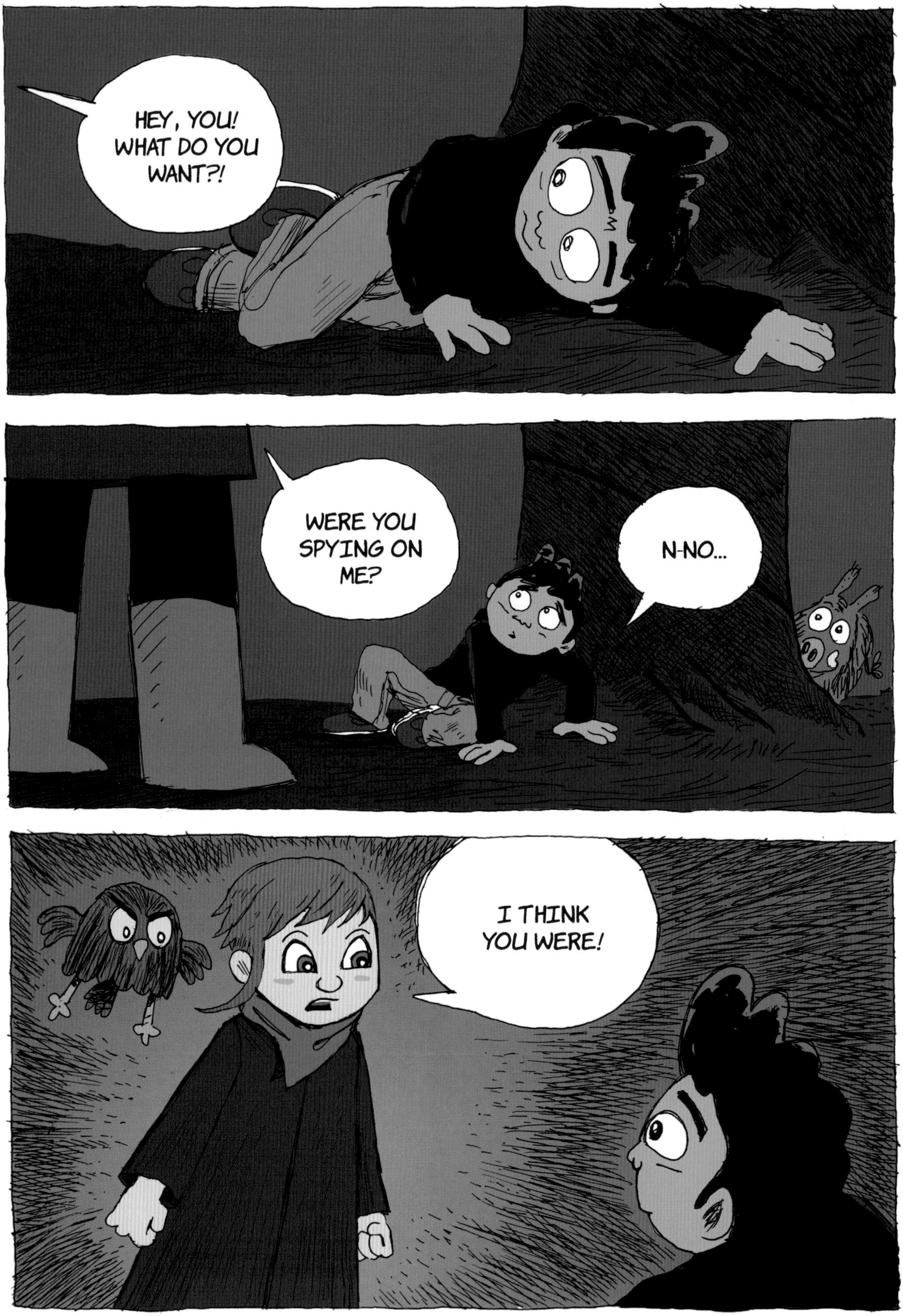
HEY, YOU!
WHAT DO YOU
WANT?!
WERE YOU
SPYING ON
ME?
N-NO...
I THINK
YOU WERE!

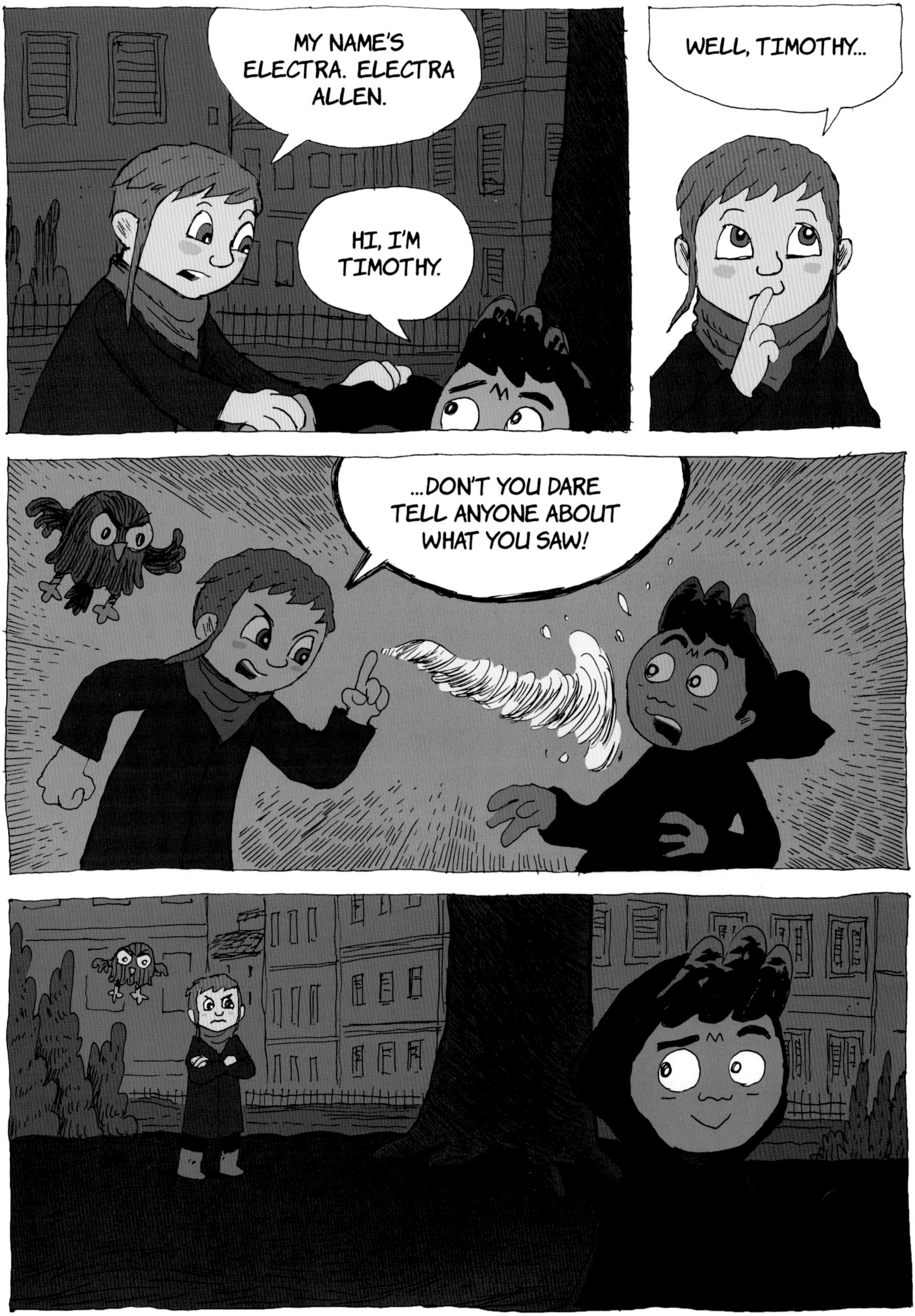
MY NAME'S ELECTRA. ELECTRA ALLEN.
HI, I'M TIMOTHY.
WELL, TIMOTHY...
...DON'T YOU DARE TELL ANYONE ABOUT WHAT YOU SAW!

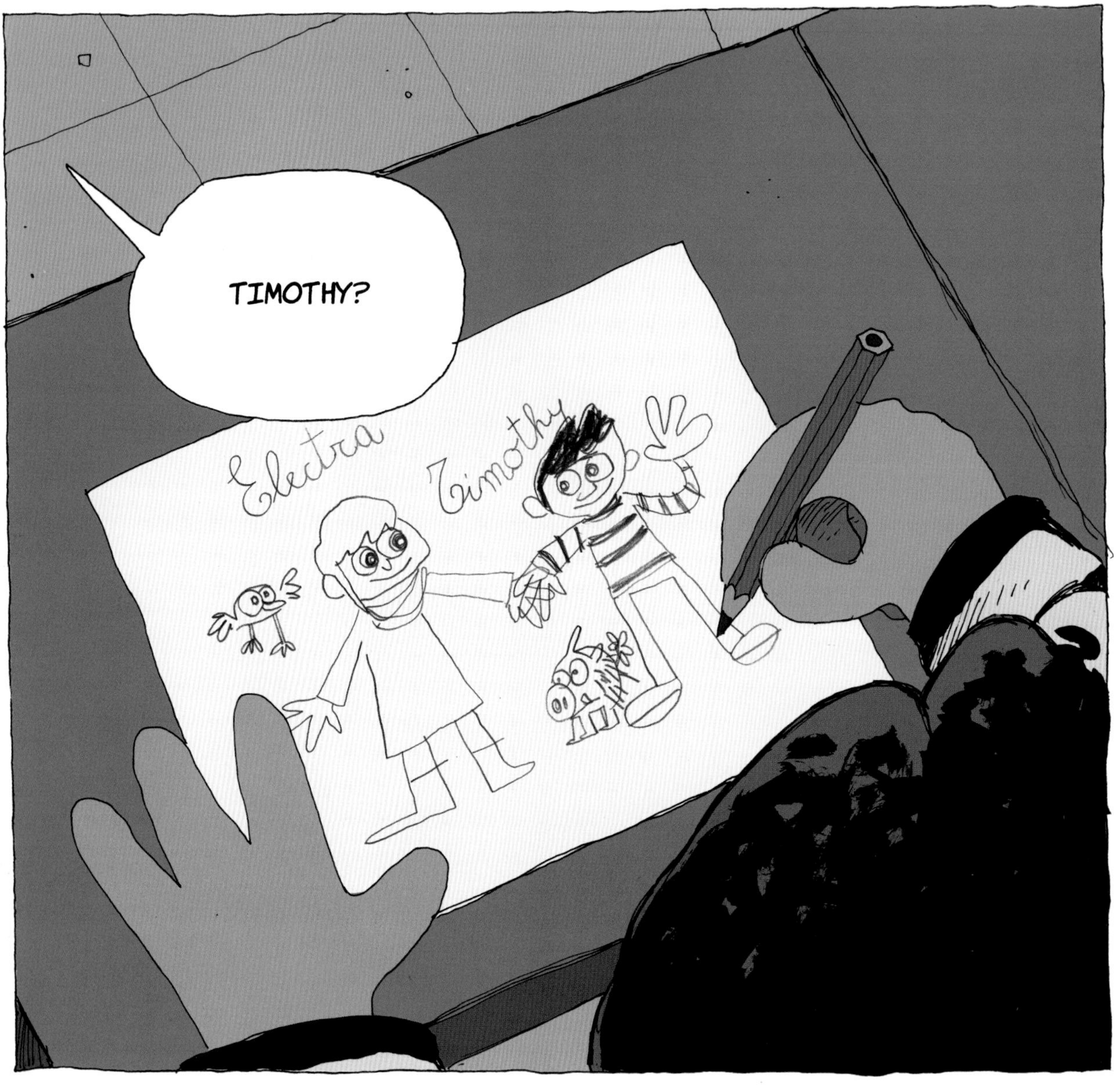
TIMOTHY?
Electra
Timothy

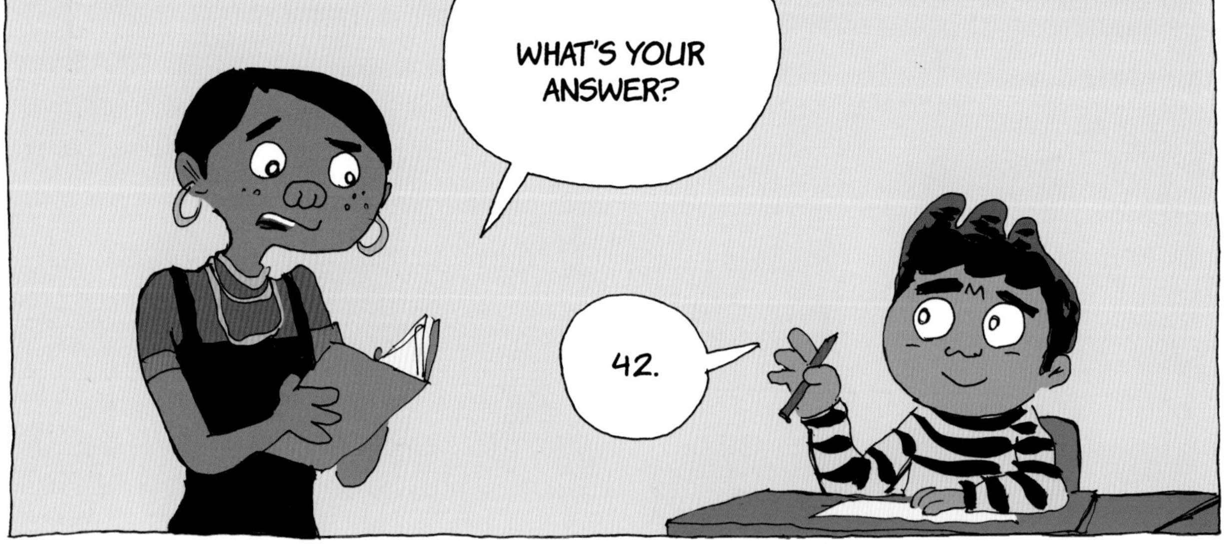
WHAT'S YOUR ANSWER?
42.

CHAPTER FOUR
SILVIA AND TONY

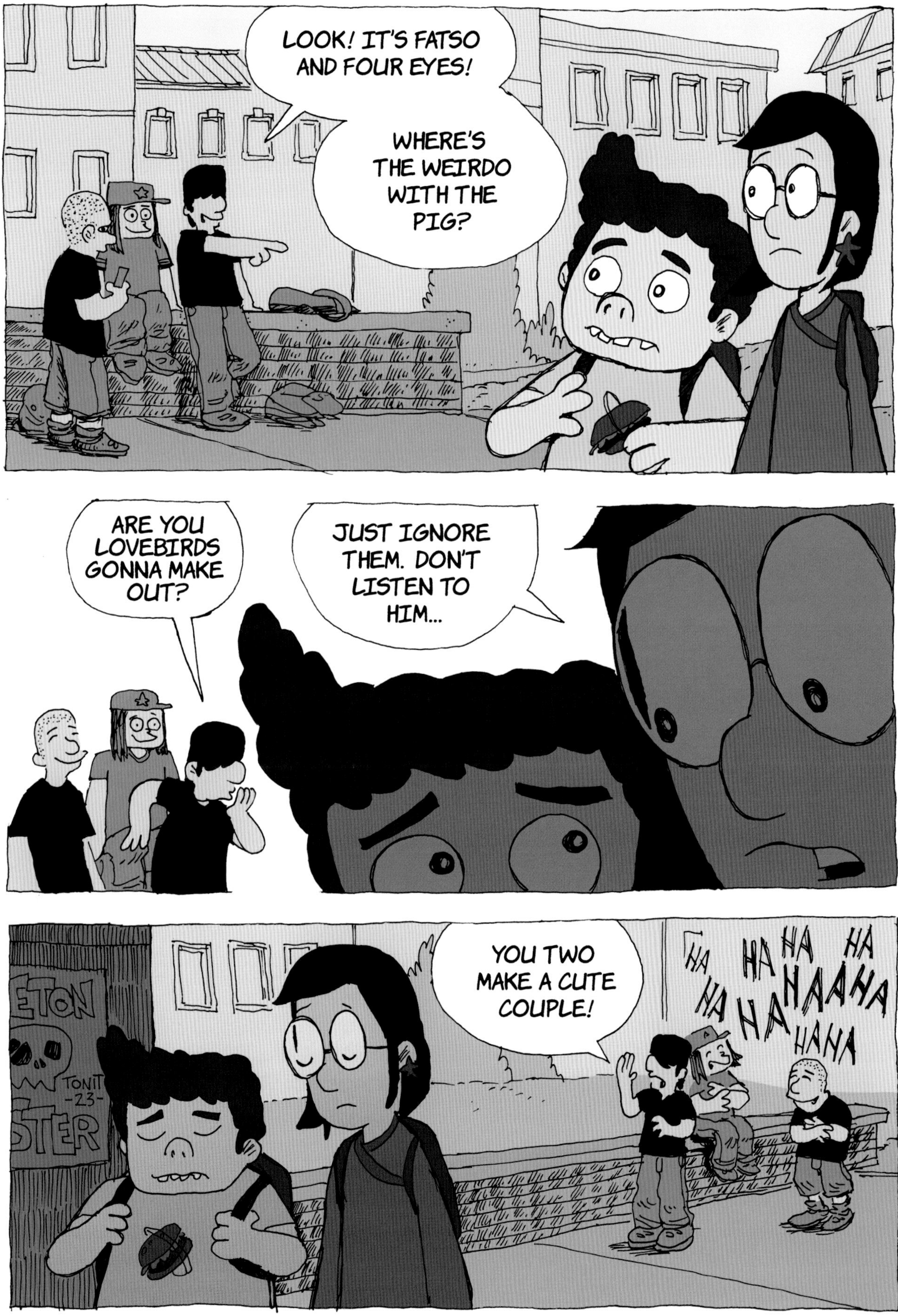
LOOK! IT'S FATSO AND FOUR EYES!
WHERE'S THE WEIRDO WITH THE PIG?
ARE YOU LOVEBIRDS GONNA MAKE OUT?
JUST IGNORE THEM. DON'T LISTEN TO HIM...
YOU TWO MAKE A CUTE COUPLE!
HA HA HA HA HA HAHAHA HA HAHA

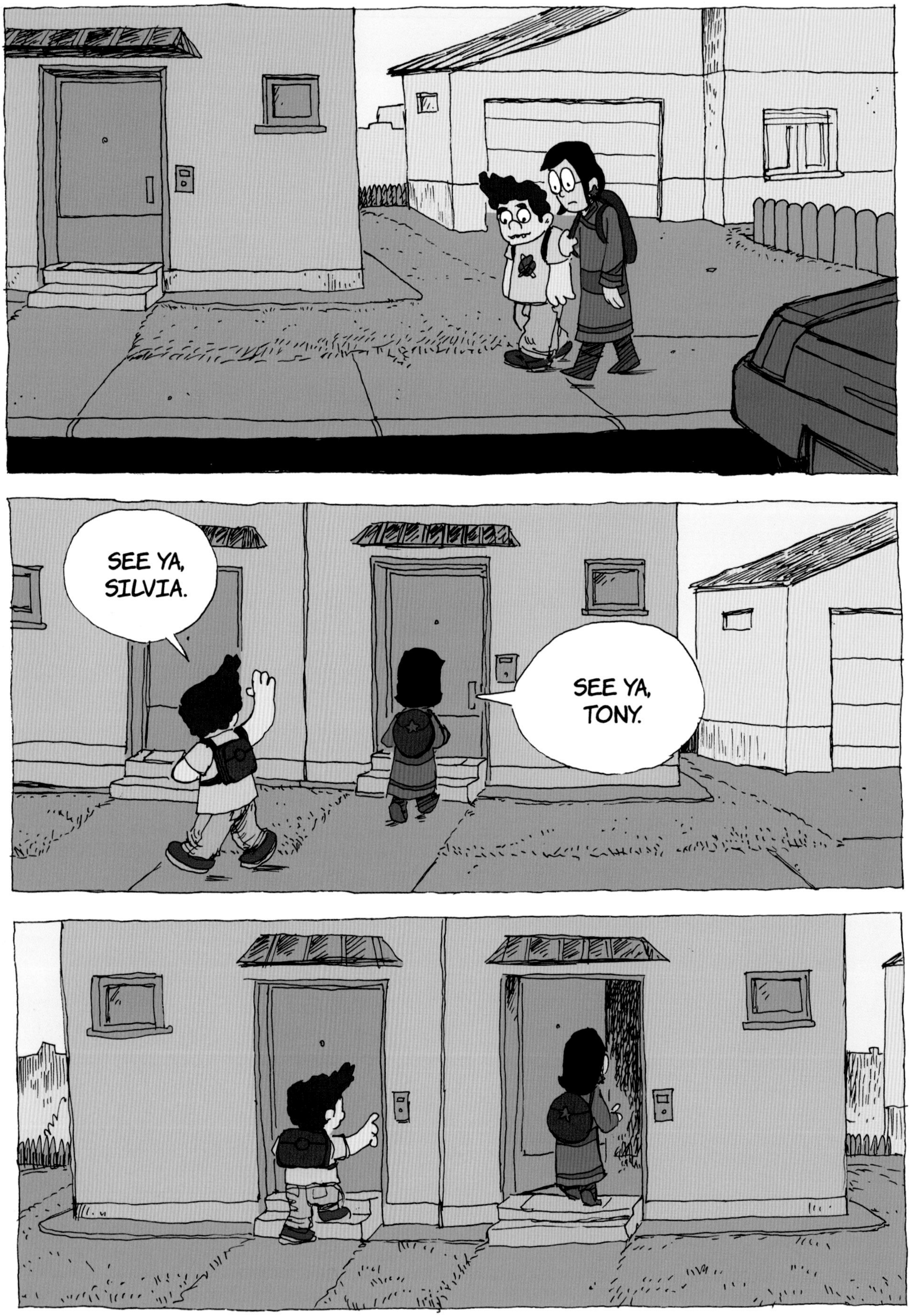
SEE YA, SILVIA.
SEE YA, TONY.

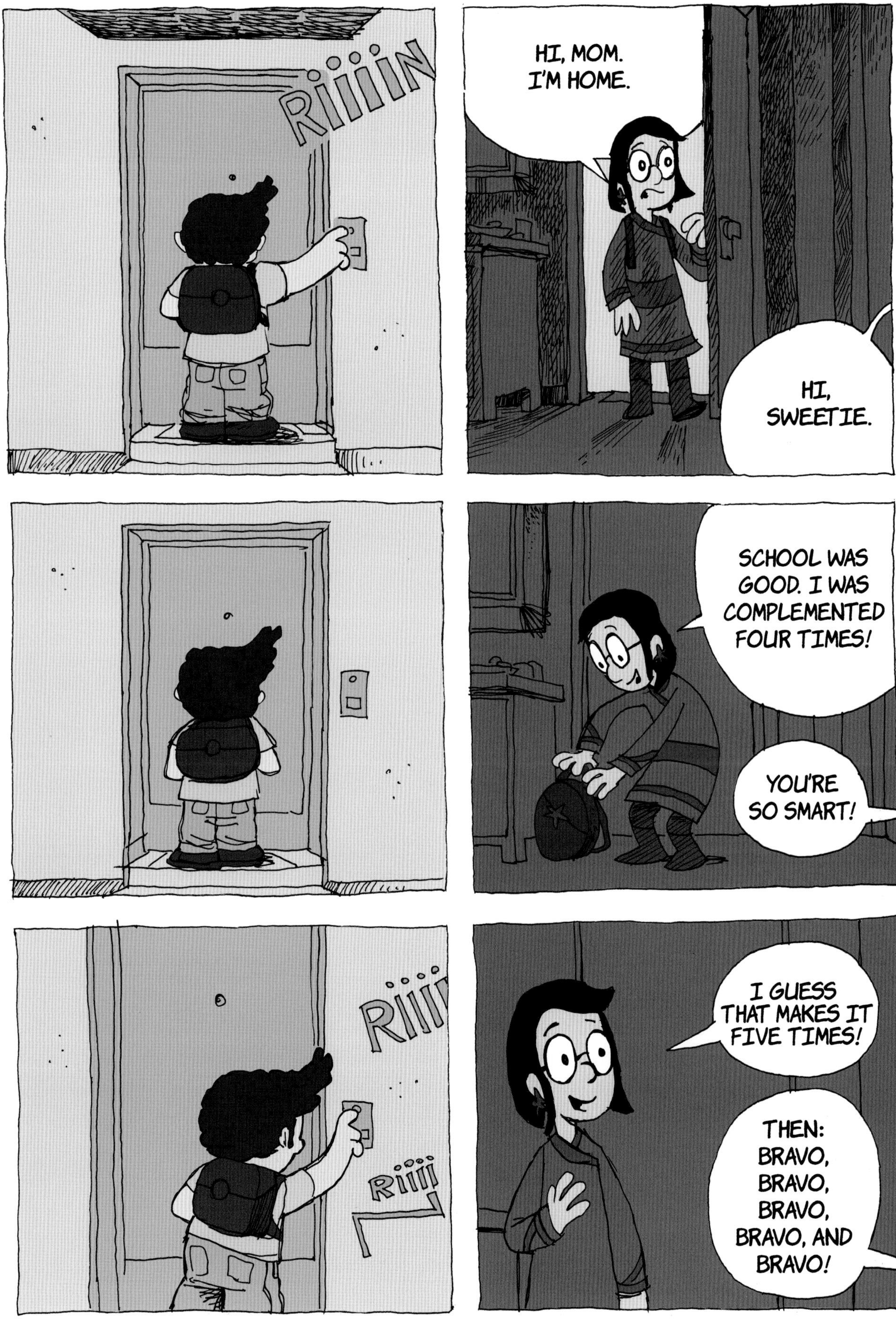
RIIIIN
HI, MOM. I'M HOME.
HI, SWEETIE.
SCHOOL WAS GOOD. I WAS COMPLEMENTED FOUR TIMES!
YOU'RE SO SMART!
RIIII
RIIII
I GUESS THAT MAKES IT FIVE TIMES!
THEN: BRAVO, BRAVO, BRAVO, BRAVO, AND BRAVO!

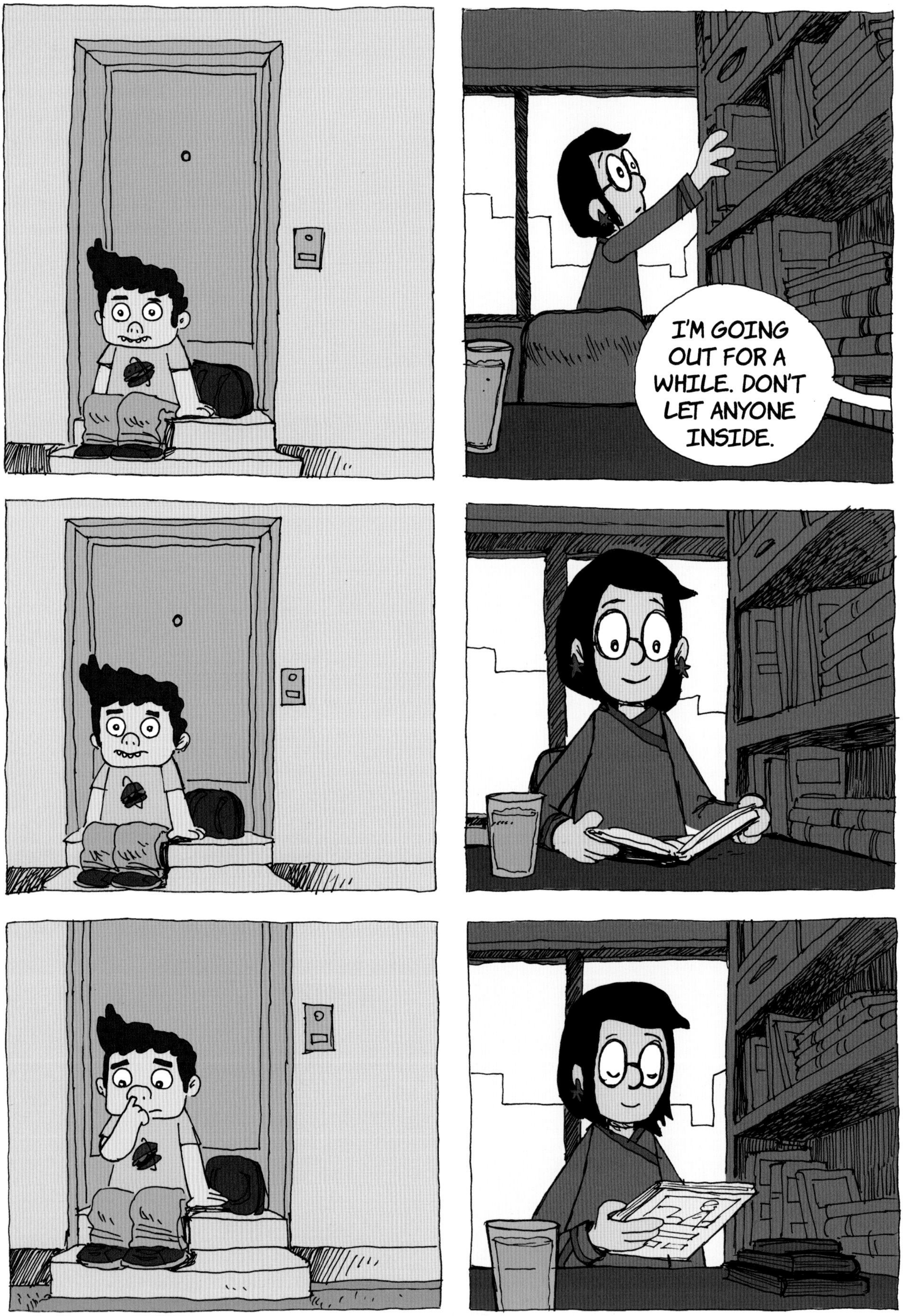
I'M GOING OUT FOR A WHILE. DON'T LET ANYONE INSIDE.

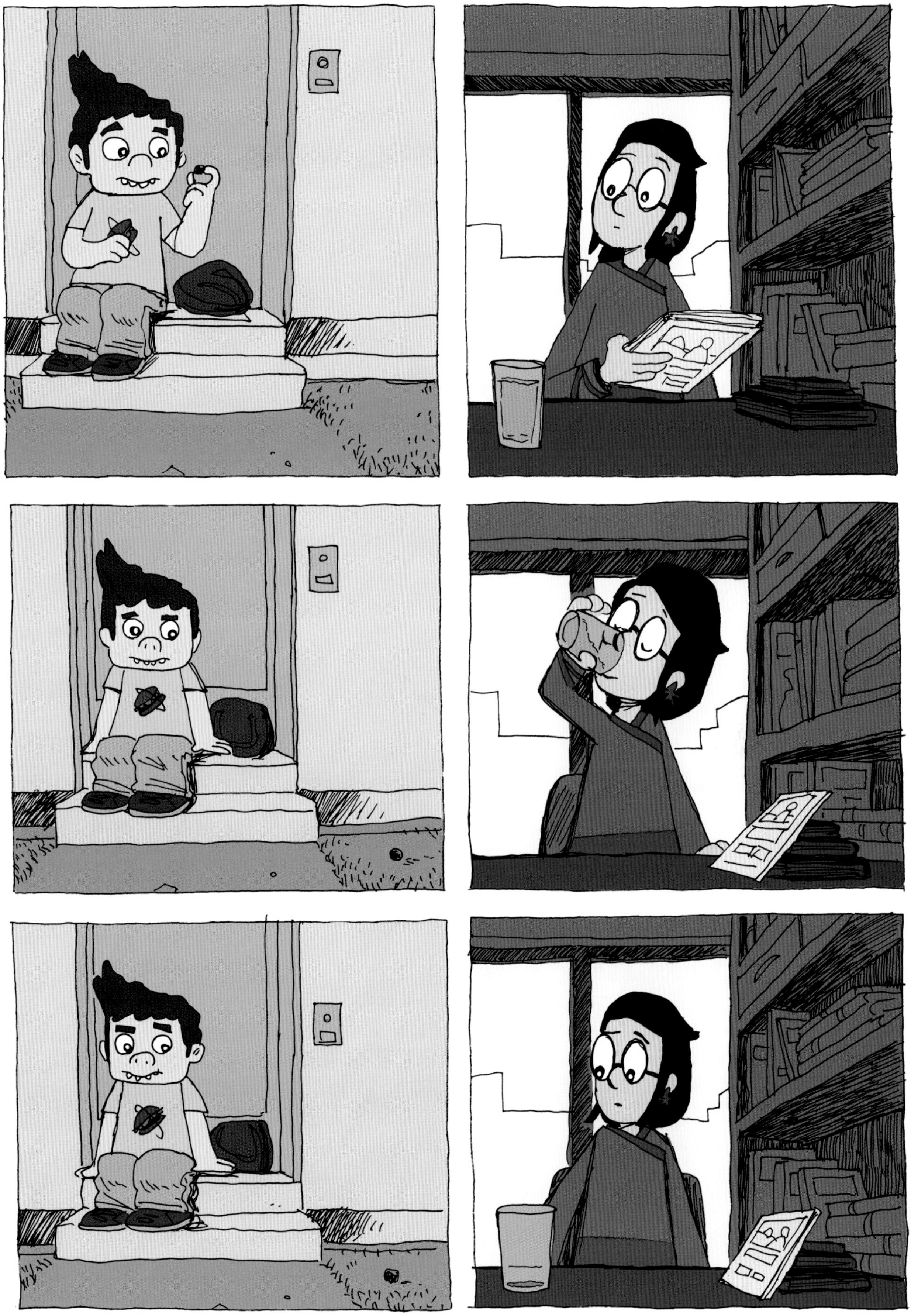

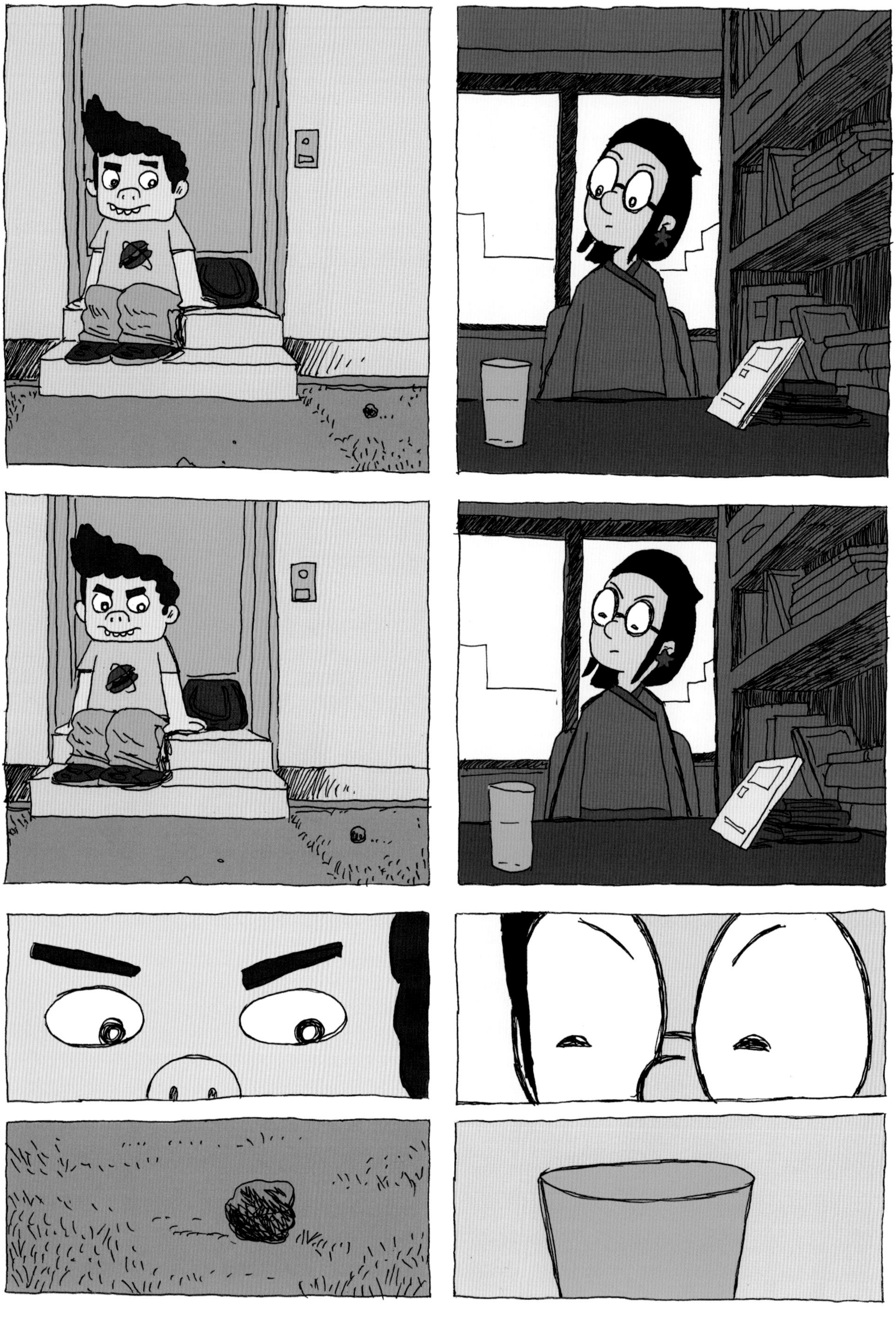

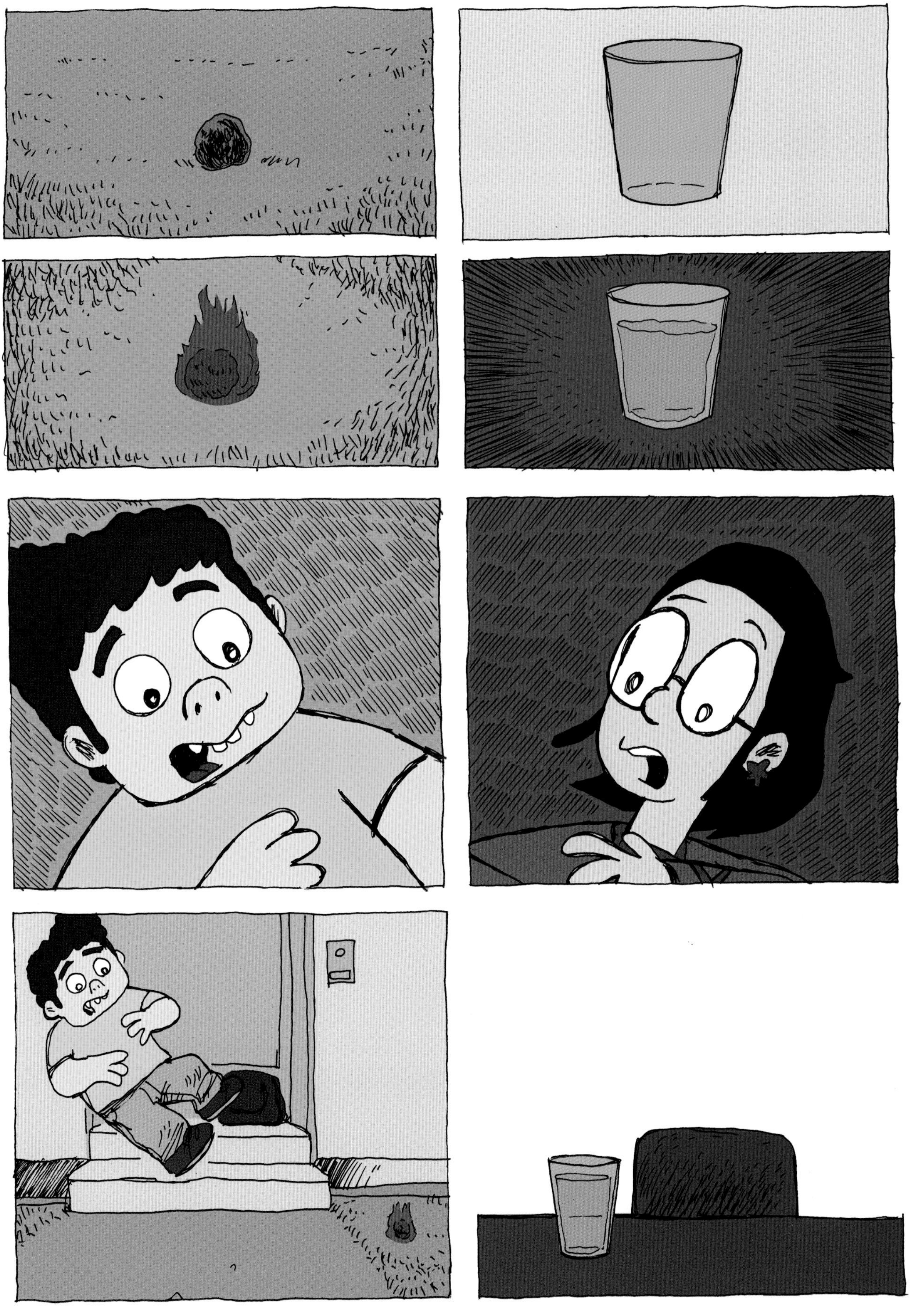

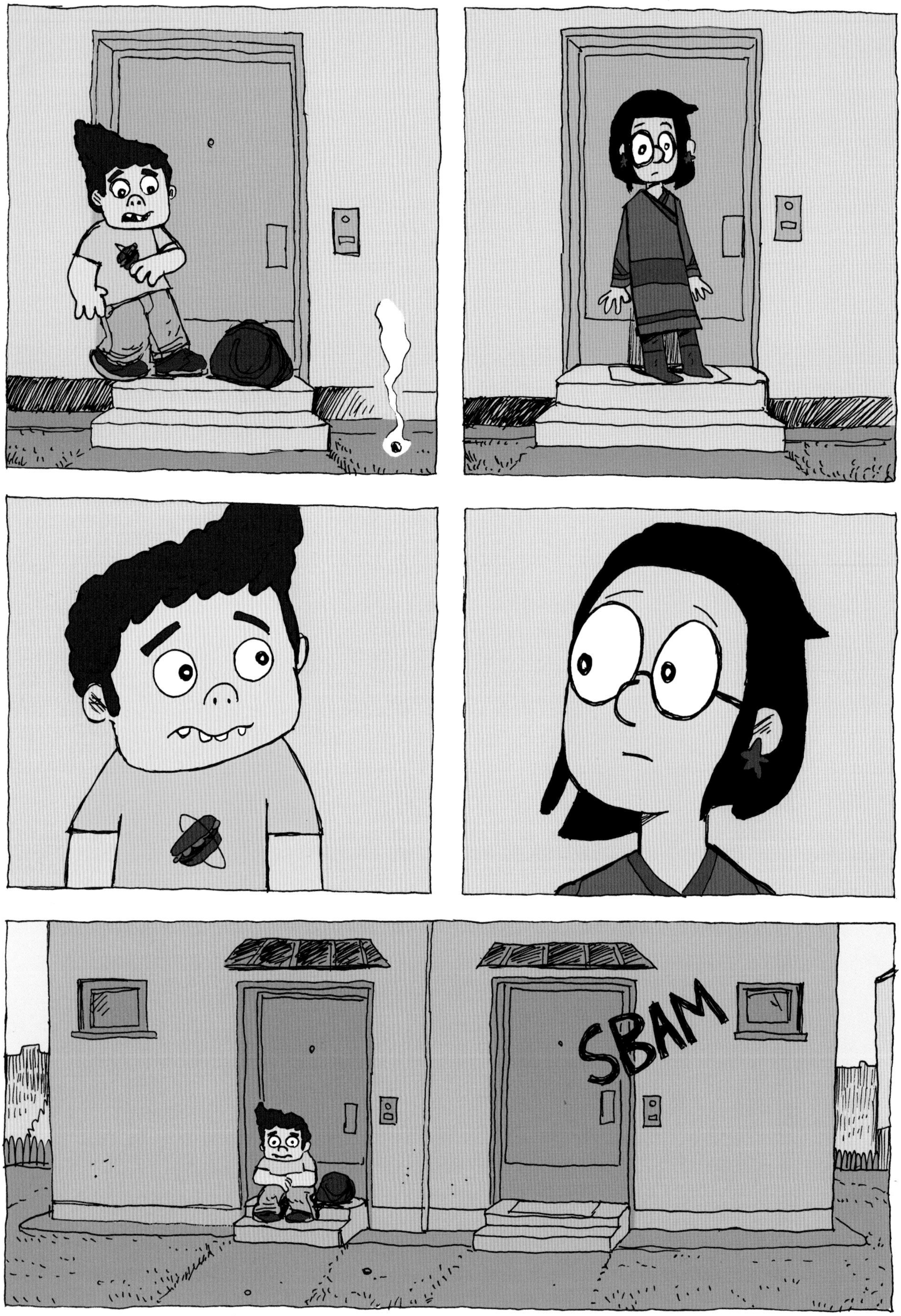
SBAM

CHAPTER FIVE
GIANT ROBOTS

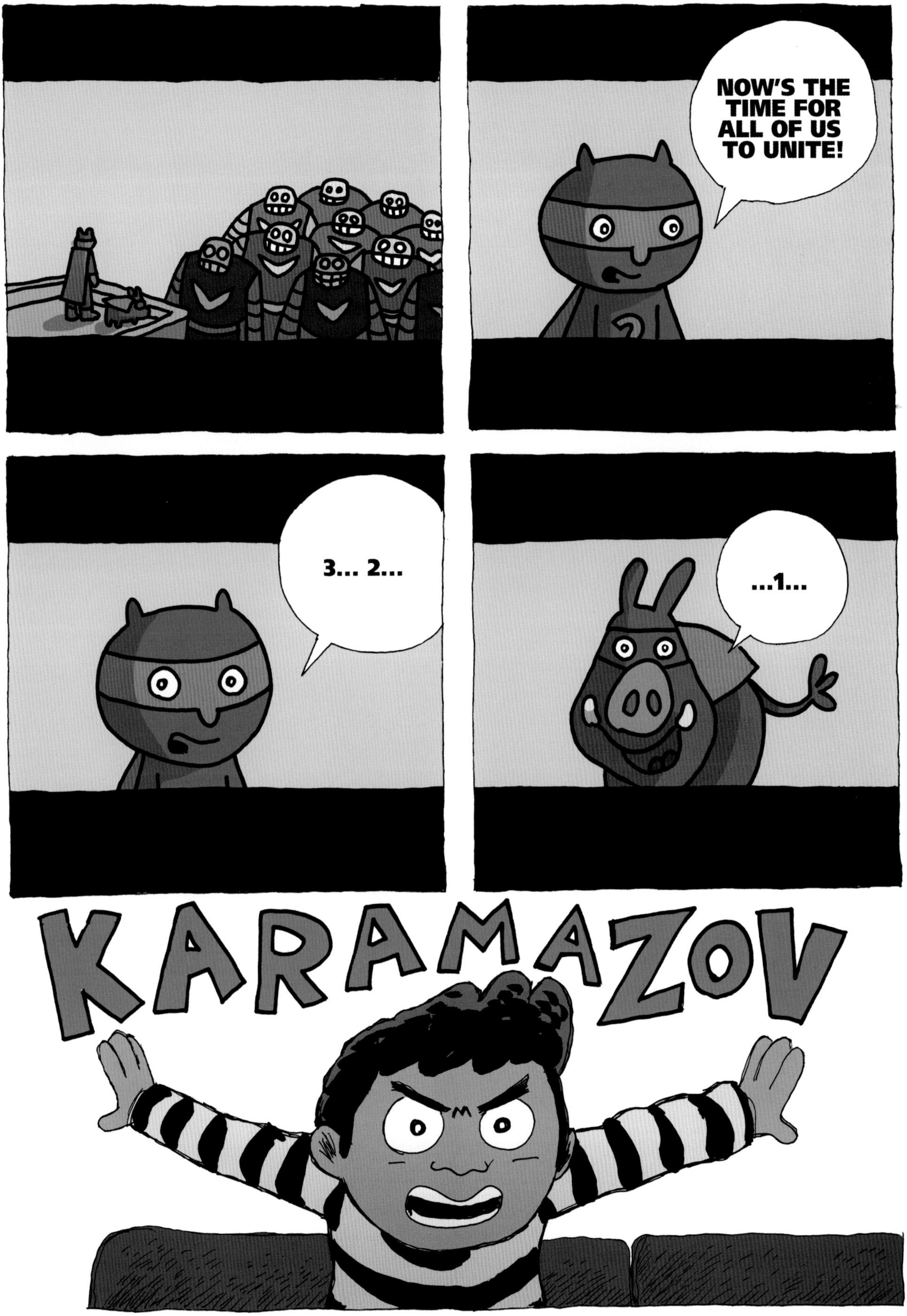
NOW'S THE TIME FOR ALL OF US TO UNITE!
3... 2...
...1...
KARAMAZOV

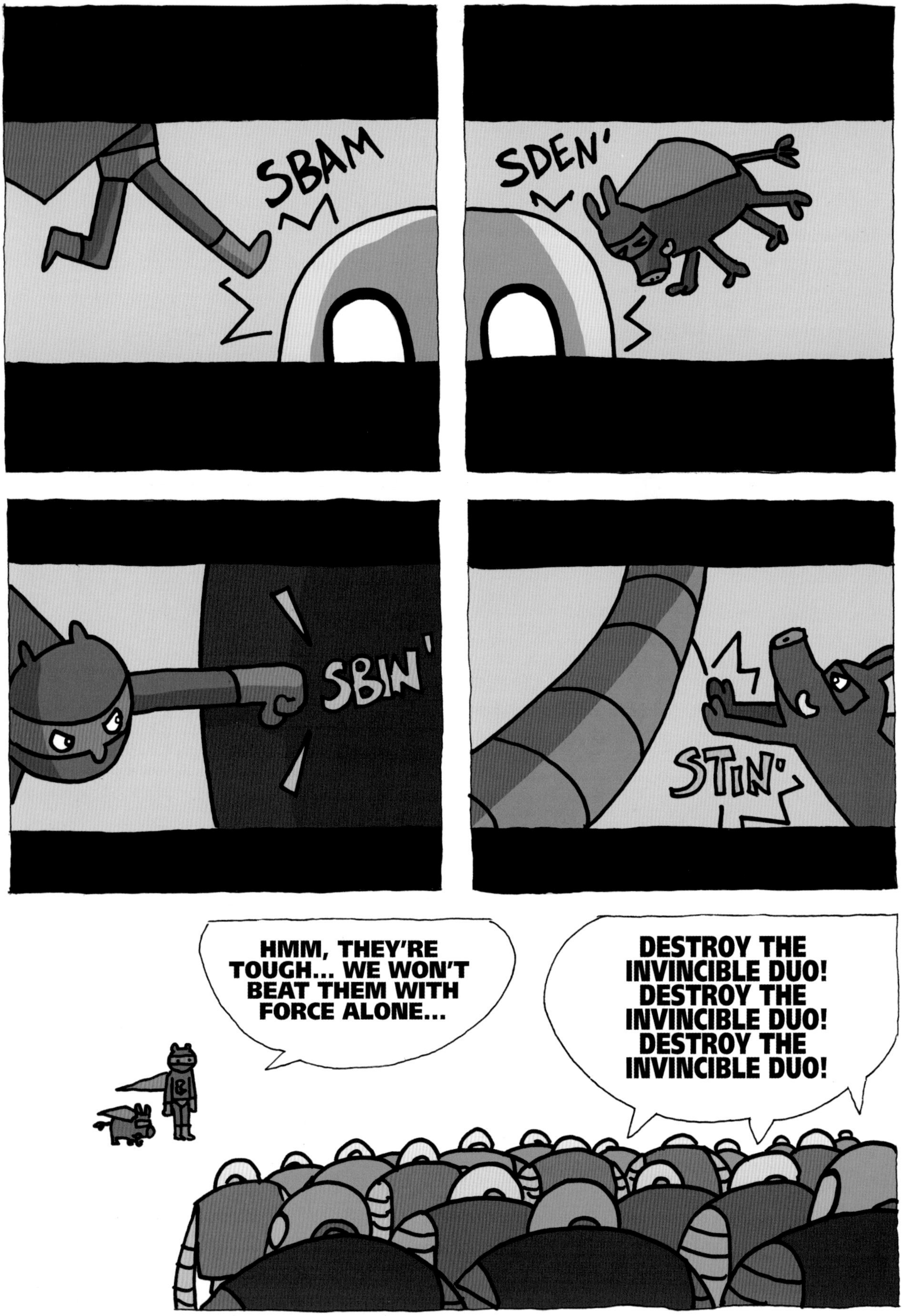
SBAM
SDEN'
SBIN'
STIN'
HMM, THEY'RE TOUGH... WE WON'T BEAT THEM WITH FORCE ALONE...
DESTROY THE INVINCIBLE DUO! DESTROY THE INVINCIBLE DUO! DESTROY THE INVINCIBLE DUO!

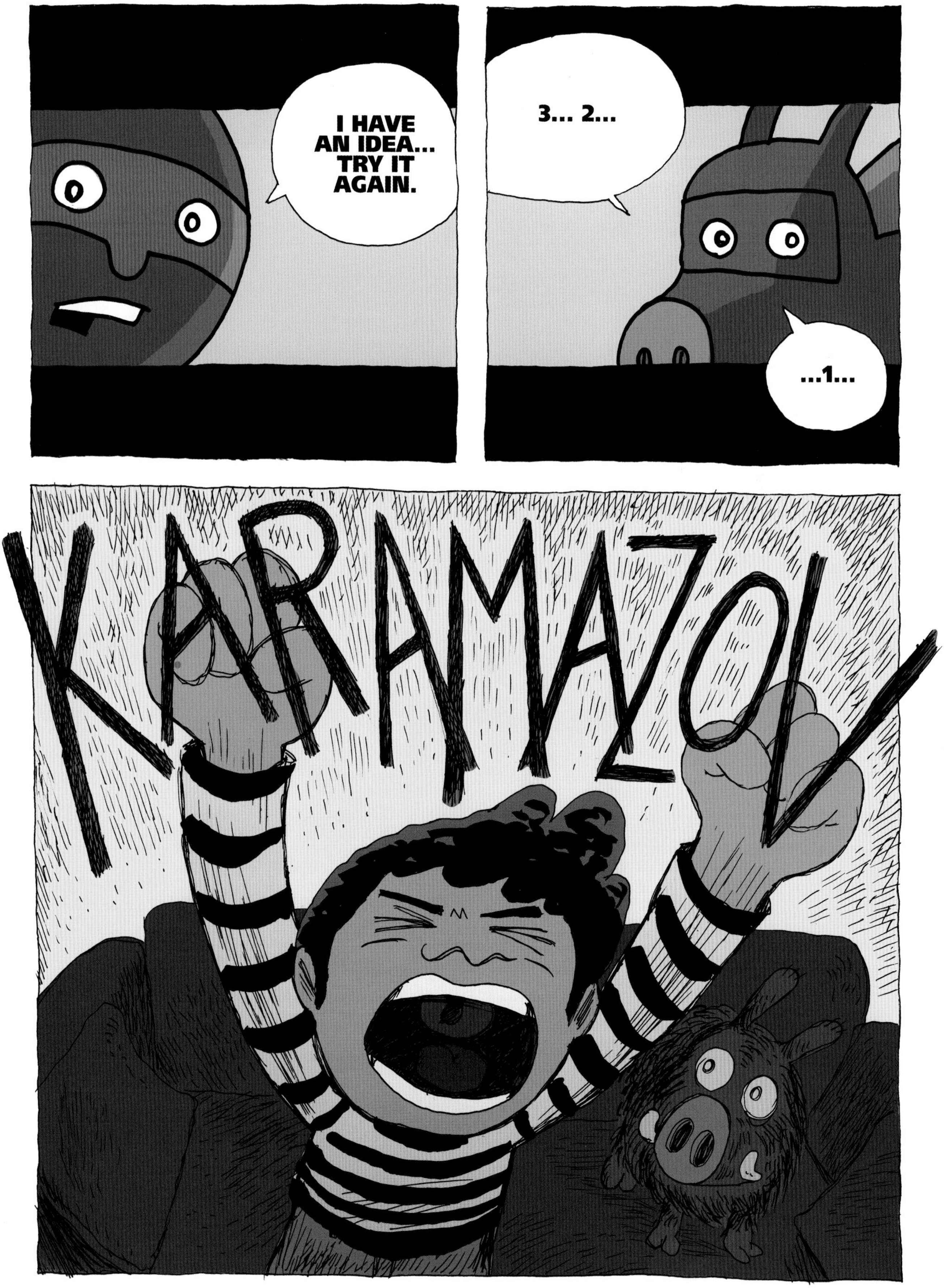
I HAVE AN IDEA... TRY IT AGAIN.
3... 2...
...1...
KARAMAZOV

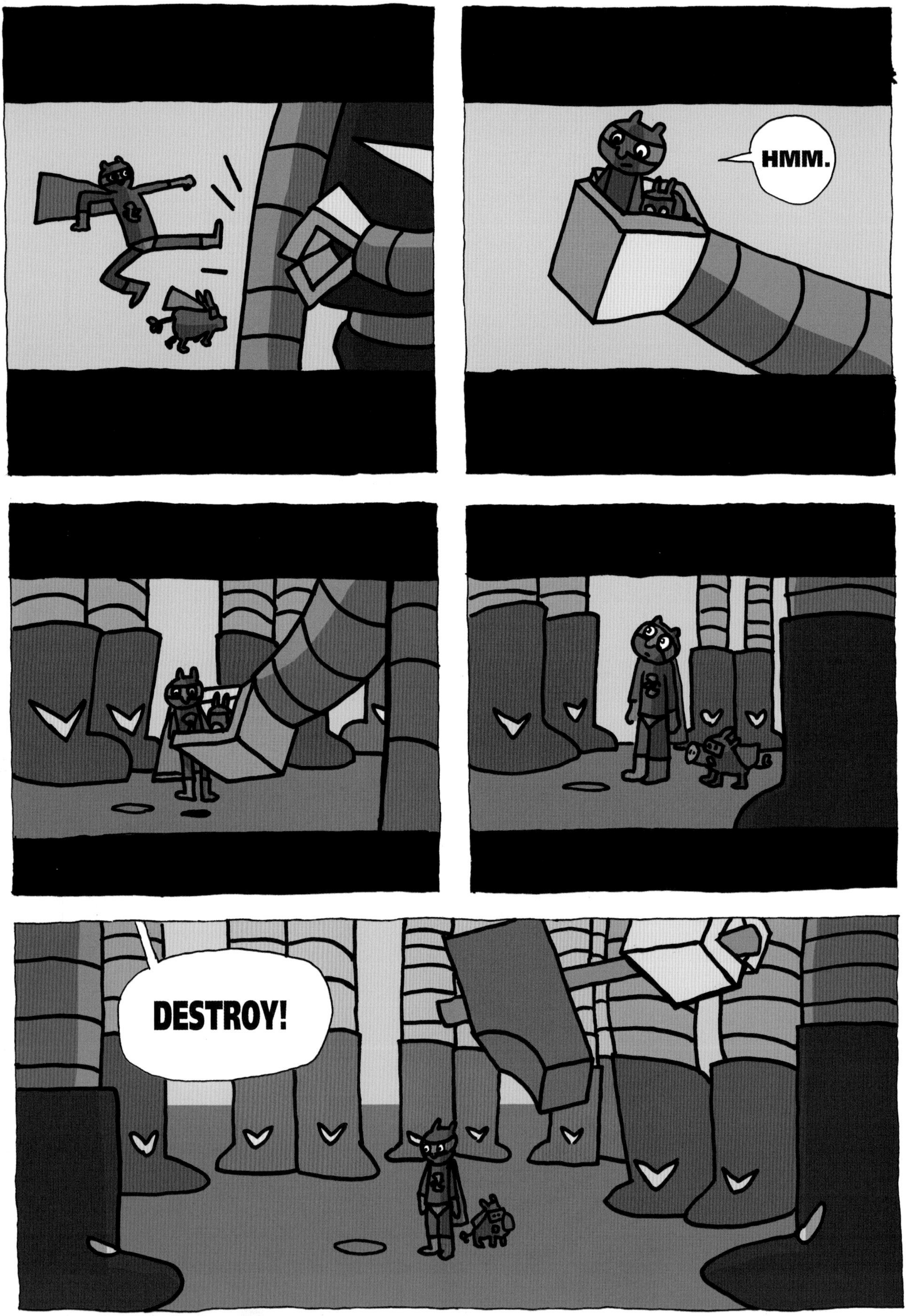
HMM.
DESTROY!

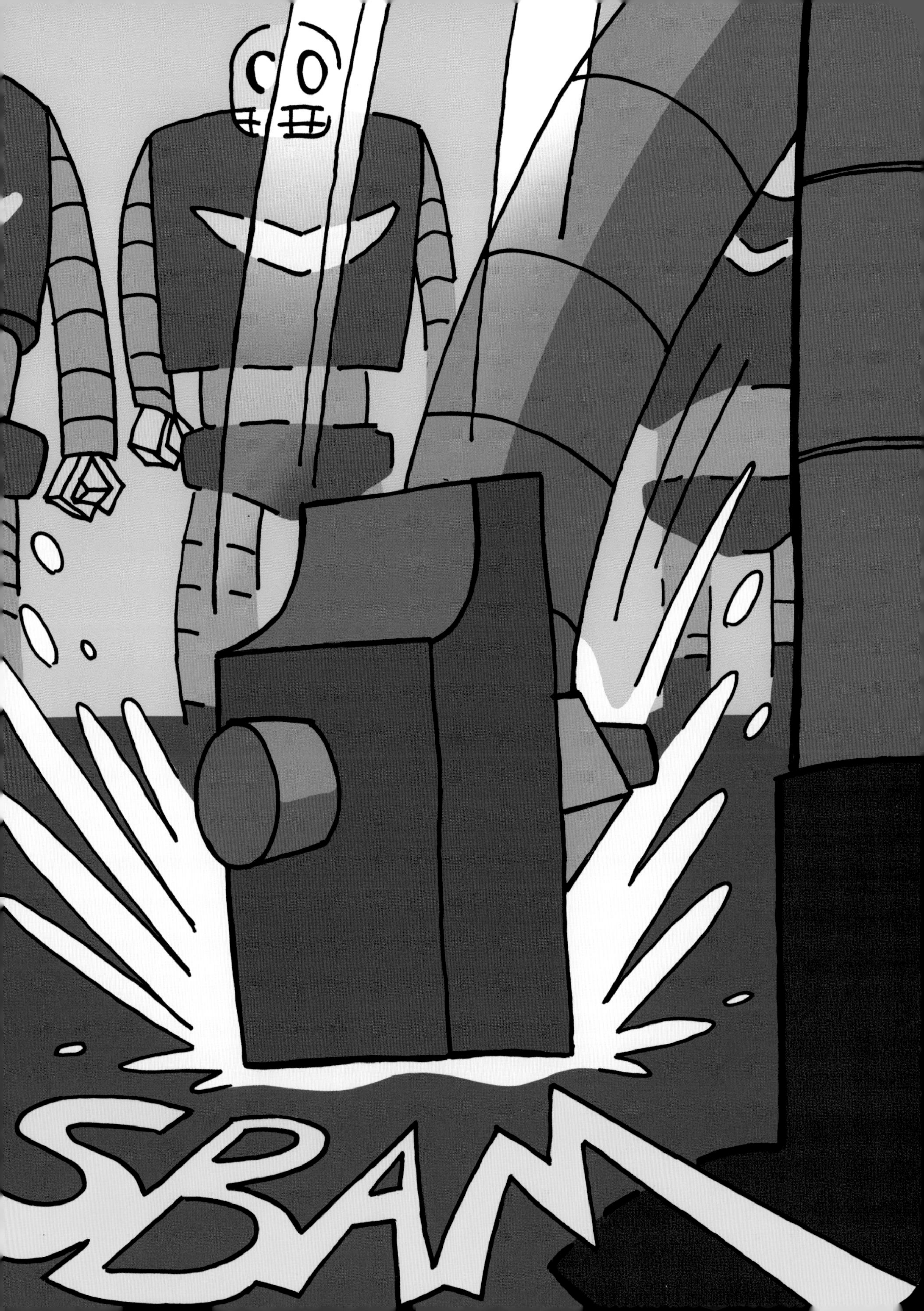
SBAM

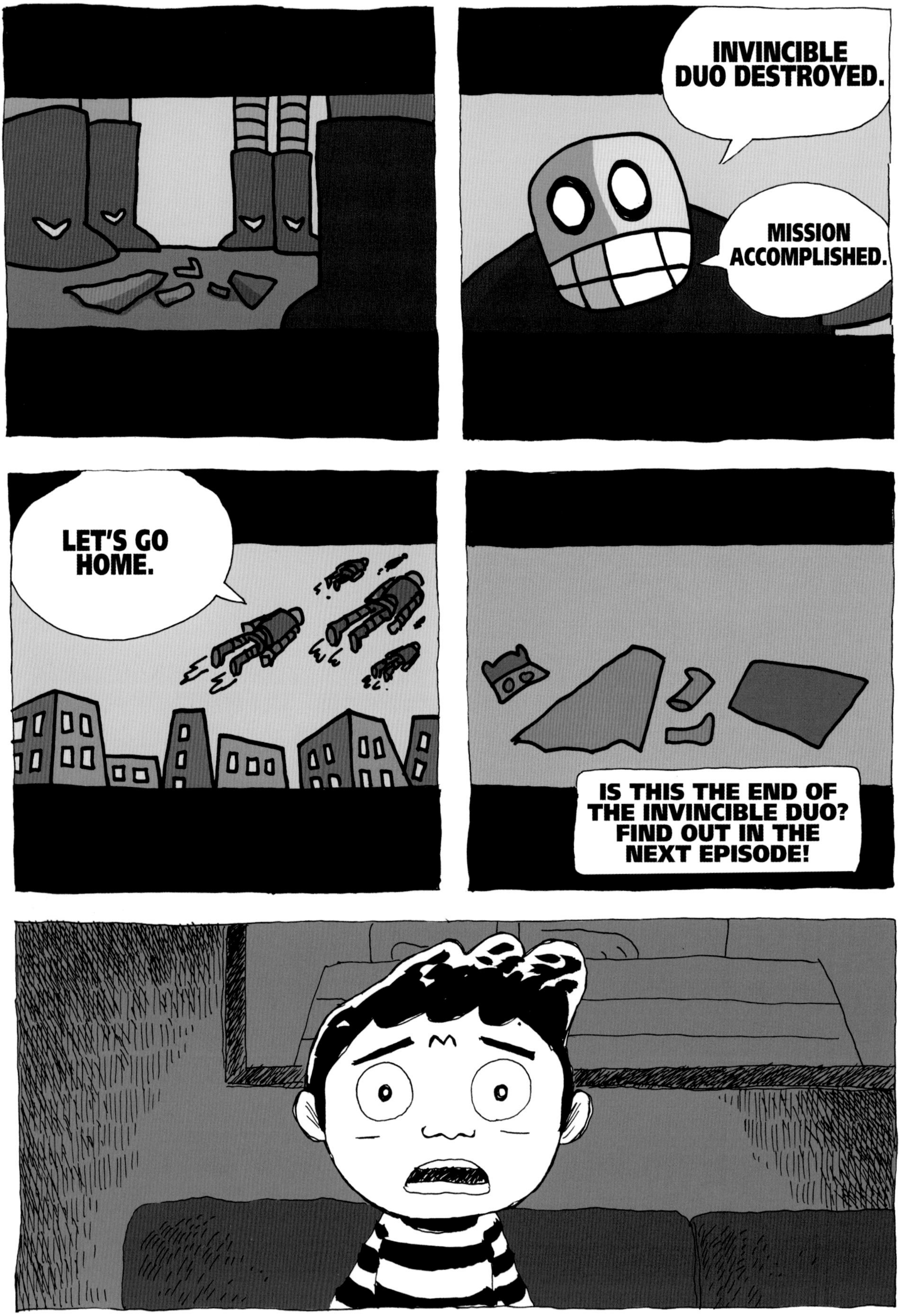
INVINCIBLE DUO DESTROYED.
MISSION ACCOMPLISHED.
LET'S GO HOME.
IS THIS THE END OF THE INVINCIBLE DUO? FIND OUT IN THE NEXT EPISODE!

CHAPTER SIX
NEW HEROES

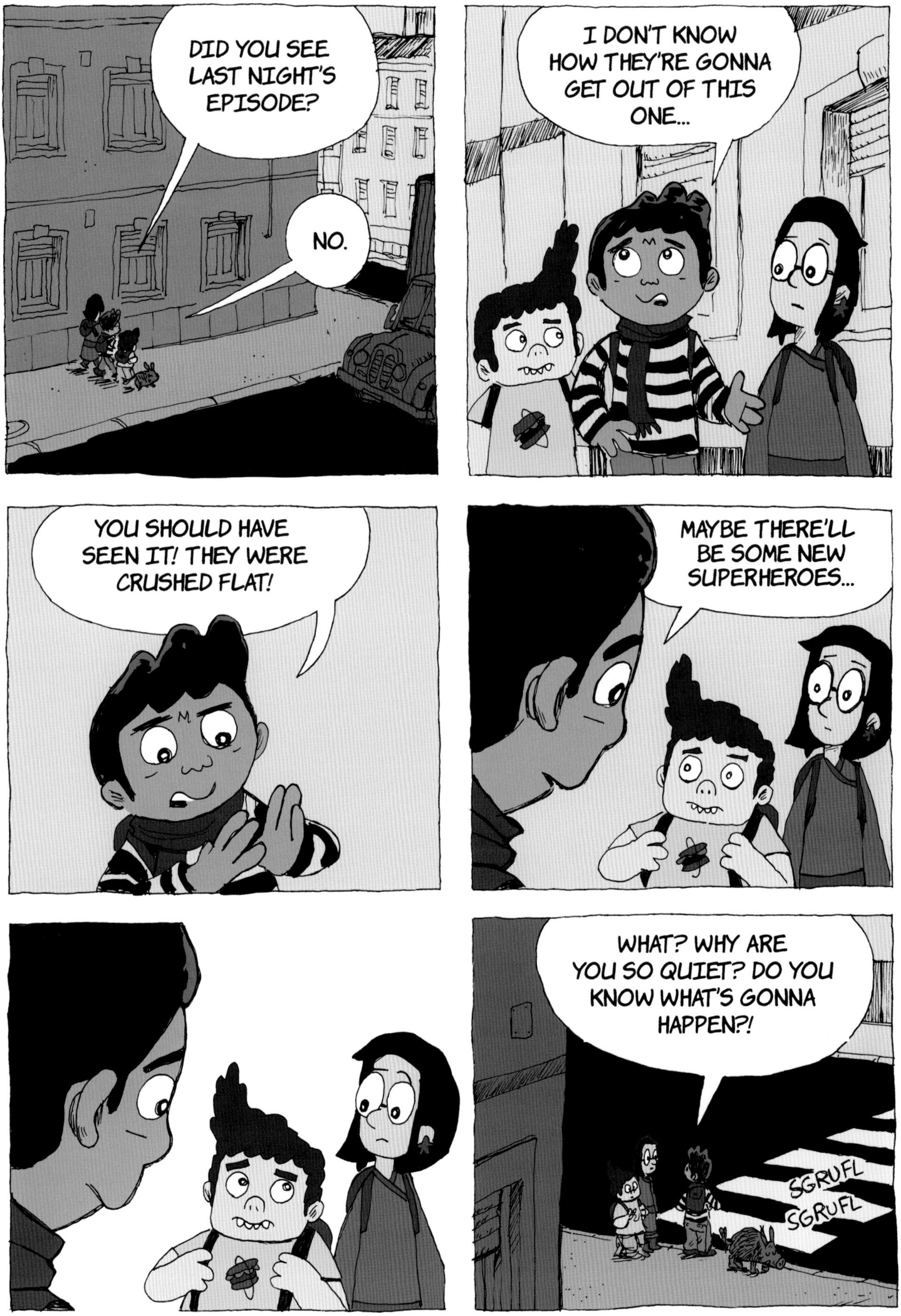
DID YOU SEE LAST NIGHT'S EPISODE?
NO.
I DON'T KNOW HOW THEY'RE GONNA GET OUT OF THIS ONE...
YOU SHOULD HAVE SEEN IT! THEY WERE CRUSHED FLAT!
MAYBE THERE'LL BE SOME NEW SUPERHEROES...
WHAT? WHY ARE YOU SO QUIET? DO YOU KNOW WHAT'S GONNA HAPPEN?!
SGRUFL
SGRUFL

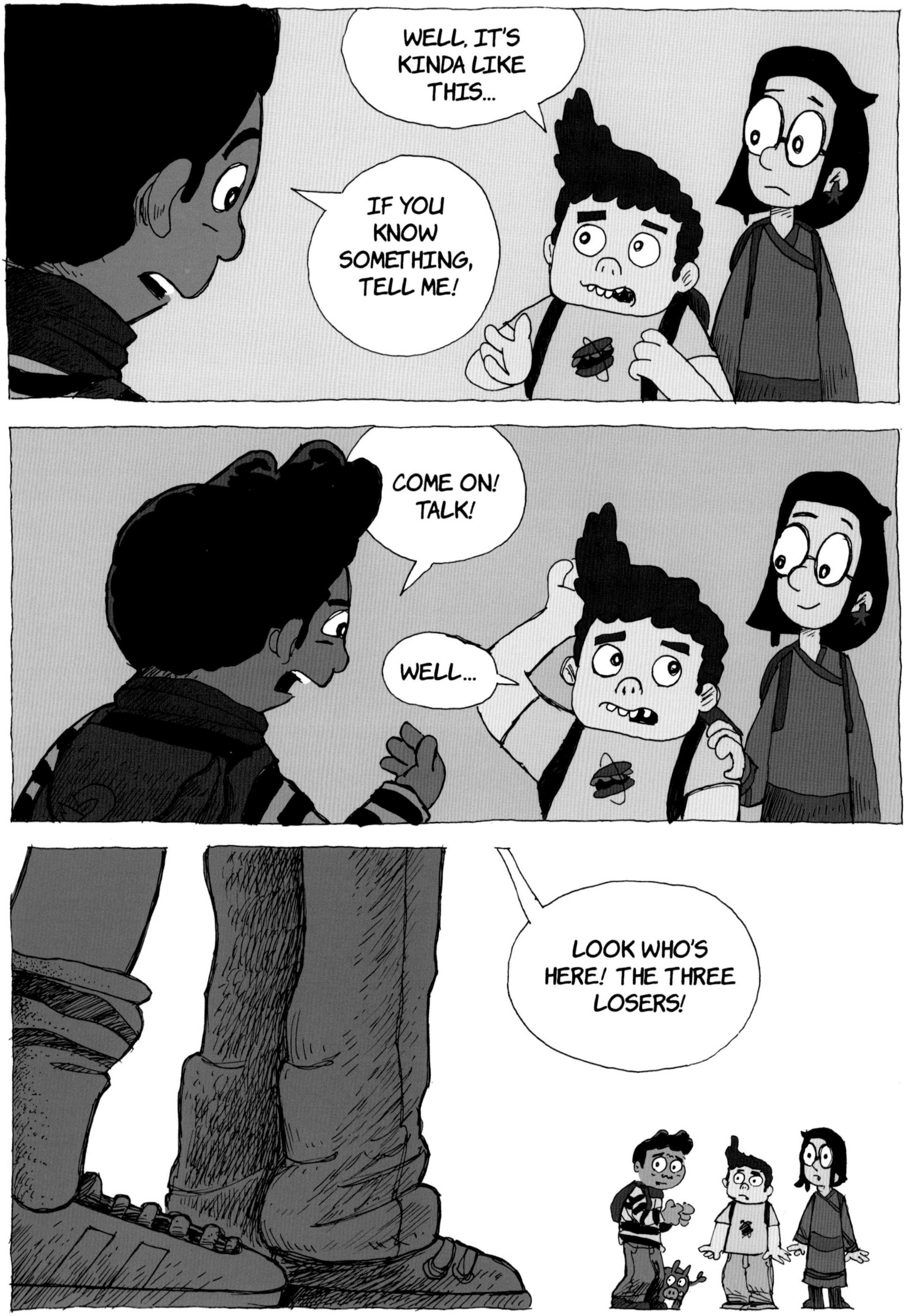
WELL, IT'S KINDA LIKE THIS...
IF YOU KNOW SOMETHING, TELL ME!
COME ON! TALK!
WELL...
LOOK WHO'S HERE! THE THREE LOSERS!

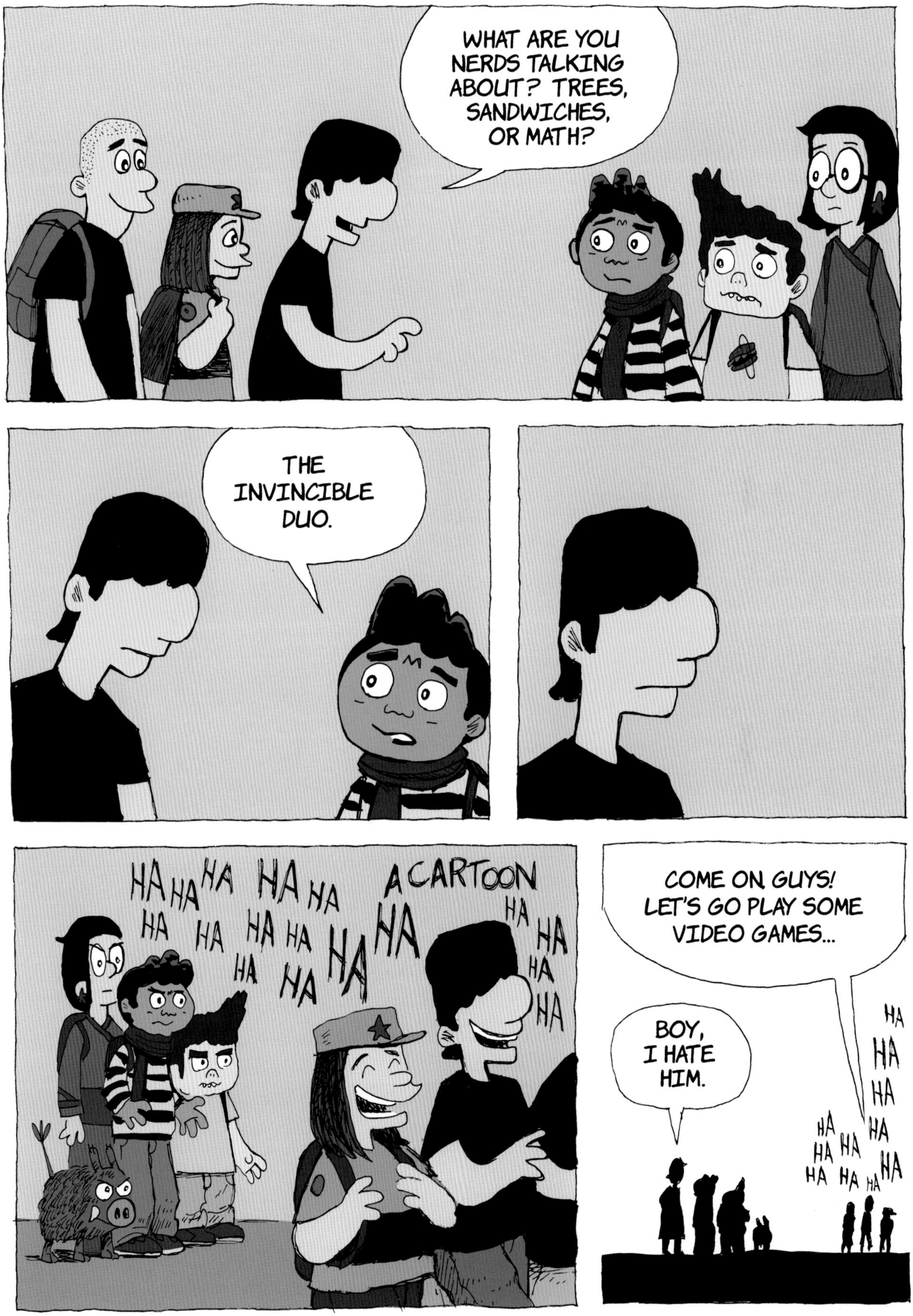
WHAT ARE YOU NERDS TALKING ABOUT? TREES, SANDWICHES, OR MATH?
THE INVINCIBLE DUO.
HA HA HA HA HA A CARTOON HA HA HA HA HA HA HA HA HA HA HA HA HA HA
COME ON GUYS! LET'S GO PLAY SOME VIDEO GAMES...
BOY, I HATE HIM.
HA HA HA HA HA HA HA HA HA HA

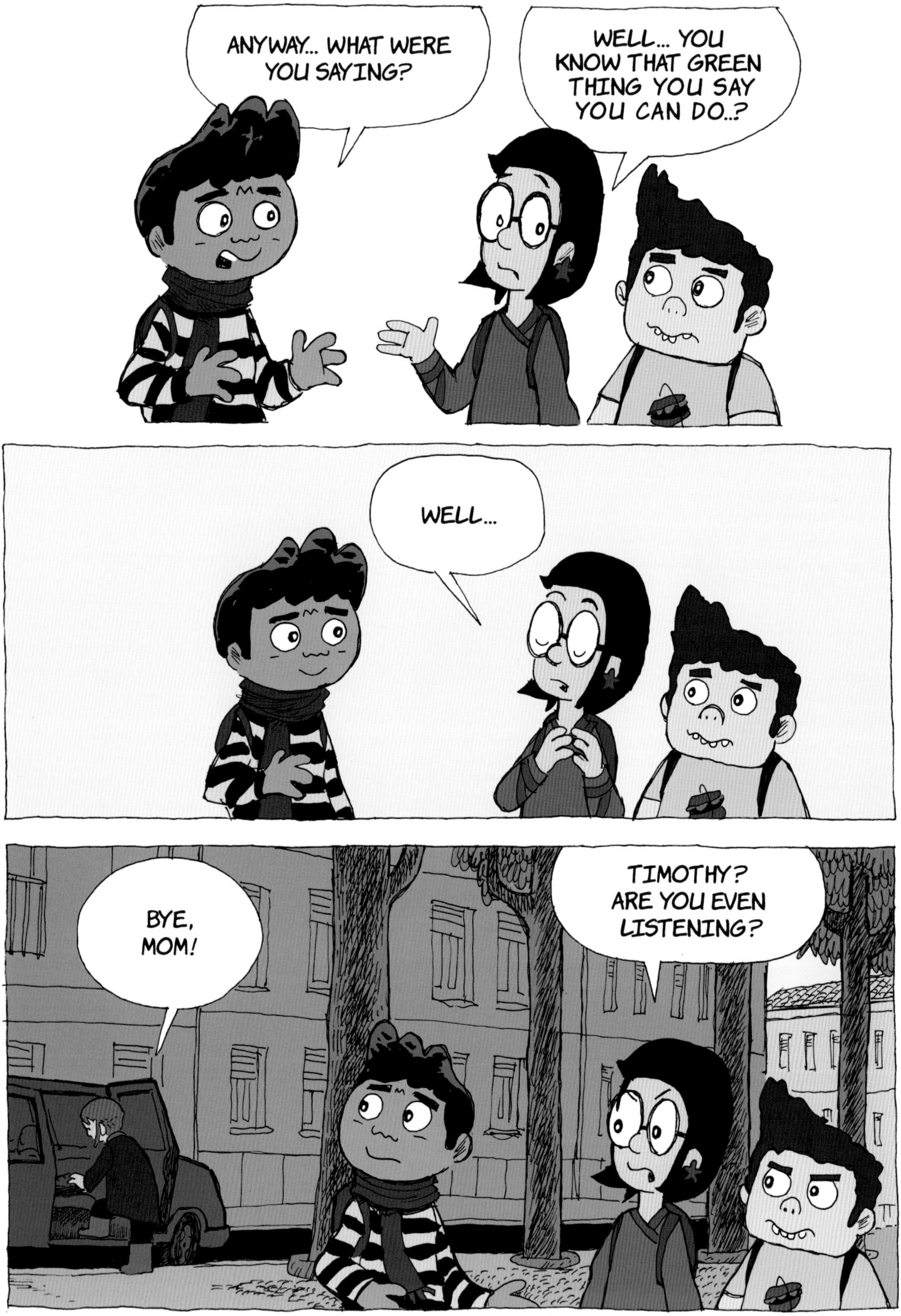
ANYWAY... WHAT WERE YOU SAYING?
WELL... YOU KNOW THAT GREEN THING YOU SAY YOU CAN DO..?
WELL...
BYE, MOM!
TIMOTHY? ARE YOU EVEN LISTENING?

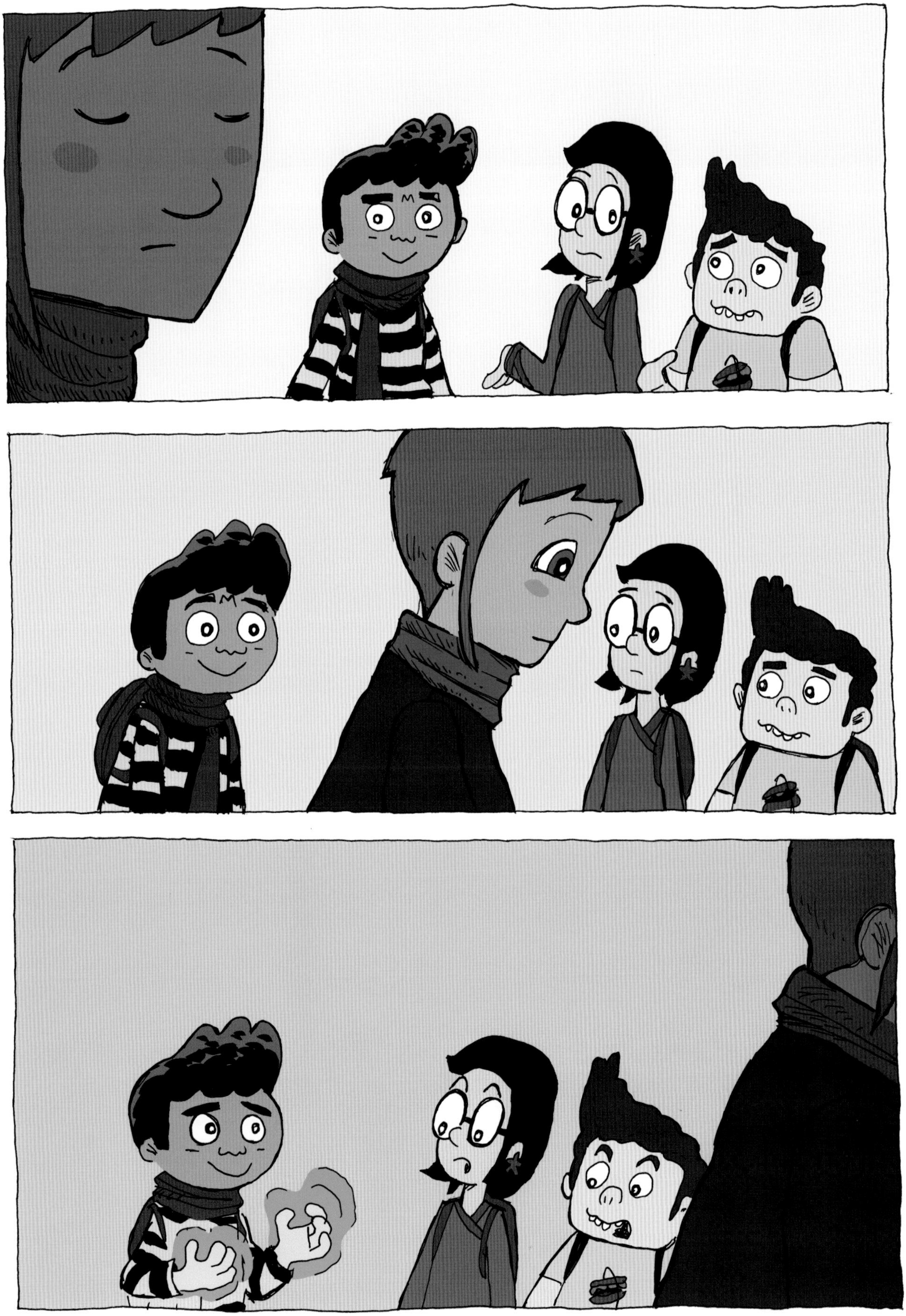

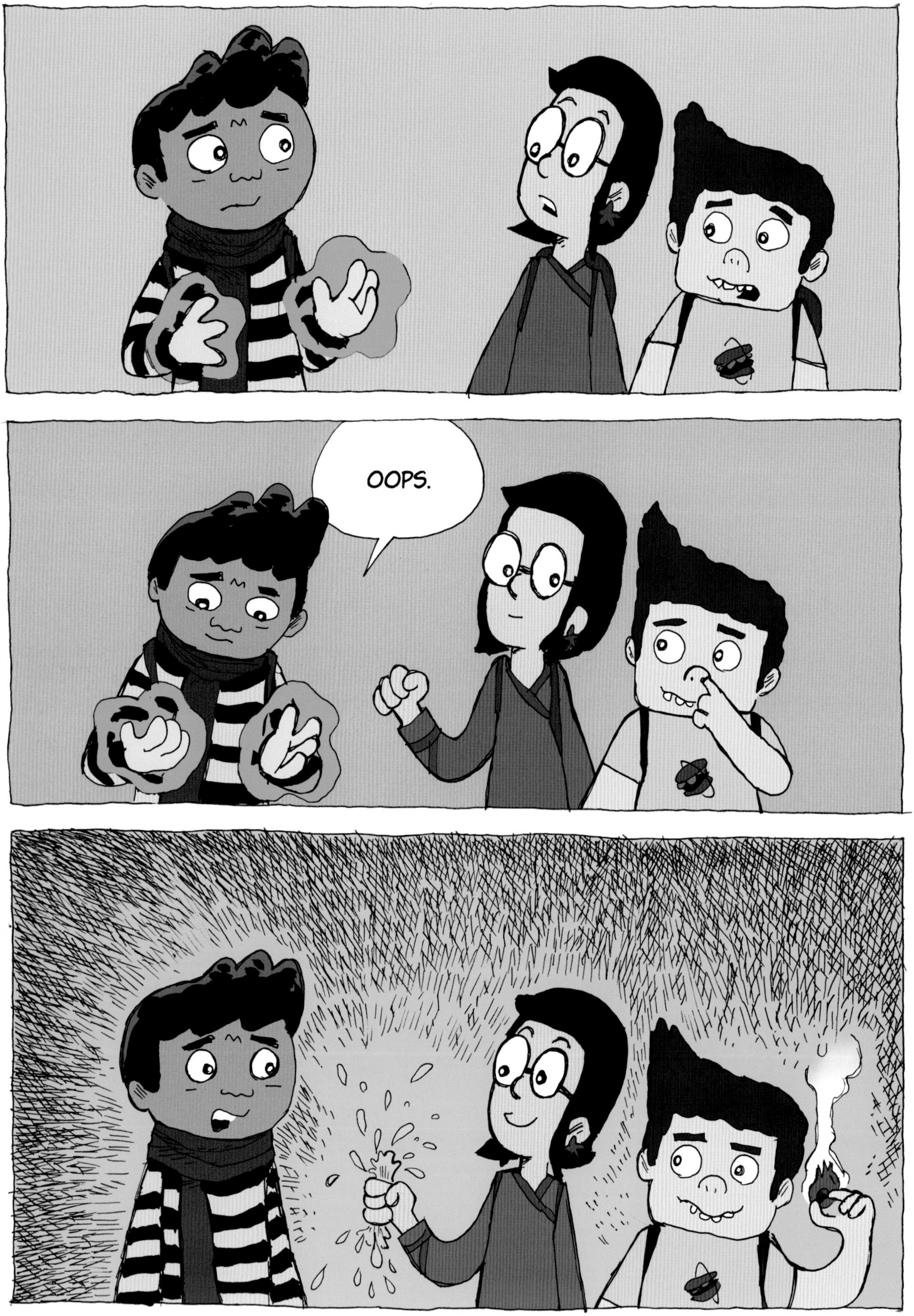
OOPS.

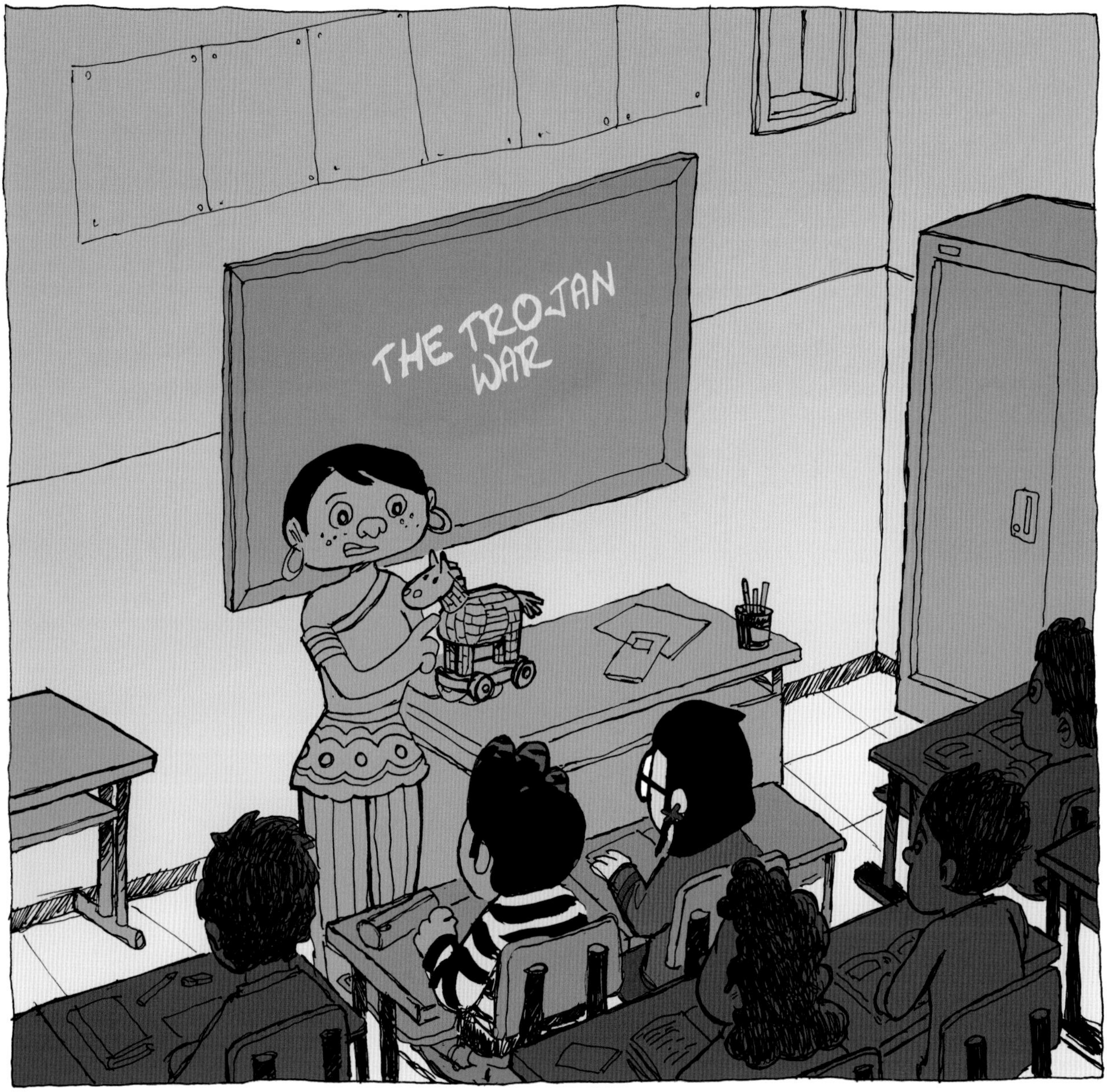
THE TROJAN WAR
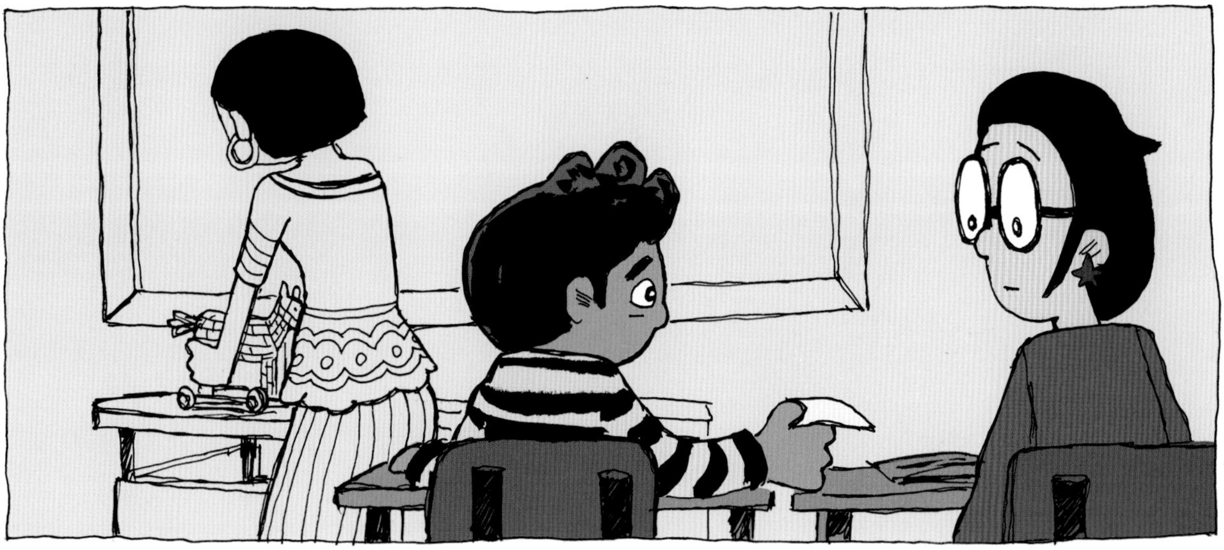

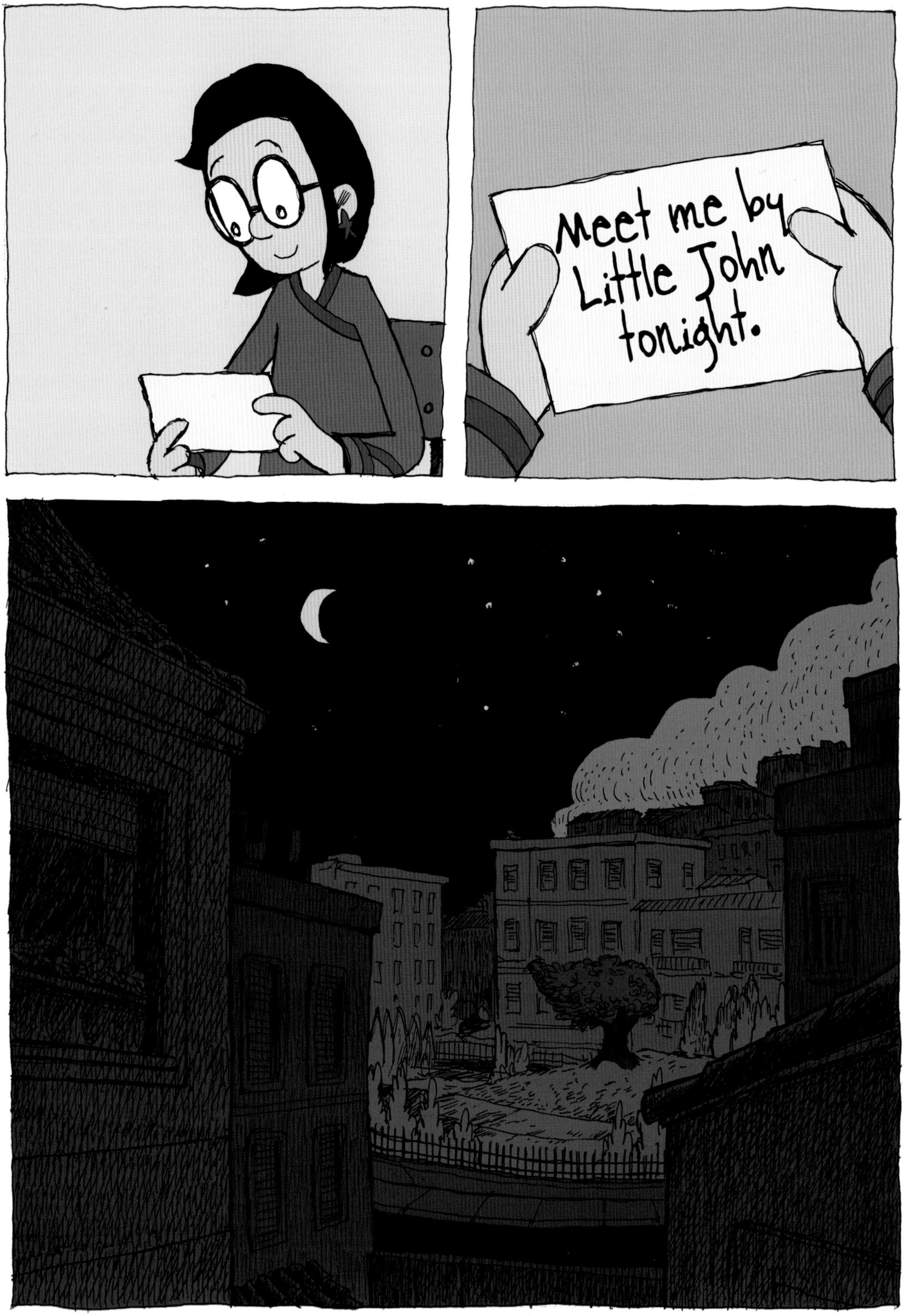
Meet me by Little John tonight.

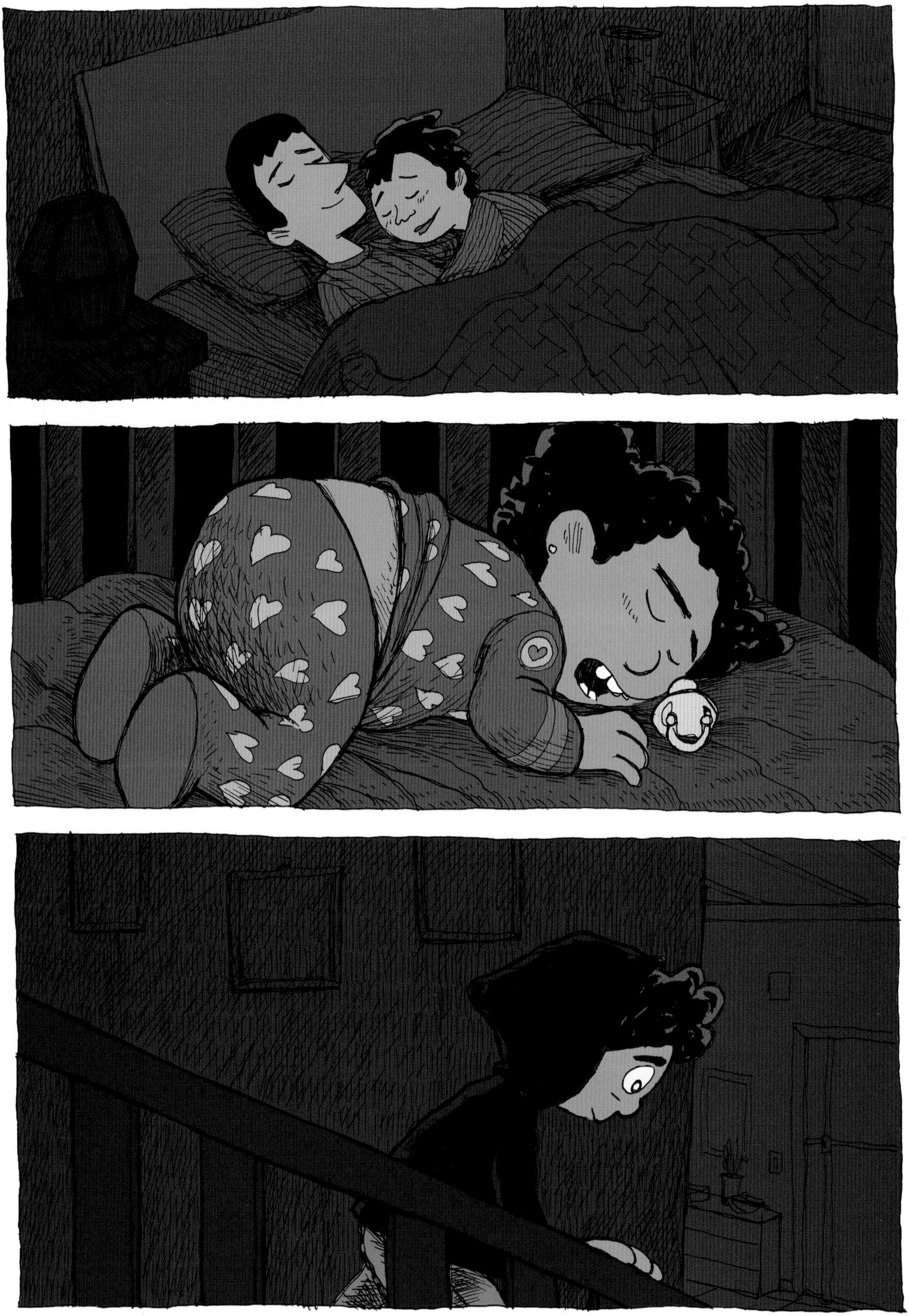

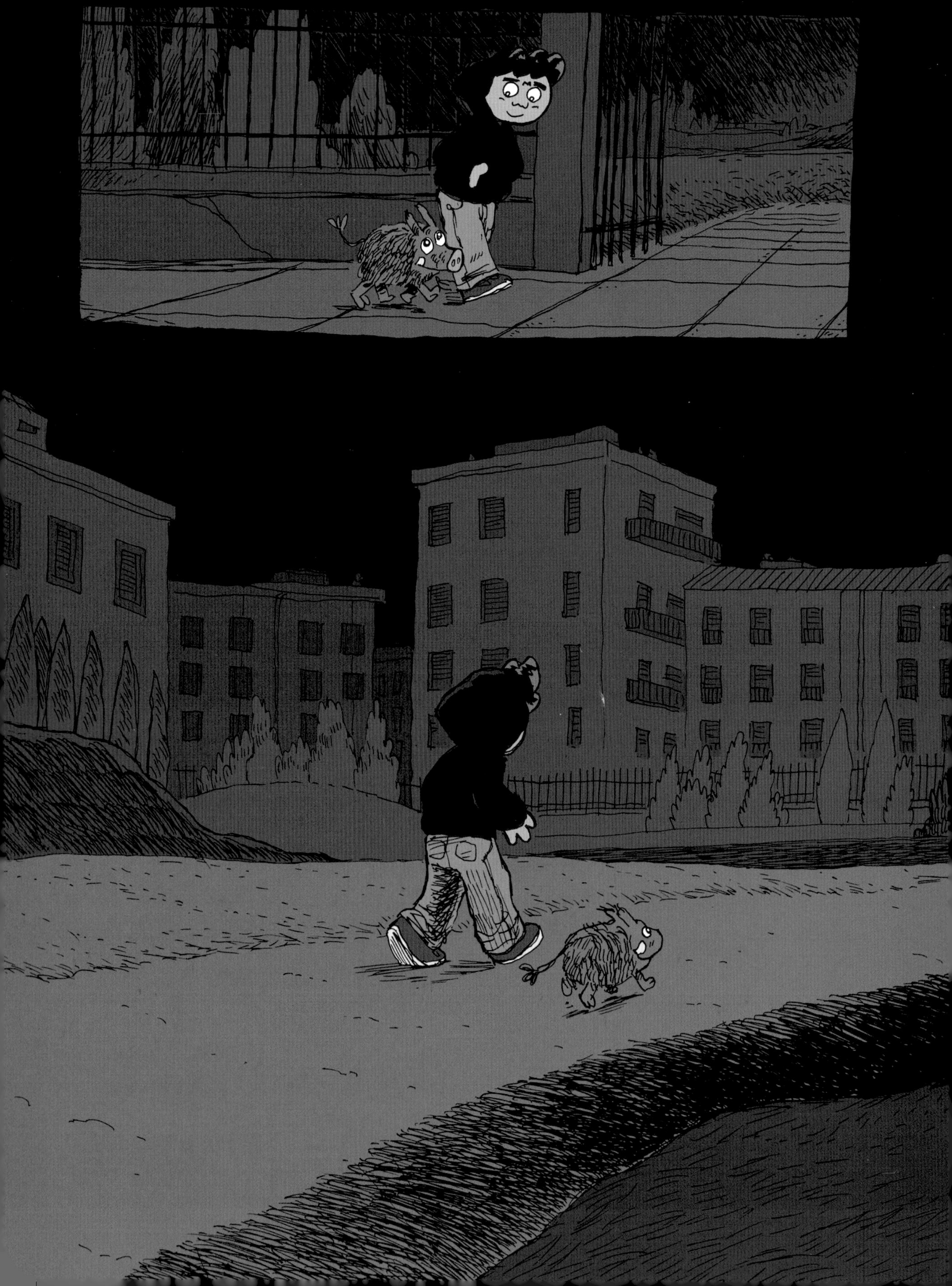

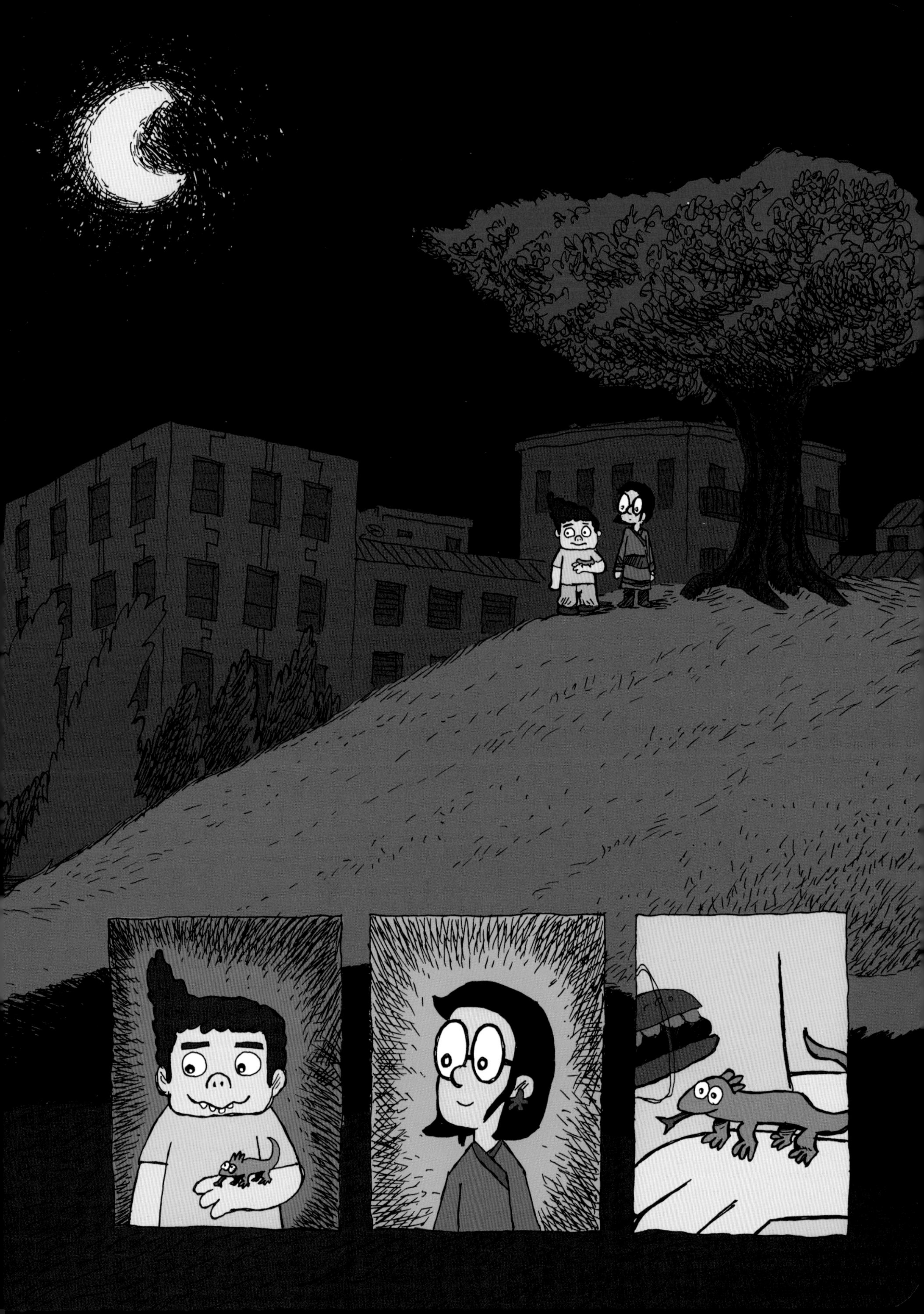

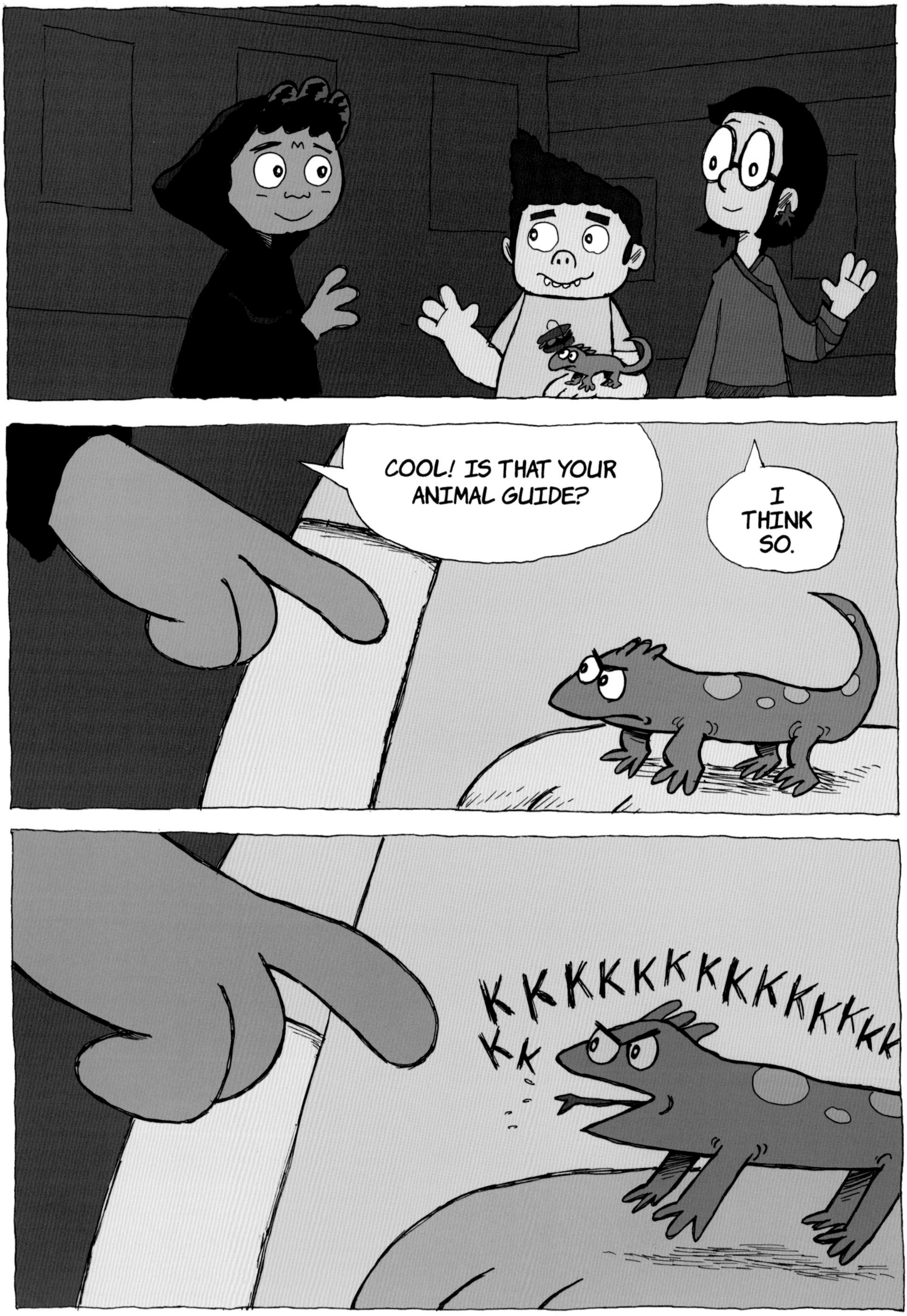
COOL! IS THAT YOUR ANIMAL GUIDE?
I THINK SO.
KKKKKKKKKKKKKKKK
KK

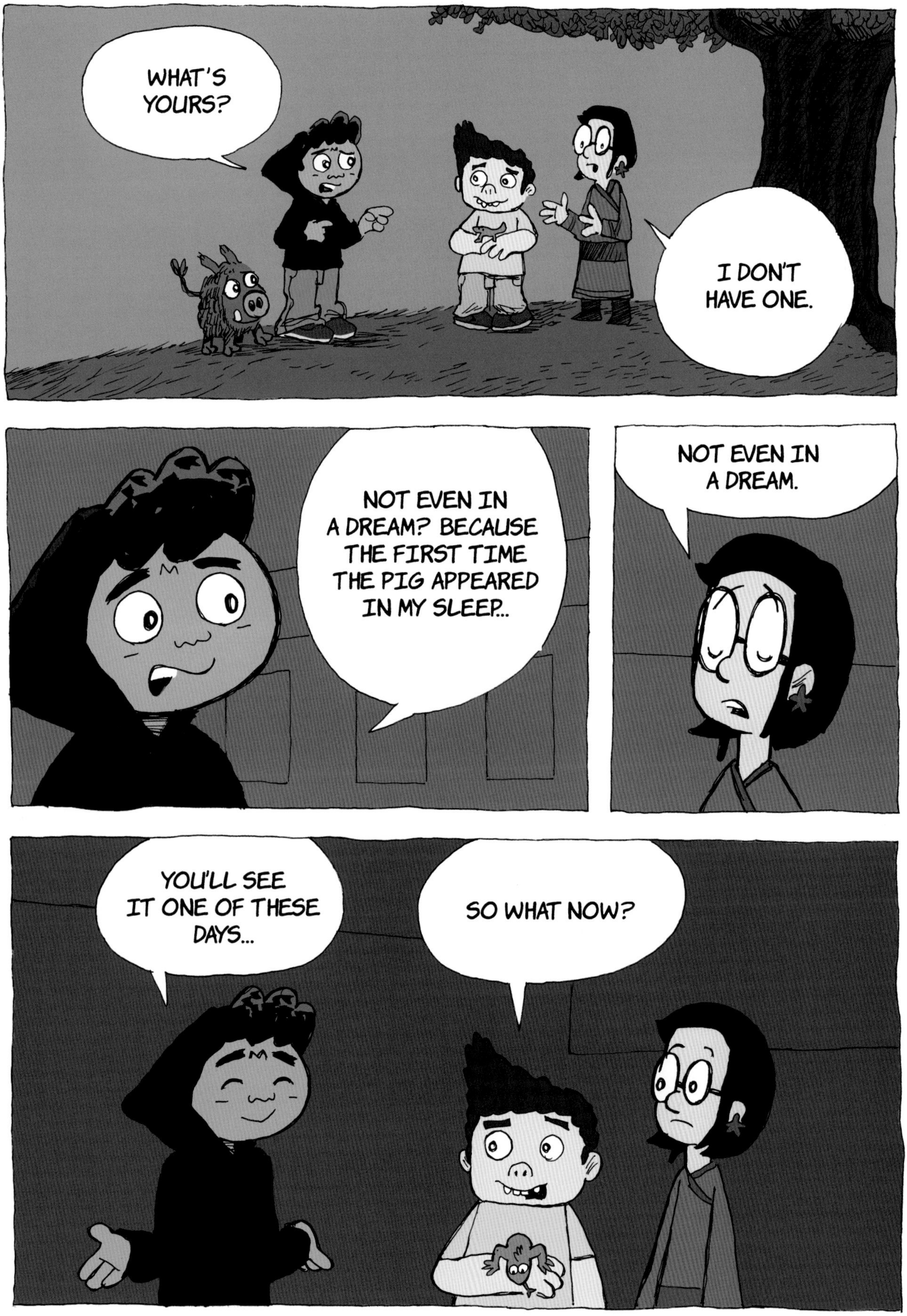
WHAT'S YOURS?
I DON'T HAVE ONE.
NOT EVEN IN A DREAM? BECAUSE THE FIRST TIME THE PIG APPEARED IN MY SLEEP...
NOT EVEN IN A DREAM.
YOU'LL SEE IT ONE OF THESE DAYS...
SO WHAT NOW?

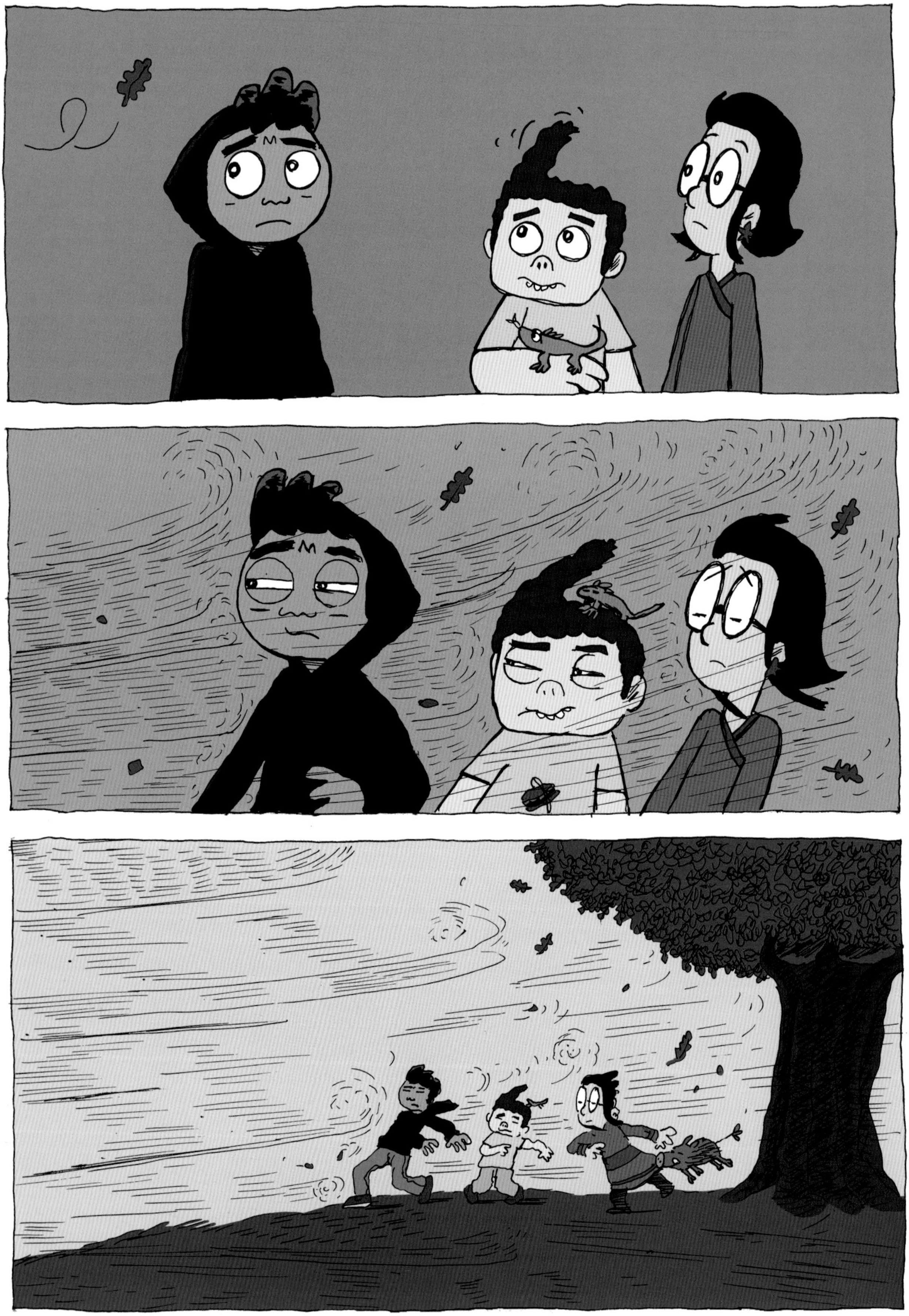

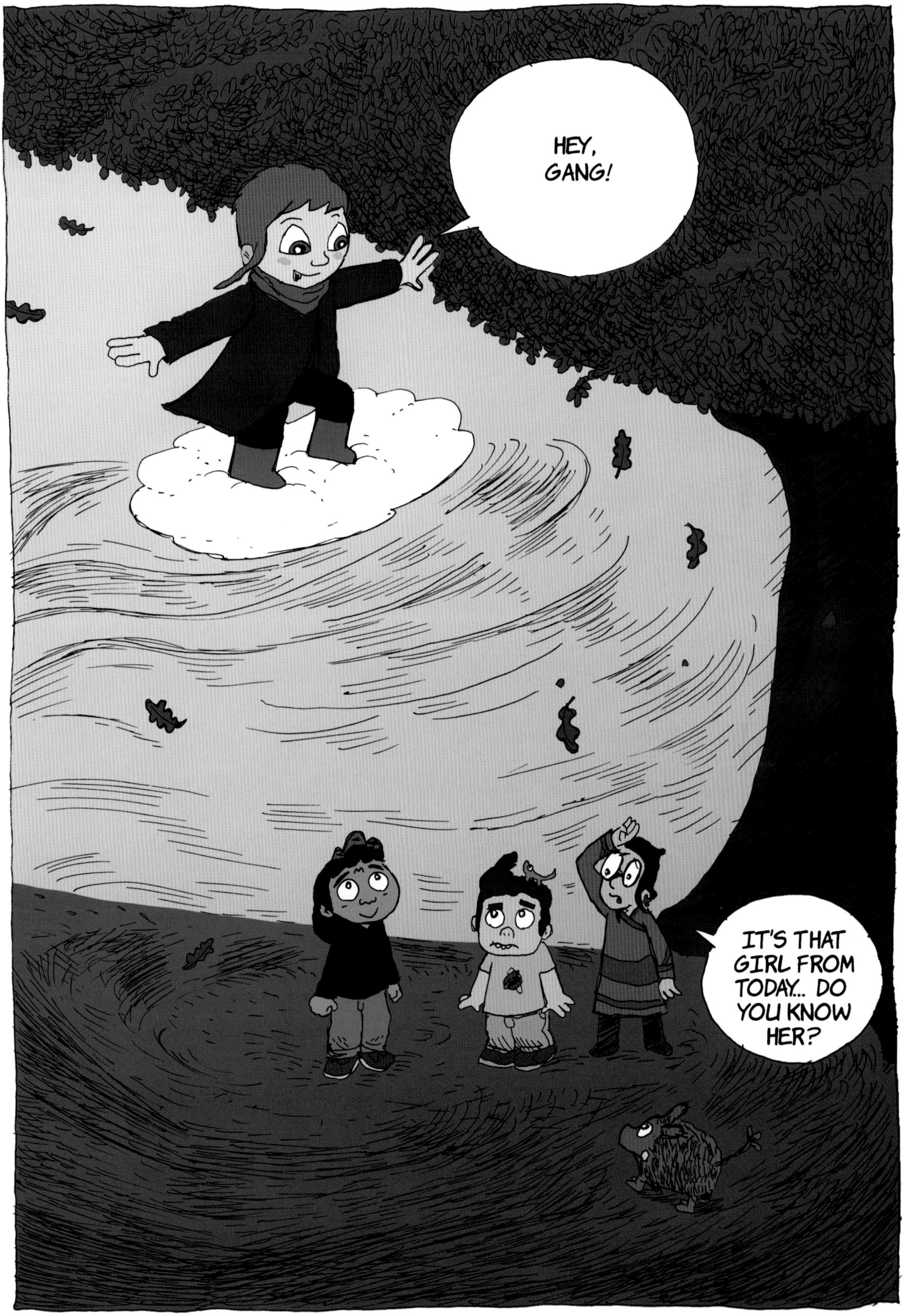
HEY, GANG!
IT'S THAT GIRL FROM TODAY... DO YOU KNOW HER?

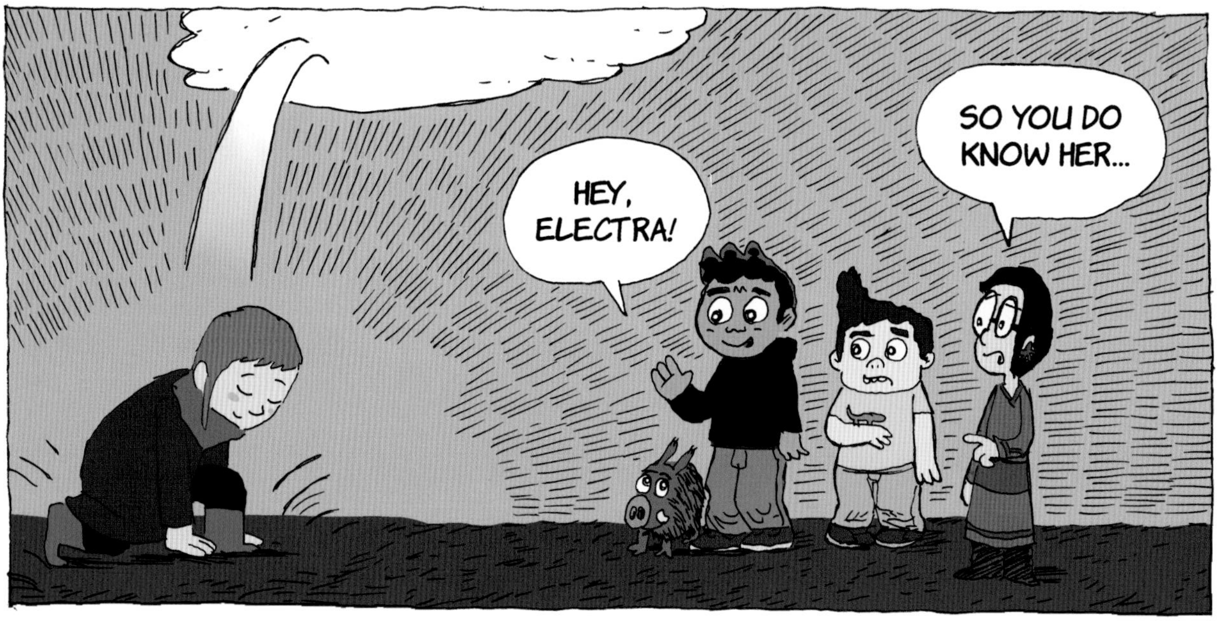
HEY, ELECTRA!
SO YOU DO KNOW HER...

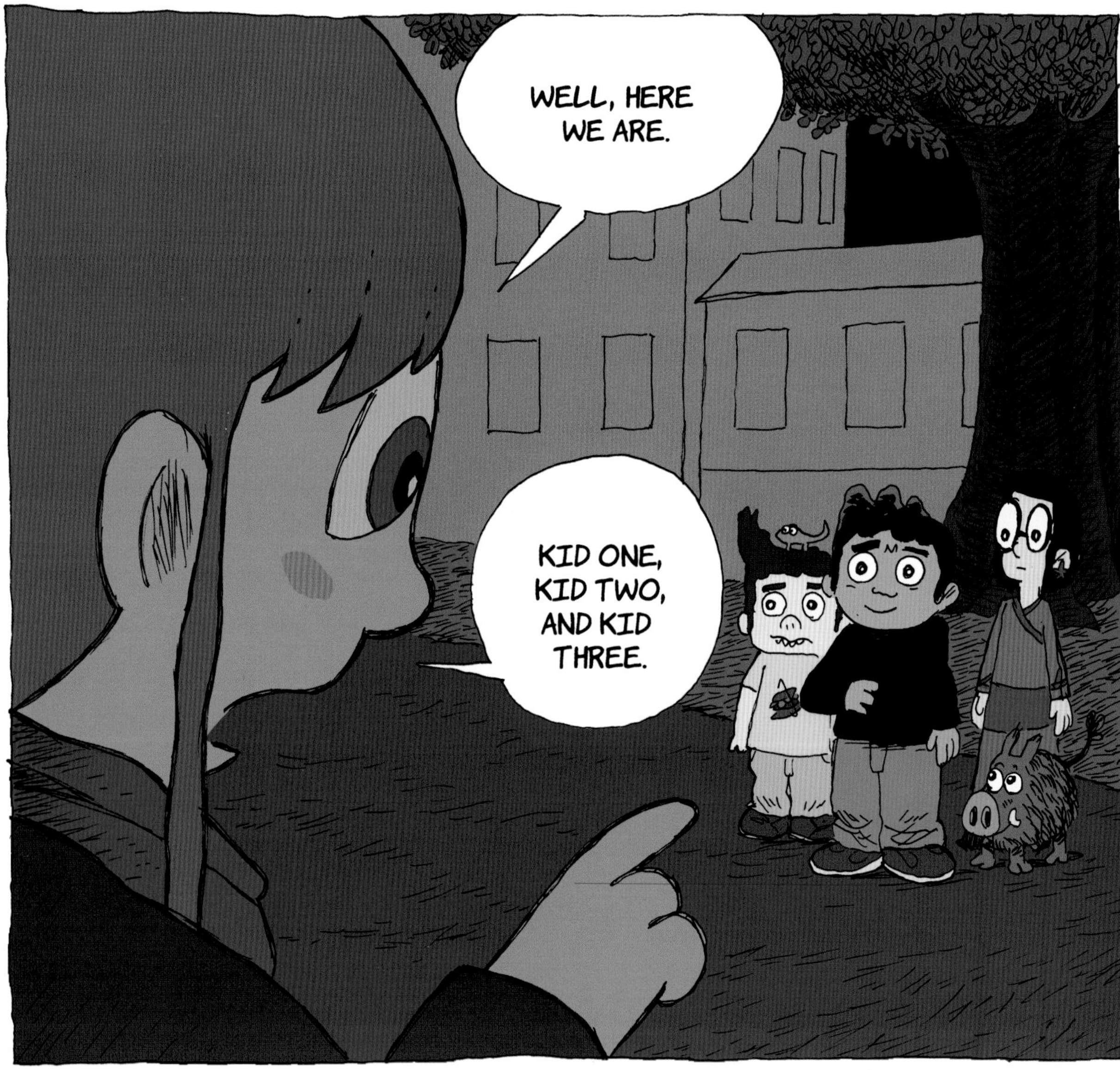
WELL, HERE WE ARE.
KID ONE, KID TWO, AND KID THREE.

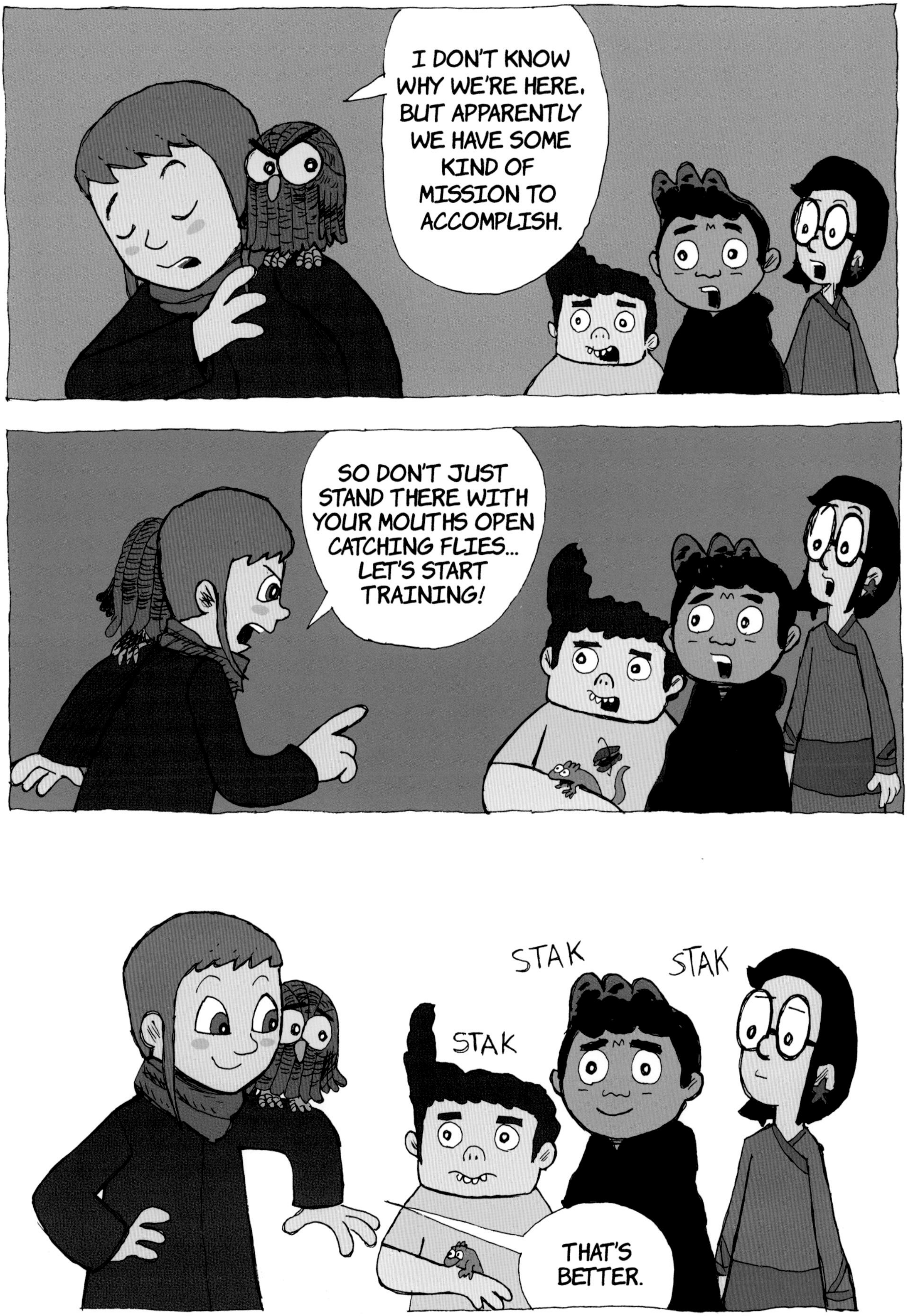
I DON'T KNOW WHY WE'RE HERE, BUT APPARENTLY WE HAVE SOME KIND OF MISSION TO ACCOMPLISH.
SO DON'T JUST STAND THERE WITH YOUR MOUTHS OPEN CATCHING FLIES... LET'S START TRAINING!
STAK
STAK
STAK
THAT'S BETTER.

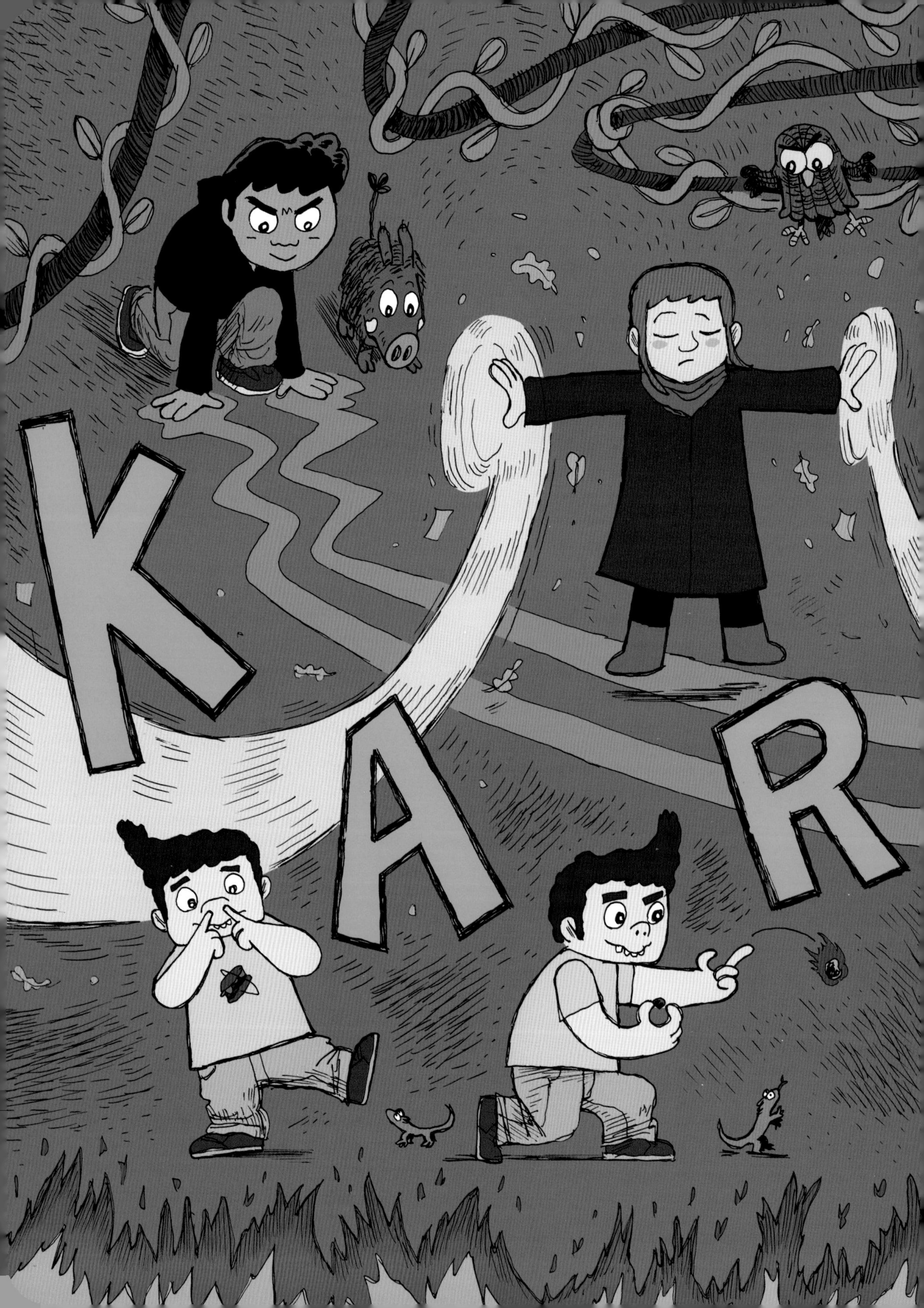
KAR

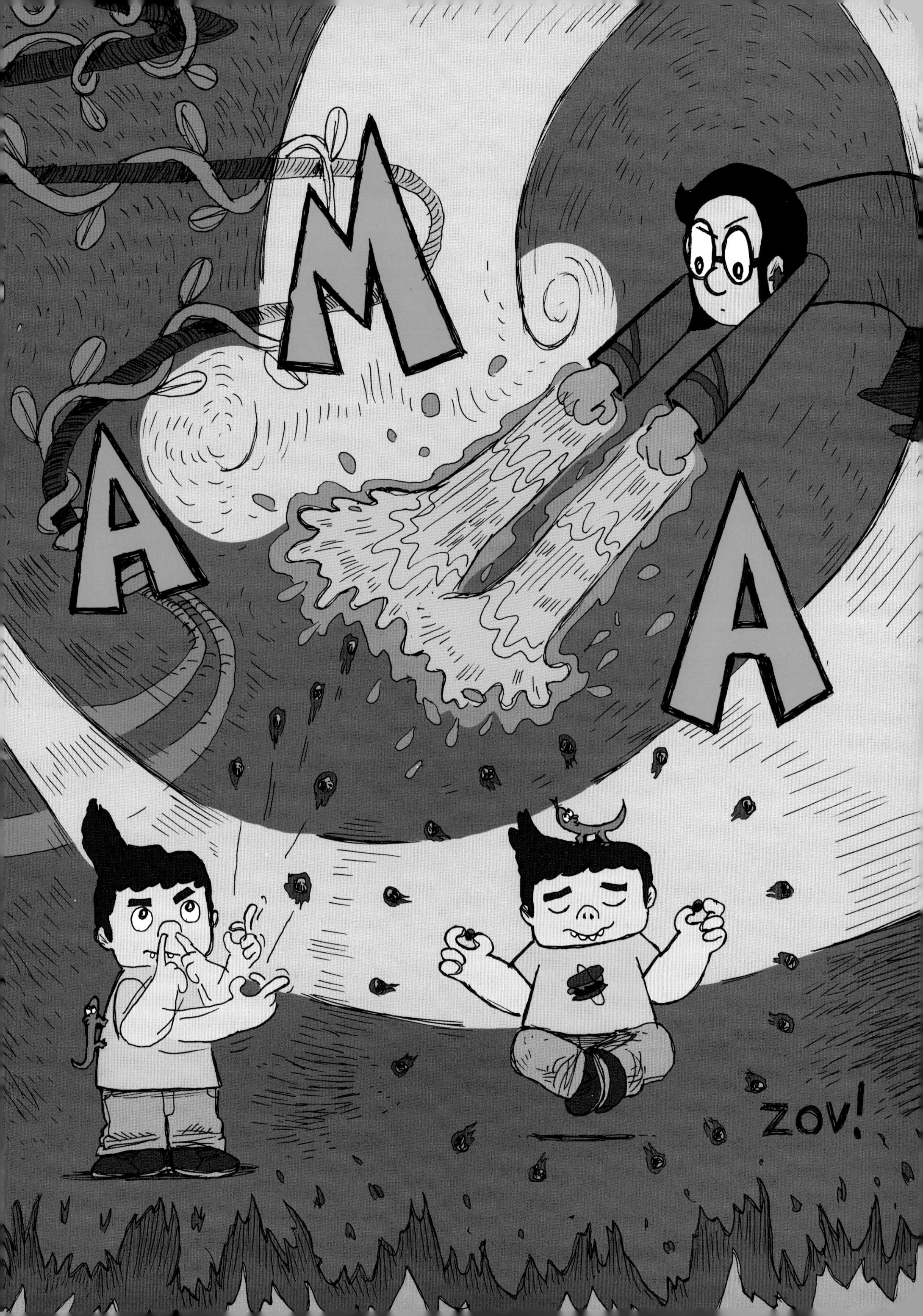
AMUA
ZOV!

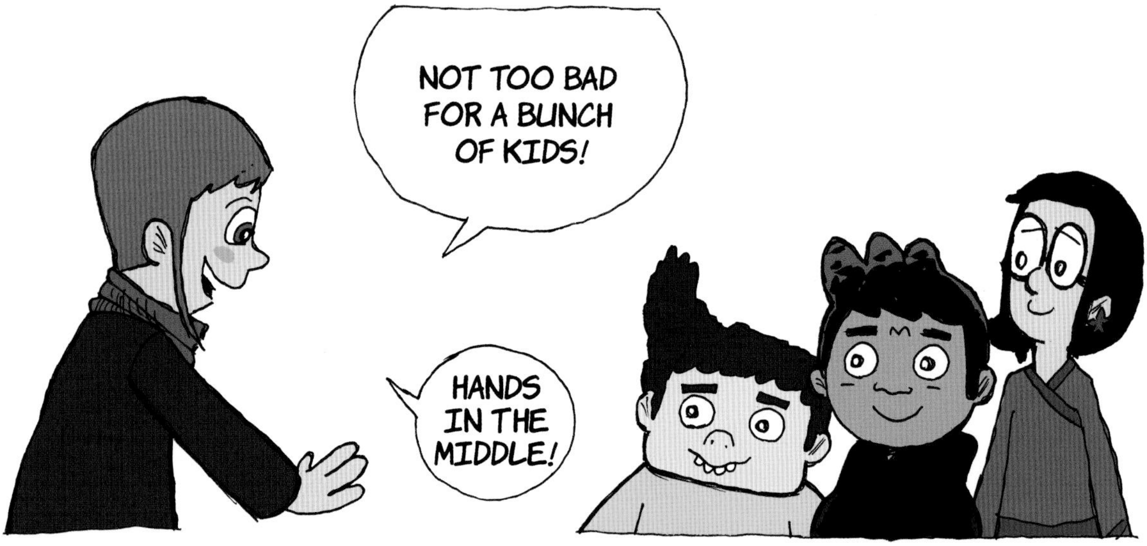
NOT TOO BAD FOR A BUNCH OF KIDS!
HANDS IN THE MIDDLE!

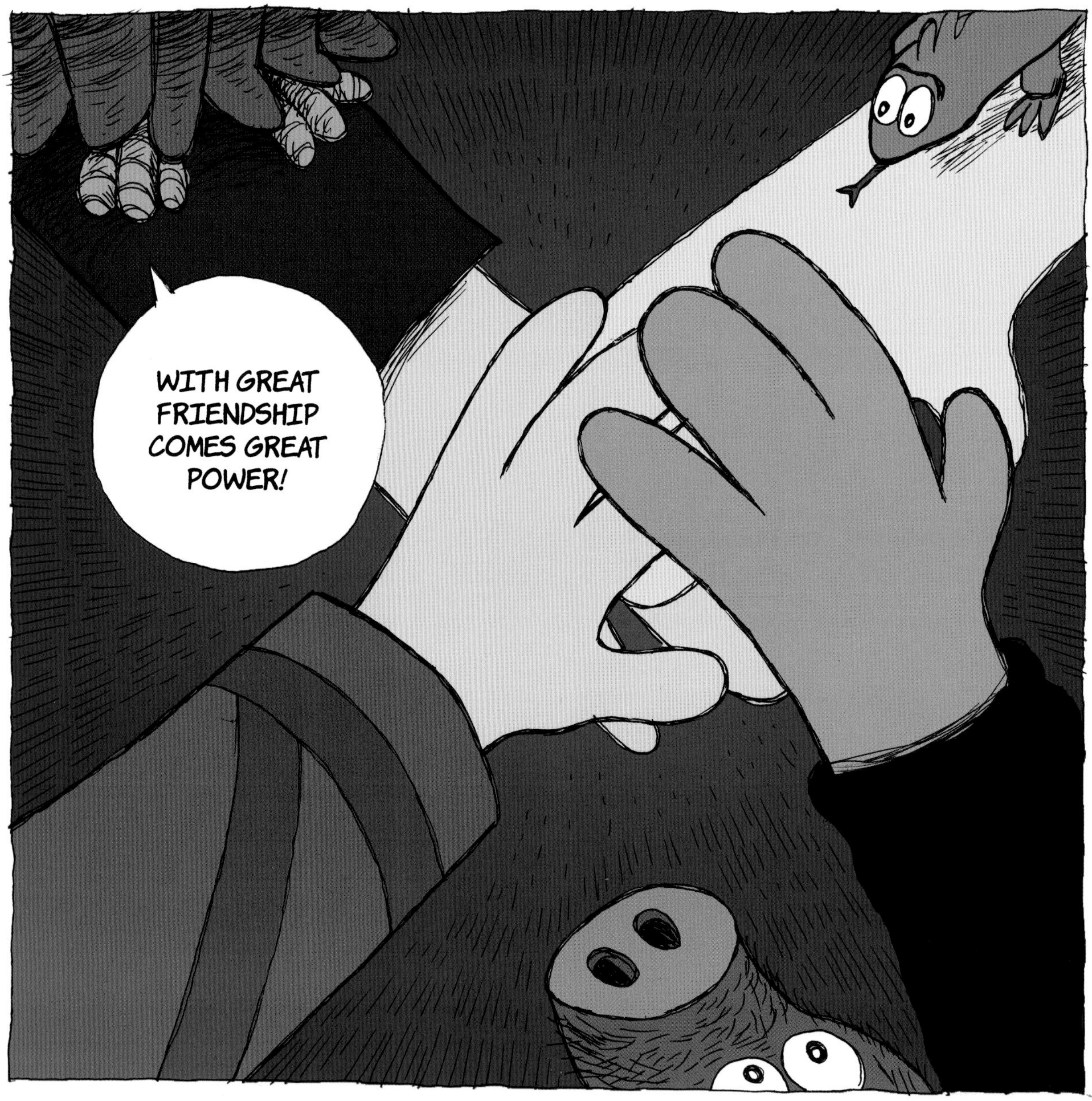
WITH GREAT FRIENDSHIP COMES GREAT POWER!

CHAPTER SEVEN
THE PLAN

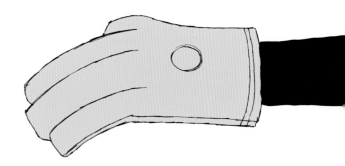

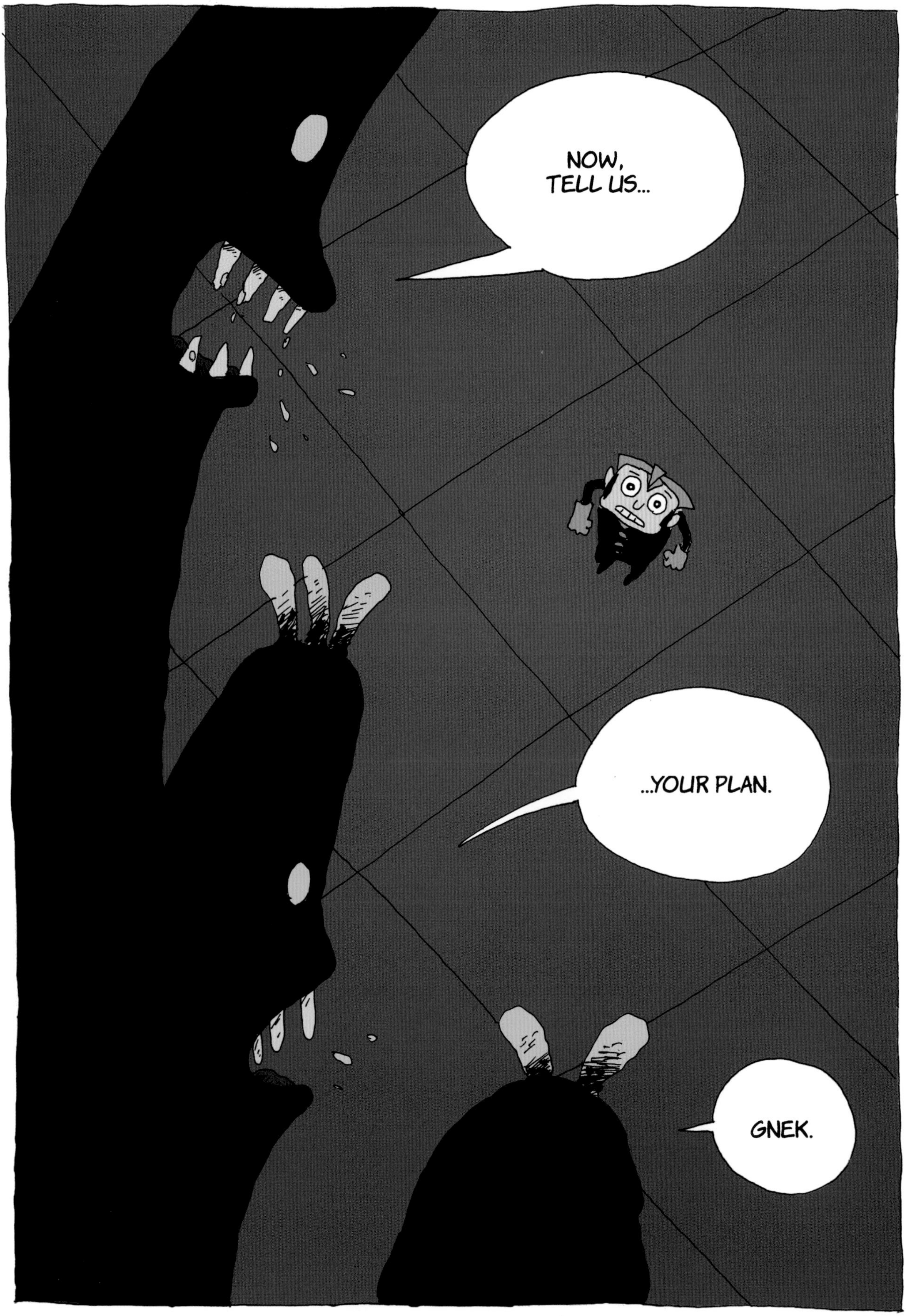
NOW, TELL US...
...YOUR PLAN.
GNEK.

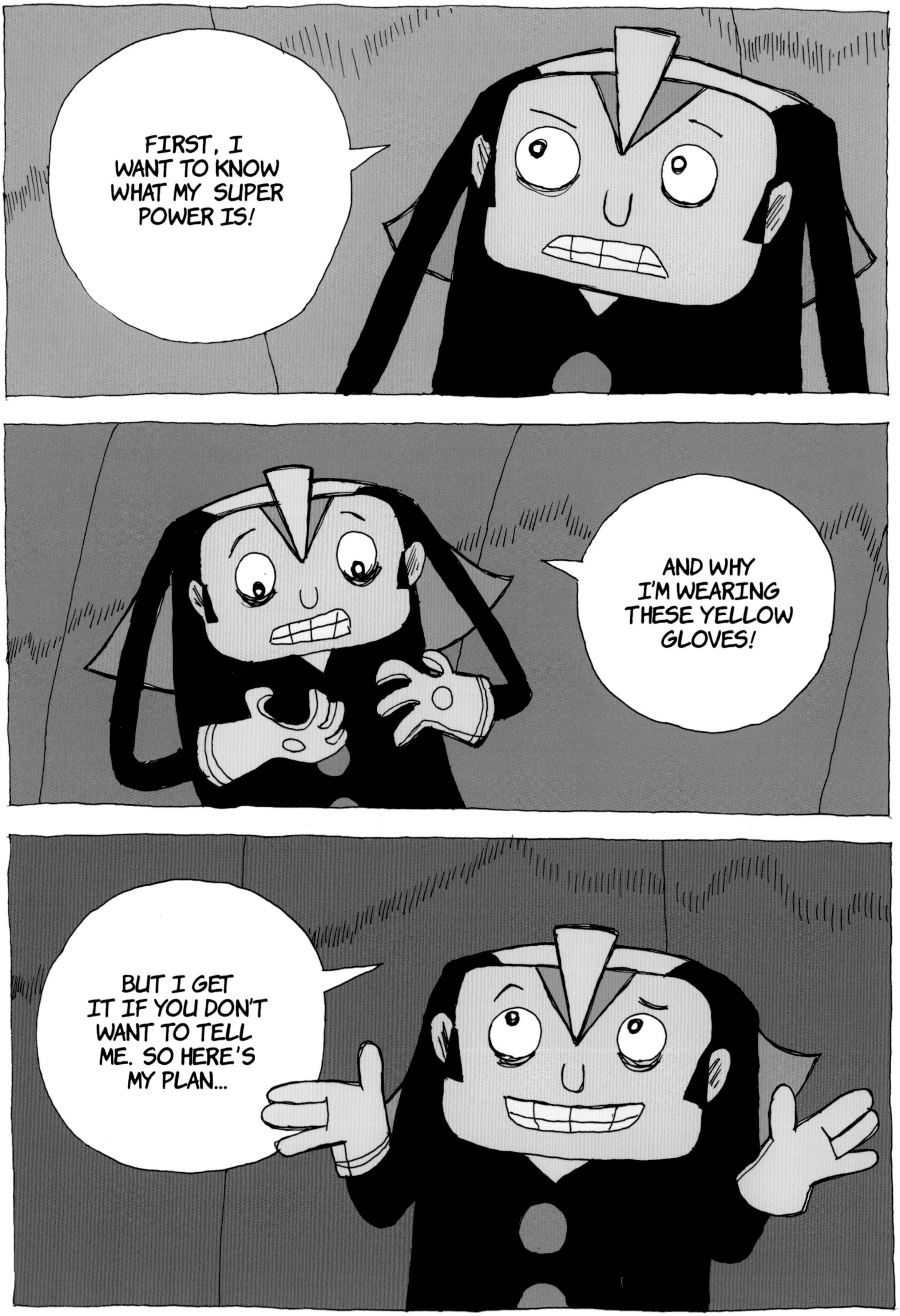
FIRST, I WANT TO KNOW WHAT MY SUPER POWER IS!
AND WHY I'M WEARING THESE YELLOW GLOVES!
BUT I GET IT IF YOU DON'T WANT TO TELL ME. SO HERE'S MY PLAN...

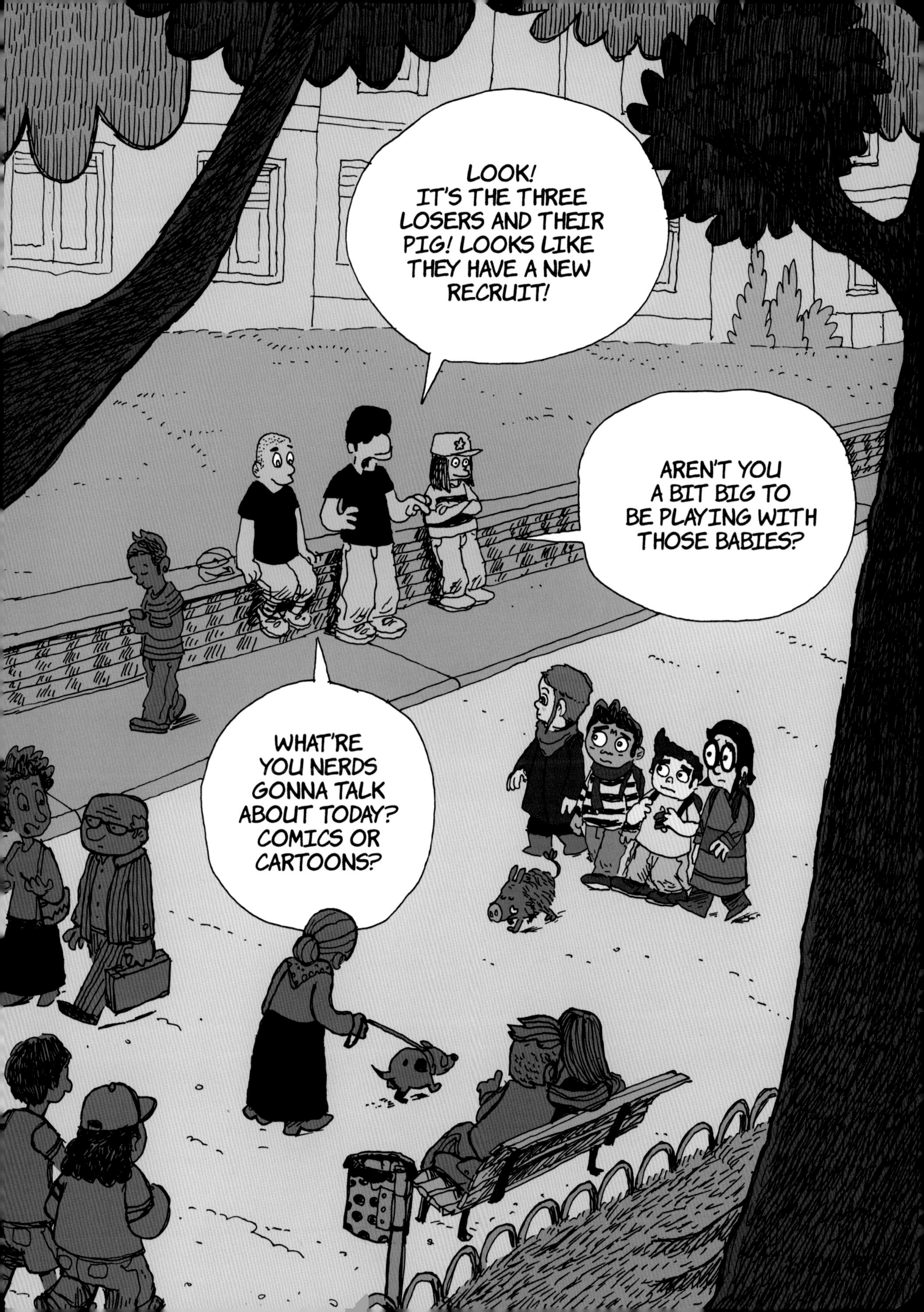
LOOK! IT'S THE THREE LOSERS AND THEIR PIG! LOOKS LIKE THEY HAVE A NEW RECRUIT!
AREN'T YOU A BIT BIG TO BE PLAYING WITH THOSE BABIES?
WHAT'RE YOU NERDS GONNA TALK ABOUT TODAY? COMICS OR CARTOONS?

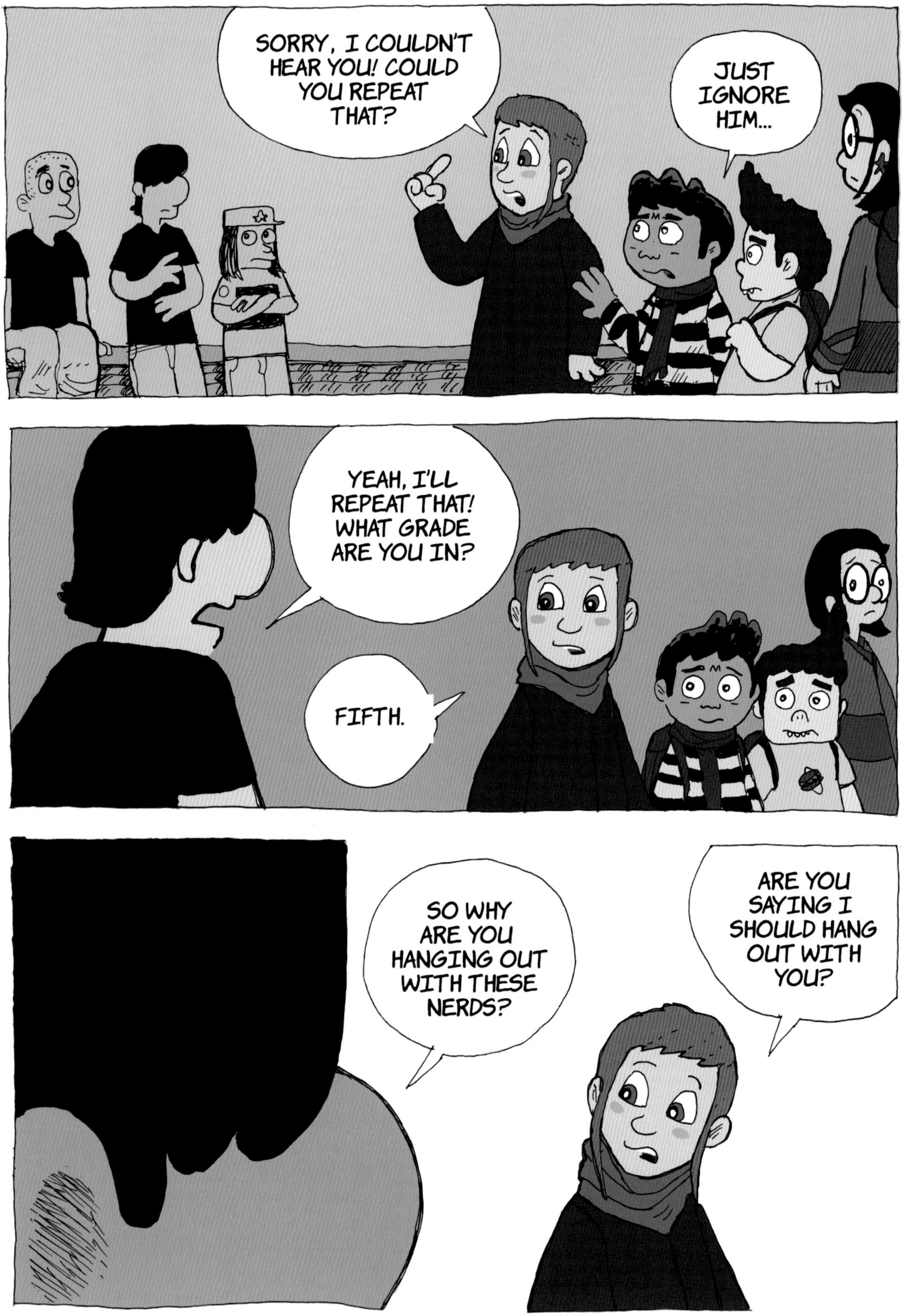
SORRY, I COULDN'T HEAR YOU! COULD YOU REPEAT THAT?
JUST IGNORE HIM...
YEAH, I'LL REPEAT THAT! WHAT GRADE ARE YOU IN?
FIFTH.
SO WHY ARE YOU HANGING OUT WITH THESE NERDS?
ARE YOU SAYING I SHOULD HANG OUT WITH YOU?

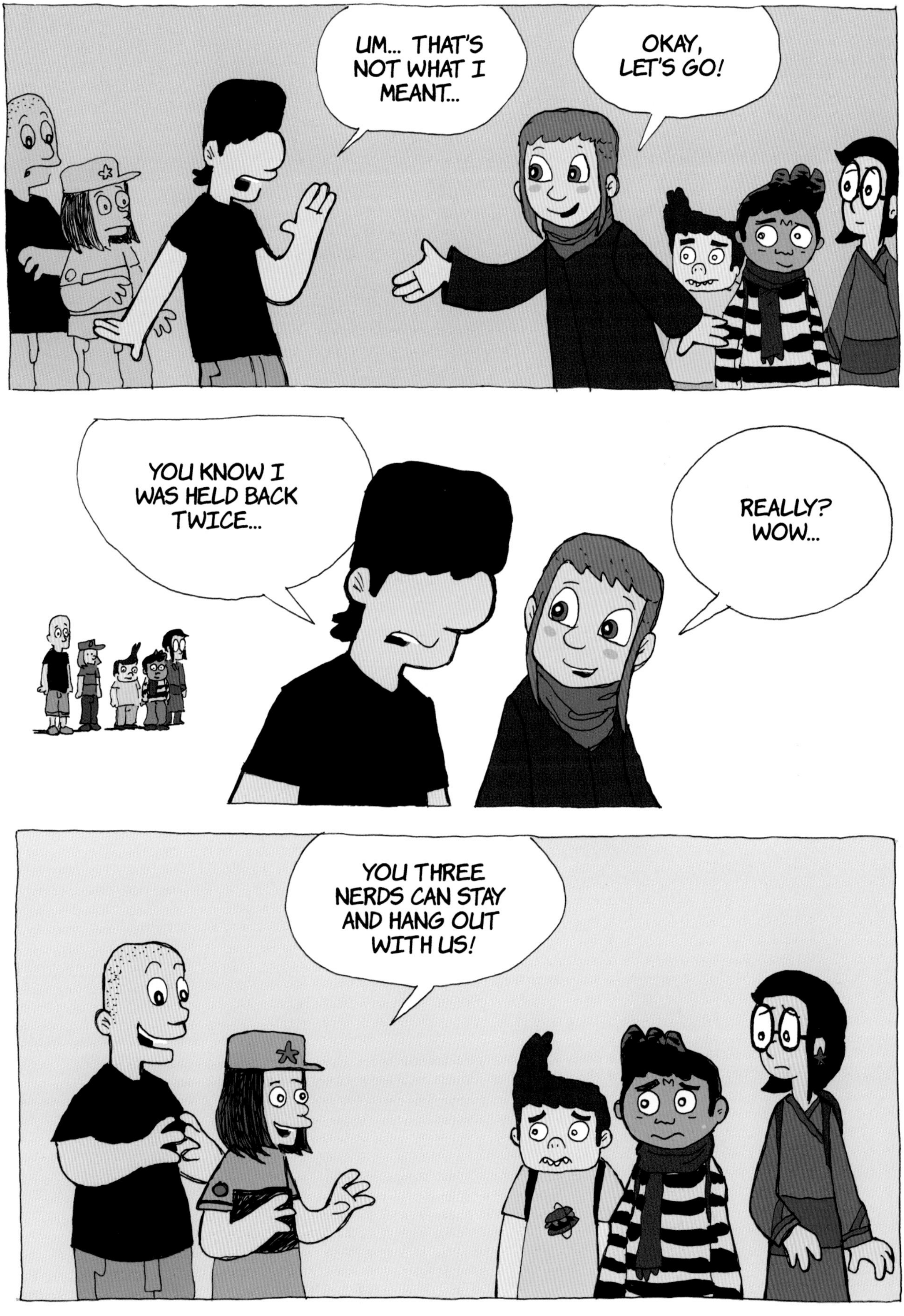
UM... THAT'S NOT WHAT I MEANT...
OKAY, LET'S GO!
YOU KNOW I WAS HELD BACK TWICE...
REALLY? WOW...
YOU THREE NERDS CAN STAY AND HANG OUT WITH US!

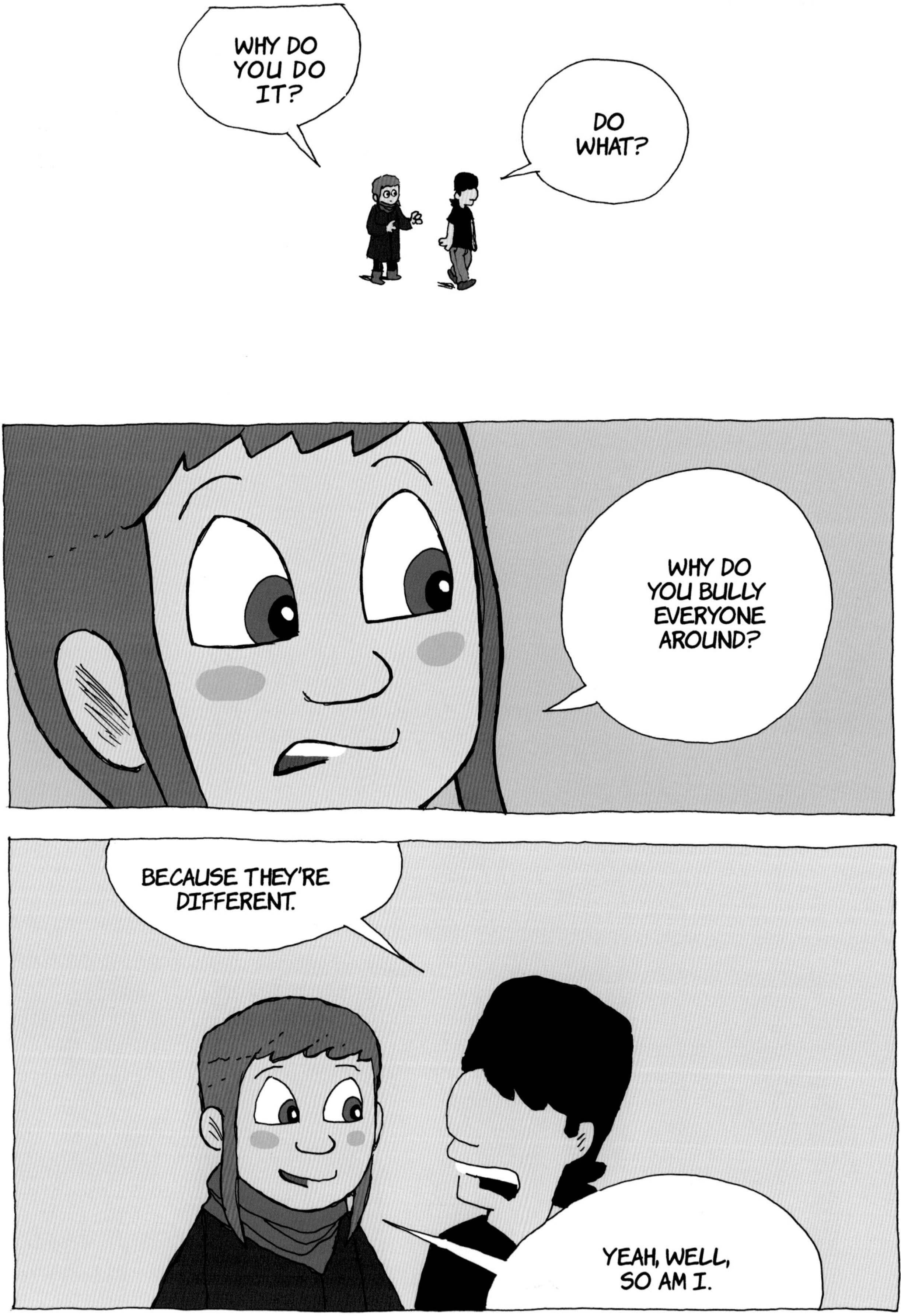
WHY DO YOU DO IT?
DO WHAT?
WHY DO YOU BULLY EVERYONE AROUND?
BECAUSE THEY'RE DIFFERENT.
YEAH, WELL, SO AM I.

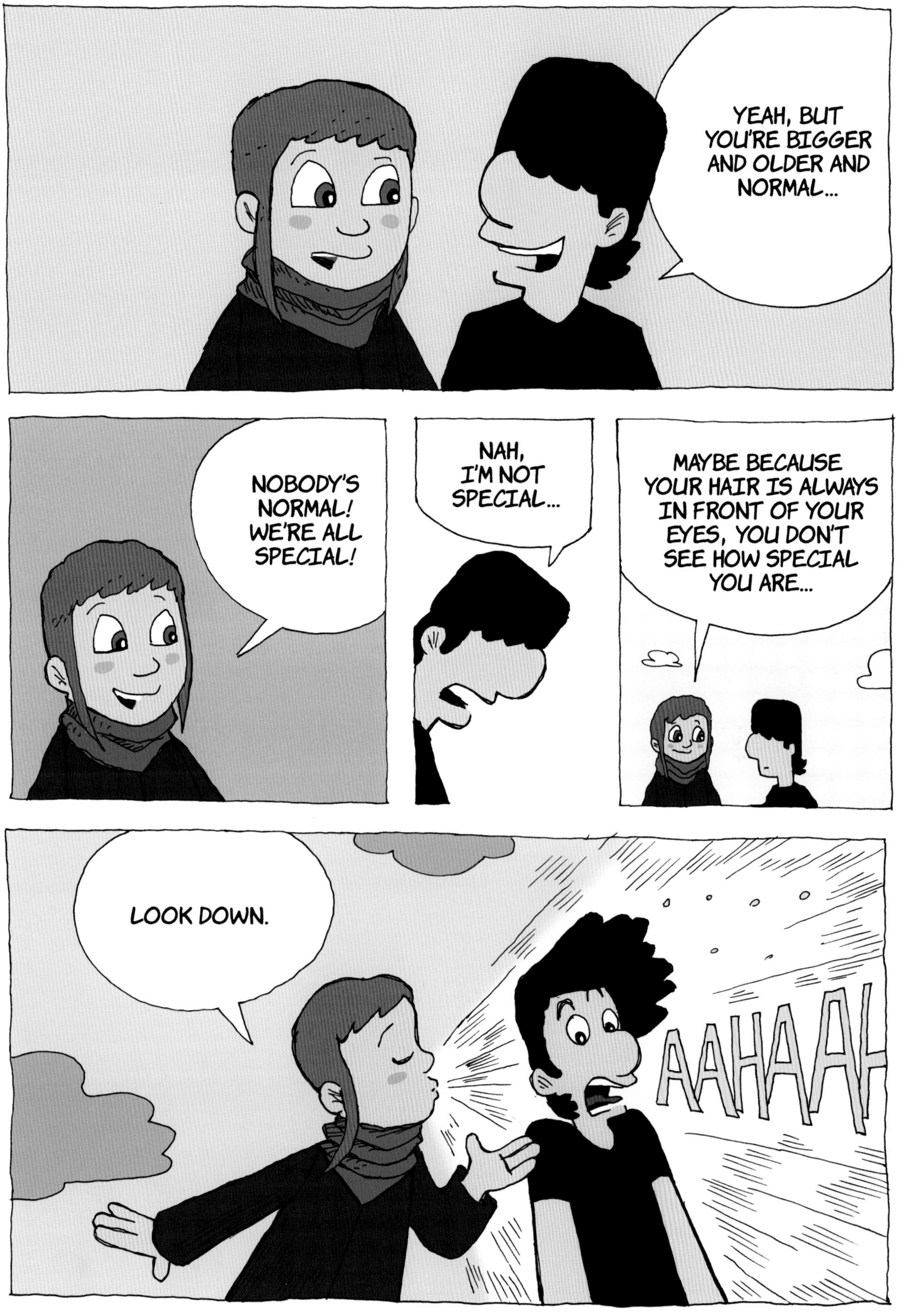
YEAH, BUT YOU'RE BIGGER AND OLDER AND NORMAL...
NOBODY'S NORMAL! WE'RE ALL SPECIAL!
NAH, I'M NOT SPECIAL...
MAYBE BECAUSE YOUR HAIR IS ALWAYS IN FRONT OF YOUR EYES, YOU DON'T SEE HOW SPECIAL YOU ARE...
LOOK DOWN.
AAHAAAH

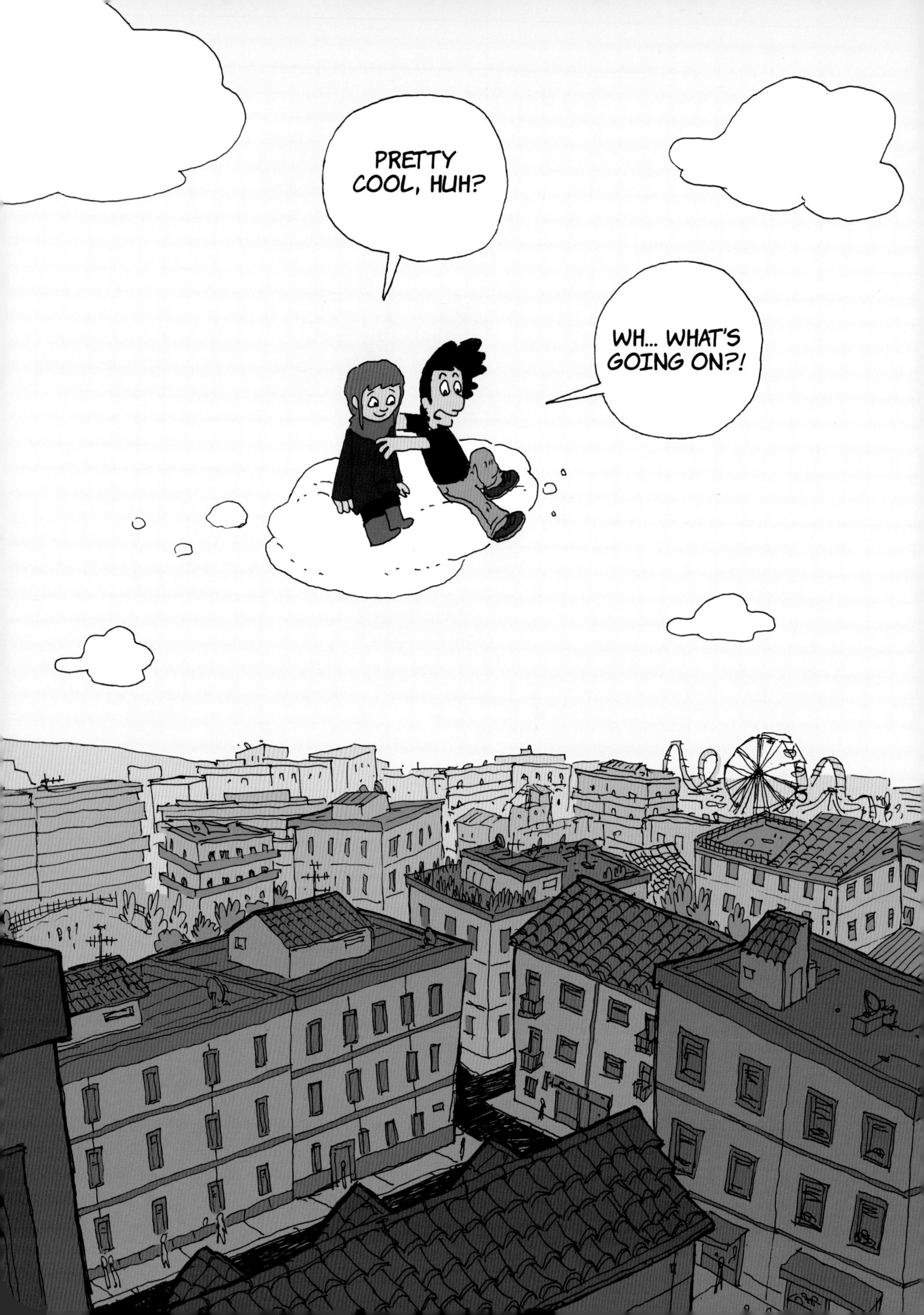
PRETTY COOL, HUH?
WH... WHAT'S GOING ON?!

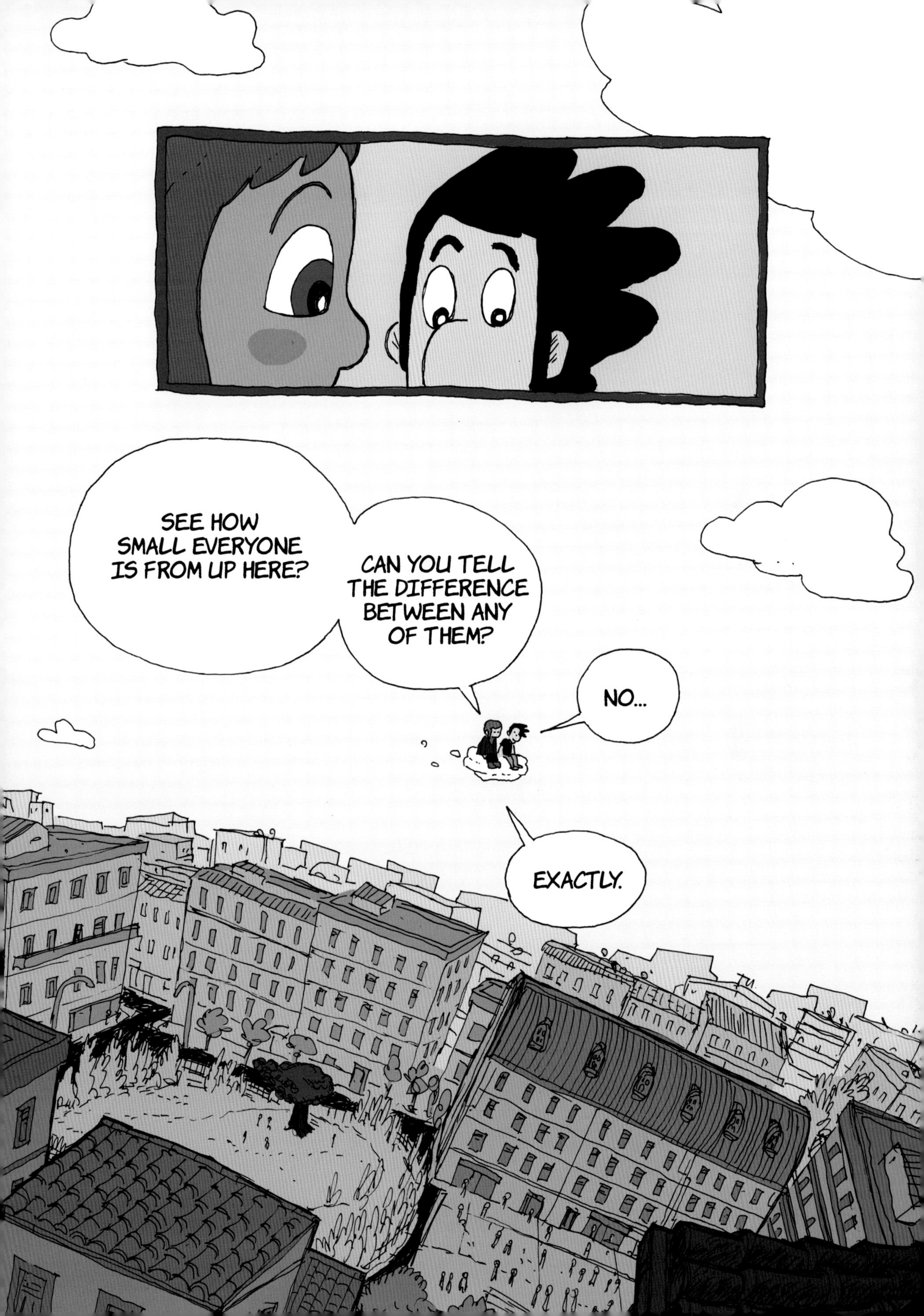
SEE HOW SMALL EVERYONE IS FROM UP HERE?
CAN YOU TELL THE DIFFERENCE BETWEEN ANY OF THEM?
NO...
EXACTLY.

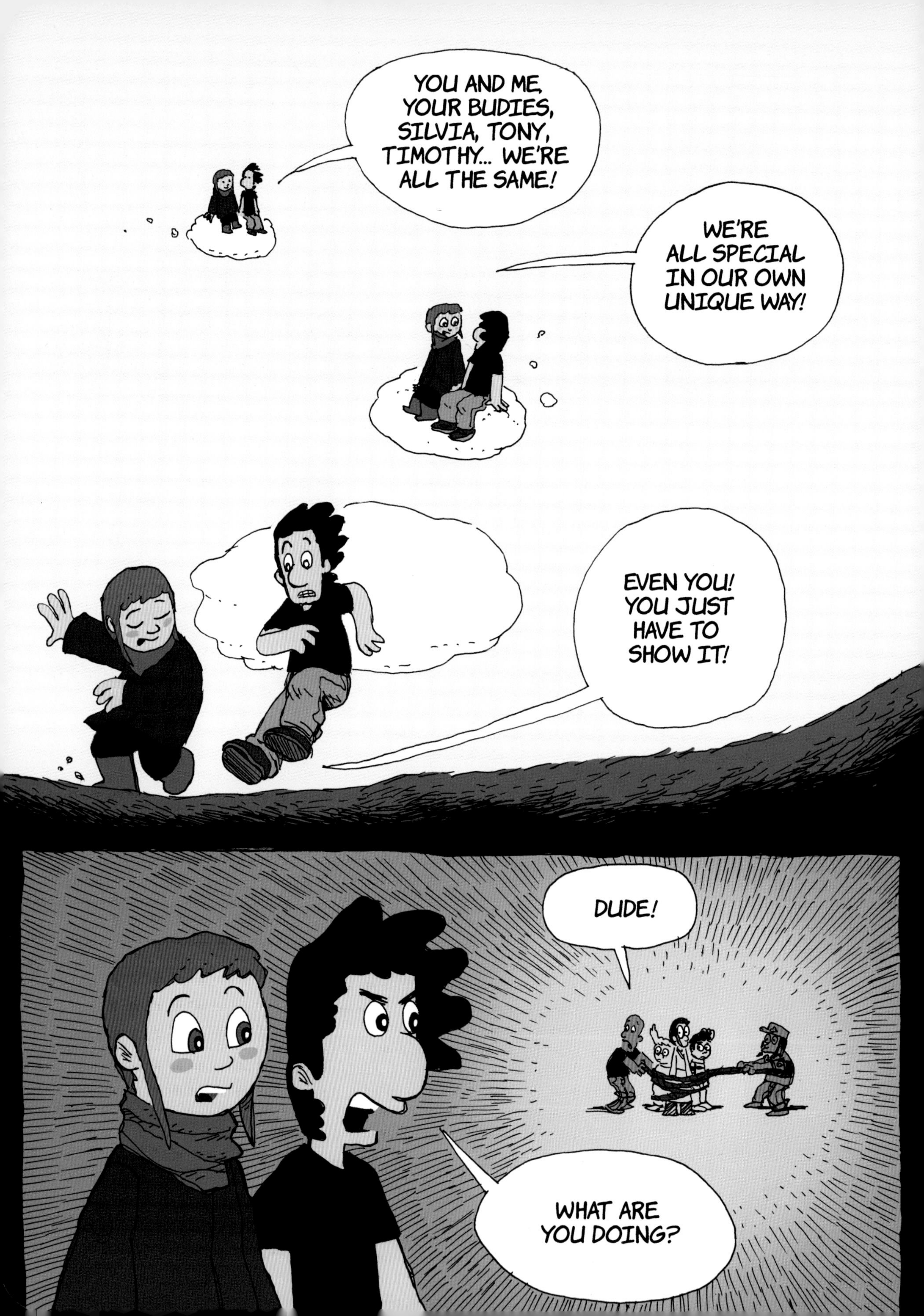
YOU AND ME, YOUR BUDIES, SILVIA, TONY, TIMOTHY... WE'RE ALL THE SAME!
WE'RE ALL SPECIAL IN OUR OWN UNIQUE WAY!
EVEN YOU! YOU JUST HAVE TO SHOW IT!
DUDE!
WHAT ARE YOU DOING?

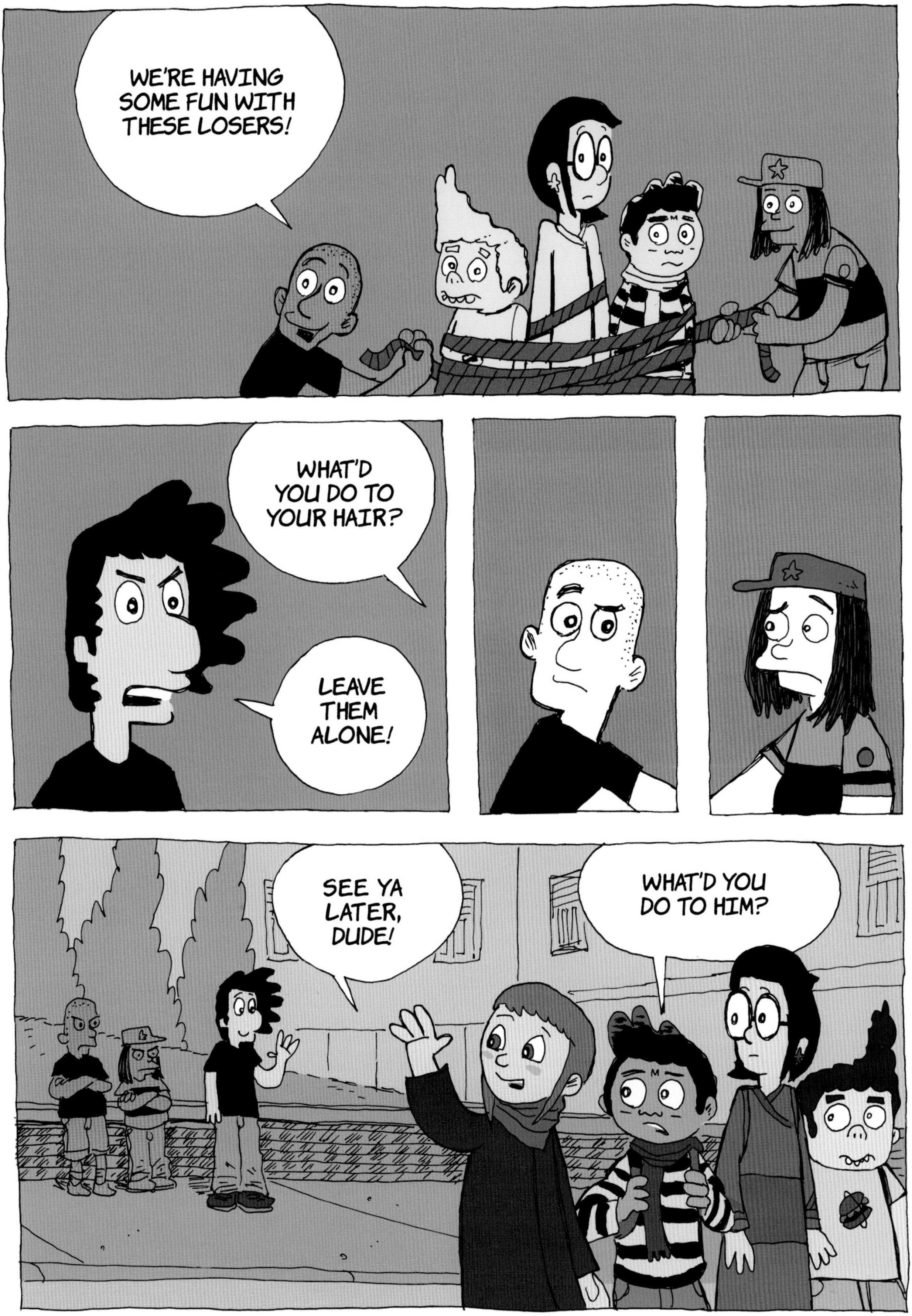
WE'RE HAVING SOME FUN WITH THESE LOSERS!
WHAT'D YOU DO TO YOUR HAIR?
LEAVE THEM ALONE!
SEE YA LATER, DUDE!
WHAT'D YOU DO TO HIM?

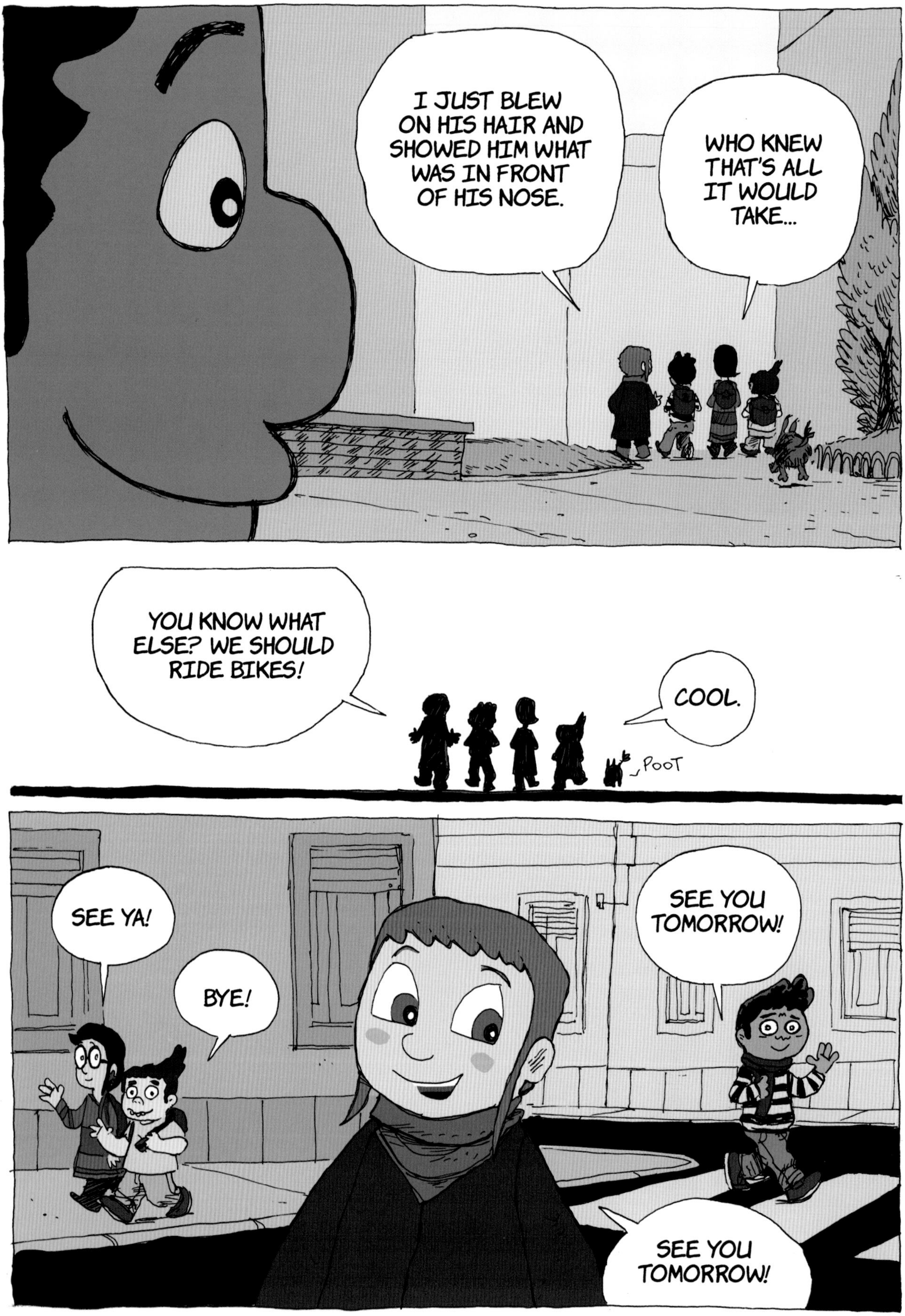
I JUST BLEW ON HIS HAIR AND SHOWED HIM WHAT WAS IN FRONT OF HIS NOSE.
WHO KNEW THAT'S ALL IT WOULD TAKE...
YOU KNOW WHAT ELSE? WE SHOULD RIDE BIKES!
COOL.
POOT
SEE YA!
BYE!
SEE YOU TOMORROW!
SEE YOU TOMORROW!

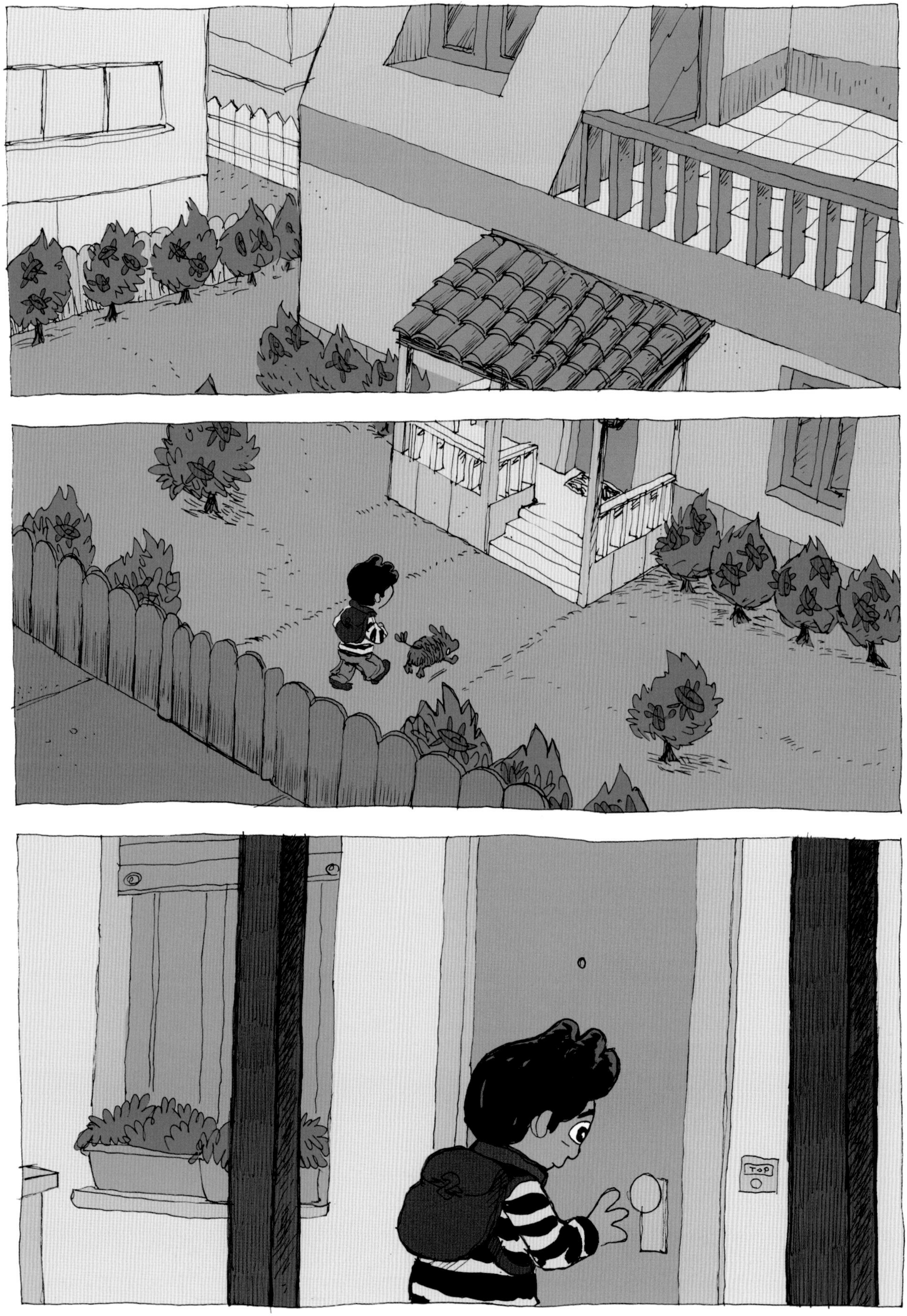
TOP

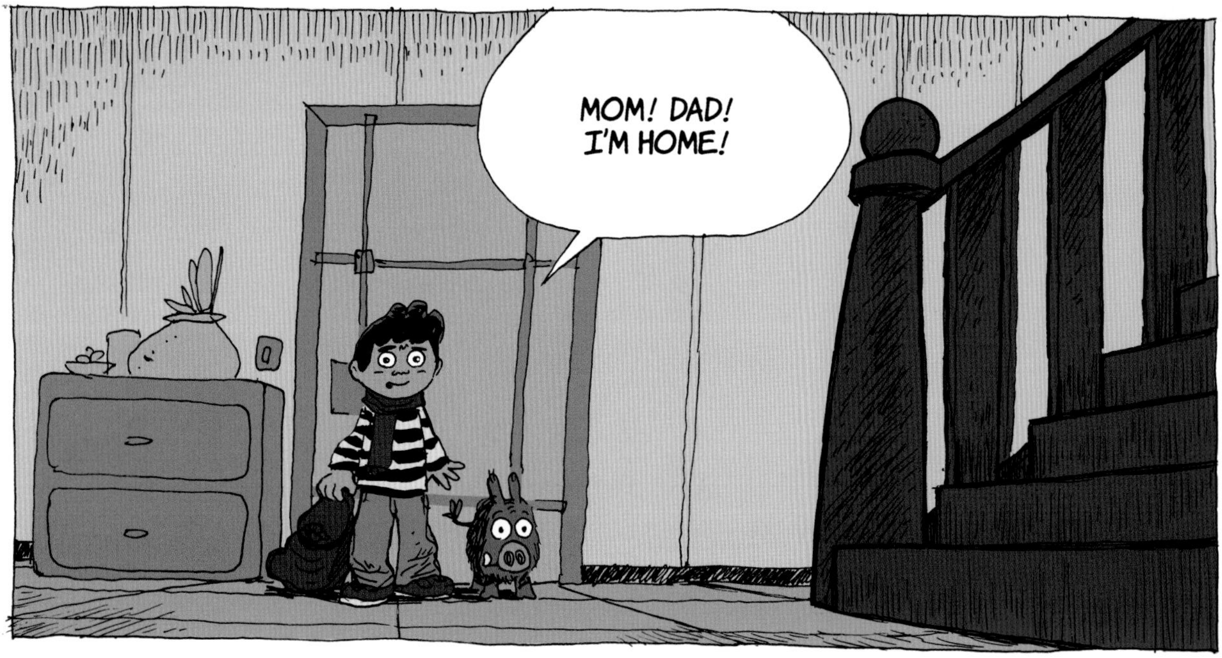
MOM! DAD!
I'M HOME!

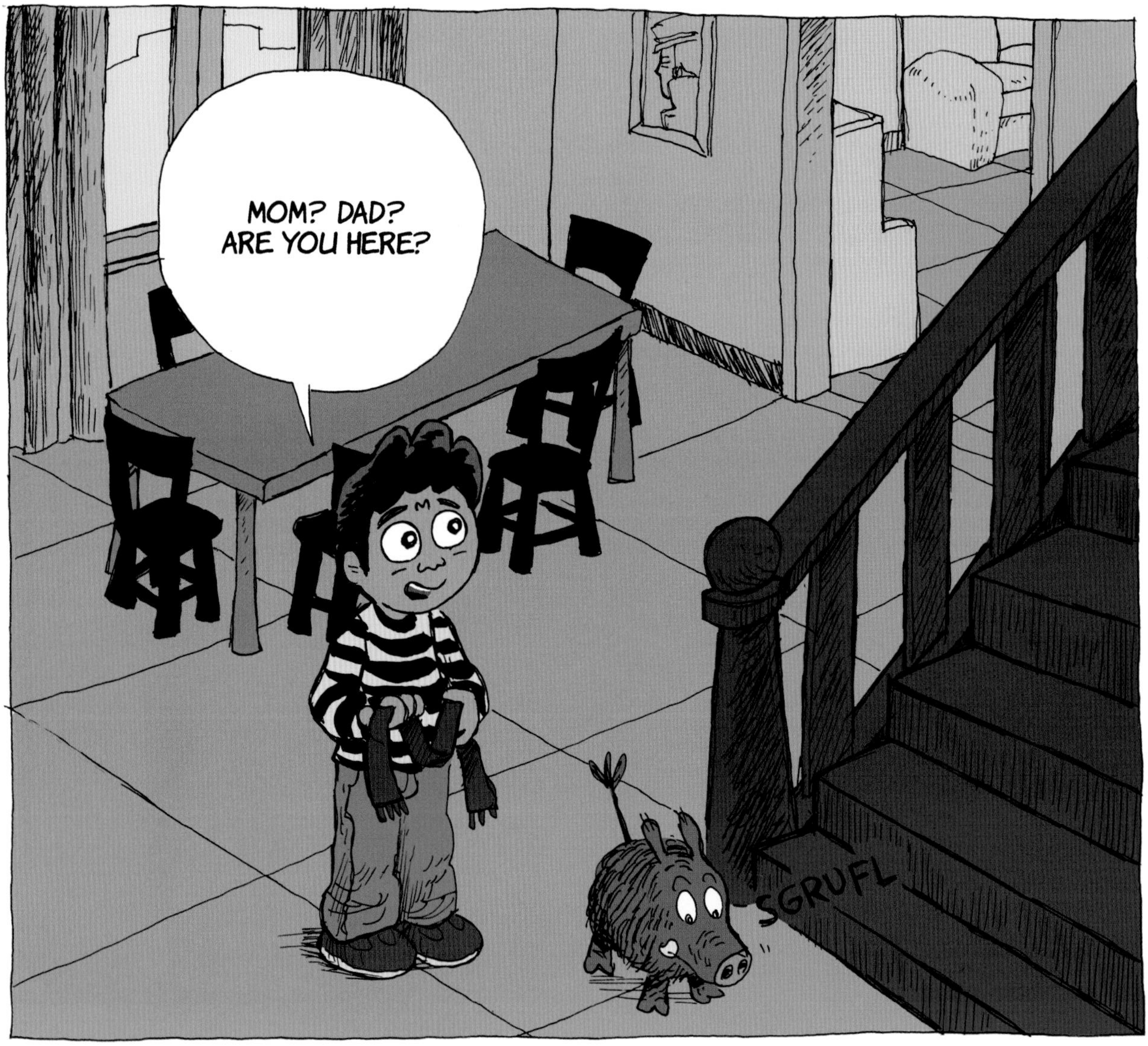
MOM? DAD?
ARE YOU HERE?
SGRUFL

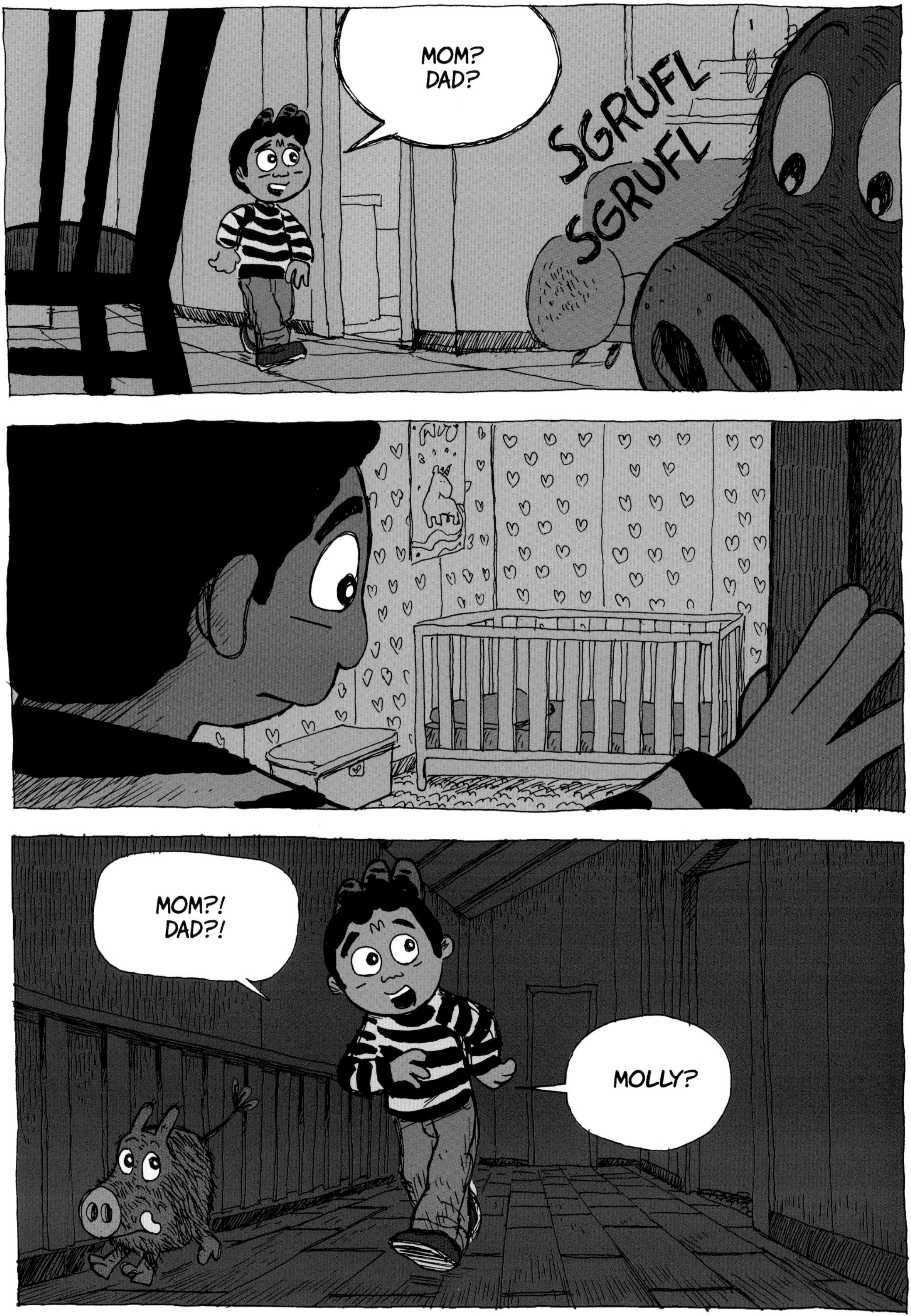
MOM?
DAD?
SGRUFL
SGRUFL
MOM?!
DAD?!
MOLLY?

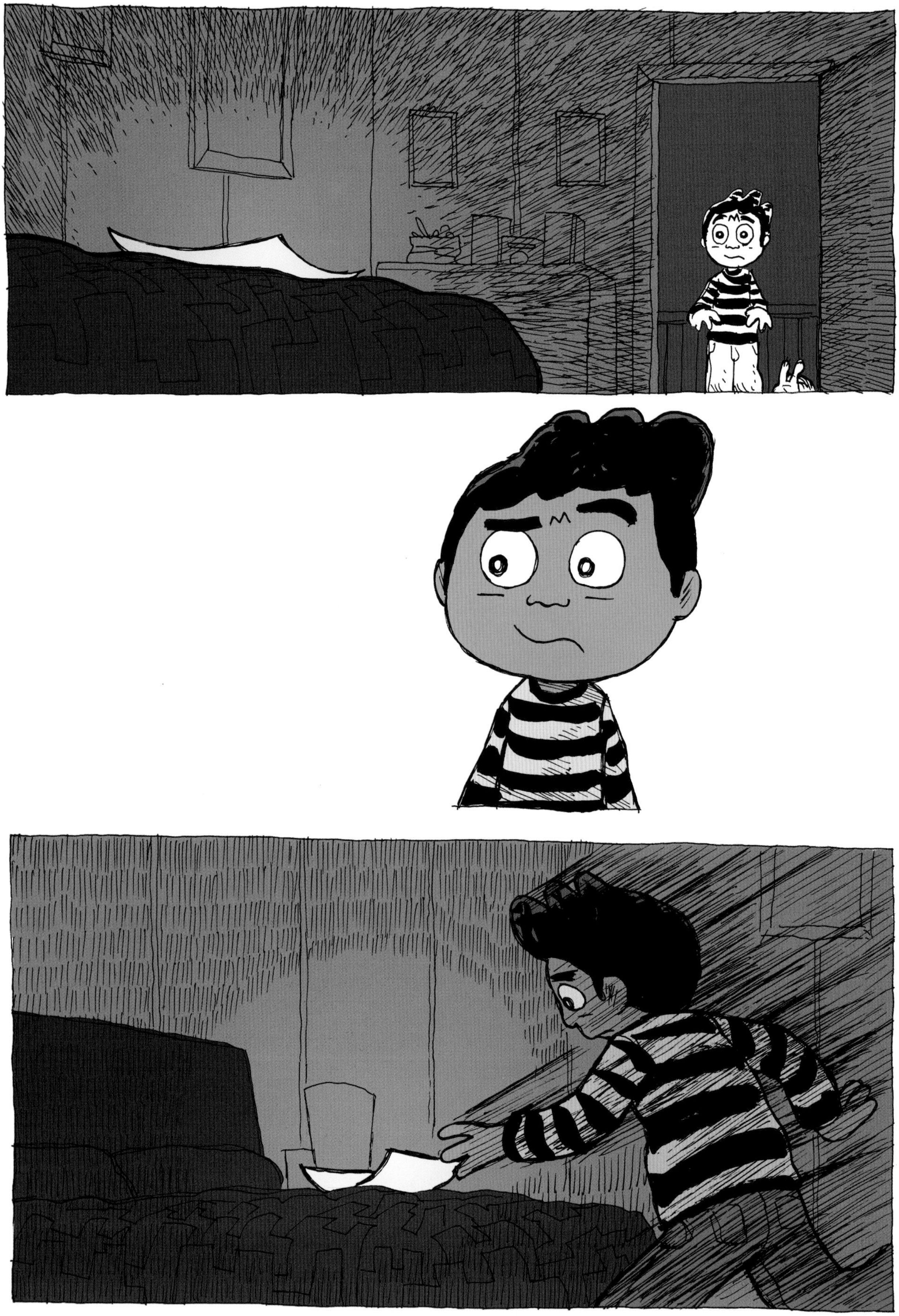

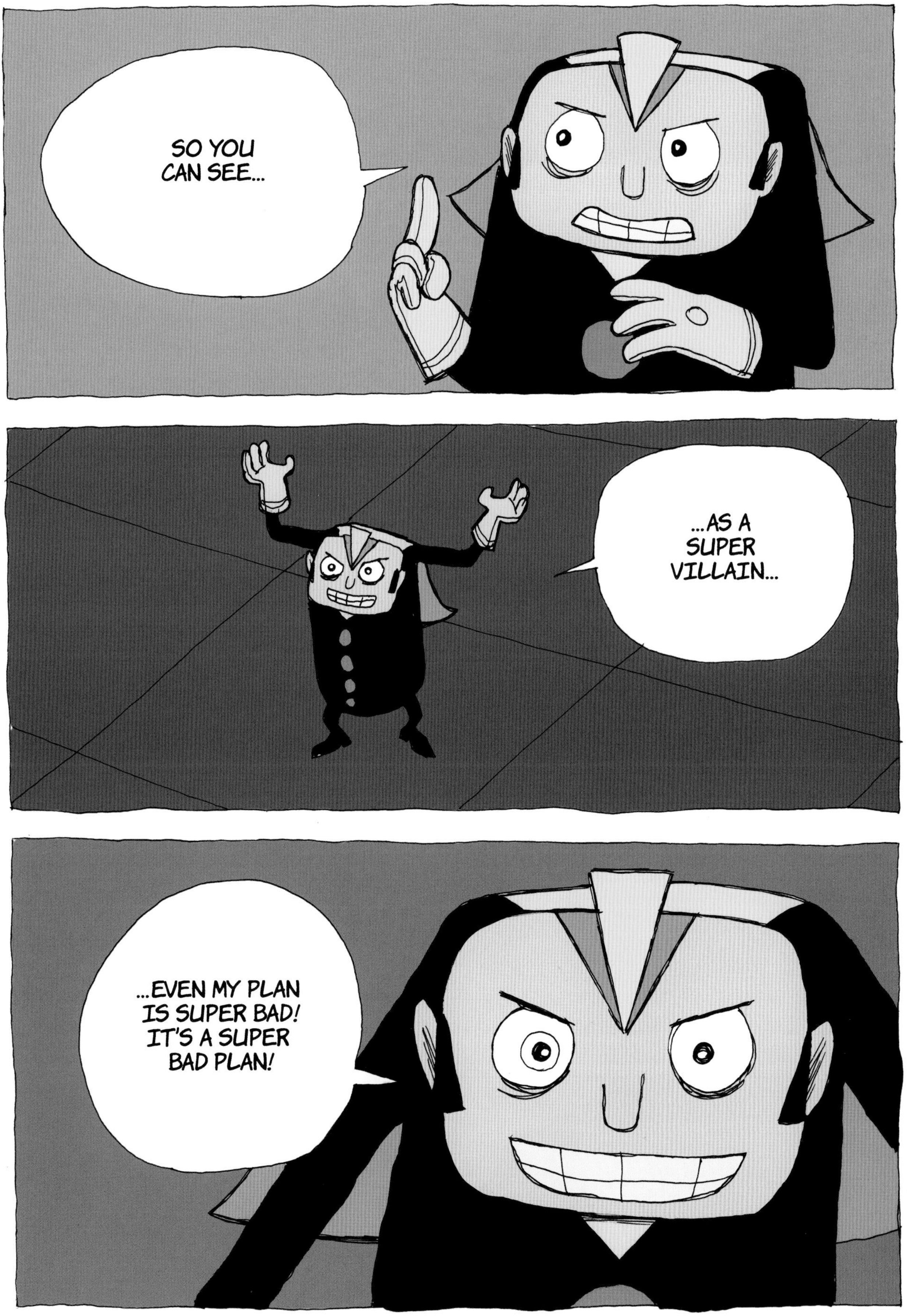
SO YOU CAN SEE...
...AS A SUPER VILLAIN...
...EVEN MY PLAN IS SUPER BAD! IT'S A SUPER BAD PLAN!

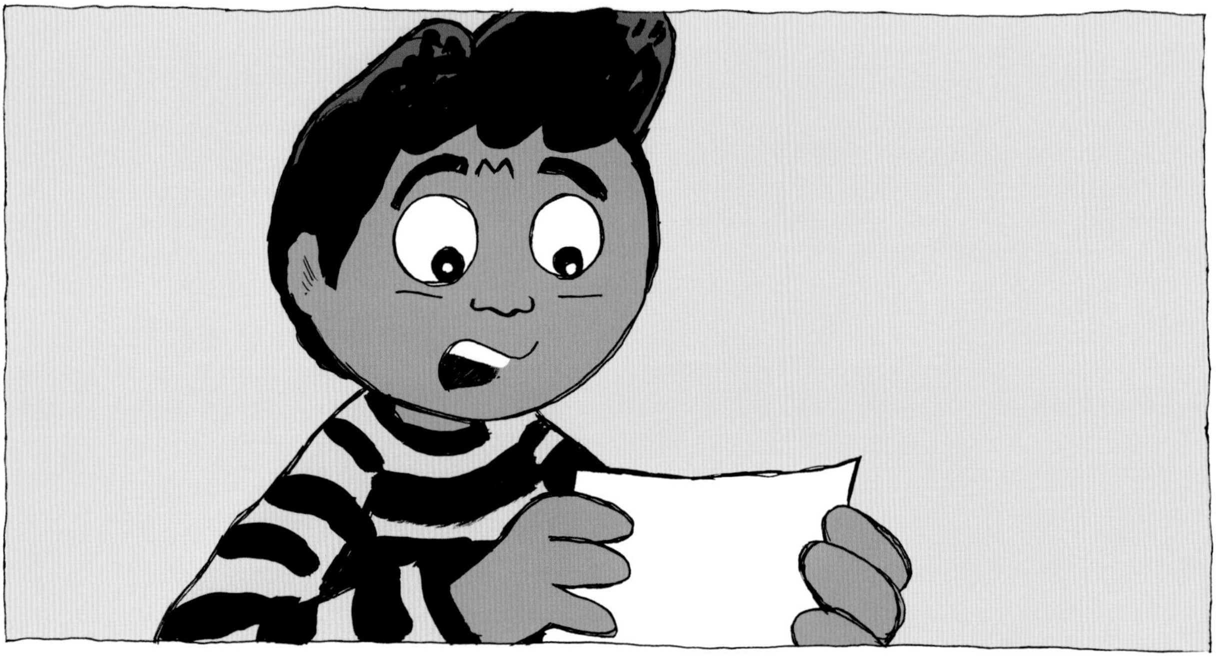

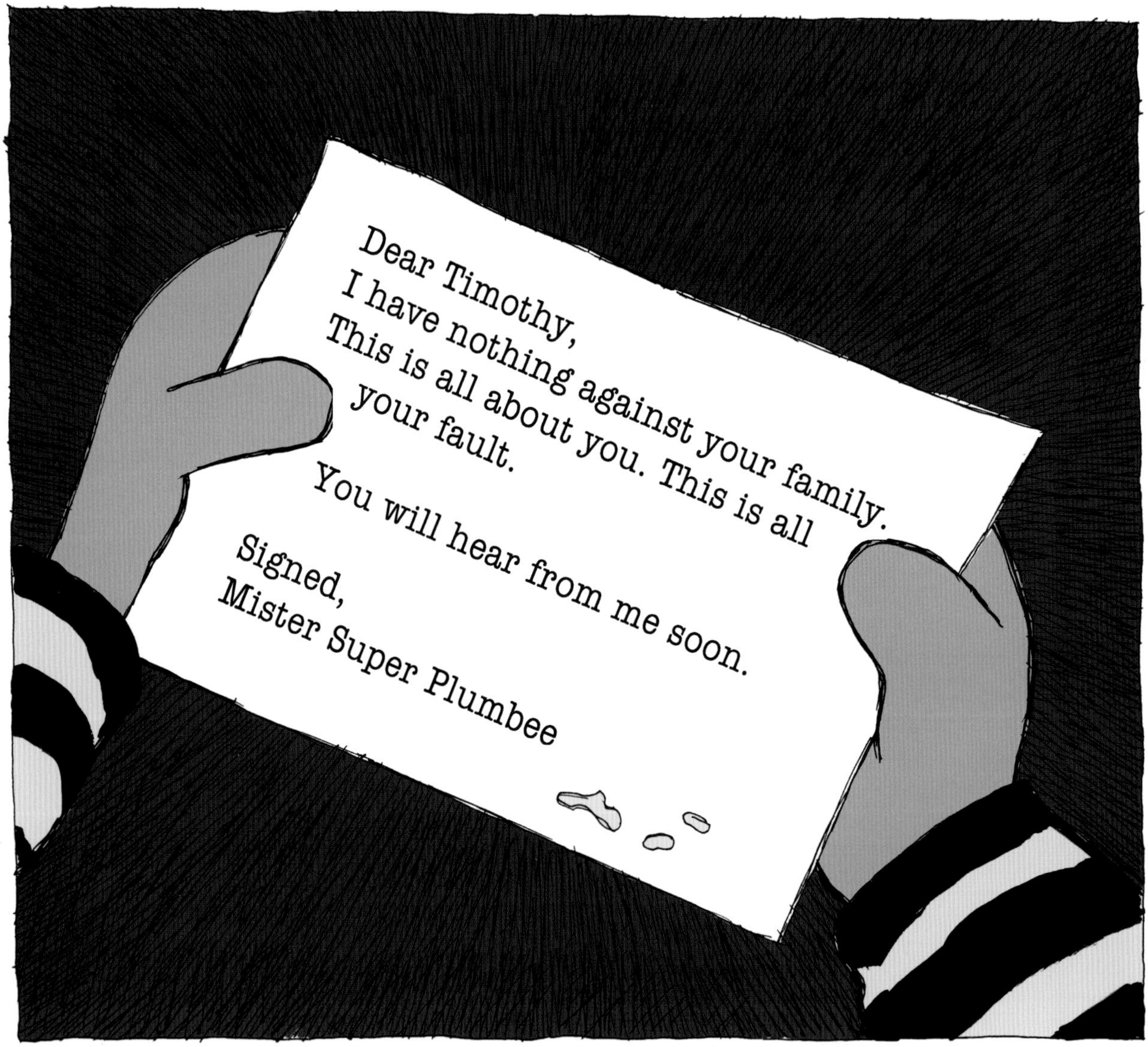
Dear Timothy,
I have nothing against your family.
This is all about you. This is all your fault.
You will hear from me soon.
Signed,
Mister Super Plumbee

CHAPTER EIGHT
BIG MEANY

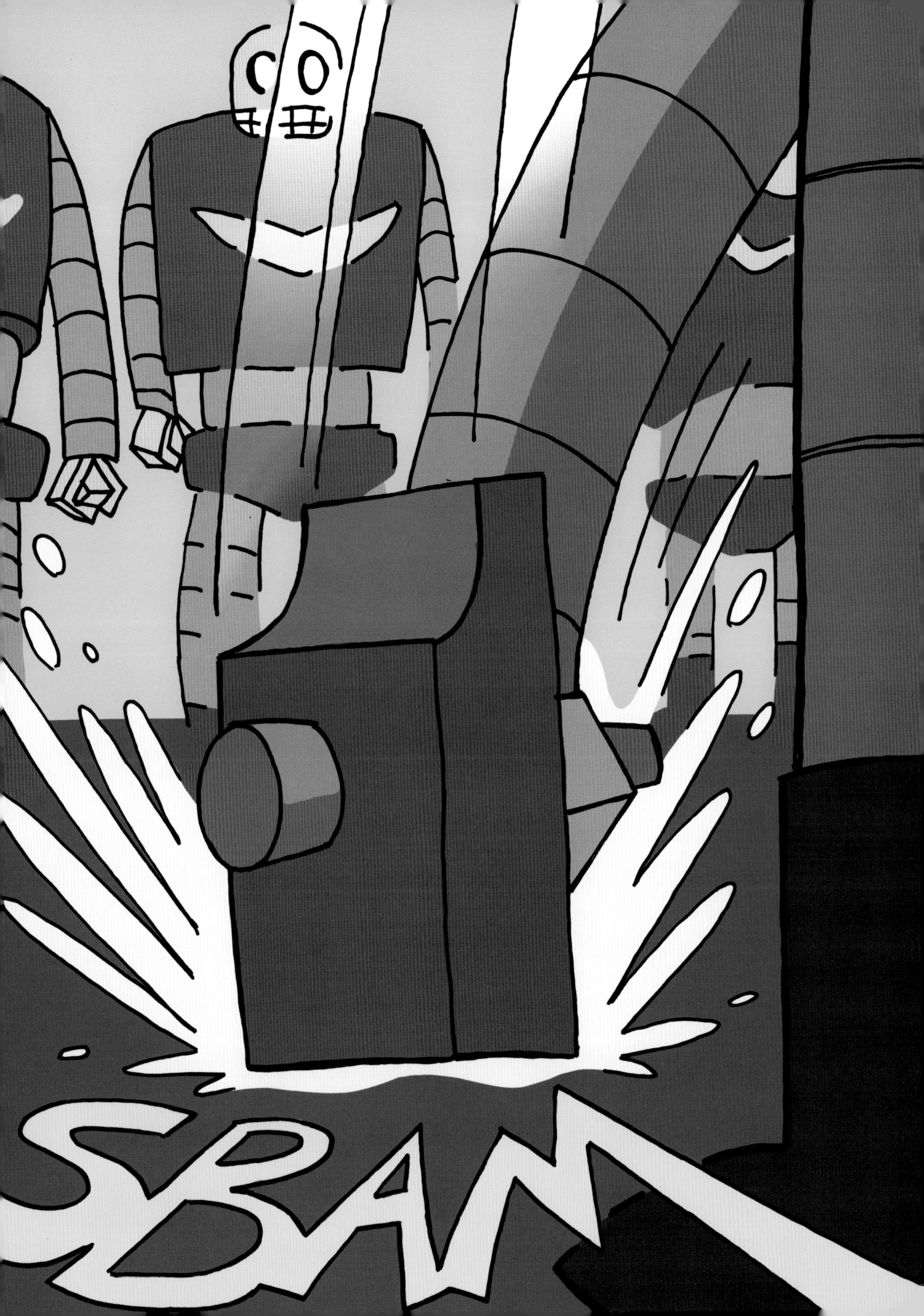
SBAM

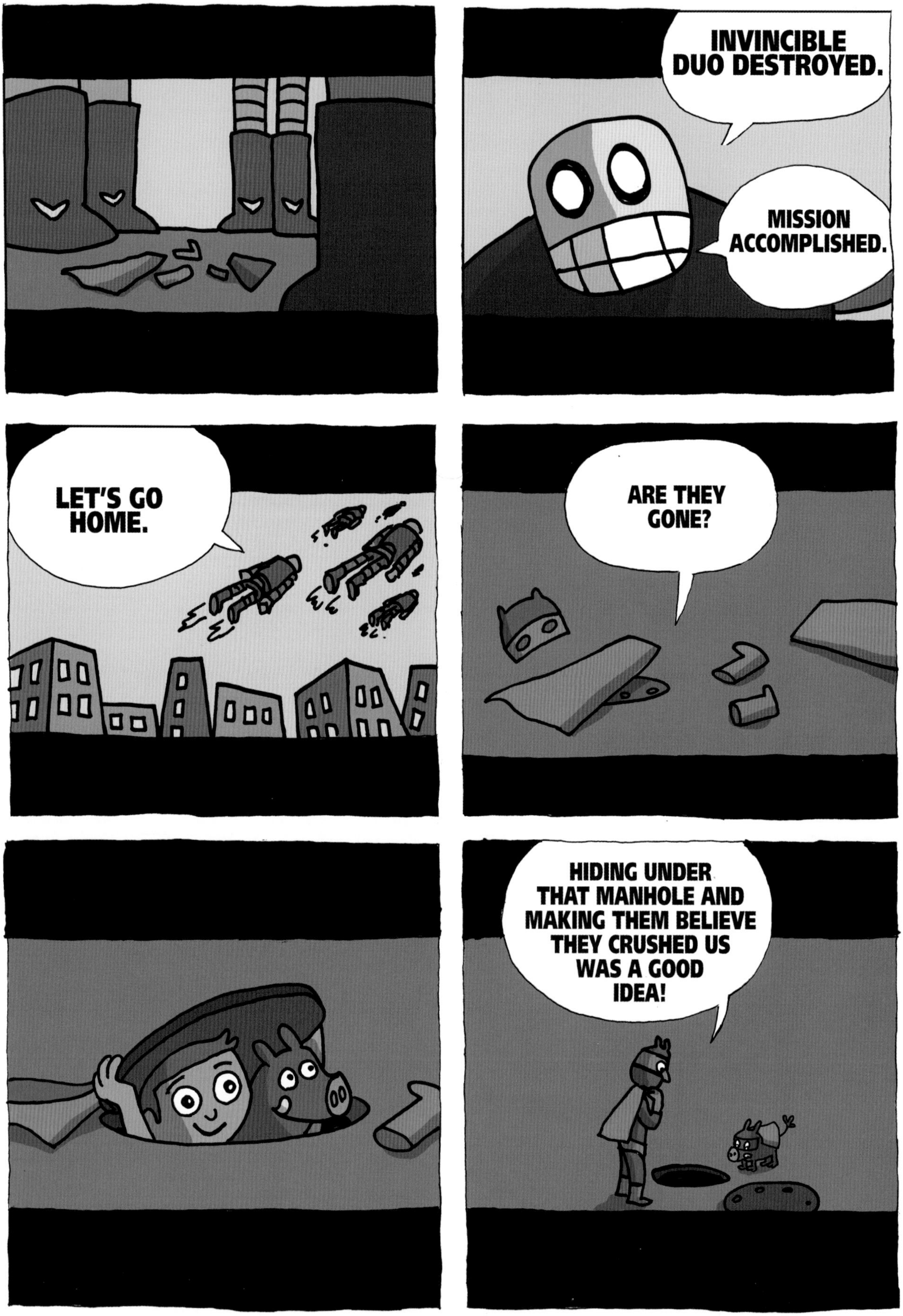
INVINCIBLE DUO DESTROYED.
MISSION ACCOMPLISHED.
LET'S GO HOME.
ARE THEY GONE?
HIDING UNDER THAT MANHOLE AND MAKING THEM BELIEVE THEY CRUSHED US WAS A GOOD IDEA!

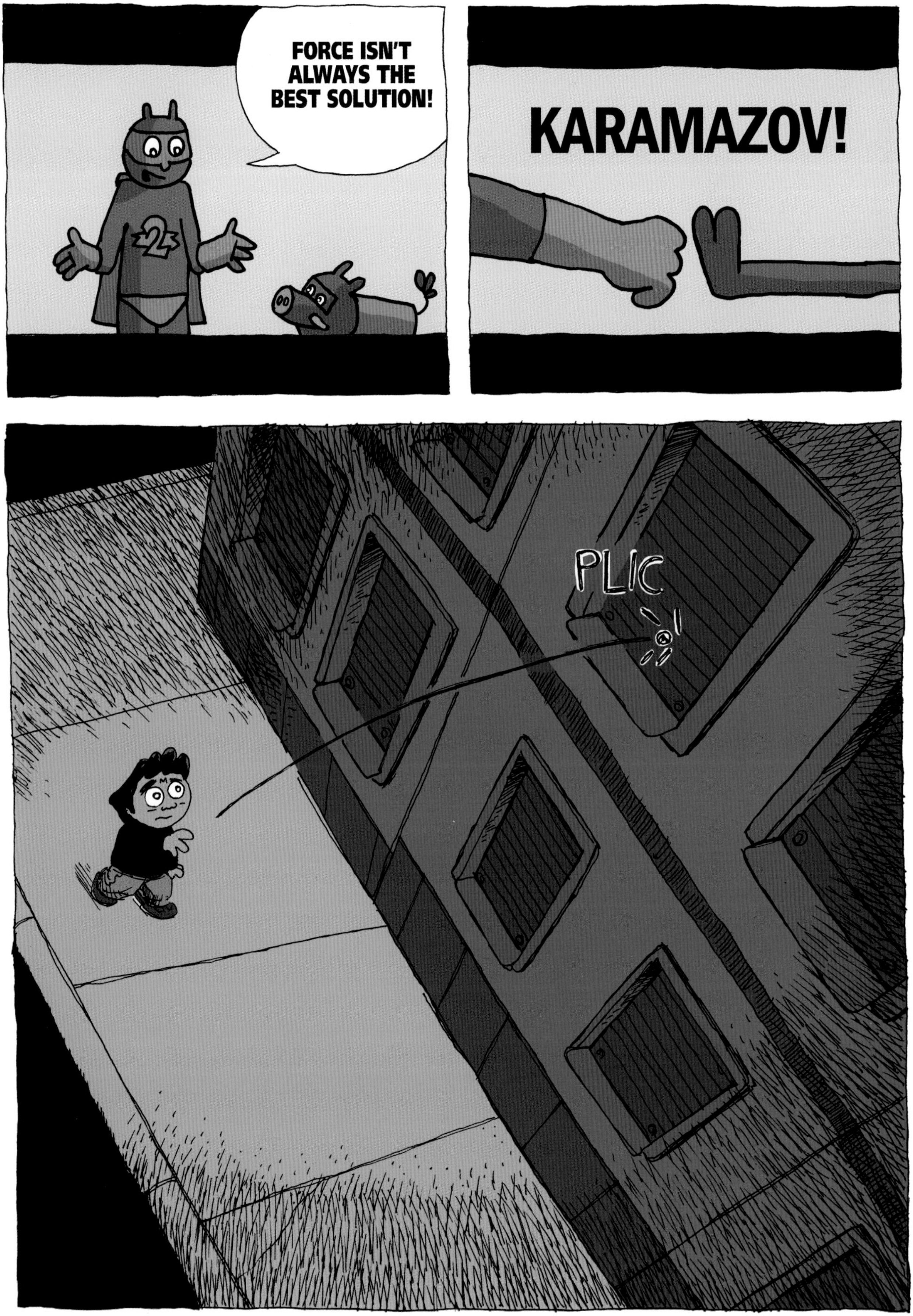
FORCE ISN'T ALWAYS THE BEST SOLUTION!
KARAMAZOV!
PLIC

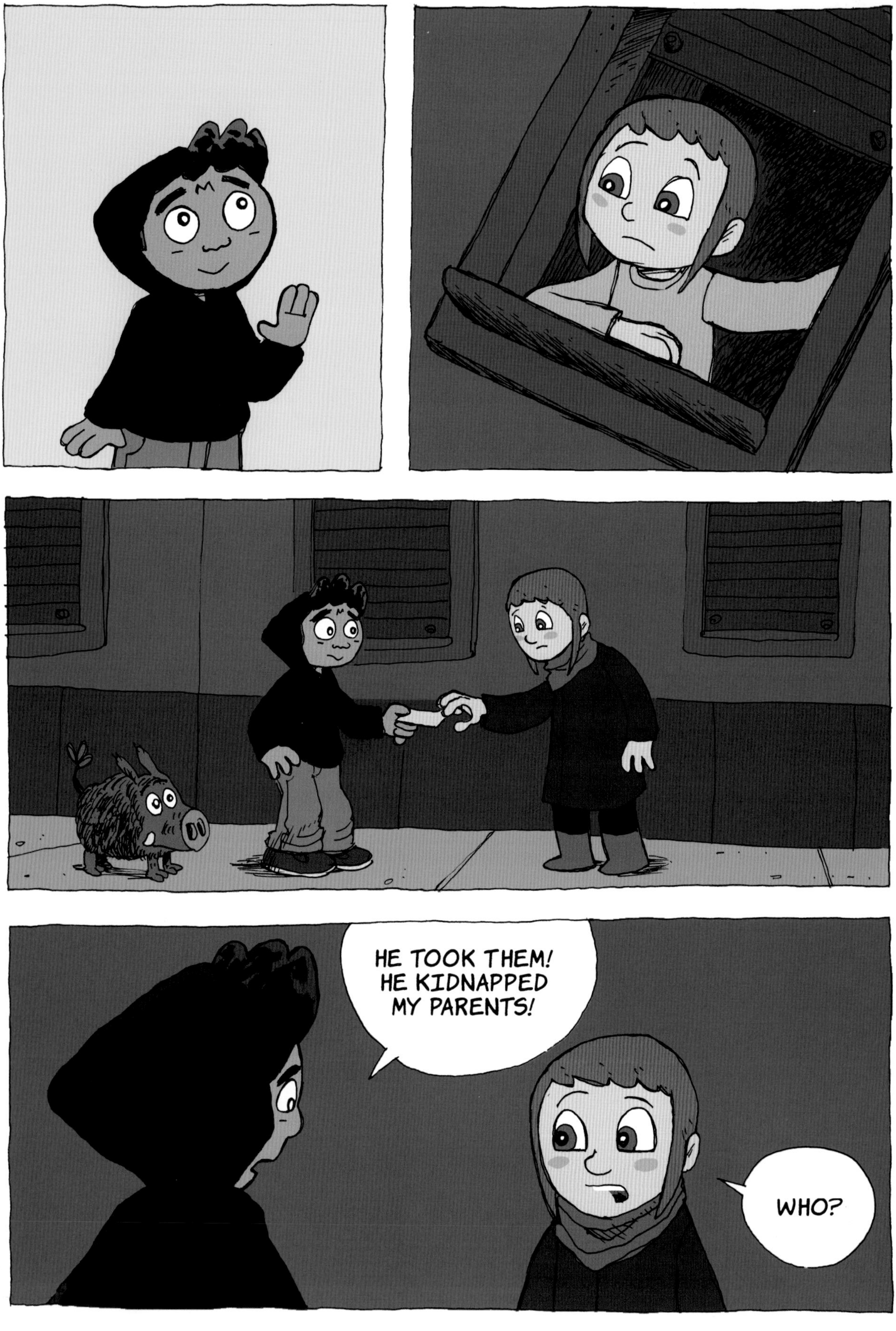
HE TOOK THEM! HE KIDNAPPED MY PARENTS!
WHO?

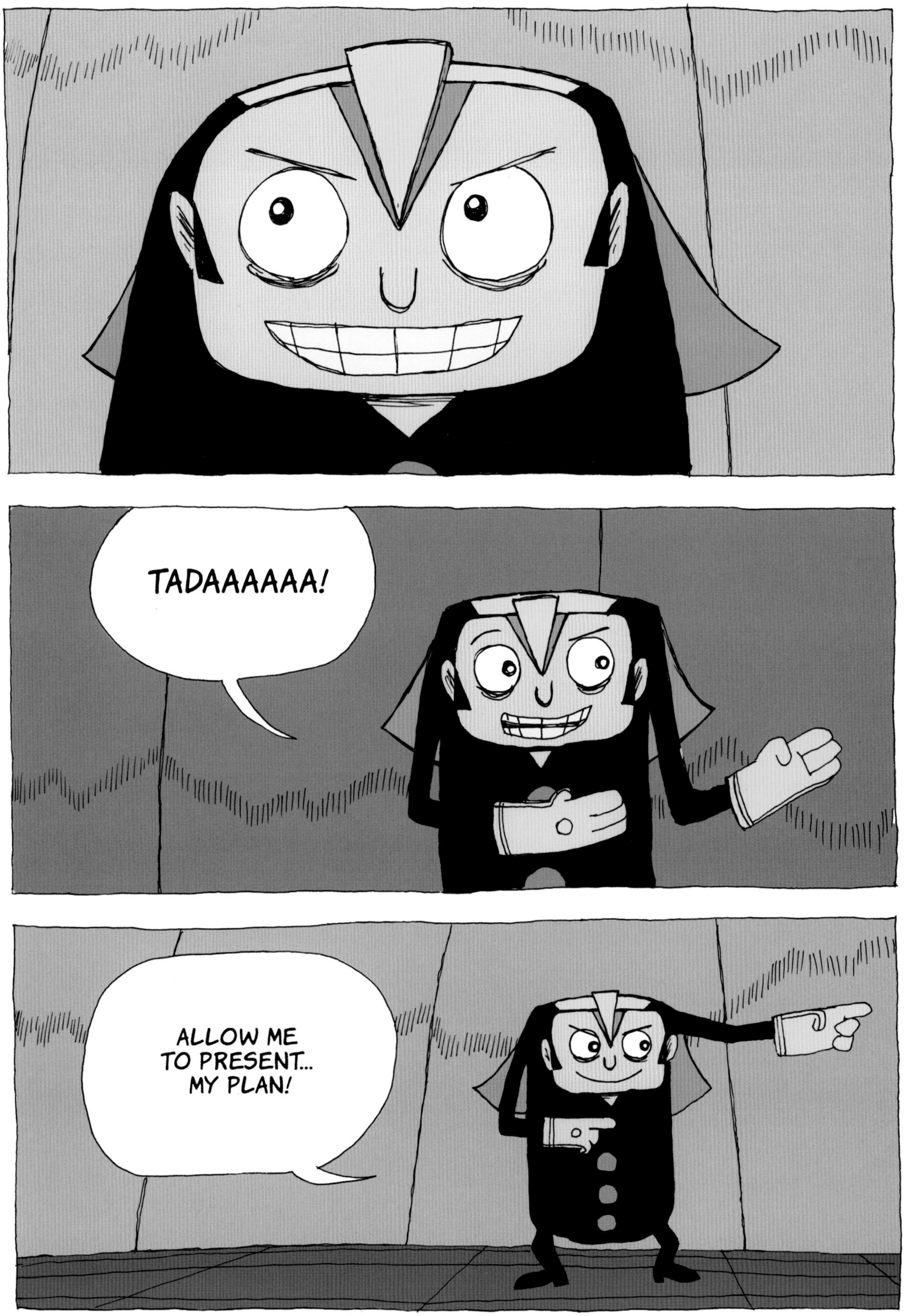
TADAAAAAA!
ALLOW ME TO PRESENT... MY PLAN!

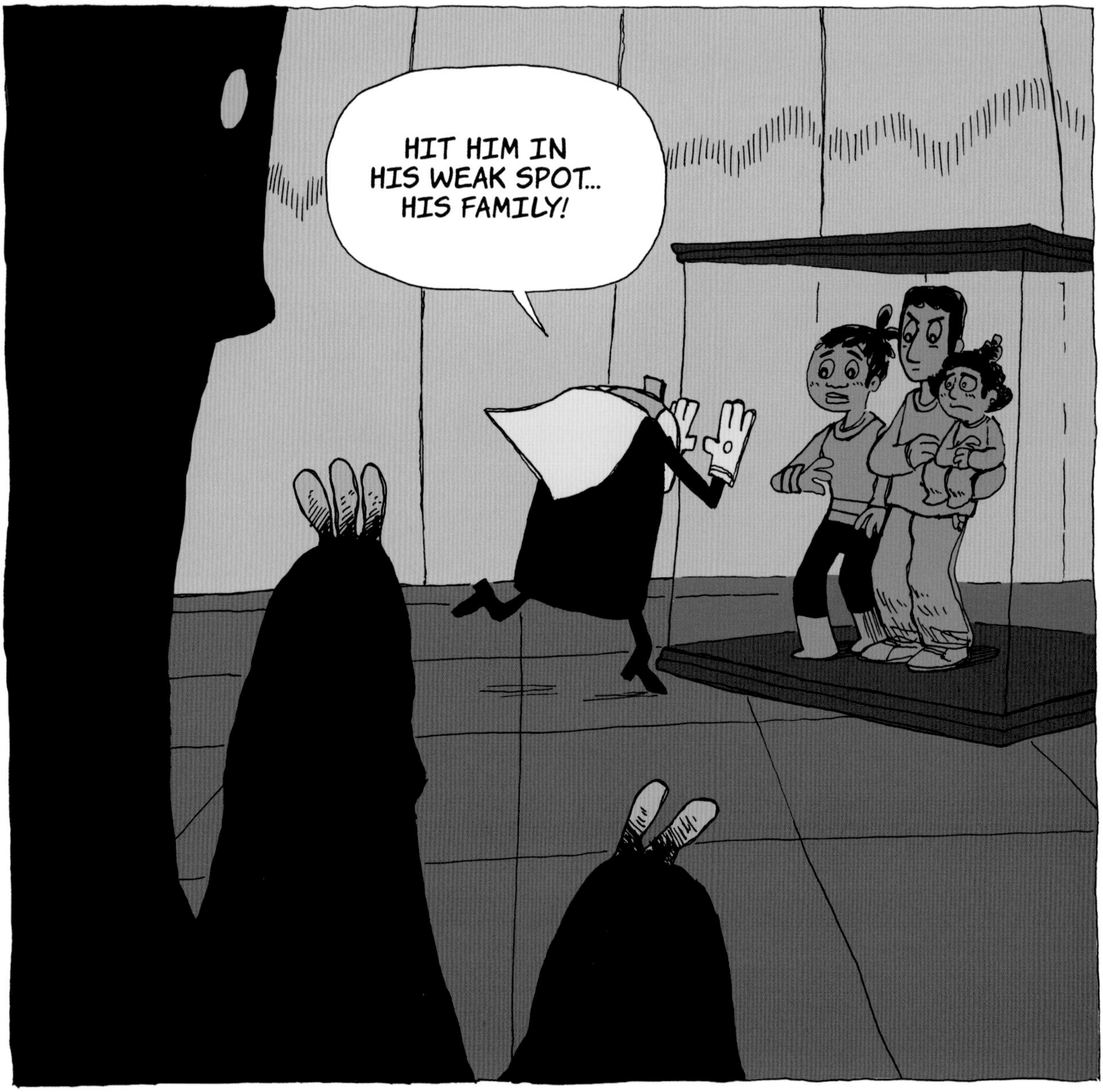
HIT HIM IN HIS WEAK SPOT... HIS FAMILY!

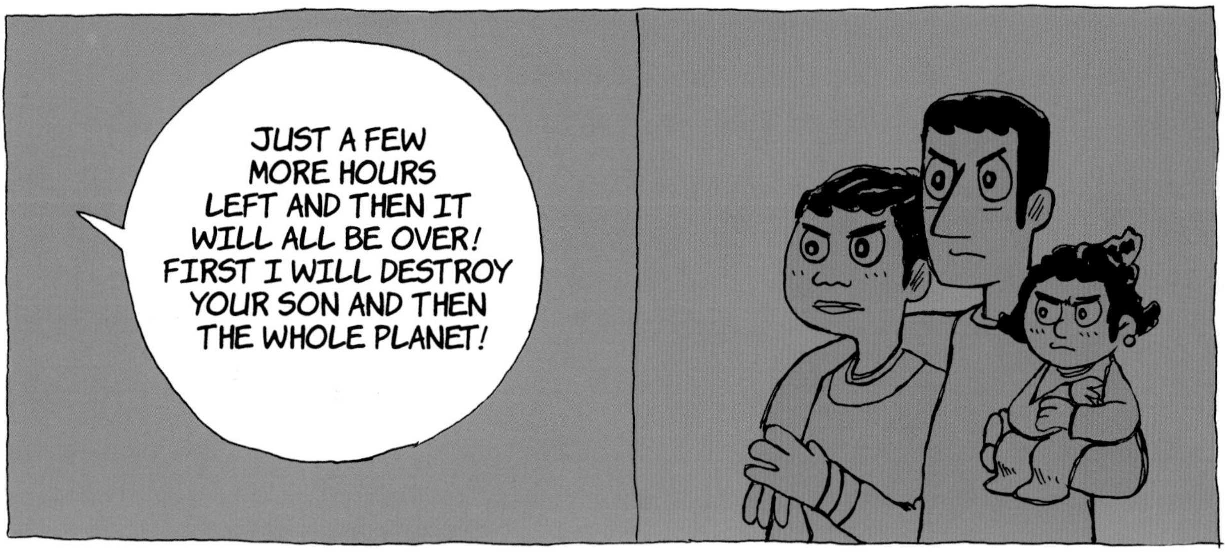
JUST A FEW MORE HOURS LEFT AND THEN IT WILL ALL BE OVER! FIRST I WILL DESTROY YOUR SON AND THEN THE WHOLE PLANET!

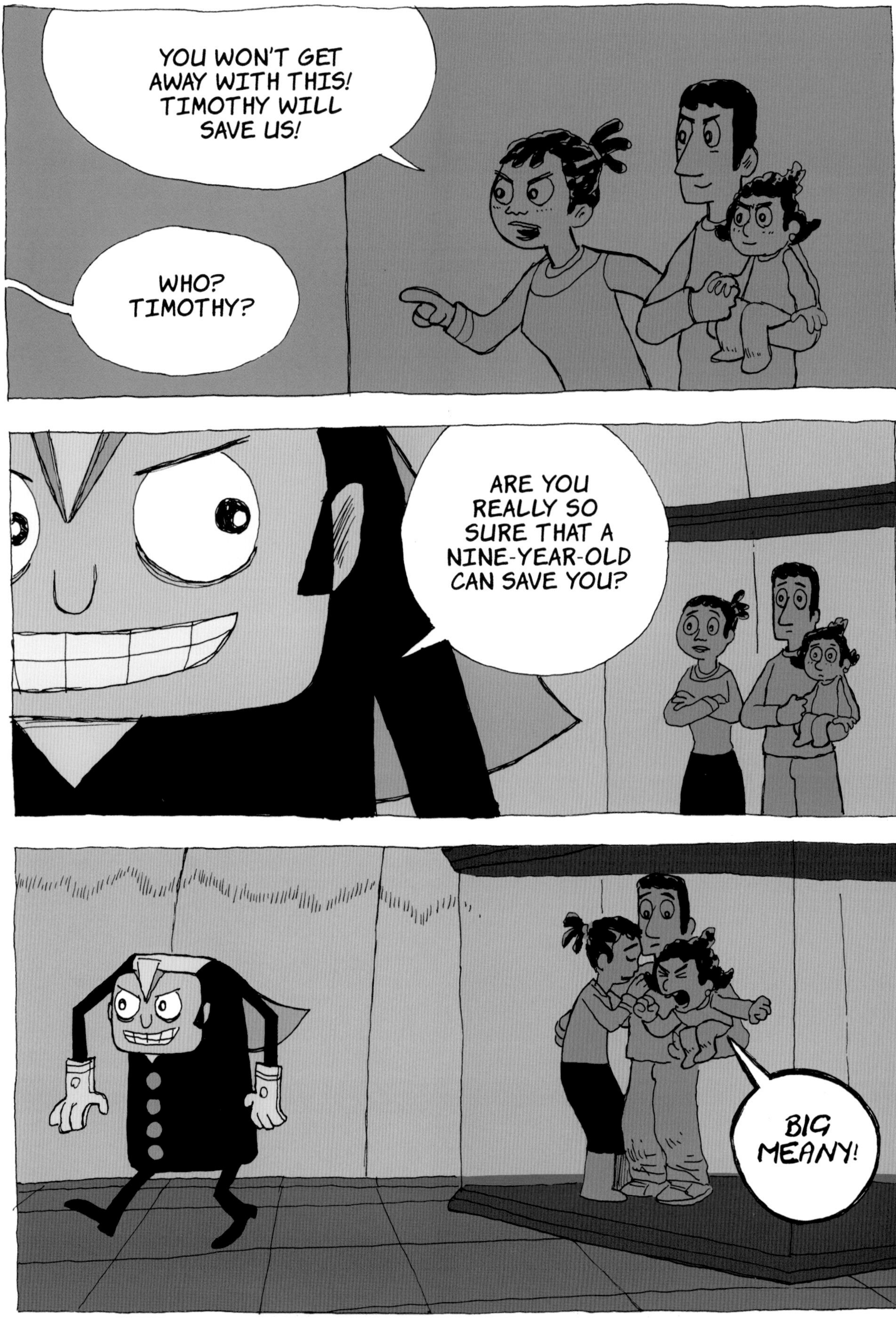
YOU WON'T GET AWAY WITH THIS! TIMOTHY WILL SAVE US!
WHO? TIMOTHY?
ARE YOU REALLY SO SURE THAT A NINE-YEAR-OLD CAN SAVE YOU?
BIG MEANY!

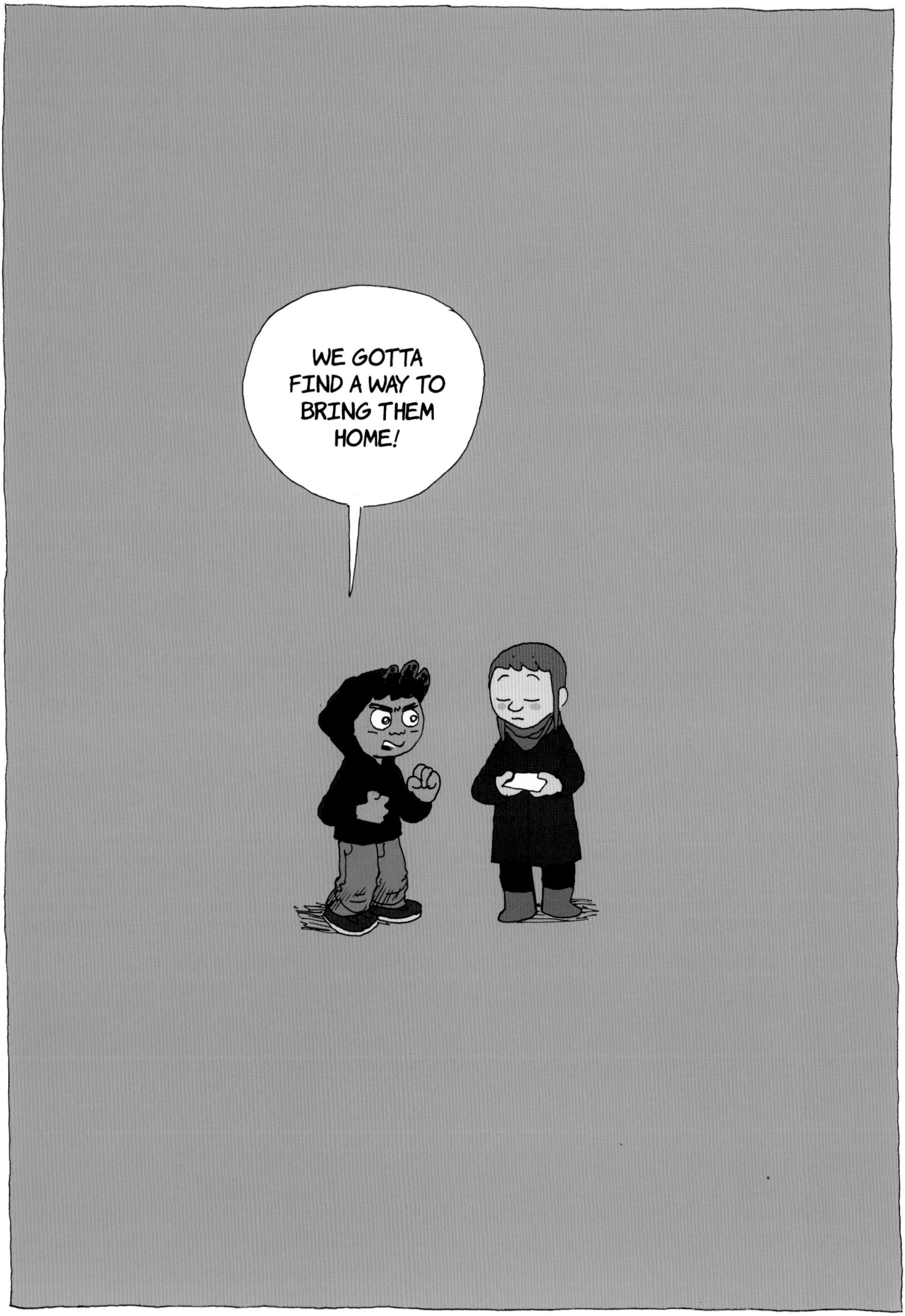
WE GOTTA FIND A WAY TO BRING THEM HOME!

CHAPTER NINE

THE YELLOW WHALE

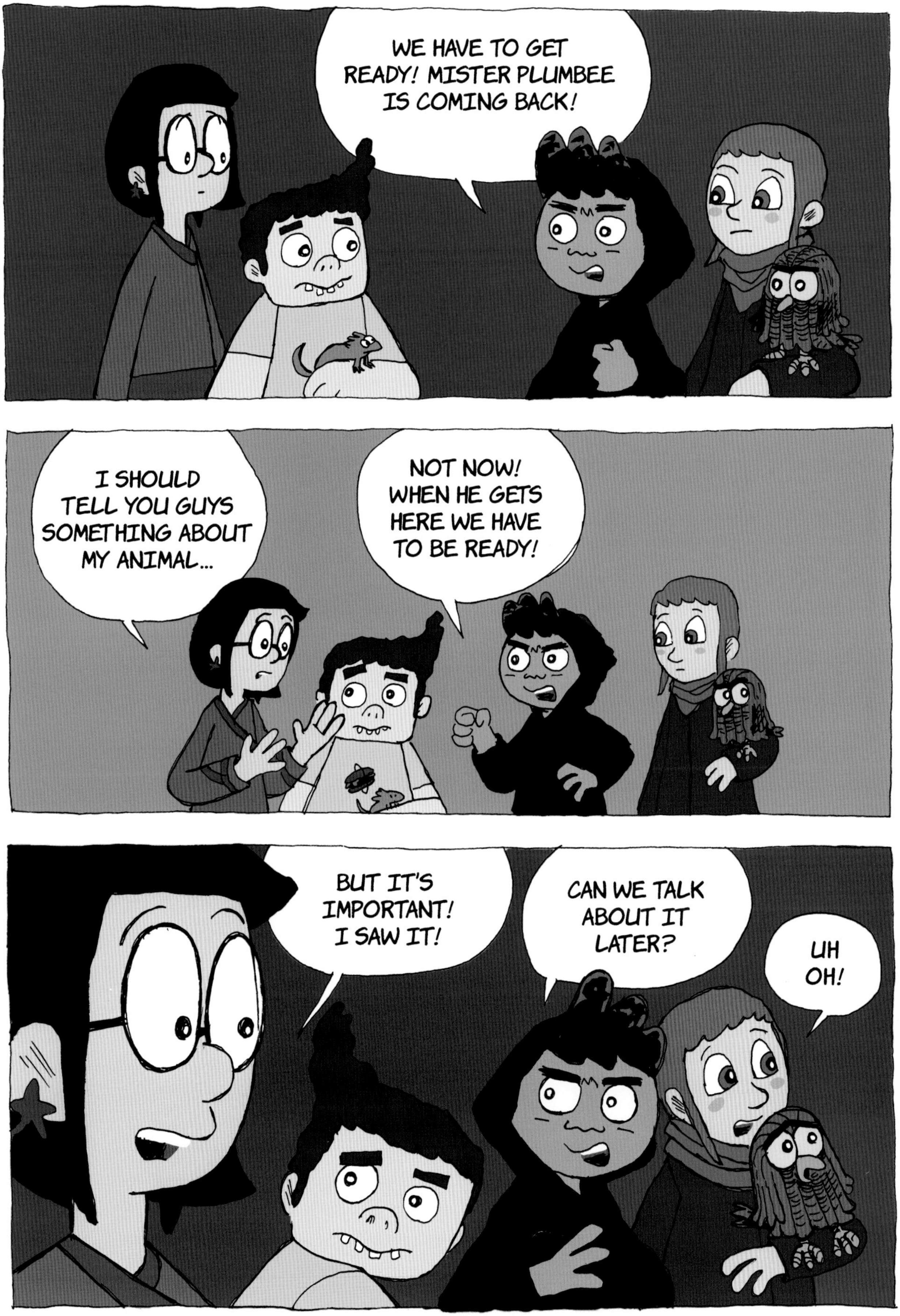
WE HAVE TO GET READY! MISTER PLUMBEE IS COMING BACK!
I SHOULD TELL YOU GUYS SOMETHING ABOUT MY ANIMAL...
NOT NOW! WHEN HE GETS HERE WE HAVE TO BE READY!
BUT IT'S IMPORTANT! I SAW IT!
CAN WE TALK ABOUT IT LATER?
UH OH!

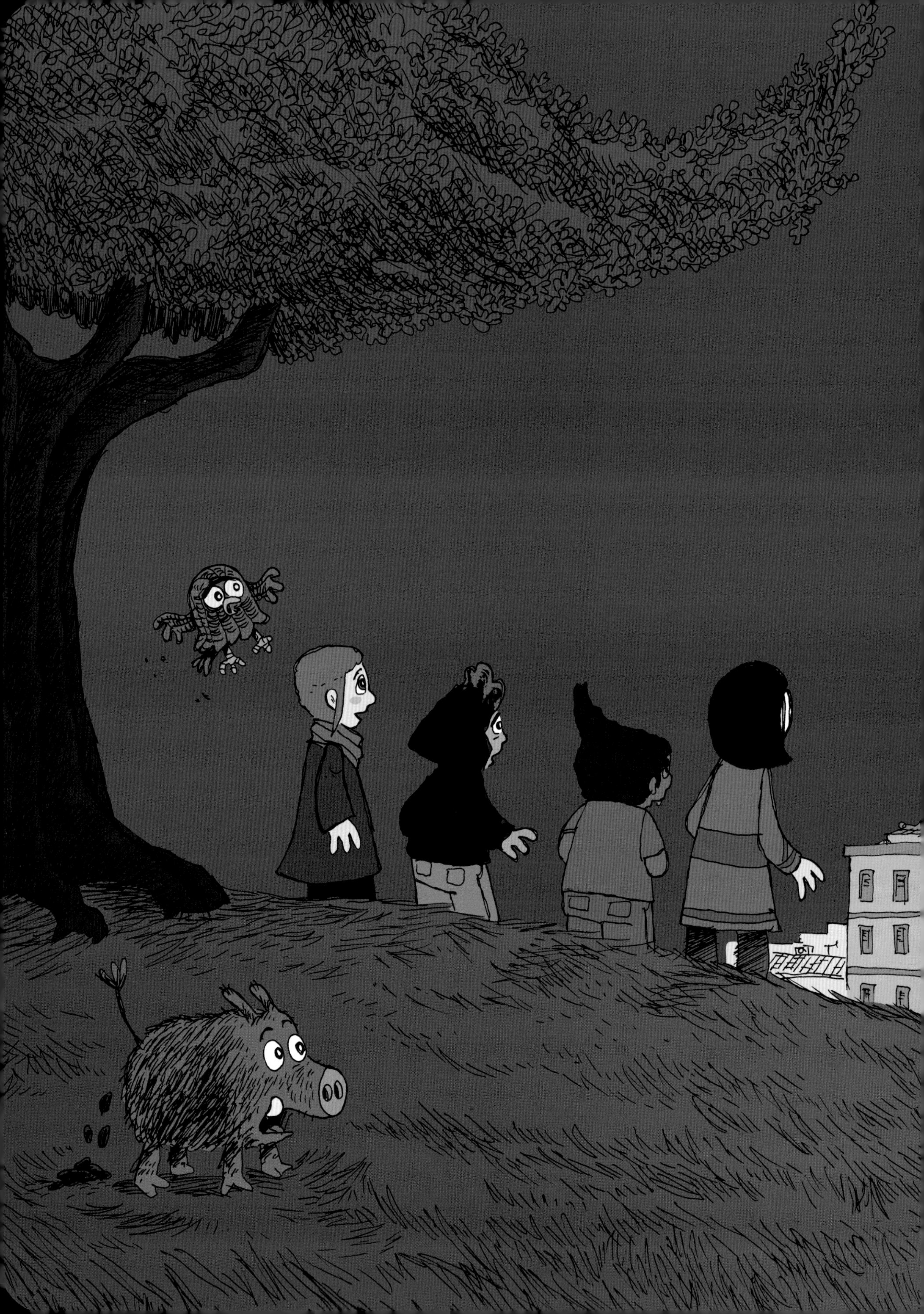

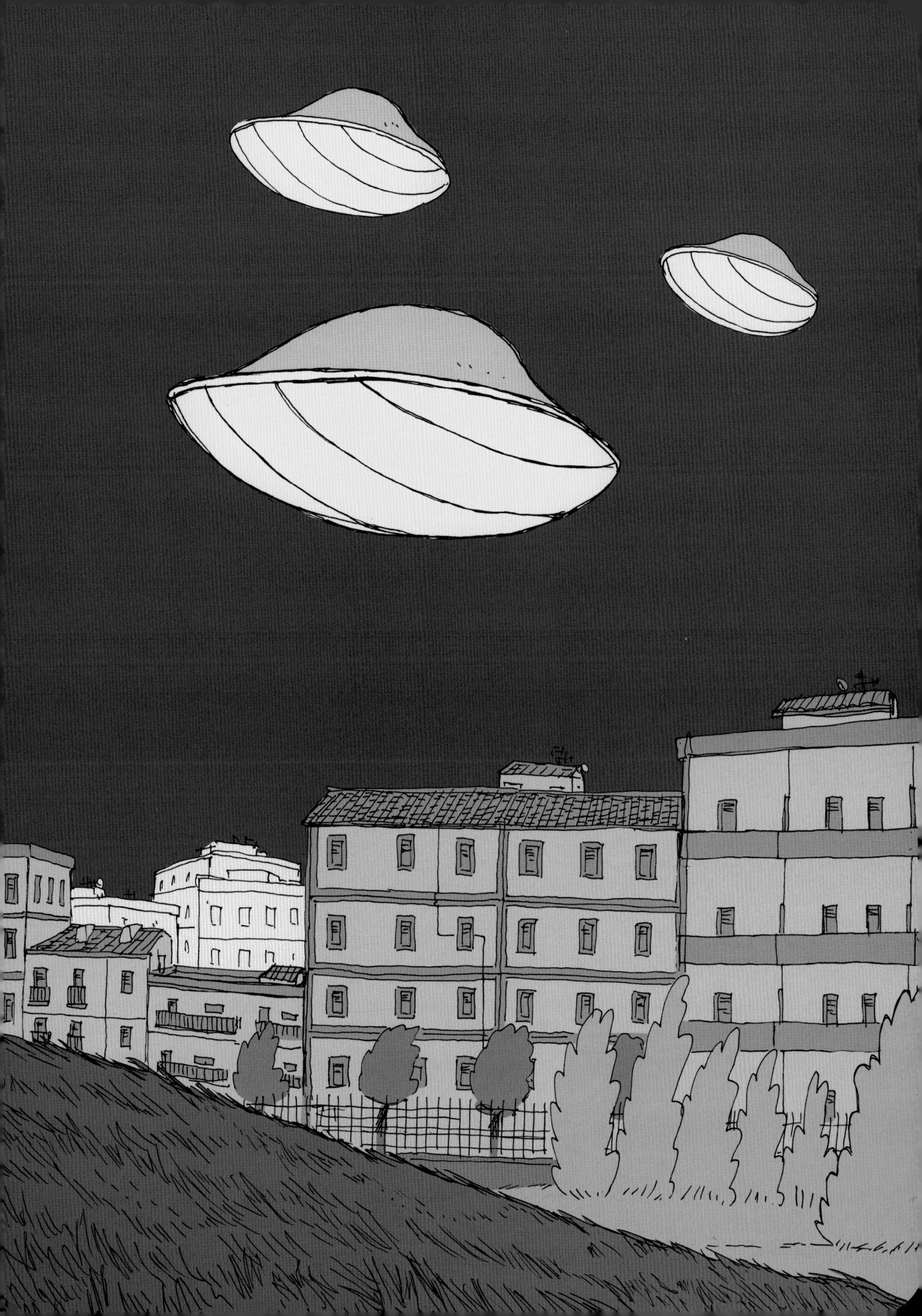

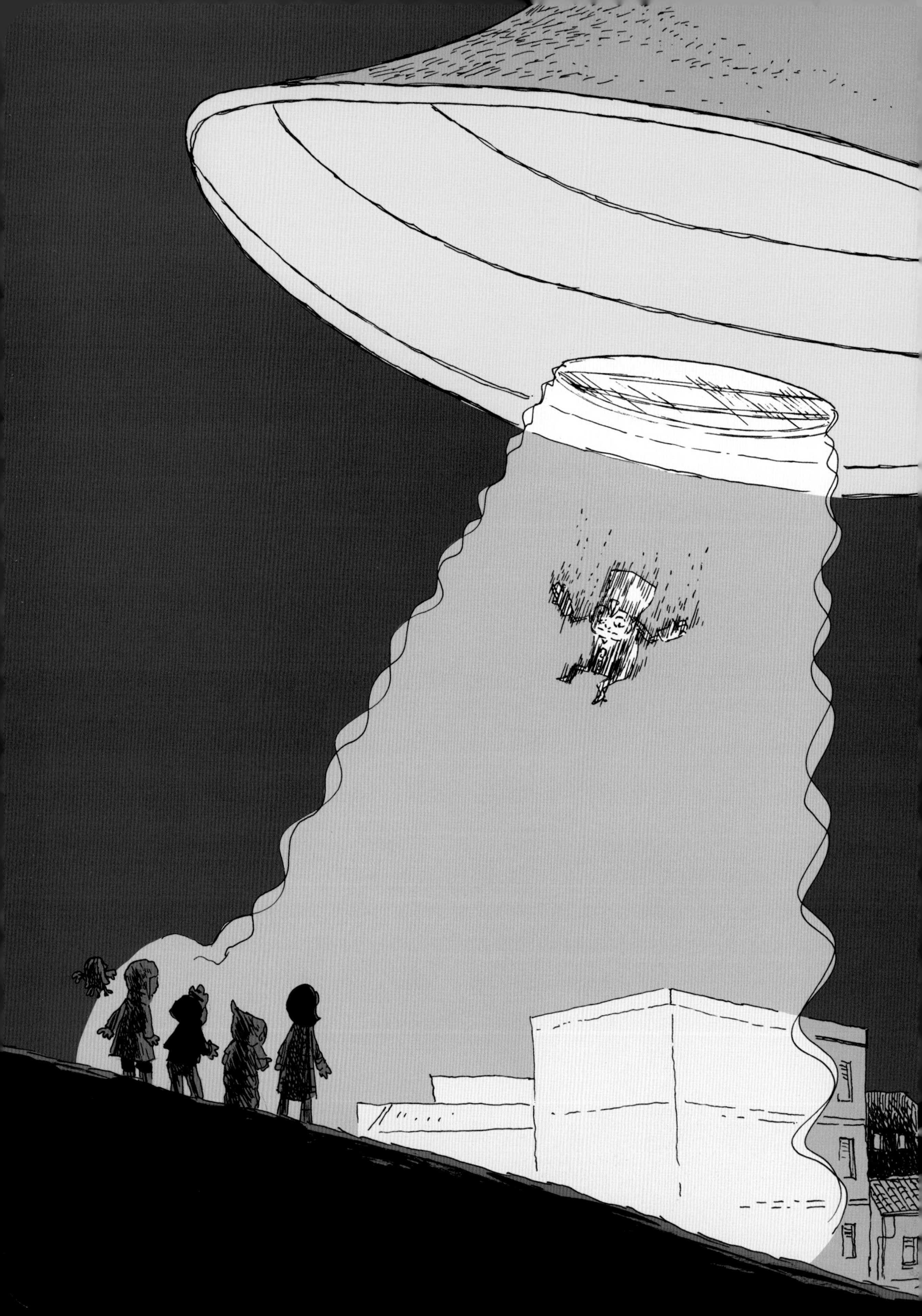

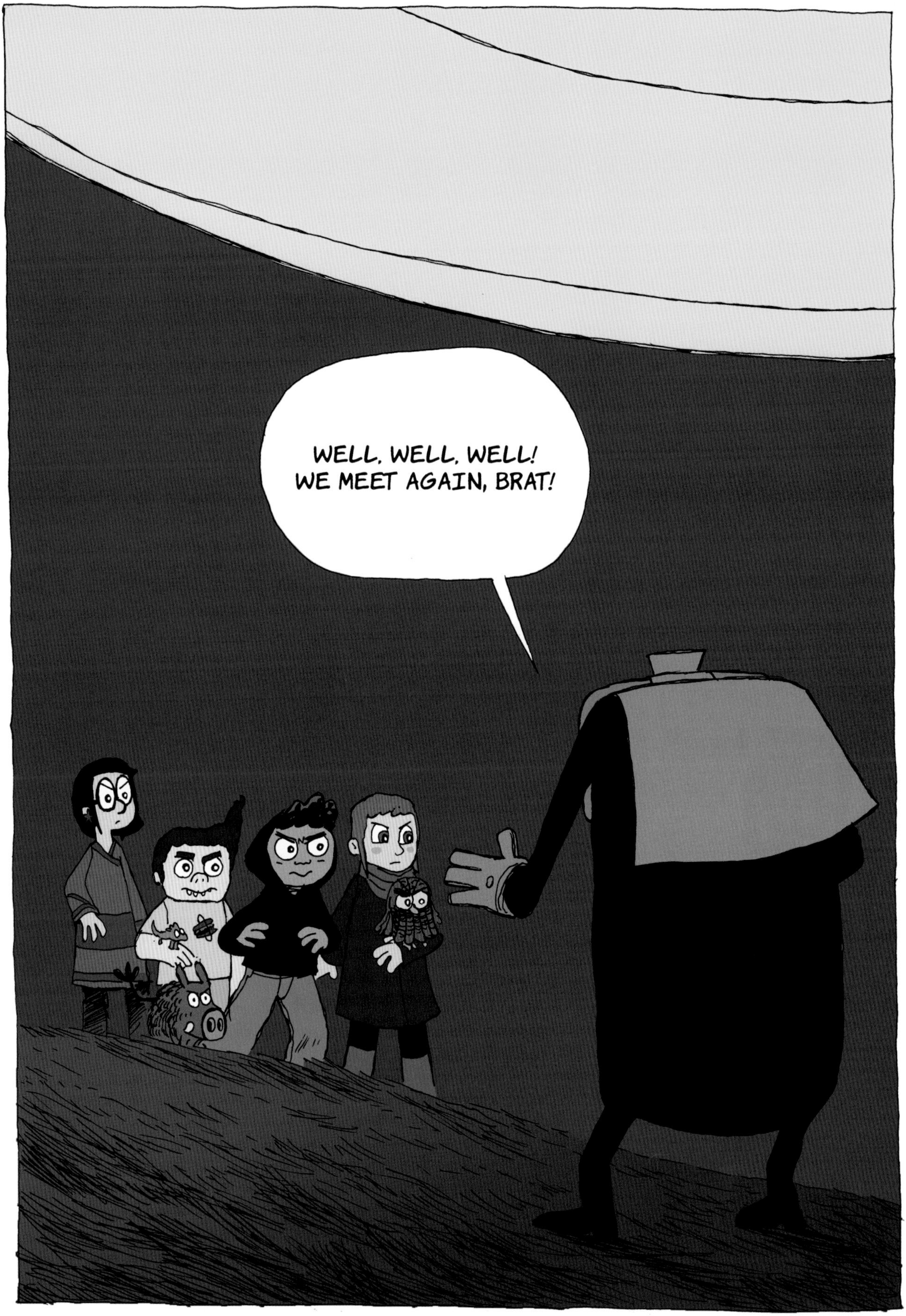
WELL, WELL, WELL! WE MEET AGAIN, BRAT!

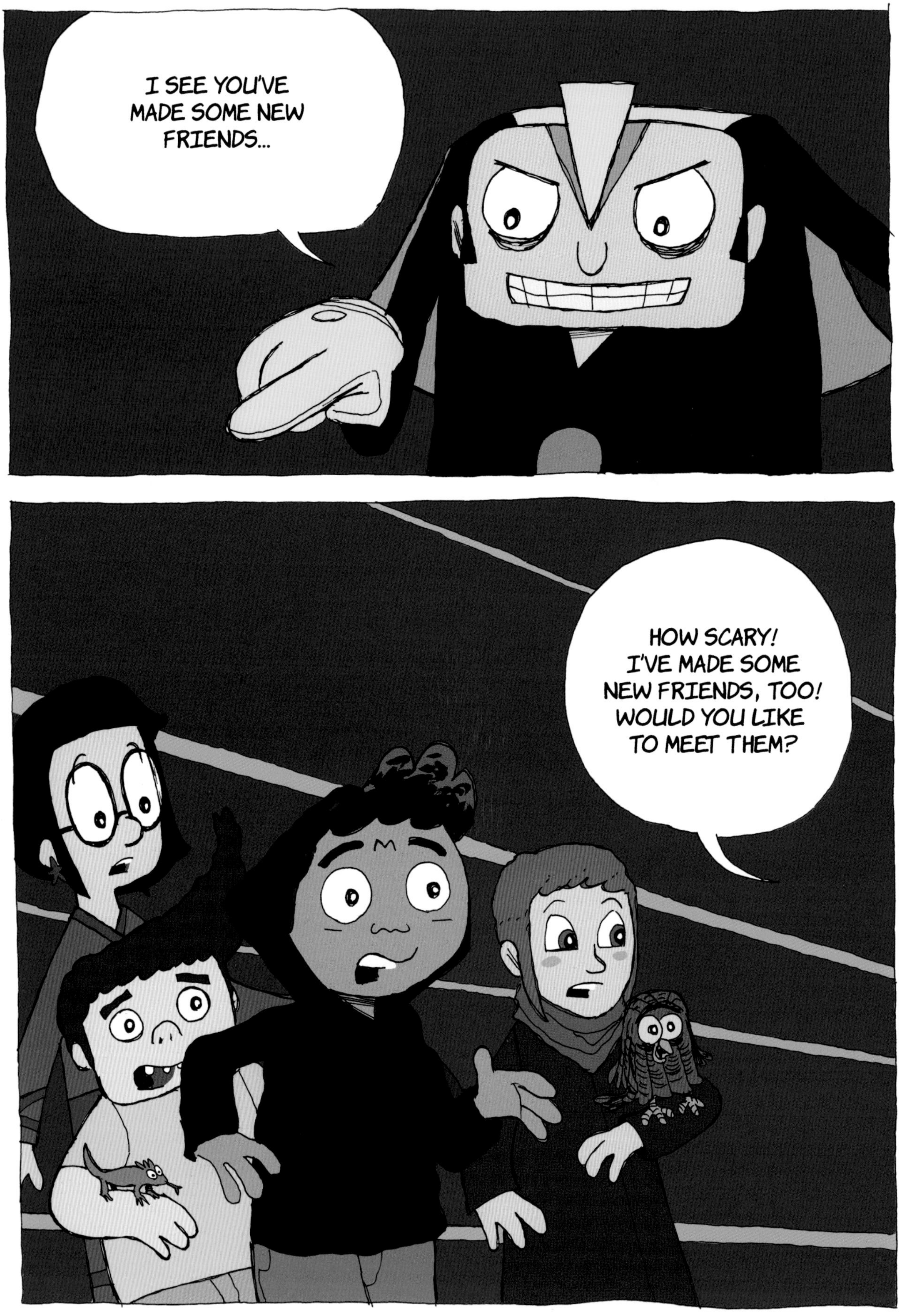
I SEE YOU'VE MADE SOME NEW FRIENDS...
HOW SCARY! I'VE MADE SOME NEW FRIENDS, TOO! WOULD YOU LIKE TO MEET THEM?

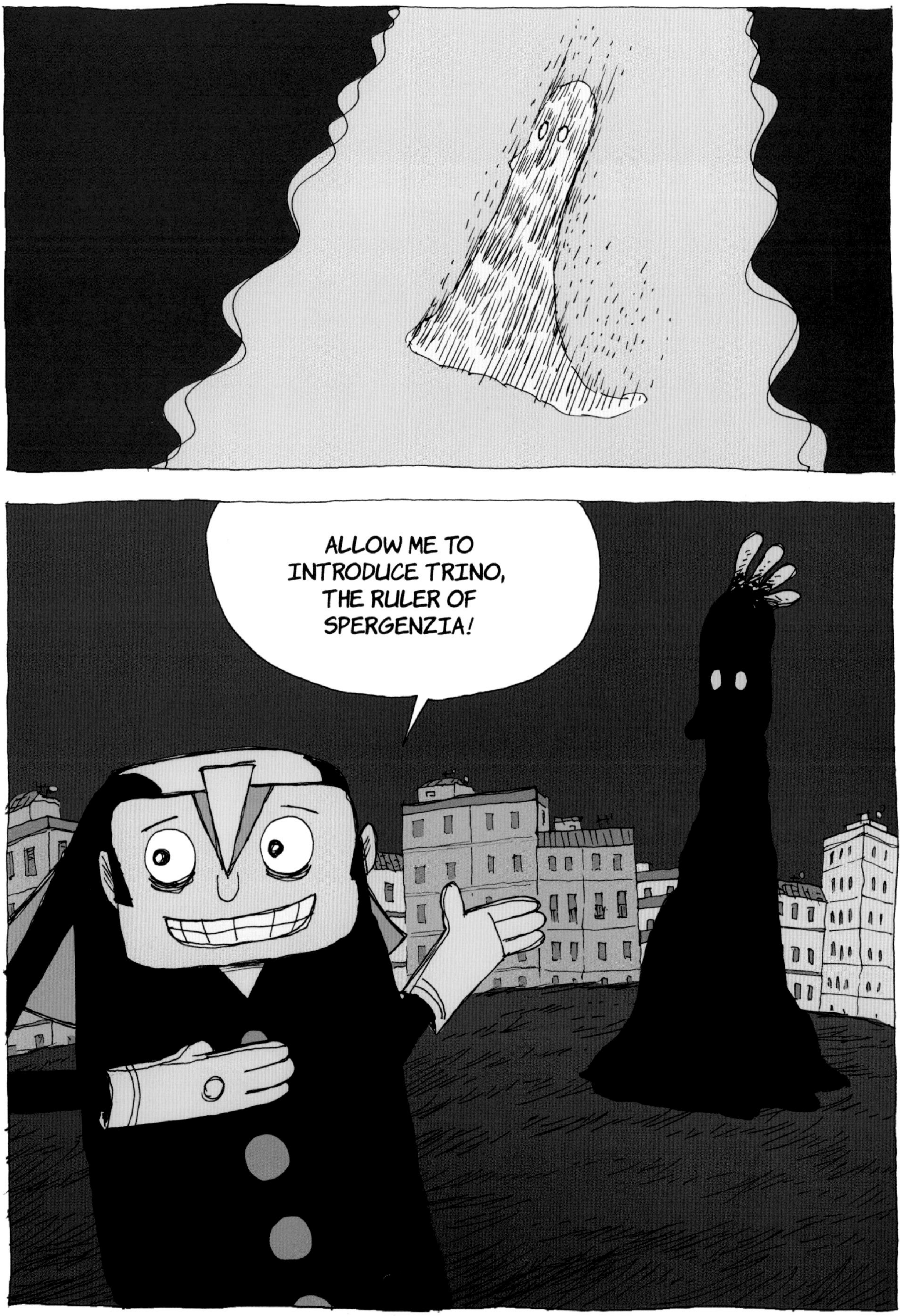
ALLOW ME TO INTRODUCE TRINO, THE RULER OF SPERGENZIA!

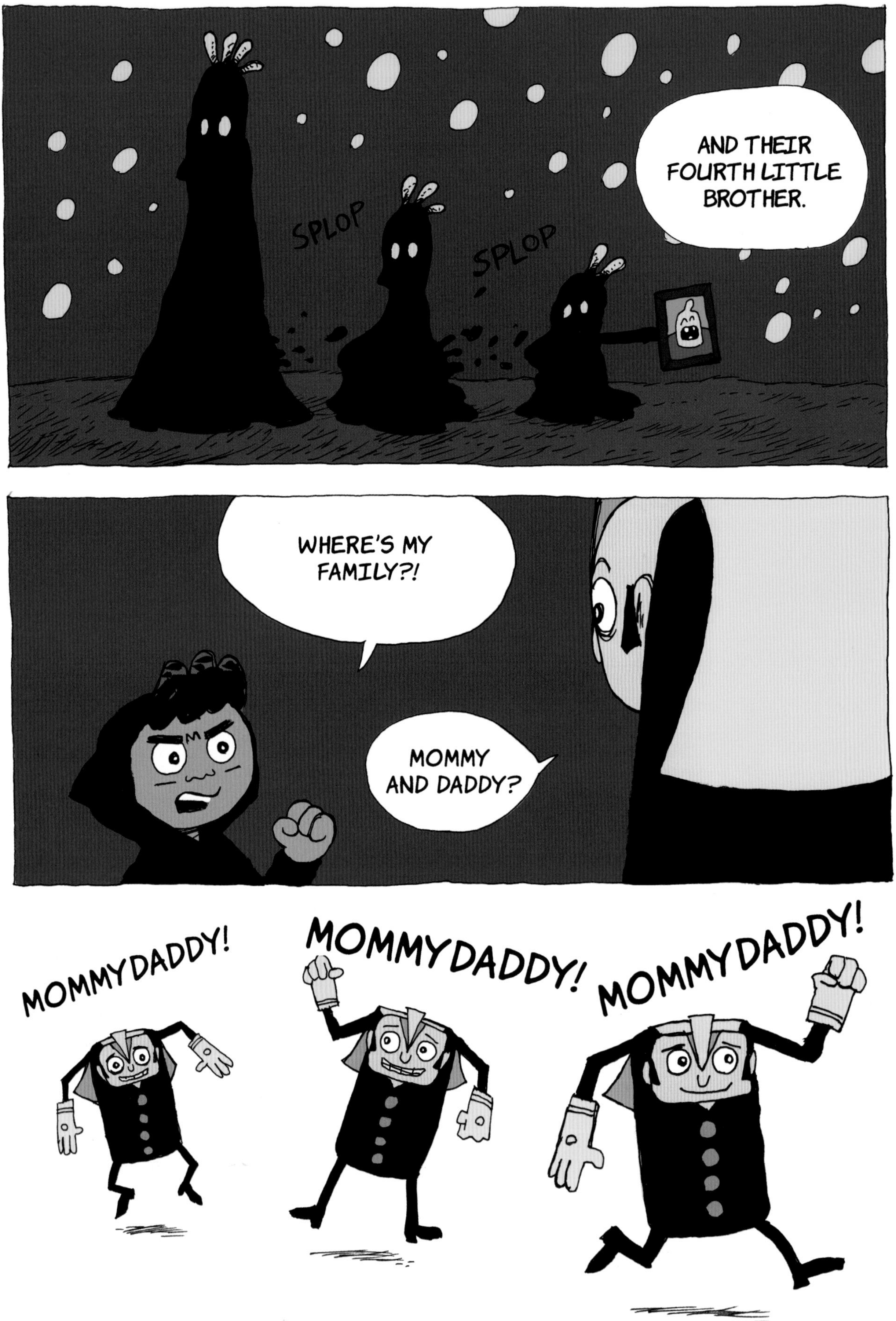
AND THEIR FOURTH LITTLE BROTHER.
SPLOP
SPLOP
WHERE'S MY FAMILY?!
MOMMY AND DADDY?
MOMMYDADDY!
MOMMYDADDY!
MOMMYDADDY!

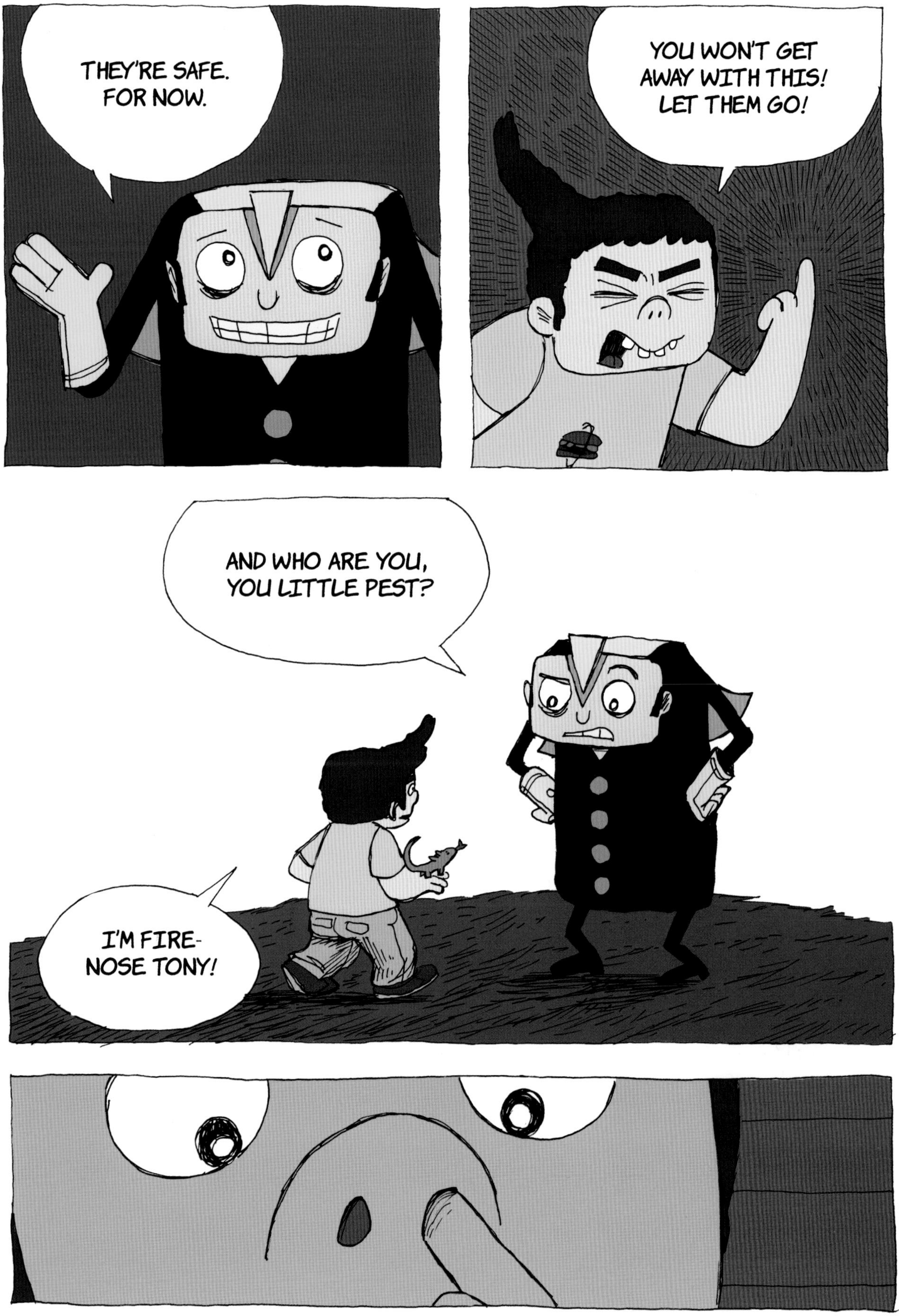
THEY'RE SAFE. FOR NOW.
YOU WON'T GET AWAY WITH THIS! LET THEM GO!
AND WHO ARE YOU, YOU LITTLE PEST?
I'M FIRE-NOSE TONY!

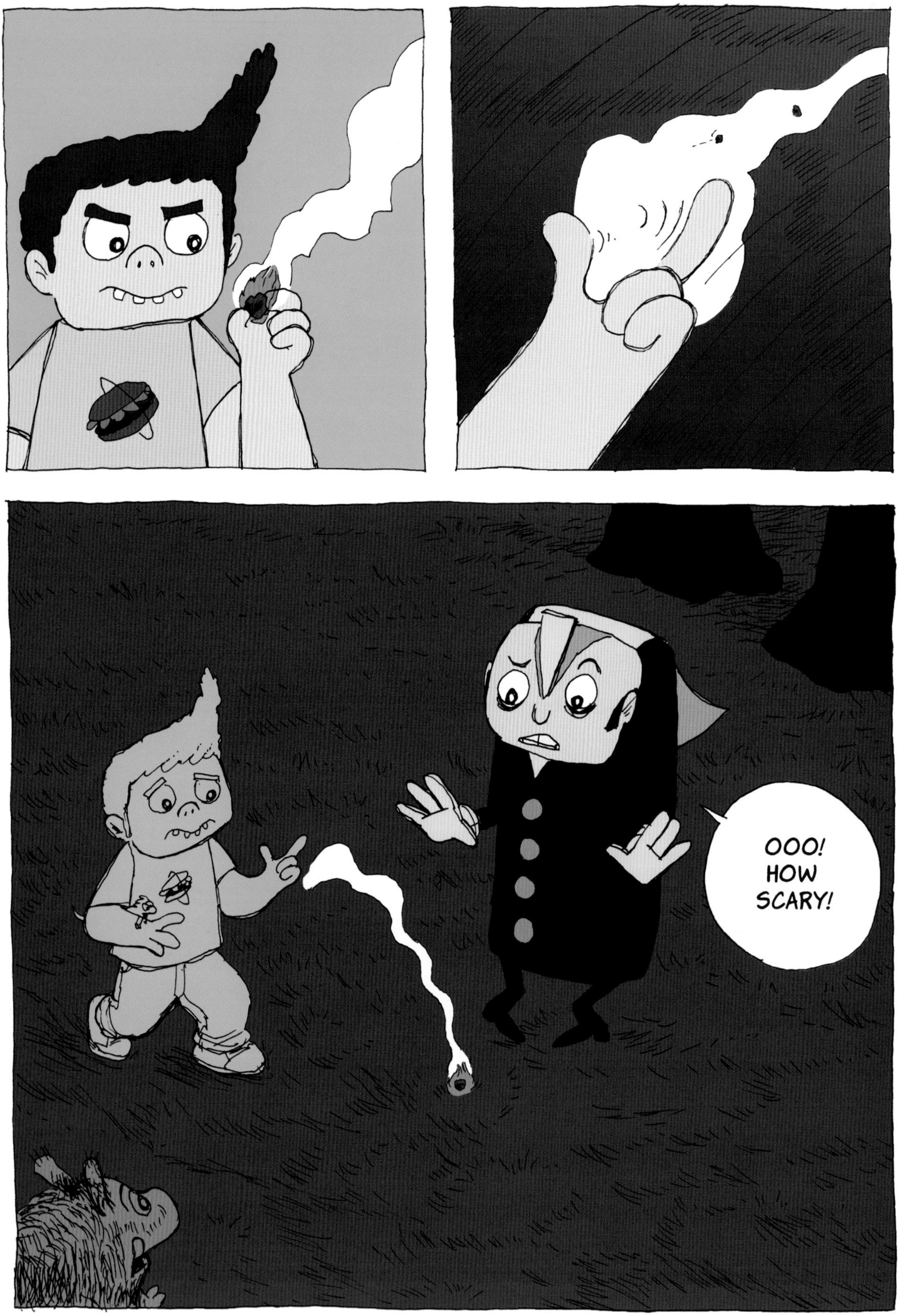
OOO! HOW SCARY!

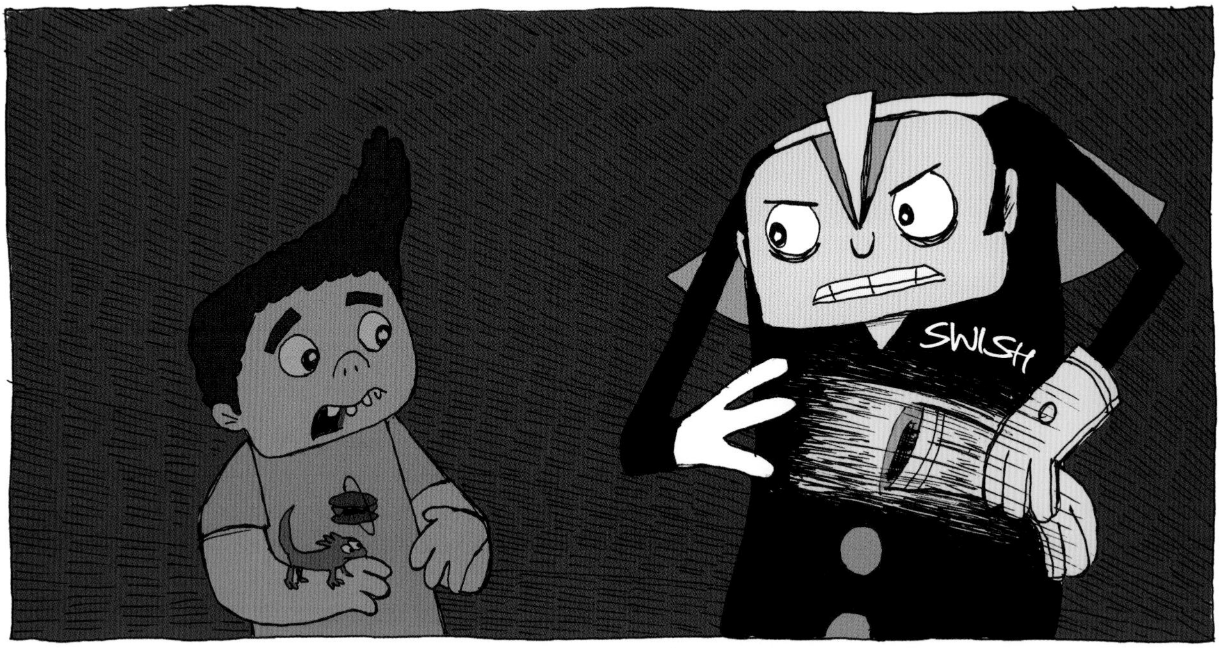
SWISH

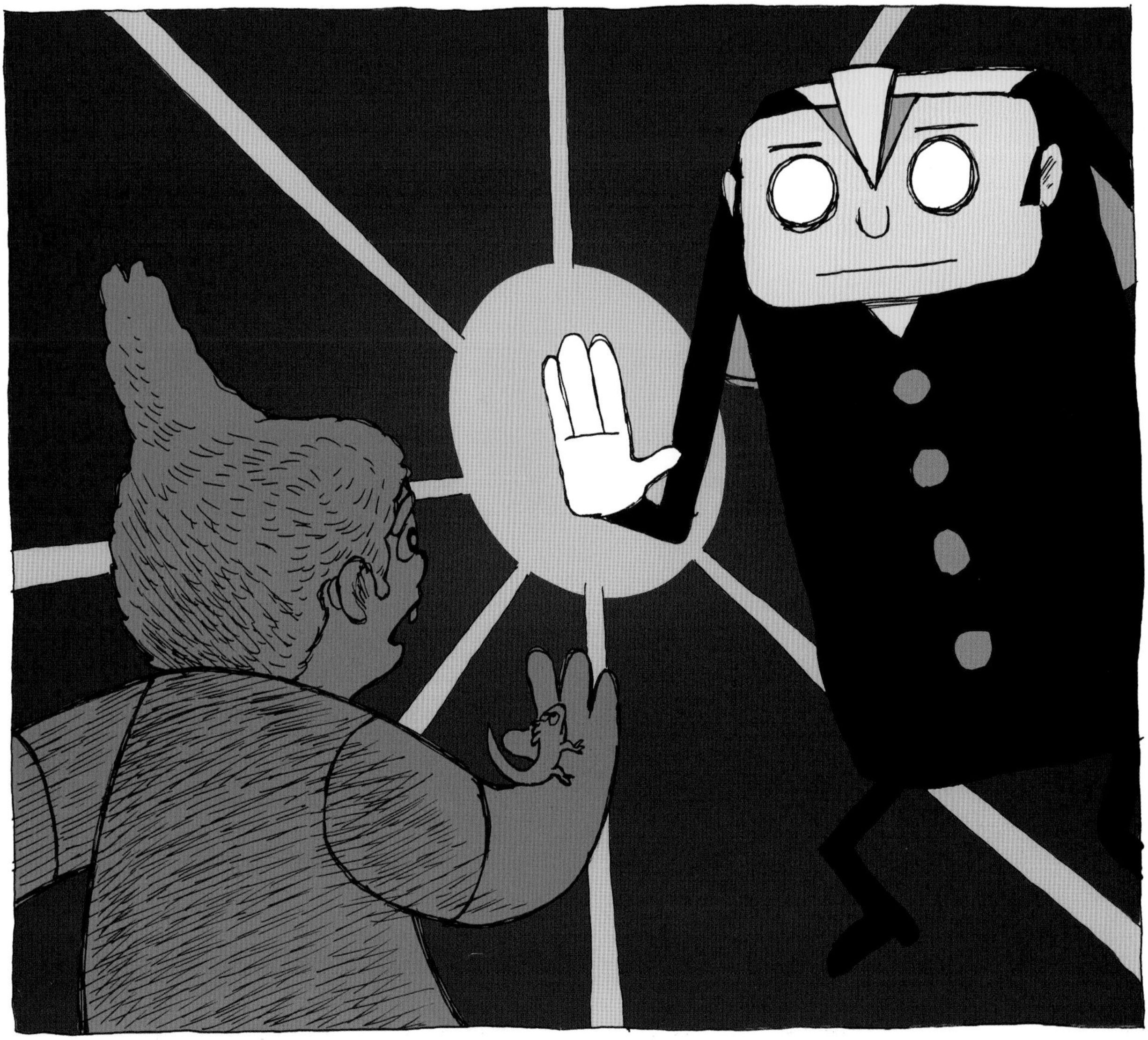

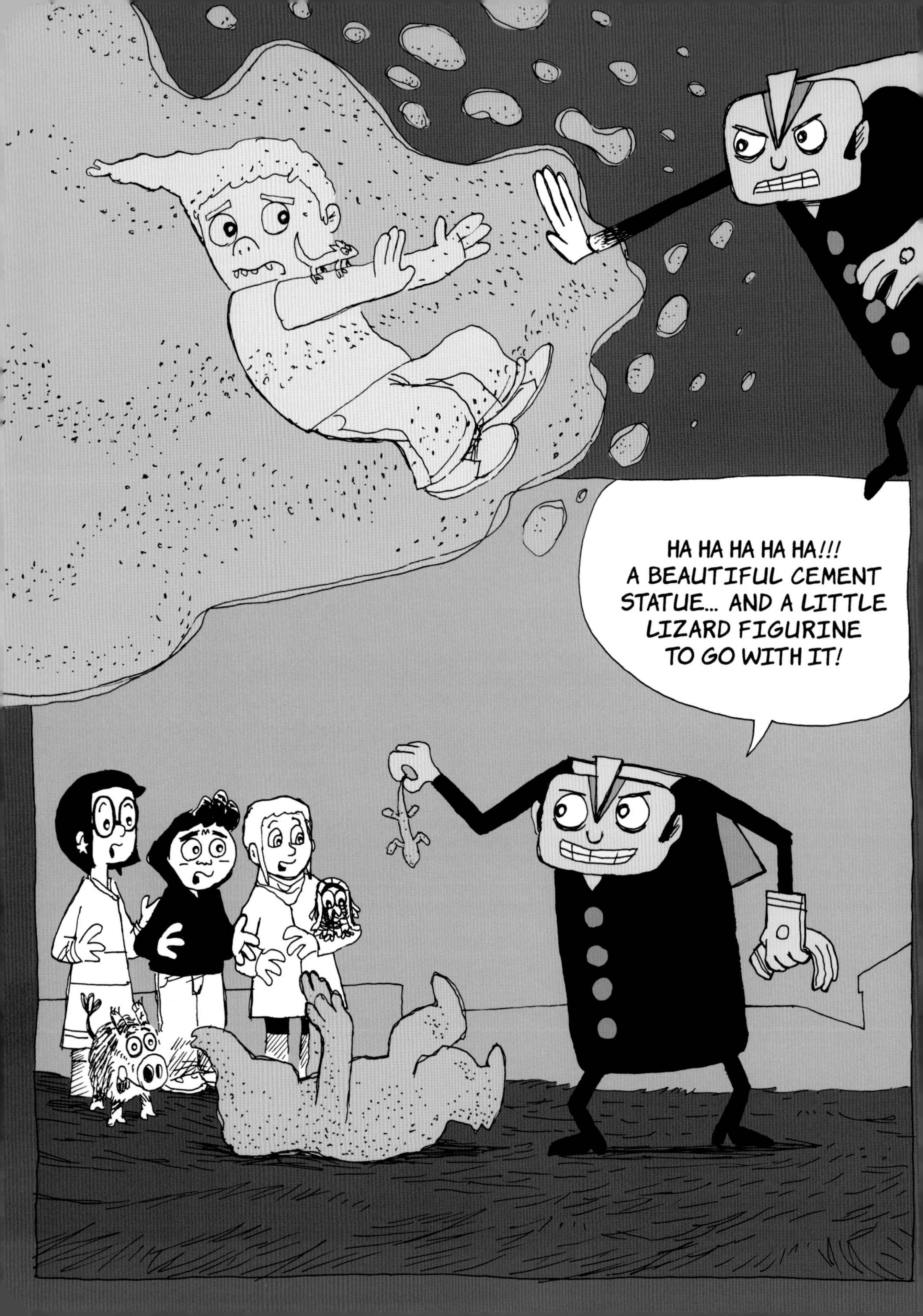
HA HA HA HA HA!!! A BEAUTIFUL CEMENT STATUE... AND A LITTLE LIZARD FIGURINE TO GO WITH IT!

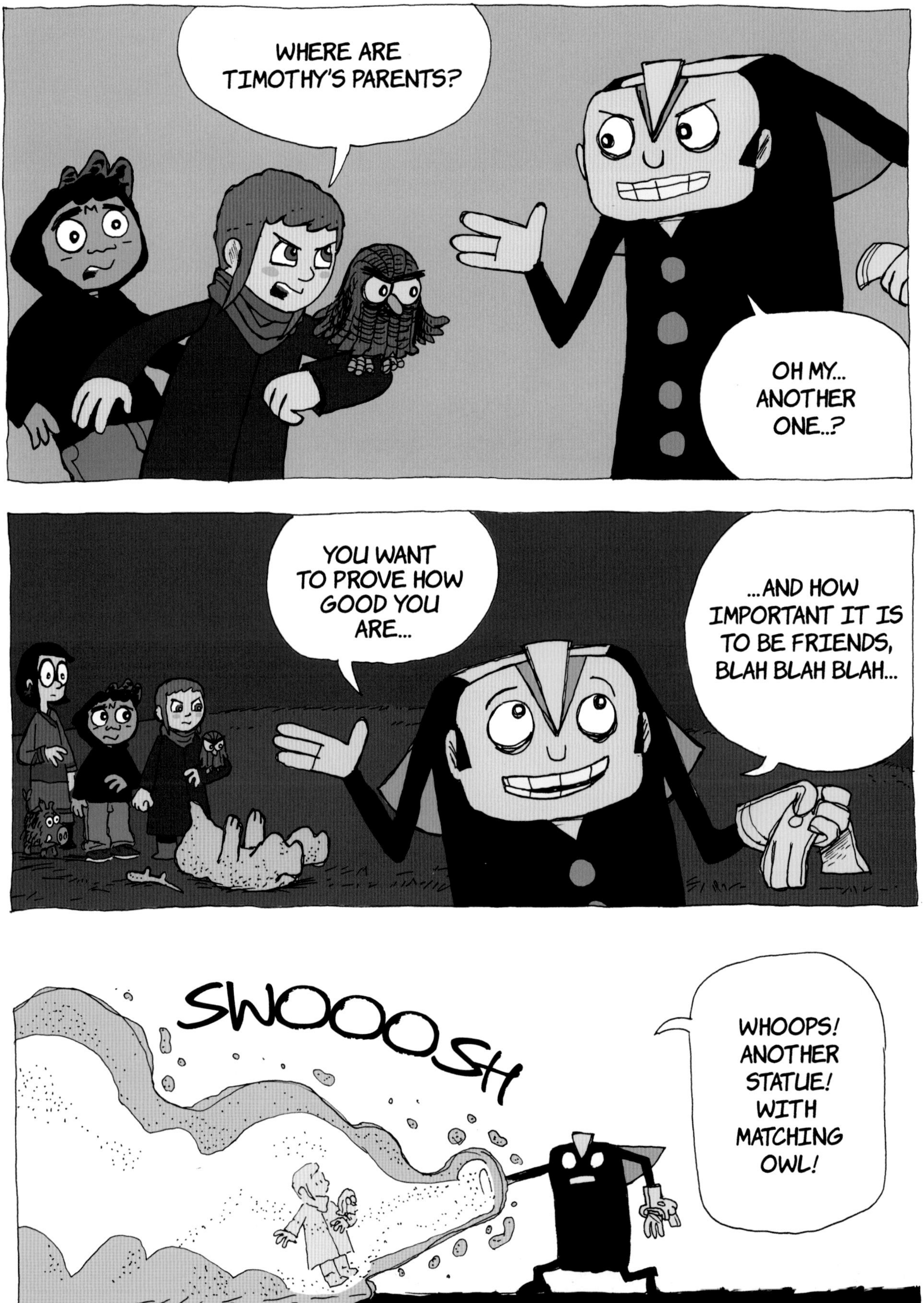
WHERE ARE TIMOTHY'S PARENTS?
OH MY... ANOTHER ONE..?
YOU WANT TO PROVE HOW GOOD YOU ARE...
...AND HOW IMPORTANT IT IS TO BE FRIENDS, BLAH BLAH BLAH...
SWOOOSH
WHOOPS! ANOTHER STATUE! WITH MATCHING OWL!

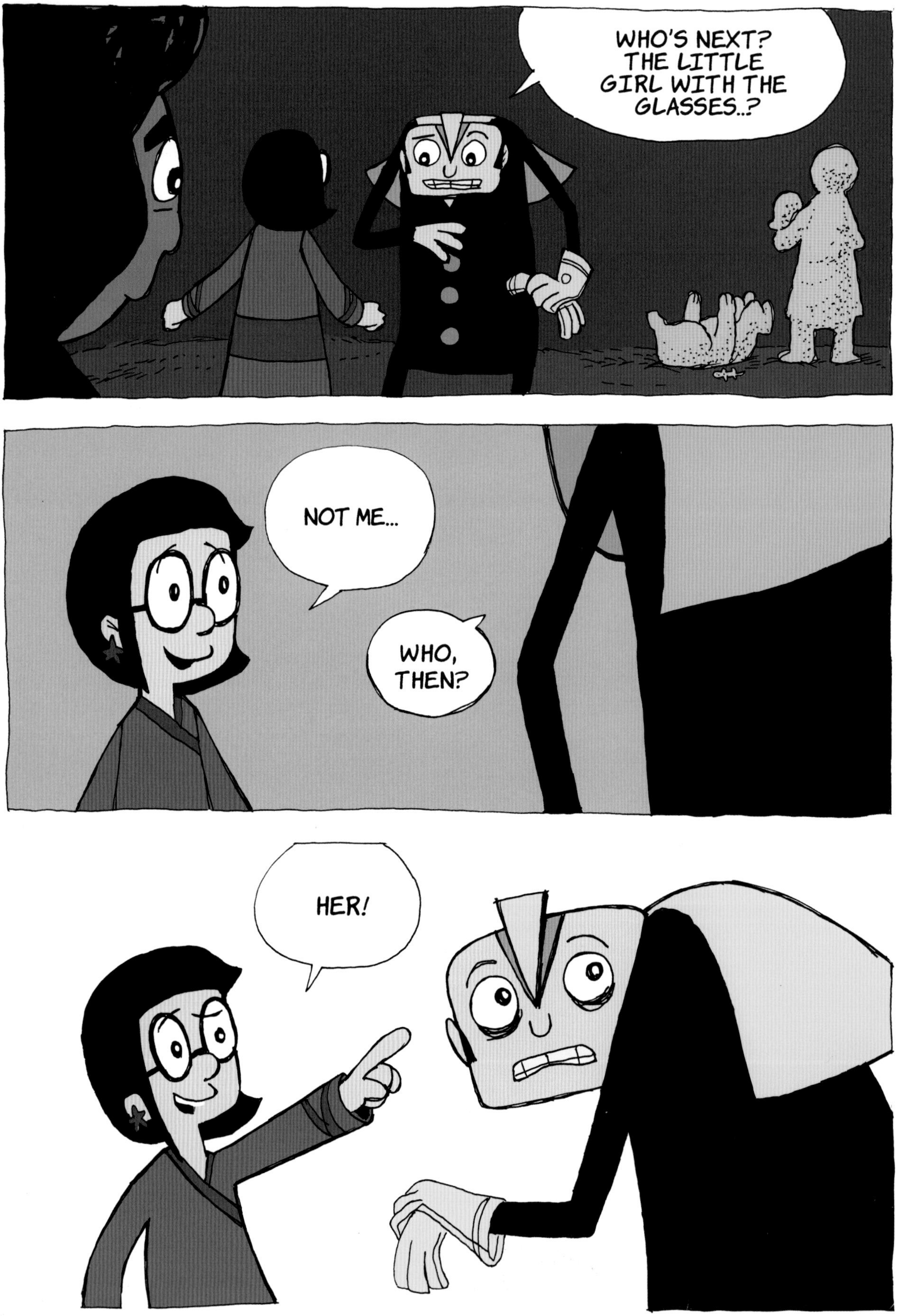
WHO'S NEXT? THE LITTLE GIRL WITH THE GLASSES..?
NOT ME...
WHO, THEN?
HER!

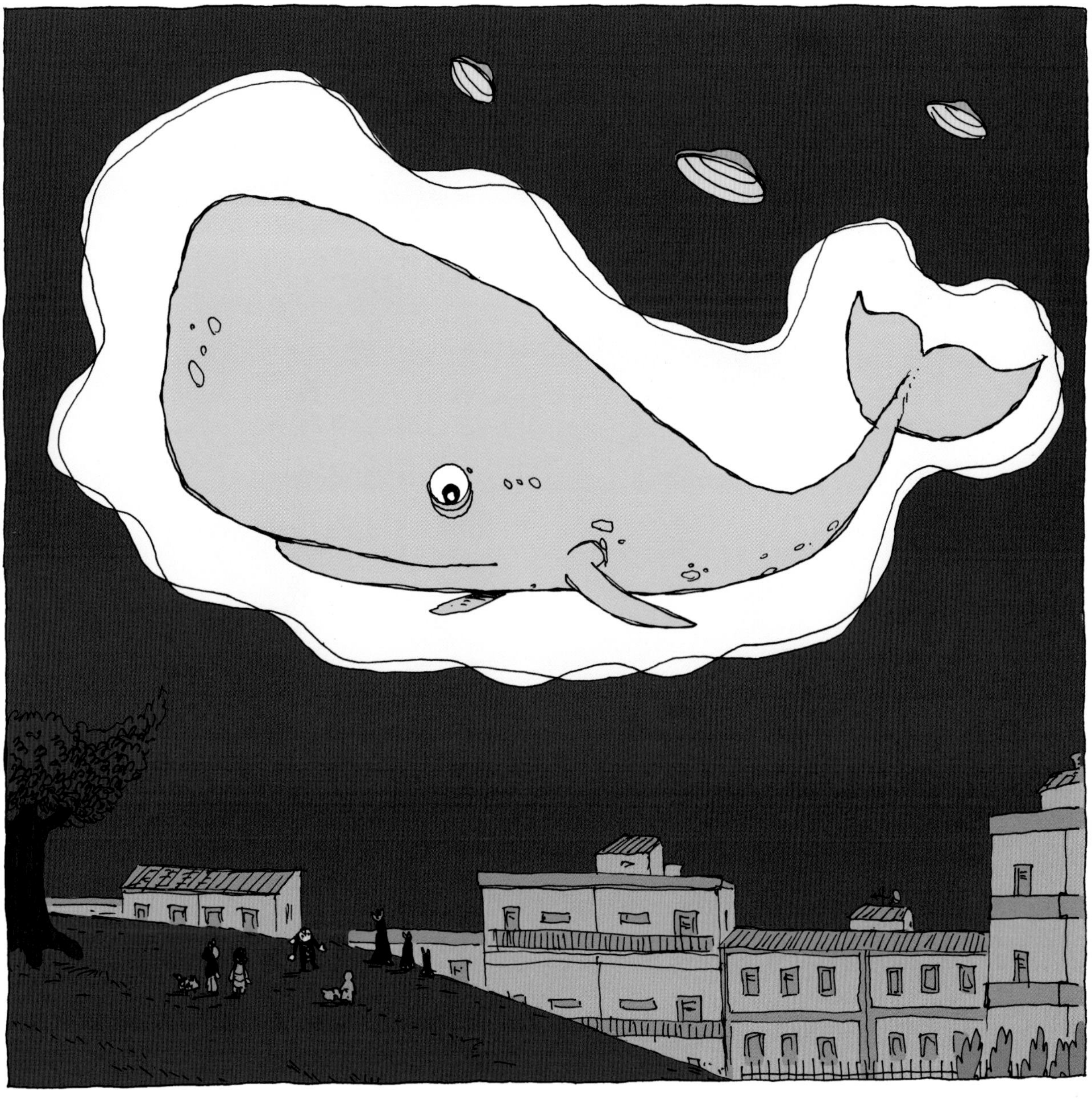

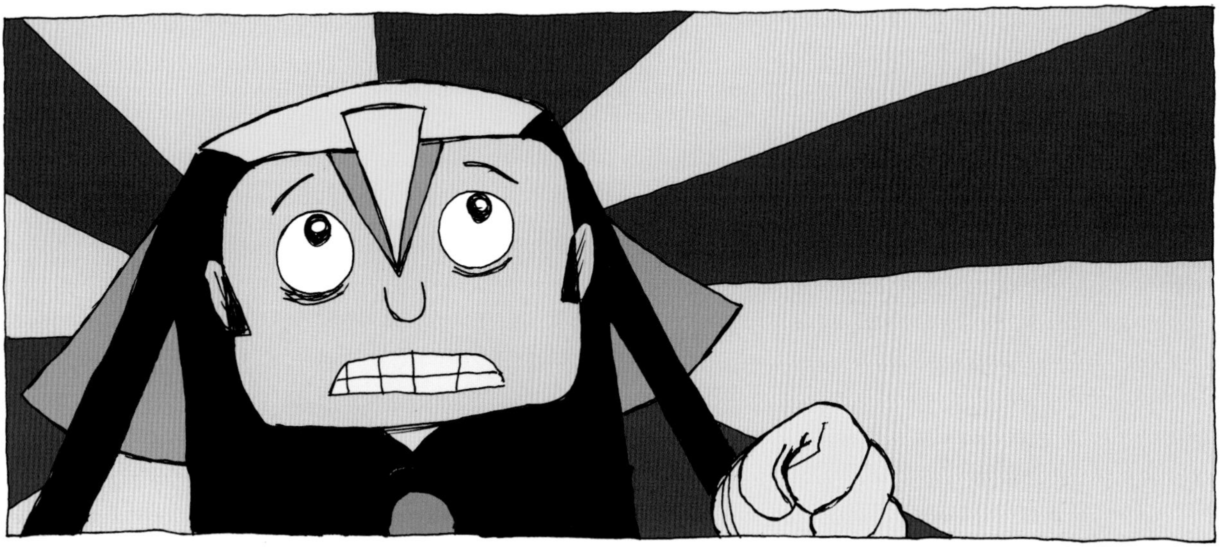

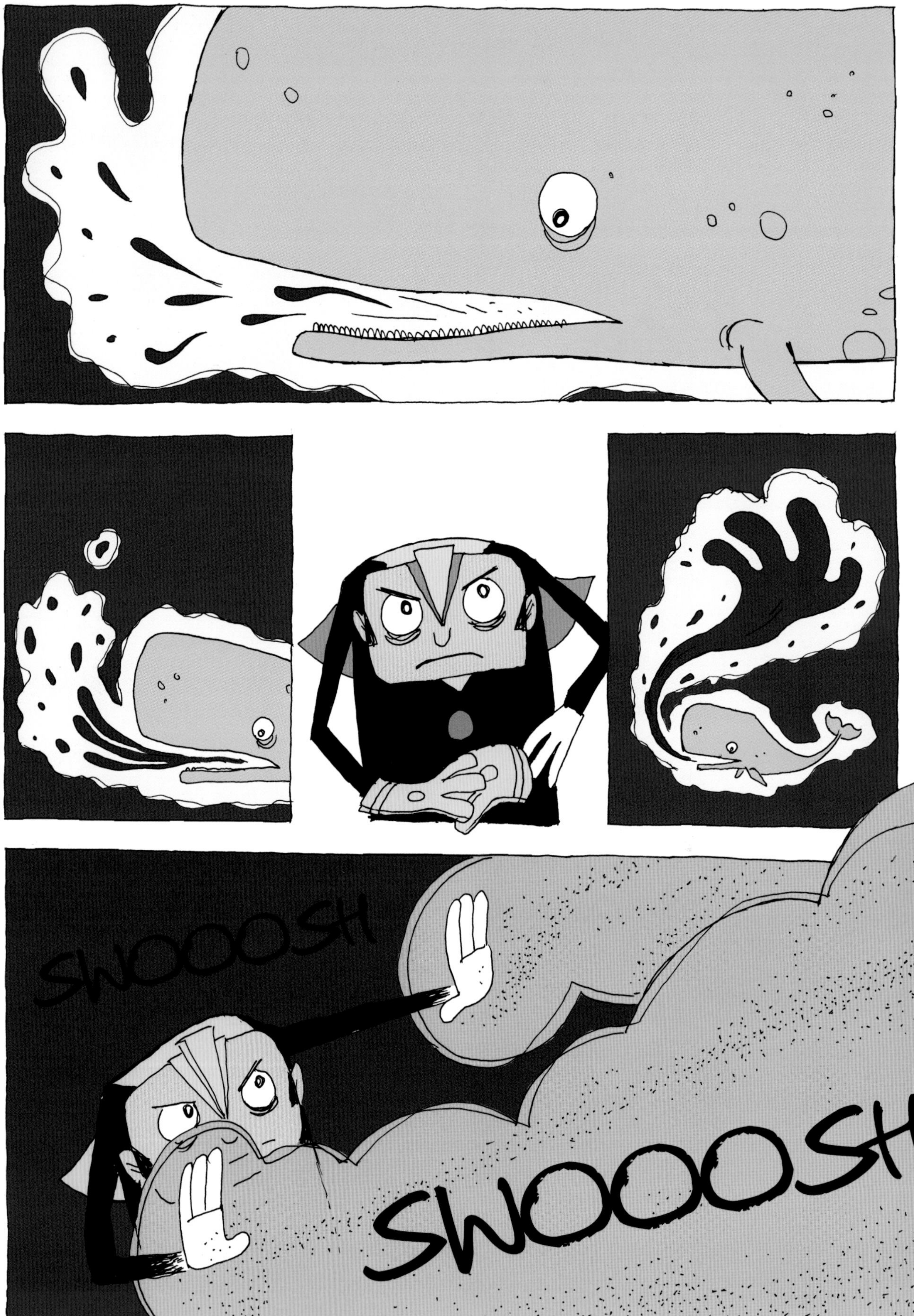
SWOOOSH
SWOOOSH

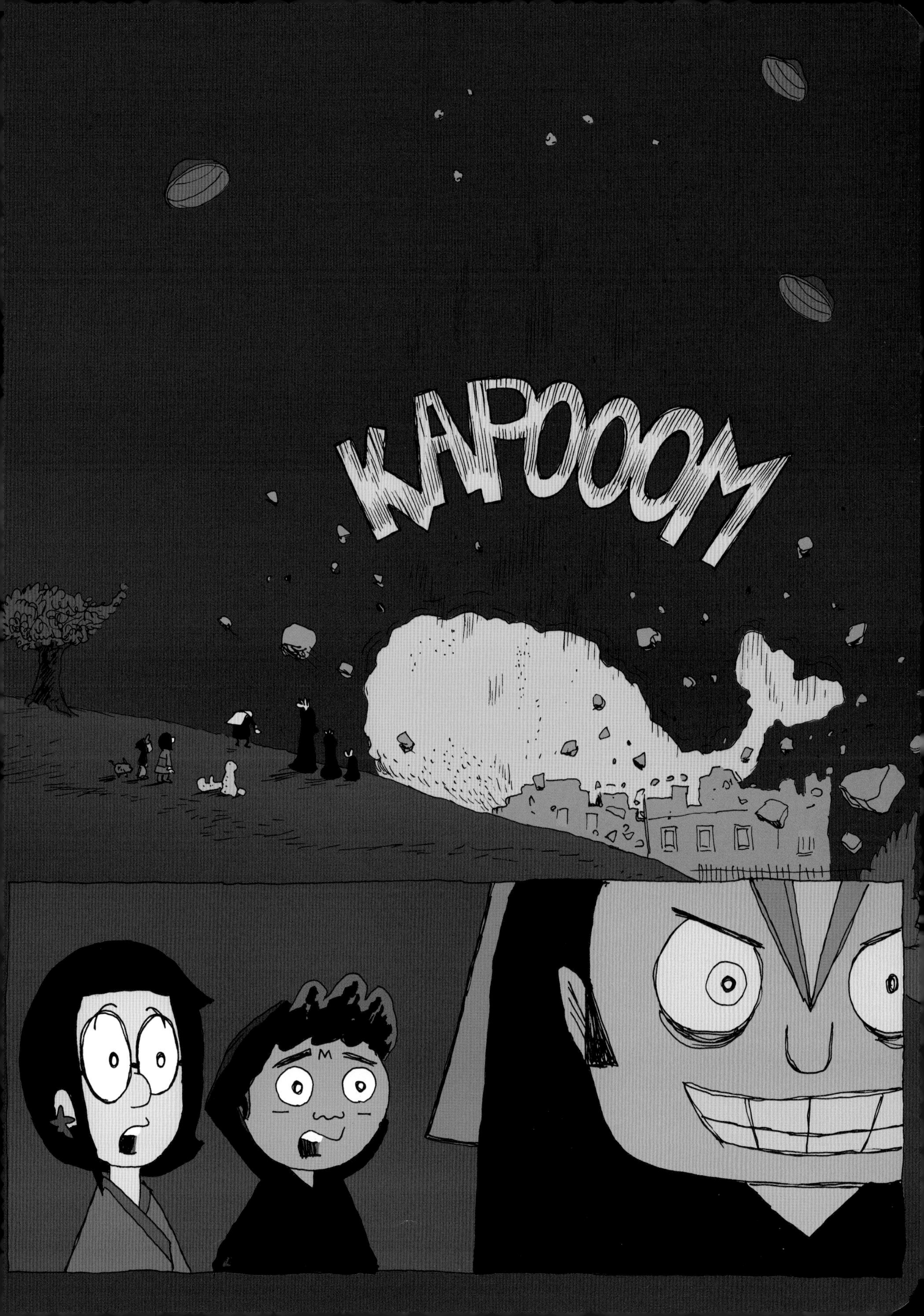
KAPOOOM

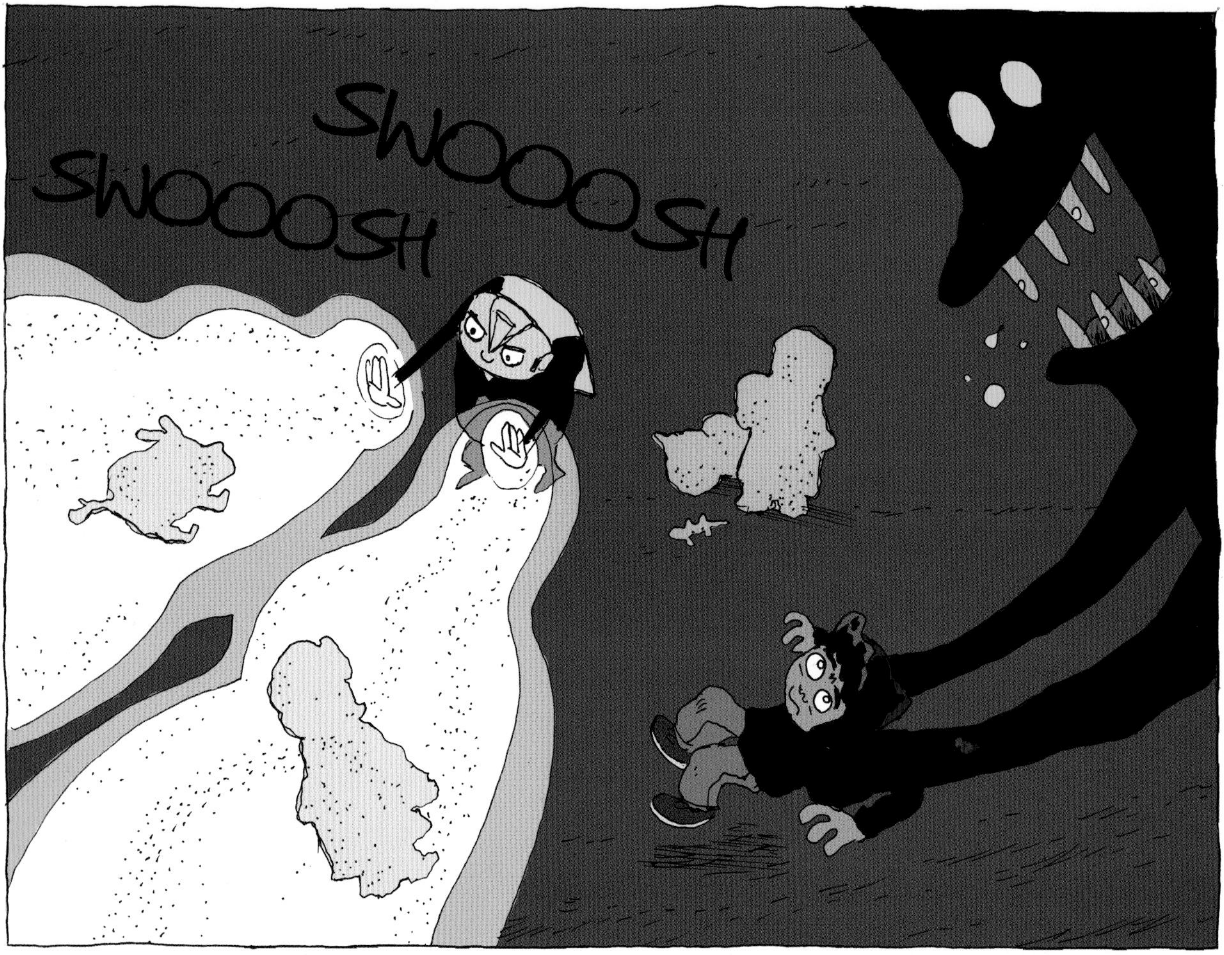
SWOOOSH
SWOOOOSH

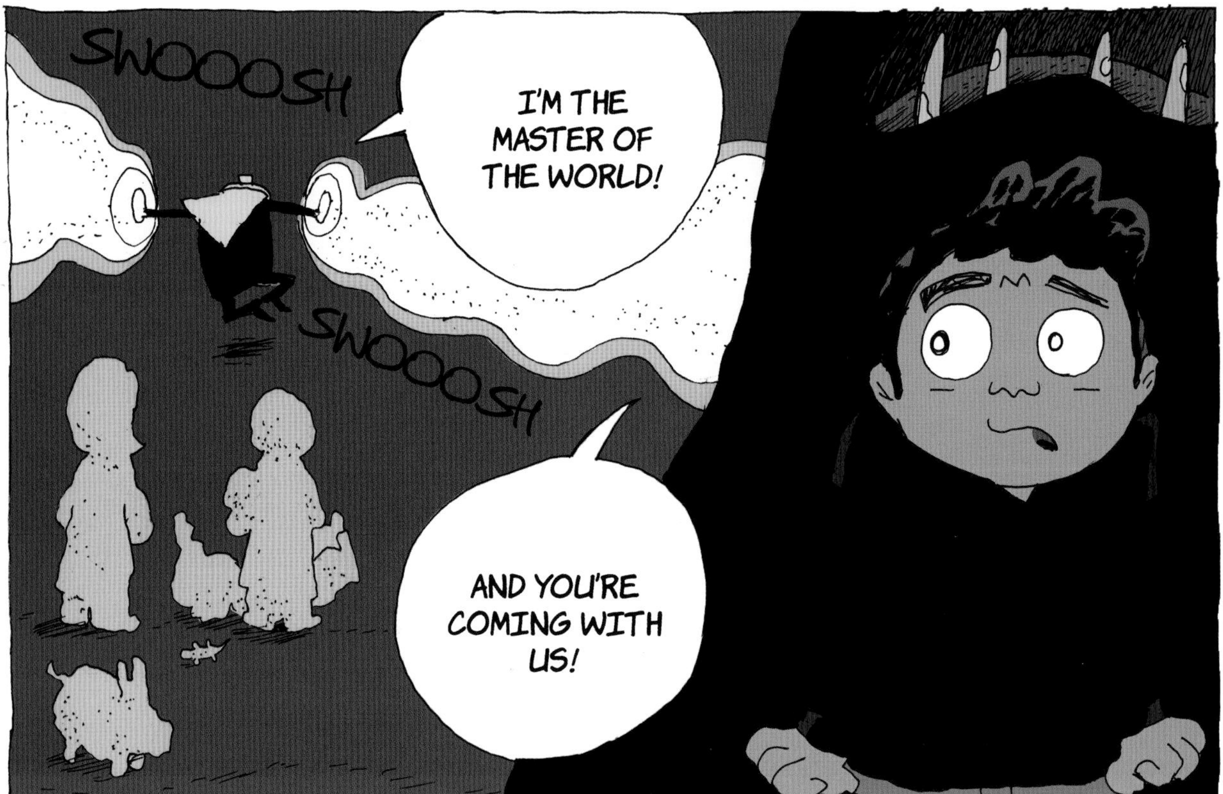
SWOOOSH
I'M THE MASTER OF THE WORLD!
SWOOOSH
AND YOU'RE COMING WITH US!

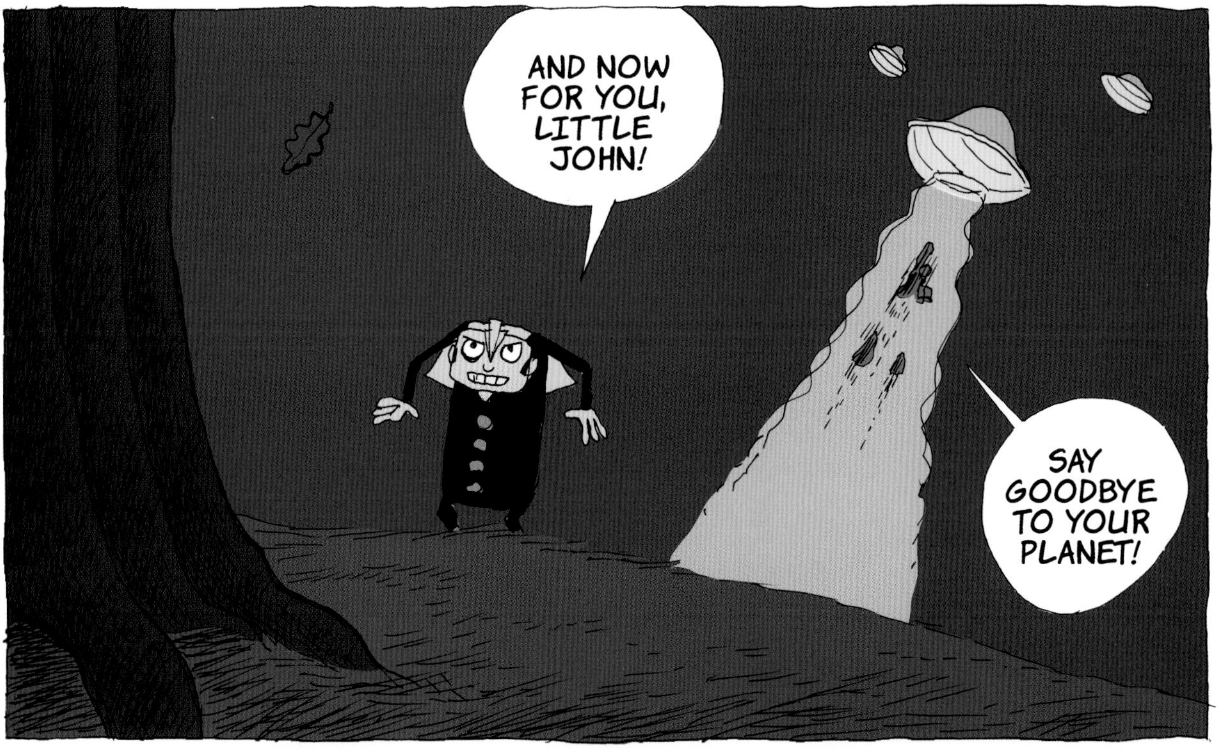
AND NOW FOR YOU, LITTLE JOHN!
SAY GOODBYE TO YOUR PLANET!

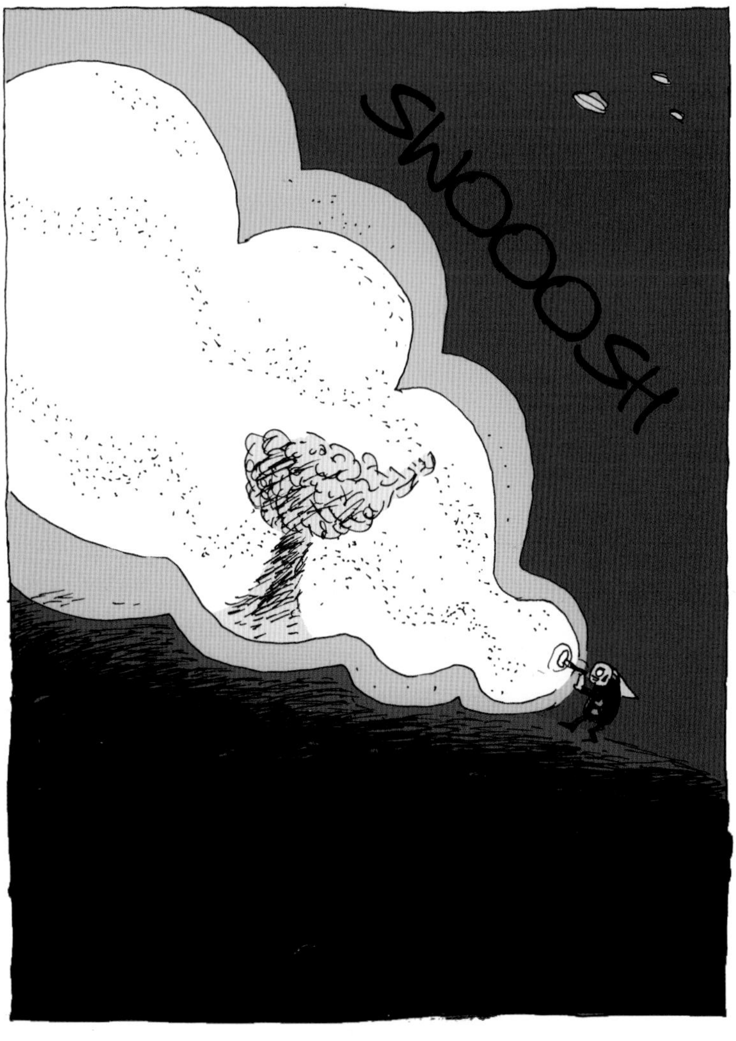
SWOOOSH

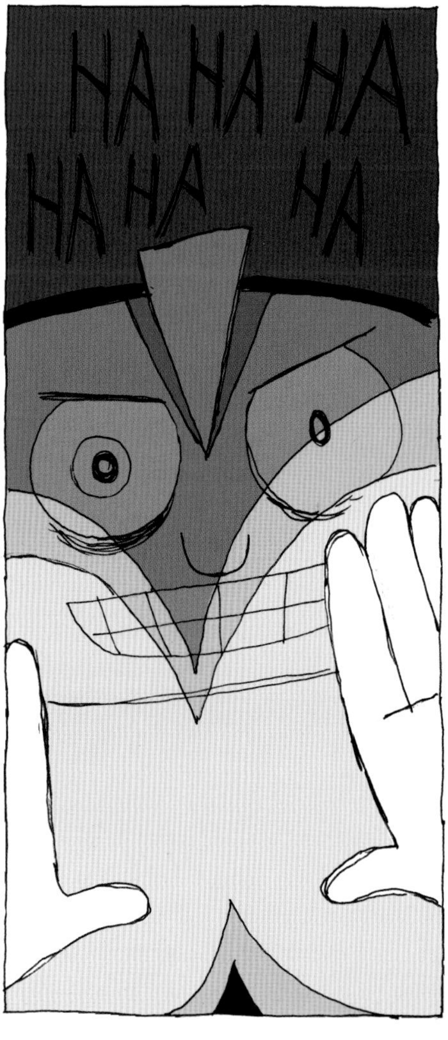
HA HA HA HA HA HA HA

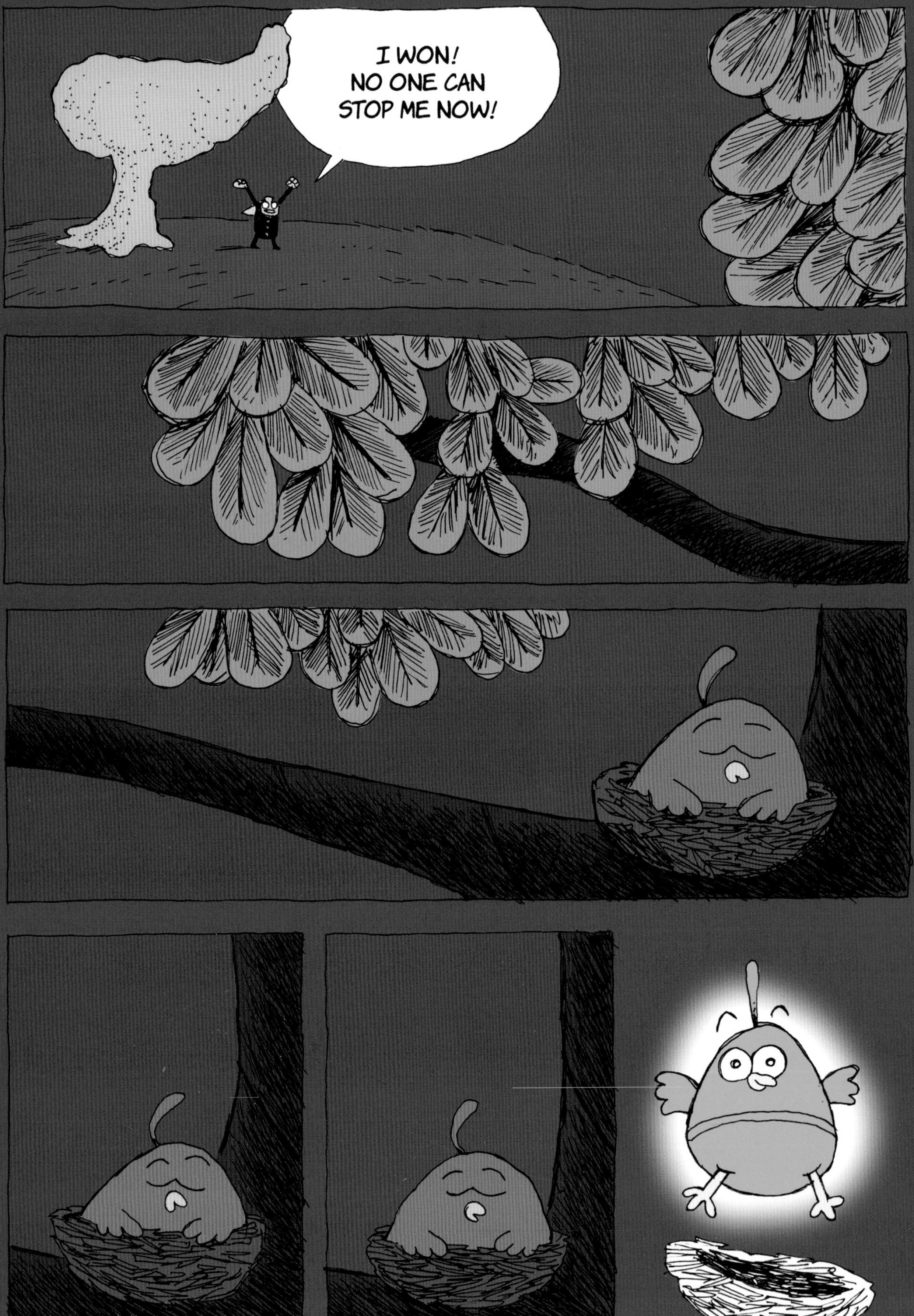
I WON!
NO ONE CAN
STOP ME NOW!